CORK CITY LIBRARY
Leabharlann Cathrach Chorcaí

www.corkcitylibrary.ie

Tel./Guthán (021) 4924900

This book is due for return on the last date stamped below.
Overdue fines: 10c per week plus postage.

MOONLIT EYES

Also by Emma Blair

WHERE NO MAN CRIES
NELLIE WILDCHILD
HESTER DARK
THIS SIDE OF HEAVEN
JESSIE GRAY
THE PRINCESS OF POOR STREET
STREET SONG
WHEN DREAMS COME TRUE
A MOST DETERMINED WOMAN
THE BLACKBIRD'S TALE
MAGGIE JORDAN
SCARLET RIBBONS
THE WATER MEADOWS
THE SWEETEST THING
THE DAFFODIL SEA
PASSIONATE TIMES
HALF HIDDEN
FLOWER OF SCOTLAND
AN APPLE FROM EDEN
GOODNIGHT, SWEET PRINCE
WILD STRAWBERRIES
FORGET-ME-NOT

MOONLIT EYES

Emma Blair

LITTLE, BROWN AND COMPANY

A *Little, Brown* Book

First published in Great Britain in 2002
by Little, Brown

A CIP catalogue record for this book
is available from the British Library.

HARDBACK ISBN 0 316 85578 2
C FORMAT ISBN 0 316 85585 5

Typeset by Palimpsest Book Production Ltd,
Polmont, Stirlingshire

Printed and bound in Great Britain by Clays Ltd, St Ives plc

Little, Brown
An imprint of
Time Warner Books UK
Brettenham House
Lancaster Place
London WC2E 7EN

www.TimeWarnerBooks.co.uk

MOONLIT EYES

Chapter *E*

'**B**lack!'

Jess Sykes almost laughed out loud at her husband's dumbfounded expression. She might have announced that the couple who'd moved in next door were from Mars.

'As the ace of spades I'm told,' she added.

'Bloody hell,' Albert muttered, giving a shake of his head. He was dead beat having just come off shift after a long and particularly hard day. 'So you haven't seen them yourself yet?'

'I have,' their son Paul piped up.

'Don't speak with your mouth full,' Jess admonished. 'How often have I told you that.'

Albert eyed his ten-year-old. 'What are they like?'

'She's big and fat while he's got grey woolly hair and funny eyes.'

'Why are they funny?' Jess queried, intrigued. 'Did the man have a cast, or what?'

Paul shrugged. 'I don't know. They just are.'

'I've never seen a black person in the flesh,' Ellie, Paul's older sister, declared. 'In films, yes, but never in real life like.'

'They arrived this morning,' Jess explained. 'A huge van that was there for hours. Mrs Diamond across the street saw it, and them. As did old Ma Jenkins whom I spoke to earlier.'

'Black eh?' Albert mused, scratching his chin.

'Are you going to want any more steak and kidney?' Jess asked him. 'There's plenty left. That and mash.'

'I'll have some,' Paul volunteered eagerly. 'It's scrummy.'

'You've already had enough to fill an Irish navvy. Don't be greedy,' his sister rebuked him. 'You're a right guts and no mistake.'

'I am not!'

'Yes you are.'

Jess sighed. These two were always getting at one another. If she hadn't known better she'd have thought they hated each other. 'He's only a growing lad,' she declared eagerly to Ellie.

Ellie snorted. 'At the rate he eats he'll be eight foot tall and five wide before he's finished.'

'Enough,' Albert growled, glaring first at Ellie, then Paul. 'I haven't come home from work just to listen to you two going at it hammer and tongs. Understand?'

Both Ellie and Paul nodded that they did.

'Good.'

Albert turned his attention again to his wife. 'I won't have any more, thanks.'

Paul's face brightened and he looked expectantly at Jess who steadfastly ignored him.

'I wonder what he does?' Albert queried, more to himself than as a question to the others.

'Who?' Jess frowned.

'The black chappie. He must work, presumably.'

'No idea.'

'Maybe he's a cannibal,' Paul said, suddenly a little frightened that it might be true.

Jess laughed. 'Don't be daft! There aren't any cannibals in England, far less London. They're all in Africa.'

'But if the man is black he must have come from Africa,' Paul argued.

'You saw him, did he have a bone through his nose?' Albert asked.

The lad shook his head.

'Then he isn't a cannibal. All cannibals have a bone through their nose.'

Paul's eyes were wide. 'Really?'

'Really,' Albert stated matter-of-factly, though he was micky-taking. 'I read that somewhere once.'

Ellie glanced over at the clock ticking on the mantelpiece. 'Can I get down?' she requested urgently.

Friday, of course Jess thought. 'Are you seeing George tonight?'

Ellie nodded. 'I'd better get a move on or he'll be knocking the door and I won't be ready.'

'It won't do him any harm to wait,' Albert declared. 'When I was courting your ma I always had to wait. Many's the long hour I've spent kicking my heels while she titivated herself.'

Jess smiled in memory knowing that to be true. It wasn't something she'd done intentionally, it had simply happened that way.

'Please, Ma?' Ellie pleaded.

'Where are you off to?'

'The flicks probably and then back to The Florence for a drink afterwards, I should imagine.'

'What's on?'

'A new Greta Garbo. Should be good.'

'Oh, I like Greta Garbo,' Jess enthused. 'Especially when she's with John Gilbert. Now there's a handsome man for you.'

Albert pushed his plate away and yawned. It would be a sleep in the chair for him when Ellie had gone out. He could hardly keep his eyes open and the warm food had made him feel even more tired.

'Maybe we could go one night?' Jess suggested to him.

'Maybe,' he replied vaguely.

'It finishes tomorrow,' Ellie pointed out.

'It'll come round again. They always do,' Albert replied.

Jess hid her disappointment. But Albert was right, films always did. Or nearly always anyway.

'On you go then,' Jess nodded to Ellie who immediately left the table and hurried from the kitchen.

Paul was still thinking about the remainder of the steak and kidney. 'Ma?'

'What, son?'

'Don't forget what you say about food being wasted. That it's a sin when so many folk go hungry.'

Jess smiled. He was a persistent little bugger, you had to give him that. And he was right, it was a saying of hers. 'Oh, all right then, give me your plate,' she conceded.

Paul beamed as he handed it over. 'Thanks, Ma.'

Albert slumped into his comfy chair by the side of the fire. Black people coming to live in Islington? he mused. Whatever next?

When Jess spoke to him a few minutes later he was already fast asleep.

'Maybe it's because I'm a Londoner . . . !'

Albert recognised the voice as belonging to Mike, one of the Pratts who lived just down the road from them in Florence Street. 'Sounds like Mike's enjoying himself,' he commented to Jess as they went through the doors into the pub. Being a local they knew more or less everyone present so the usual nods and waves were exchanged.

Jess glanced around, spotting Ellie and George sitting in a corner. 'Shall we join them?' she asked Albert.

He noted they were deep in conversation. 'No, they're all lovey-dovey. They don't want us old folk spoiling it for them.'

'Speak for yourself. I don't consider myself old,' Jess retorted sharply. At forty-one she thought herself in her prime. Old! Why, she didn't have a single grey hair on her head.

Albert smiled at her protestation. 'You know what I mean. To them we probably seem ancient.' Then, as a sop, 'Though you and I know better, darling.'

That mollified Jess, delighted that he'd called her darling. Terms of endearment from Albert were few and far between.

Oh, he loved her, there was no question about that, but his acknowledging it in any way, shape or form was almost like getting blood from the proverbial stone.

'Usual?' he queried.

'Please.'

There was one table recently vacated, so Jess headed for that while Albert went up to the bar.

Mike Pratt finished his song to loud cheers and clapping. He then broke into 'Roll Out The Barrel'.

Albert ordered a port and lemon for Jess, considered having a pint of mild and then decided on bitter instead. It was his weekend off so there was no worry about getting up in the morning, or having to wake with a clear head. When you were a fireman hangovers could be lethal, not only for yourself but others as well. Your mind had to be fully concentrated on the job.

'Nice to see you, Albert,' declared Hazel, the guv'nor's wife who was dealing with his order. She was a tarty woman, brassy as anything with a razor-sharp wit. The customers all loved her, the men never failing to appreciate the low-cut blouses she invariably wore, blouses she more than amply filled.

'Hello, Mr Sykes. You were sparko when I called by earlier.'

Albert turned to find George standing beside him holding empty glasses. Albert liked and approved of George whom he considered a steady young man. 'Hello, son. How was the picture then?'

George pulled a face. 'Mushy stuff, romantic nonsense, not my taste at all. But Ellie enjoyed it and that's all that matters.'

'Let me get these,' Albert said, taking the glasses from George. 'My treat.'

'That's kind of you, Mr Sykes. Thanks very much.'

George was an apprentice who didn't earn a lot. He had a year to go till he was time served at which point his pay would jump considerably.

'A pint and a gin and orange,' George informed Albert.

'Right then.'

'Are you going to give us a song tonight, Albert? I think you should,' Hazel wisecracked. It was a longstanding joke between the pair of them, Hazel well aware that Albert couldn't hold a note to save his life.

'I'll sing when you start giving out free beer,' Albert riposted with a grin.

'Would that just be one for yourself, like?' she replied, laughter in her voice.

'No, everyone in the pub. Through till closing time.'

'Oh, I couldn't afford that, ducks.'

'Get on,' he teased. 'You're the richest woman in the street. Everyone knows it. This place is a little goldmine.'

'Well, they know more than I do.' She sniffed. 'Richest woman indeed, as if!'

Their banter continued until she'd finished serving him and he moved away, George having already returned to Ellie.

'There you are then,' he declared, setting their drinks on the table and sitting beside Jess.

'I saw you with George there. Did they enjoy the picture?'

'Ellie did. George thought it mushy, romantic nonsense. Not his cup of tea at all.

Sounds rather nice, Jess mused. There was nothing wrong with a bit of mush after all, even if it did embarrass men like her Albert. He was a big softie really, just undemonstrative, that's all.

It was about half an hour later, Albert and Jess on their second drink, when the pub suddenly fell silent. Albert looked round in surprise, wondering what had caused that to happen.

Everyone was staring at the newcomer who'd come in moments before. Jess hadn't been exaggerating, Albert thought. The chap *was* as black as the ace of spades.

The black man, a little older than himself Albert reckoned, slowly made his way to the bar where customers moved aside to let him in.

'Can I have a beer, please?' he politely asked a bemused Hazel.

'Pint or half?'

The man clearly didn't understand. 'One of those,' he said, pointing at a pint pot further along the bar.

'Coming up. A pint of best.'

People started to speak again, but quietly, almost in whispers. It didn't take a genius to work out what the subject of conversation was.

The black man placed a ten-shilling note on the bar then glanced nervously about. Jess could see then why Paul had said he had funny eyes. They were pale blue which appeared incongruous in such a black face.

'Are we going to allow niggers in here?'

The belligerent voice cut through the low hum of conversation like a knife, causing the black man to wince. The speaker was Taffy Roberts who was universally disliked in the street. A self-styled tough guy, he boasted of once having boxed professionally. No one knew whether or not that was true.

'Enough of that, Taffy!' Hazel snapped, wishing her husband Harry was there but he'd nipped out earlier on an errand and hadn't yet come back.

Taffy swaggered over till he was next to the black man. 'You're not welcome here, nigger, so why don't you just piss off.'

'I said enough, Taffy. This gentleman is as welcome as anyone else who minds their manners and behaviour. Neither of which you are at the moment.'

'Well, I'm not drinking with the likes of this scum. And I'm a regular don't forget, someone you're never shy to take money off.'

'I'll go,' the black man said. 'I don't want to cause no trouble. That's the last thing I need.'

Taffy poked him in the chest. 'And that's exactly what you'll get if you try and stay.'

Albert would have admitted to having many faults, but intolerance wasn't one of them. He also had a very strong sense of fairmindedness. He watched as the black man reached for his ten-bob note.

There and then he made up his mind. This was obviously

beyond Hazel who looked frightened, for once lost for words and unable to deal with the situation. Well, Taffy didn't frighten him, not by a long chalk. If no one else was going to interfere then he damned well would. He slowly rose to his feet.

'Albert, be careful,' Jess whispered.

'Why don't you shut it, Roberts!'

Taffy wheeled to face Albert. 'What's this got to do with you, Sykes?'

A grim-faced and determined Albert walked over to Roberts and the black man. 'This chap has come to live next door to me, I believe, so I'm going to ask him to sit with the wife and myself, neighbours getting to know one another like. If you have any objections to that then we'll step outside and discuss the matter further.'

Taffy's eyes narrowed, he hadn't expected this. There was an air about Albert that made him uneasy. It dawned on him it was the air of someone supremely confident in his capabilities. For the first time ever he became aware of how fit he looked and some instinct warned him it would be a big mistake to take on Albert Sykes.

'Well?' Albert queried, steel in his voice.

Taffy sneered. 'If you want that sort of company that's up to you. Just keep him away from me, that's all.'

Albert stood his ground, he wasn't going to be the first to move. There was a few seconds' hiatus, then Taffy turned away and made for the other side of the bar.

Hazel nodded her appreciation to Albert. When Harry returned she'd have him speak to Taffy. She didn't want a repetition of what had just happened. Loud-mouthed Welsh bastard, she thought to herself.

'Will you join us?' Albert asked the black man.

'My pleasure, sir.'

Albert smiled to be called that.

Hazel served the black man and quietly told him the pint was on the house, going on to emphasise he'd be welcome back any time he wished.

Jess had been holding her breath throughout the confrontation, as had many others. She was proud of Albert for what he'd just done. None of the other chaps present had been prepared to stand up to the Welshman.

'I'm Albert Sykes and this is my wife Jess,' Albert said when they reached the table.

'And I'm Pee Wee Poston.'

Jess frowned, recognising the accent from the movies. 'Are you an American?'

'All the way from New York City, ma'am. I'm right pleased to meet you folks and for getting me out of a tight corner.'

'Think nothing of it,' Albert replied, and gestured Pee Wee to sit.

Not only a black man but an American into the bargain as a neighbour! It was just one surprise after another.

'So what did you think?' Albert asked Jess later as they were getting undressed for bed.

'I liked him. And so courteous too. He couldn't have been more polite or charming.'

Albert shook his head. 'The last thing I expected was a Yank.' He suddenly laughed. 'So much for Paul worrying about him being a cannibal!'

Jess smiled as she struggled with her corset. That was funny, especially after having met the man. 'Strange name though. I found it difficult to call someone Pee Wee.'

'Lots of jazz musicians have nicknames,' Albert declared knowingly.

'And what would you know about either jazz or musicians?' she teased.

'You'd be surprised at what I know,' he replied, kicking off his shoes. 'Don't forget I get lots of spare time at the station between call-outs, time I often spend reading. Why, at the moment I'm working my way through a stack of National Geographics that was brought in. All interesting stuff.'

Jess never knew whether or not Albert was fibbing,

micky-taking again. He could be a terrible micky-taker when he had the mind. That was a side of him she'd always found endearing.

'I wonder what it means, Pee Wee, that is? I thought it would be rude to ask him.'

Albert shrugged his shoulders. 'An American expression of some sort no doubt. We'll find out in time.'

'He talked so strangely, there were so many words I didn't understand.'

'It's probably the same for him, listening to us that is.'

Jess stopped to stare at Albert. 'That was a brave thing you did tonight. No one else had the gumption to speak up against that horrible Taffy. Dreadful man.'

Albert could see the pride in her face which made him feel good inside. 'Someone had to do it,' he replied softly. 'Couldn't let Pee Wee get bullied like that. It isn't his fault he's black. And, as you said, look how nice he turned out to be.'

'You were still brave.'

'Perhaps. It was just a pity Harry wasn't there at the time. He would have sorted it out without me having to intervene. Anyway, he's had a word with Taff and that sort of thing won't happen again. If Taff tries it he'll be barred.'

Jess wriggled into her nightdress. 'I'm tired and all that port has gone to my head rather. I had far too much.'

'Go on, you enjoyed yourself. Nothing wrong with that. It's good for you once in a while. Anyway, it's a lie-in tomorrow.'

Jess laughed. 'For you that is. When do I ever lie in? You know I don't. Can't with a family to take care of.'

He considered that, appreciating how conscientious she'd always been. 'Then I think tomorrow we should change the pattern. Paul is old enough to get his own breakfast and Ellie certainly is. It's high time you stopped waiting on them hand and foot. An extra hour out the week isn't going to hurt after all. They can do for themselves for a change.'

'Oh, I couldn't, Albert!' Jess protested. 'It wouldn't be right.'

'Who says?'

She didn't have an answer to that. But it wouldn't feel right, as a wife and mother it was her duty to be up and about before the rest of the family.

'So?'

'We'll see,' she prevaricated.

He'd talk her into it, he told himself. Persuade her somehow. And that's what they'd do from here on in every time he had a weekend off, a lie-in both days.

Now in his pyjamas Albert slipped into bed and a few moments later, having switched off the light, Jess had too.

'You know something?' she whispered in the darkness.

'What?'

'I'm glad I married you.'

That touched him. He grunted in reply.

'Well?'

'Well what?'

'Aren't you going to say the same?'

'That I'm glad I married me?'

She giggled. 'Don't be ridiculous.' And with that she pinched his thigh.

'Ouch! That hurt.'

'It was meant to.'

He took her hand and squeezed it. 'I think you know how I feel.'

'But you could say it nonetheless.'

'I'm glad I married you too,' he replied in a low, gruff voice. 'Now let's get some sleep, for God's sake. You'd think it was you and not Ellie who'd been to see that romantic guff of a picture. Now, good night.'

She smiled. 'Good night.'

Jess felt gloriously, wondrously at peace. But then, she always did when in bed with Albert. It was one of the joys of being happily married.

Hell and damnation, she was going to be late! Ellie thought as she slammed the front door behind her. Miss Oates, the head of her department, would give her a right finger-wagging. The old cow!

At least it was Saturday which meant she'd be finished by dinnertime. And that evening she and George were going dancing at the Roxy, the Poxy Roxy as it was locally known. Still, it was cheap and the bands they had weren't all that bad.

She stopped in amazement to admire the car parked at the kerb. A car in Florence Street! That was a turn-up for the books. Usually the only car to be seen parked round here belonged to the doctor.

A smart machine too, she noted, all nicely polished with comfy-looking leather upholstery. It was outside the new people's house so it must belong to them. Funny, it hadn't been there when she'd come home the night before. It must have arrived after that or earlier that morning.

Maybe those black people were rich? But if so why come to live in Florence Street? It didn't make sense.

No time to spend dawdling, she berated herself, and hurried on her way to the bank in Upper Street where she worked as a clerk and where an irate, if she was any later, Miss Oates would be waiting for her.

Jess wiped her hands on her pinny, the apron she, and most housewives, habitually wore during the day, before answering the knock at the door.

An extremely fat black lady beamed at her, exposing the most amazing set of gleaming white teeth.

'Are you Mrs Sykes?'

'I am.'

'I's Beulah Poston, Pee Wee's wife. I've come round to personally thank you for what you and your husband did last night. Pee Wee's told me all about it.'

Beulah? Another peculiar name. 'Think nothing of it. We were glad to help.'

Impossibly Beulah's beam became even broader. 'I was wonderin' if I could speak to you, Mrs Sykes?'

'Of course. Of course,' Jess replied hurriedly, standing aside so Beulah could enter. 'And the name's Jess, by the way.'

'And I's Beulah.'

Jess ushered her through to the kitchen. 'I was just about to put on the kettle. Would you like a cup of tea?'

Beulah hesitated. 'You wouldn't happen to have coffee?'

Jess smiled. 'Yes, I do.' She didn't always have coffee in the house as it was something of a luxury due to the cost. But right then she did.

'How are you settling in, Beulah?'

'Just fine. Jim dandy. Though I must say England is going to take a deal of gettin' used to. It's so different from back home.'

'This is your first trip here then?' Jess probed, opening a cupboard to get the coffee. She'd use the best china, she decided.

'It's my first trip outside the good ole US of A. Same for Pee Wee. We're both absolutely thrilled to bits.'

Jess wished she had some cakes or scones to offer, but hadn't. Not even a plain biscuit, Paul having scoffed the last of those the previous night when they were out at the pub.

'He mentioned he's here to play in a band?'

'That's right. He jumped at the chance when offered as it means we can be with our son Julius for a spell. He works in London and has done for nearly a year now.'

'Really?' Jess thought that interesting.

'Yeah, he's with the State Department currently posted to our Embassy here. He sure was pleased when we wrote him the news about our comin' over. He thought it was a great idea.'

Embassy! Jess was impressed. 'And is he living with you?'

'Has an apartment in town, comes with the job, but is givin' it up to be with us. Says he sure misses his old ma's home cookin'.'

Jess laughed.

'No offence to your English food, Jess, but Julius says it just ain't the same.'

Jess put out the cups and saucers, again wishing she had something else to offer.

'Anyway, the other reason I came by is Pee Wee and me was wonderin' if you and your family would care to come to lunch next Sunday, a week tomorrow that is? We'd sure like that.'

Jess was taken aback to say the least, this the last thing she'd been expecting. Lunch at an American house, and with a black couple at that. What on earth would Albert say?

'I eh . . .' Oh dear.

'Maybe you want to ask your husband before answering?' Beulah said, a trace of disappointment in her voice.

Jess made up her mind. A refusal would be downright rude. And it would be different. Yes, certainly that. Bound to be. 'We'd love to come, Beulah.'

The broad beam returned. 'Excellent. Now, just tell me how many of you are there?'

'Four,' Jess replied. 'We have a boy of ten and a daughter of nineteen.'

'Then four it is,' Beulah declared, smacking meaty hands together.

Chapter 2

'If you'll just sit here, Jess, and Albert you there.' They'd all come through to the kitchen where a splendid table had been laid. A frankly gawping Jess did as she was instructed.

'It's meat loaf,' Beulah declared from the newly installed electric stove where she was busying herself. 'I hope you folks like that.'

'What's meat loaf?' a frowning Paul queried.

Beulah laughed. 'Is that new to you? Well it's just what you would call mince, done in a sort of loaf shape and covered in tomato sauce. It's real traditional where we come from. Ain't that right, honey?'

Pee Wee nodded. 'Sure is.'

Jess stared about her in astonishment, she'd never in her entire life seen a kitchen so well equipped. 'It's amazing the transformation here in just a week,' she commented.

'We got Julius to thank for that,' Pee Wee replied proudly. 'Workin' as he does at the Embassy that boy can get almost anythin'. And quick too.'

'Is that a refrigerator?' Ellie inquired, pointing.

'You got it,' Beulah beamed. 'Though out of habit I still call it the ice box.'

'I've noticed vans outside your house all week long,' Jess said. 'Now I know what they were delivering.'

'And installin',' Pee Wee added. 'All thanks to Julius.'

Don't be envious, Jess chided herself. But she'd have given anything for a kitchen like this.

'How about another beer there, Albert?' Pee Wee offered.

Albert shook his head. The bottle he'd had on arrival, something called Schlitz, had tasted foul, and so cold! The refrigerator explained the latter.

Jess couldn't help herself. 'I presume that's a washing machine in the corner?'

'Uh-huh!' Beulah confirmed, placing a large plate of vegetables on the table. More vegetables followed that then a plate of yellow-coloured bread.

'Can I get you anythin', Jess? A glass of wine perhaps? We got lots.'

She was about to say no, then changed her mind. She needed a drink after the shock of all this.

'Red or white?'

'Red please.'

'And you, Ellie?'

'The same, thanks,' she answered, almost as bemused as her mother.

Pee Wee delved into a cupboard to produce a bottle which he proceeded to open.

'Don't forget me there, honey. I'd like one too.'

Pee Wee smiled hugely at his wife. 'I ain't forgettin' you, Mama. How could I ever do that?'

Beulah laughed almost girlishly as she placed the meat loaf alongside the vegetables. 'I should hope not.'

'What instrument do you play, Mr Poston?' Ellie inquired politely.

'The saxophone. Alto sax actually.'

'And real sweet music he plays too,' Beulah chipped in. 'When I listen to him play I swears I's in dreamland.'

Pee Wee preened at the compliment. 'Do you know anythin' about jazz?' he asked Ellie.

She shook her head. 'Nothing at all.'

'I don't think any of us do,' Albert said, having finally relaxed and now beginning to enjoy himself. He hadn't been at all sure about this but Jess had accepted the invitation so he'd had to come. More than anything the food had worried him, he was used to plain, no-nonsense, English fayre and the thought of anything exotic or . . . horror of horrors . . . spicy filled him with dread. Still, this meat loaf didn't look too bad. Mince was mince after all and he was well used to that. Though not with tomato sauce plastered all over it!

Beulah eased herself into the chair at the bottom of the table, facing Pee Wee at the top. 'Will you say grace, honey?'

That startled the entire Sykes family who weren't used to such niceties, Jess indicating for Paul to bow his head.

Pee Wee said a few short words followed by a hearty amen. 'Now let's eat, folks, I'm starvin'.'

Albert refused the bread when it was handed round, thinking he didn't like the look of that, but Jess and the children had some. It certainly wasn't like any bread Jess had ever come across before. It was coarser than she was used to, and why yellow? She slowly buttered her piece and then gingerly tasted it.

'Interesting,' she commented after she'd swallowed.

'You never had corn bread before?' Beulah queried.

Corn bread, that explained the colour. 'I'm afraid I haven't.'

'So what do you think?'

Jess considered that. 'I like it. It's certainly different.'

'And what about you, Paul?'

He shrugged non-committally.

Minutes later Jess watched Albert tentatively taste the meat loaf, then smiled to herself in relief as he took a full mouthful. It had met with his approval, thank God!

Every so often, the conversation never flagging, Jess found her eyes straying to the stove, refrigerator, washing machine and various other paraphernalia that she wished she owned. Beulah didn't know how lucky she was.

'And when do we get to meet Julius?' Albert asked at one point, on his second helping of meat loaf which he'd found delicious. He'd already made a mental note that Jess should get the recipe for their own use.

'Hopefully before you all leave. He's out on business I'm afraid,' Beulah replied.

'He works Sundays?' Albert queried with a frown.

'Sure. Though not every week. There's always a skeleton staff at least at the Embassy,' Beulah explained.

'And what exactly does he do there?'

Pee Wee laughed. 'No idea, Albert. That boy sure is close-mouthed about his work. Ain't allowed to tell anyone anythin' apparently. It's all a big secret.'

'Is he a spy?' a wide-eyed Paul asked.

'Naw, nothin' fancy like that,' Pee Wee assured him. Then, seeing the boy's crestfallen expression, 'Though, who's to say? I don't know. Maybe he is at that.'

'Gosh!' Paul exclaimed softly. Just wait till he told his pals at school!

'Here, let me help you,' Jess offered when Beulah began clearing the table.

'You just set where you are, Jess. You're a guest here which means you just set and enjoy yourself.'

'At least let Ellie help. Please?'

Ellie was instantly on her feet. 'I insist, Mrs Poston.'

'But you's . . .'

'Ma will be furious with me if I don't,' Ellie interjected, knowing that to be true enough.

Beulah gave in. 'OK then, child, just stack the dirty stuff in the sink while I get the dessert ready.'

'What is it?' Paul demanded eagerly.

'Paul!' Jess rebuked, while Albert glared at him.

'Sorry,' a suddenly red-faced Paul mumbled, glancing down into his lap.

Beulah was amused, thinking that was just like a kid. Julius had been exactly the same. 'Well, let's see now,' she demurred. 'You got a choice.'

Paul looked up at her, but said nothing.

'There's strawberry shortcake with cream, or chocolate ice cream.' She paused, a smile twinkling her face. 'There again, you could have both.'

Paul had no idea what strawberry shortcake was, and decided not to ask. He'd already blotted his copybook by being too eager.

The strawberry shortcake was a circular sponge flan with strawberries inside, the latter encased in a sort of gelatin. Jess watched in amazement as Beulah shook a can from the refrigerator and squirted cream over the top.

Albert shook his head. What will they think of next! Trust the Yanks to come up with cream in a can, he thought.

When asked, Paul elected to have the strawberry shortcake which, it transpired, he simply adored.

'Now can the kid have some ice cream as well?' Beulah asked Jess when he'd swiftly polished that off.

Jess's expression was one of disapproval. 'It seems a bit excessive. Albert?'

He too was disapproving, but didn't wish to offend their hosts. The ice cream hadn't been solicited after all. 'I suppose so. Just this once,' he agreed reluctantly.

'We do this all the time back home,' Beulah explained. 'We see nothin' unusual in it. One dessert and then another.'

No wonder she was so fat, Albert thought somewhat unkindly. 'I suppose you Americans simply have more food than we do over here,' he rationalised.

They seemed to have more of everything, Jess thought, glancing enviously yet again at the refrigerator. What a wonderful, easy life it must be in America.

'Now what say we have coffee in the other room, Beulah?' Pee Wee suggested when everyone had finished.

'Sure thing. More comfortable in there. We can spread out and relax.'

They all trouped through leaving Beulah behind. 'Now how about a brandy, or there's scotch if you prefer,' Pee Wee declared, rubbing his hands together.

'Not for me thank you,' Jess replied, sinking into a comfortable chair, so large it threatened to engulf her. She was full enough to explode. Cream in a can indeed, not at all like the cream she could buy in the shops. Now that was cream! The American version was a poor relation on the taste buds. Very poor.

'I wouldn't mind a scotch,' Albert admitted. Scotch was something of a treat he allowed himself once in a while, though beer was his usual tipple.

'Malt or Black Label?'

'Black Label please.' Now that was scotch at its best. He'd never really been partial to malt.

'Ma?'

'What is it, Paul?'

'Can I ask you something?'

'Of course.'

He crossed over and started to whisper in her ear.

'Paul, it's rude to whisper in company. Say aloud what you have to or not at all.'

He reddened for the second time. 'Can I leave and play out?'

Pee Wee intervened when he saw that Jess was about to refuse. 'We wouldn't take no offence if he does, Jess. Let the kid do as he wants.'

'Are you certain?' she demanded.

'Sure I'm certain. He don't want to be cooped up in here when the sun's shinin'.'

Jess turned again to Paul. 'All right, on you go.'

'Thanks, Ma. And thanks, Mr Poston.'

'Children,' Jess sighed when Paul was gone. 'What do you do with them?'

'I think the question is, what would you do without them. Me and Beulah have always taken the attitude that the good Lord smiled on us when He gave us Diane and Julius.'

That puts me firmly in my place, a chastened Jess thought. Pee Wee was right of course.

'Here, steady on!' Albert exclaimed as Pee Wee poured the whisky.

Pee Wee held out the glass. 'That's only three fingers' worth. Too much for you?'

Albert swallowed hard as he accepted the drink. 'No, it's just that I'm used to far smaller measures, that's all.'

'I noticed that in the pub the other night,' Pee Wee nodded. 'You Brits are sure mean with the liquor.'

Albert didn't know what to reply, so said nothing.

'You have a daughter as well?' Jess queried. 'I didn't realise.'

'Yeah, Diane, our firstborn. Older than Julius by three years. She's back in New York where she lives with her husband and baby. The baby, cute little beggar, is called Bradley after his pa. A real happy family they are too. We miss them already.'

Pee Wee laid his brandy aside. 'I have some pictures here if you'd care to see them?'

'That would be lovely.'

Ellie inwardly groaned. They were on to pictures, snaps, now. How boring. She wanted to excuse herself as Paul had done but her parents would be furious if she suggested it. Manners dictated she stay.

'Should I go and help Mrs Poston bring the coffee through?' she said to Jess.

'Good idea. On you go. And see if there's anything else you can do to help.'

Ellie came up short in the hallway when she found herself face to face with an incredibly good-looking young black man who smiled at her.

'Hello,' he said in a warm, velvety voice which made her go instantly weak at the knees. 'I'm Julius.'

'Well,' Albert declared later when they were finally back home again, Ellie having gone straight upstairs. 'What did you make of that?'

'One thing's certain,' Jess replied.

'What is?'

'We can't ask them back here for a meal.'

Albert frowned. 'Why not?'

'It's obvious, I should have thought. I can't compete with the likes of that. Refrigerator, washing machine, cream in a can. Wine, whisky . . .' She trailed off and shook her head. 'I'd be ashamed.'

Dear Jess, he thought. Dear dear Jess. And how typical of a woman. 'We have a working-class English household, Jess, not a fancy American one. They'd understand.'

'I don't care. I'd feel humiliated.'

'Then you'd be wrong.'

'Maybe,' she sniffed. 'But I won't change my mind.'

She would, he told himself. He'd see to it. 'Well I don't know about you, but I thoroughly enjoyed myself.'

'So did I. Don't get me wrong. And they did go to a lot of trouble. Even though . . .' Again she trailed off.

Albert's lips twitched. 'Cream in a *can*,' he said mockingly.

They looked at each other, and then, as one, burst out laughing. Cream in a can! How ridiculous could you get.

Danny McGiver looked up from the newspaper he was reading. 'What do you think of this Mussolini business?' he asked Albert, the pair of them having completed their routine duties round the fire station and now waiting for either a call-out or the end of their shift.

Albert, sitting in an adjacent chair, frowned. 'What Mussolini business?'

'It says here we've signed an Anglo-Italian Agreement allowing the Eyeties to annexe Abyssinia. In my book that's another sell-out to Fascism.'

Albert thought about that. 'Perhaps we had no choice?'

'Of course we did!' Danny snapped. 'I don't like it, I tell you. I don't like it at all. Once you give in to those bastards they just want more and more.' Danny snorted. 'First Hitler with Austria, now this. Where will it all end, I ask you. Where will it all end?'

They both brooded on that for a few seconds. 'Are you suggesting there might be another war?' Albert asked eventually, going cold at the thought.

'It's a possibility, I suppose.'

'Dear God in Heaven,' Albert swore softly. That would be disastrous. Unthinkable! 'It'll never come to that,' he declared, wishing he felt more sure about it. Surely they all learned their lesson last time?'

Danny regarded him thoughtfully. 'Didn't you lose your father in that?'

Albert's face clouded, his expression becoming one of deepest sadness. 'My father and three uncles. Two in France, one in Belgium.' He hesitated before going on, 'I was exempt otherwise I would have been in it too.'

'Are you sorry you weren't?'

Albert barked out a short laugh. 'That bloodbath? I'm as loyal to King and Country as the next man, but if I'm being honest I was more than relieved at not having to join up.'

'I was "over there",' Danny stated quietly.

That surprised Albert who hadn't thought Danny old enough. 'I never knew that.'

'Only for a short while towards the end.' He shuddered. 'It was hell on earth, believe me. An absolute nightmare. It just beggars belief that they'd want to go through it all again. They'd have to be bloody mental. Stark raving bonkers.'

'Let's just hope and pray it doesn't come to that,' Albert said.

'Surely it won't.' Then, vehemently, 'It can't!'

Their conversation was abruptly terminated when the bell began to clang announcing they'd been called out. The station erupted into a frenzy of activity as men appeared from wherever they'd been, all hurriedly snatching up bits of uniform and equipment.

Within minutes their engine, with Danny at the wheel, was roaring down Upper Street towards the Angel where apparently a chimney had gone up.

Ellie didn't know why she was miserable, but she was. Miserable and down in the dumps. Fed up to the back teeth.

Life seemed to have become so predictable of late. Go to

work, come home from work. Stay in one night a week to wash her hair. Friday nights with George, usually the pictures, Saturday to the Poxy Roxy. All humdrum in the extreme.

Was this what the rest of her life was going to be like? Marriage in a few years' time, children, living somewhere close by no doubt. Day in day out a repetition of the same old thing.

And what would it be like married to George? He hadn't asked her yet but she knew he intended to when he was time served and a fully fledged journeyman.

Did she love George? She frowned as she thought about that, coming to the conclusion she wasn't sure. What was love anyway? Some overpowering emotion that made you completely besotted with another person? If that was so she wasn't in love with George. Oh she certainly liked him, he could be good fun at times, and was always easy to be with. But was that enough to get married?

The trouble was there wasn't any excitement in her life, it was all so samey. And she wanted excitement, at least some before she settled down to bringing up a family.

But where would she find excitement? And what sort? There just wasn't any, at least none that she'd found.

Ellie sighed. She really did have a case of the miseries. Here she was feeling sorry for herself when there was so much she should be grateful for. She had wonderful parents, even if she did bicker with them on occasion, but that was only natural, a good home, decent job – despite that cow Miss Oates whom she was rapidly coming to loathe – with a reasonable salary considering her age and lowliness of her position.

Perhaps she should go to college and train to be a shorthand typist? Not that there would be much fun and excitement in that. But it was a thought.

There again that would mean her father having to keep her while she studied which was hardly fair, not at her age when she'd already been working for a number of years and bringing money into the house. If she'd wanted to go to college she should have come up with the idea on leaving school, not now.

Anyway, what would be the point if she got married in the not-too-distant future. None at all. A complete waste of time and energy.

She thought again about George, and smiled. He wasn't a bad-looking chap, fairly handsome actually, and he adored her, the latter going a long way in her opinion. Safe, yes that was George, safe and dependable.

Her heart sank. How boring safe and dependable sounded, though there were many round here who'd give their eye teeth for such a bloke.

He enjoyed a drink, but didn't go over the top. She simply couldn't imagine George reeling in pissed on a Friday night having blown most of his wages in the pub. There were many like that. Nor could she envision him being a womaniser, someone who got wed and then continued to chase a bit of skirt whenever the opportunity presented itself. There were a lot like that too, she'd heard her mother talking about them often enough, her tone hushed and pitying as she and whoever discussed the poor wronged wife in question.

Her dad wasn't at all like that, she doubted he'd even looked at another woman since marrying Mum, the two of them as much a couple as they'd ever been. But then they were in love, or certainly appeared to be. Happy as Larry together, the pair of them.

Ellie yawned, it was later than she'd realised. She should get some sleep. She didn't want to turn up for work in the morning all bleary-eyed which would earn her a frosty, disapproving look from Miss Oates and some cutting remarks during the course of the day.

With a jolt it dawned on her then that she'd never ever dreamt about George. If she had she hadn't recalled afterwards. Now wasn't that strange! Odd to say the least.

She bit her lip. Was that indicative of something? It could be for she dreamt about all sorts of people she knew, including the dreadful Miss Oates, but never George.

How very, very odd.

She worried about that, turning it over and over in her mind, till eventually she nodded off.

'I wish the bus would hurry up,' Jess fretted, glancing up at the sky. 'I'm sure it's going to rain.'

'And when it does come there'll be three more right behind it,' Ellie commented, for wasn't that so often the case.

A car, which Ellie instantly recognised, drew up alongside them and the window was rolled down. 'I'm going into the West End, is that any good?' Julius Poston queried with a smile.

'Oh my!' Jess exclaimed. 'Are you offering to give us a lift?'

'Sure am.'

'Well, the West End is where we're off to.'

'Then hop in.'

Jess settled herself into the seat beside Julius while Ellie, to her disappointment, was relegated to the back. 'This is the first time I've ever been in a private car,' Jess admitted as they sped away. 'I feel ever so grand.'

Julius was incredulous. 'Really?'

'The first time,' Jess reiterated. 'Won't Albert be surprised when I tell him.'

Julius glanced in his rear-view mirror. 'How about you, Ellie?'

'Me too.'

He laughed. 'Well, well, well. I never.'

'You don't see all that many round here,' Jess went on. 'When you do they usually belong to commercial travellers.'

Julius frowned. 'Commercial traveller?'

'Travelling salesmen,' Ellie interpreted.

'Oh! I understand.'

'Are you going anywhere near Oxford Street?' Jess queried.

'Can do.'

'If it's not out of your way.'

'No trouble at all, Mrs Sykes. My pleasure.'

She might have been royalty being whizzed along like this, Jess reflected with satisfaction. 'We're going in to buy a few underthings for Ellie who badly needs them,' Jess explained.

Ellie blushed bright scarlet. 'Mum!' she exclaimed, mortified.

Julius glanced in his rear-view mirror again, amused by Ellie's discomfiture. 'We all wear them, kid,' he said over his shoulder.

She very nearly snapped back for him not to call her kid, she wasn't a child but quite grown up, thank you very much.

Jess was also amused by Ellie's reaction which she hadn't anticipated. 'And a new blouse for me,' she went on. 'If I can find a suitable one that is.'

Ellie felt her face die down again. She was aware of Julius staring at her in the mirror but refused to meet his gaze.

'What's that smell?' Jess suddenly demanded.

'Smell, Mrs Sykes?'

'Like . . . like . . . flowers. Yes, that's it, flowers.'

A puzzled Julius thought about that for a moment. 'Do you mean my cologne?'

Jess was scandalised. 'You wear cologne?'

'I do.'

'Well, blow me! I never heard of such a thing. A man wearing cologne. I'd be horrified if Albert tried that.' She was about to add it was most unmanly, but decided not to. She didn't want to offend Julius after all. 'I suppose it's because you're an American,' she said instead.

'I suppose,' Julius agreed, tongue firmly in cheek.

Ellie could smell it now, and thought it was rather nice. She wouldn't have minded wearing it herself.

Jess thanked Julius profusely when he later dropped them in front of Selfridges. 'My pleasure. My pleasure entirely, ma'am.' A hint of laughter twitched the corners of his lips upwards. 'It's sure been entertainin'.'

Jess wondered what he meant by that as he continued on his way. Why entertaining?

Albert was aghast when she told him about the cologne that evening.

Chapter 3

Julius glanced about him, wondering what an English audience was going to be like. They appeared extremely stiff and reserved to him, not at all what his pop and the rest of the band were used to.

It was opening night at The Chicory House, a new cellar nightclub situated in Soho. Was the night going to be a huge success or disaster? A few hours would tell.

Beulah sipped her champagne and worried about Pee Wee. He'd been terribly nervous at home and on the way here, which was most unlike him. He'd hardly uttered a single word all day.

Beulah leant across the table so she could whisper to Julius. 'See that guy with the grey suit and red hair? That's Lord Fitzaran who hired your pop in New York and brought him and the others over.'

Julius picked out the gentleman in question, already knowing the story behind this venture. Lord Fitzaran was a jazz fanatic who'd come up with the idea of bringing American musicians across the Atlantic so that the English could hear the sound of genuine Dixieland. Every member of the band had been hand-picked and considered a true, if not great, artist on his particular instrument.

As he watched, Fitzaran made his way to the small stage and

climbed up onto it. Standing behind a microphone he held up a hand for silence.

Thankfully, the speech of welcome was brief, Fitzaran exuding excitement and confidence. The end of his speech was greeted with polite applause.

Oh dear, Julius thought. A New York audience would have been far more responsive than that. These Joes were half dead.

'You OK, Mom?'

Beulah nodded. 'OK, but all tight inside. This sure is nerve-rackin'.'

Julius could well imagine what it must be like for the band opening in a country quite foreign to them. There were British jazz musicians of course, but this band were the authentic article, only one of whom, John Parlour, was white.

The lights dimmed and the curtains fronting the stage drew back to reveal the band all ready to go.

John Parlour came forward, having been elected by the others, to speak a few words. And then, with a gesture of his cornet, they began to play, the opening number being 'Ole Rocking Chair's Got Me', followed by 'Woodchopper's Ball'.

Julius smiled as he felt the audience start to relax.

Pee Wee, face wreathed in a huge smile, collapsed into what had become his chair. 'I'll say it again, if that don't beat all!'

'You hungry, hon?'

He looked across at Beulah. 'How about a peanut butter and jelly sandwich?'

'Sure. You, Julius?'

Julius shook his head. The thought of a peanut butter and jelly sandwich at that time of the morning made his stomach heave. 'How about a drink, Pop?'

'Yes sir. Bourbon.'

When he'd arrived home that evening Julius had brought his parents several boxes of supplies that he'd acquired through the Embassy, all of them American foodstuffs and alcohol, most of which couldn't be bought in England.

'I told you it would be OK,' Beulah said to Pee Wee yet again. 'Didn't I?'

He regarded her affectionately. 'You did, honey. You most certainly did.'

'And I was right.'

Pee Wee, still smiling, closed his eyes, remembering the gig. It had taken the audience about half an hour to really unwind, but when they had! Hey, man, he might have been playing the Cotton Club itself. Any worries he, and the others, had had about playing in England had gone straight out the window.

'Did you mention there were a couple of newspaper guys there?' he queried of Julius.

'Music critics apparently. They were wild about it. You're goin' to get great reviews in tomorrow's papers.'

Pee Wee sighed with contentment. 'Then it looks like we're goin' to be here for quite a spell. Hot damn!'

Julius couldn't have been more pleased, or relieved, for his father. It meant there would be no early return Stateside for his parents which, selfishly, pleased him even more.

'There you are, Pop,' he declared, handing Pee Wee a well-filled glass, the bourbon straight as Pee Wee preferred it.

'You not having one, son?'

'I've already had more than enough. Don't forget I've got to get up in the morning for work.' Then, teasing, 'Unlike some I could name.'

Pee Wee laughed, knowing he wouldn't be emerging from the bedroom till well past noon. That was his routine when he was playing.

'Goodnight then, Pop.'

'Goodnight, son.'

'It couldn't have gone better. You brought the house down.'

Pee Wee acknowledged the compliment with a nod, then had a swallow of bourbon, Jack Daniels, his favourite.

'Goodnight, Mom.'

She kissed him on the cheek. 'You want breakfast?'

'I'll make my own. You sleep in with Pop.'

'Sleep well then.'

'Oh I will,' he replied knowingly. 'Have no doubt about that.'

Enroute upstairs he wondered for what might have been the millionth time in his life how his father's musical talent had so completely bypassed him. He could hardly hold a note.

Miss Oates stopped abruptly in her tracks, her expression horror-struck, her eyes seemingly out on stalks. Ellie tensed, dreading she'd done something wrong, and if so what? Her mind raced.

'Miss Fox,' Miss Oates finally managed to get out, her voice trembling in outrage. 'Is that what I think it is on your neck?'

Ellie glanced sideways at Connie Fox, a good pal, who did the same job as herself.

Connie was looking extremely embarrassed, her hands busily readjusting the scarf round her neck.

'Well?' Miss Oates demanded.

'Yes,' Connie acknowledged in a whisper, inwardly cursing the fact her scarf must have slipped without her realising it.

'A love bite I believe it's called.'

Several typists, listening in to the conversation, began sniggering.

'Quiet!' Miss Oates snapped, and the giggling immediately ceased. She fastened her beady gaze back onto Connie. 'How disgraceful. How utterly disgraceful. I've a good mind to send you home for the rest of the week without pay.'

Connie gulped.

'How could you let such a thing happen. And then come to the office to flaunt your depravity?'

Connie hardly thought it depravity, but wasn't going to say. You didn't argue, or cross swords, with Miss Oates, not if you valued your job that is.

'I'm terribly sorry, Miss Oates. Truly I am. Please forgive me,' Connie grovelled.

That mollified Miss Oates a little. But only a little. 'See that disgusting mark remains covered as long as it's in existence. And there will be no repeat. Understand?'

Connie nodded. 'Yes, Miss Oates.'

Miss Oates glared at Ellie, and then the typists who'd been listening in. 'That goes for all of you.'

'Disgraceful,' Miss Oates muttered a second later, and swept imperiously away.

'Frustrated, bitter old bag,' Connie spat. 'It's jealousy, that's all it is. Sheer jealousy.'

Ellie had to smile. Connie was probably right. She doubted Miss Oates had ever been kissed by a man in her entire life.

Connie leant across and whispered conspiratorially. 'I wonder what she'd say if she saw the one on my right tit.'

Ellie was shocked.

Connie winked and returned to work, leaving a speechless Ellie staring at her back.

Every Wednesday afternoon Jess called in to visit old Ma Jenkins who enjoyed the company, her legs being bad and not getting out and about as much as she used to. Mr Jenkins had died years previously from cancer of the bowel.

'Another biscuit, Jess?' Ma Jenkins asked, offering a plateful.

Jess shook her head. 'No thanks. I've already had three.'

Ma Jenkins settled back in her chair and eyed Jess speculatively through rheumy eyes. 'Want to talk about it?'

That startled Jess. 'Talk about what?'

'Whatever's bothering you. For I can see that something plainly is.'

Jess sighed. Trust Ma. She never missed a trick. 'I'm not a hundred per cent certain but I think I might be expecting.'

'Oh!' The rheumy eyes bored into Jess's. 'That's good news, isn't it?'

'Depends how you look at it,' Jess replied softly.

Ma pursed her withered lips, and waited for Jess to explain herself.

'It's my age, Ma, forty-one, shortly forty-two. It's knocking on a bit to have children.'

Ma acknowledged the truth of that with a slight nod.

'And then there's Albert. I don't know what his reaction would be at having another baby round the house. I suspect he wouldn't be best pleased.'

'I see,' Ma murmured.

'Oh don't get me wrong. Albert loves children and dotes on ours, even if Paul can be something of a handful at times. But I think he believes, although he's never actually said, that we've had our quota. That that sort of thing is finished with.'

Ma's mouth stretched into a mocking smile. 'Then he should have thought of that when he made you pregnant.'

Jess shrugged. 'I think I must have misled him there. I thought my conceiving days were over, it's been ten years since Paul after all. Apparently I was wrong.'

Ma reached to the small table by the side of her chair, picked up a packet of Woodbines and lit one. 'You won't do anything silly, I hope?'

It was a couple of seconds before Jess understood. 'Good God, no! Albert wouldn't let me go near one of those butchers. He'd have a blue fit if I even so much as suggested it.'

Ma nodded her approval. She'd had a friend once who'd gone to a backstreet abortionist. Her friend had lost the baby all right, but had come close to dying in the process when septicaemia set in. 'How many periods have you missed?'

'I haven't, that's the problem and why I thought I was past such a thing. I haven't had one for ages. Not even the smallest show.'

'And yet you think you're pregnant?'

'I know the signs, Ma, only too well.'

'If you are you are and that's all there is to it.'

'I suppose so,' Jess replied glumly.

'Do you want a baby yourself?'

Jess took a deep breath. 'The truth? No. Also at my age it's a worry about what might happen. I mean, I could even pop my clogs, and then what? Albert left on his own and Paul the age he is.'

Ma didn't know what else to say or advise. She and her Reg had never been blessed with children which had always been a great sadness to both of them. And now here was Jess admitting to not wanting what, at one time, she would almost have sold her soul for. Life was hardly fair, though no one had ever said it was or promised otherwise.

'Does anyone else know about this?' Ma asked.

Jess shook her head.

'Well, you don't have to worry about me. I won't say anything.'

'Thanks, Ma.'

'But don't you think you should go and see the doctor?'

Jess had already considered that, but simply didn't want to in case he confirmed what she suspected. She wanted to put off being certain as long as she could. For who knew? It might be a false alarm. Hardly a logical way of thinking, she told herself. But that's how she wished to deal with it.

'I will,' she lied. 'I'll get round to calling into the surgery.'

Jess reached for her tea which was now stone cold. Ma said she'd put the kettle back on but Jess excused herself saying she really had to go – another lie, she just didn't want to continue talking about this.

Out in the street she felt an almost overwhelming urge to cry, but somehow, and it was a struggle not to give in to it, she didn't. She considered that to be even more proof, remembering how she'd been forever bursting into tears when carrying Ellie.

'Are you all right?' George asked Ellie, as the pair of them sat at a table in The Florence.

'I'm fine. Why?'

'You're awfully quiet tonight.'

She'd been thinking about Connie Fox's love bite and the fact George had never even tried to give her one. She'd have quickly put him off if he had, but it rankled nonetheless that he hadn't at least made the attempt.

She gazed around The Florence. Another Friday night, another drink here. And tomorrow night, the Poxy Roxy yet again. She had suggested they might go up West for a change, but George had vetoed the idea explaining he was short of cash. It was depressing.

'Would you like another?' he asked, indicating her glass.

She almost said, was he sure he could afford it? But didn't as that would have been unkind not to mention hurtful.

'Please.'

He picked up her glass and made his way over to the bar where he fell into conversation with another of the regulars.

The same old faces, Ellie thought. Night after night the same old faces. Boring.

She wondered what it was like to have a love bite? Did it hurt getting one? It must do, especially if it was on . . . She took a deep breath, her face colouring ever so slightly . . . the breast.

Had Connie kept her bra on or taken it off? And what else had happened during that encounter? She'd never previously considered Connie to be fast, but now she wasn't so sure.

George had groped her a few times, but always on the outside of her blouse or sweater. That was as much as she'd allow. And he'd certainly never attempted to put his hand up her skirt. He'd have had a right old slap if he had.

She stared at George's back, wondering what he was like without clothes on? She'd never ever seen a naked man, not even her father. Paul when he was younger, yes. But that didn't count.

Paul's willy had been a tiny little thing, quite insignificant. But a full-grown man's? That was something else entirely, at least so she'd been told by one of the girls at school who had umpteen brothers of all ages and all still, then anyway, living at home.

She supposed she'd never find out till her wedding night when the big revelation would take place. She felt warm prickles of anticipation run over her shoulders and down her front.

The trouble with all that business was it was near impossible to get information about it. She could have asked Jess of course, but nothing on earth would have made her do so. She'd die of embarrassment, and no doubt so too would her mother.

She wished she had a married friend her own age she could consult, but didn't. Her pals were all still single and virgins. At least she presumed the latter. It was a terrible shame and stigma to 'get in the club' without being wed, not only for yourself but your entire family. The risk just wasn't worth it.

Her thoughts were interrupted when Julius Poston entered the pub accompanied by a black woman. The pub didn't quite stop but suddenly these two were the centre of attention.

Ellie watched Julius escort the woman over to an empty table where the woman sat. After a brief exchange Julius went up to order.

An attractive woman, Ellie noted. Somewhere in her mid-twenties and very smartly turned out. Why, that tan-coloured suede coat she had on alone must have cost a fortune.

'Close your mouth or you'll catch flies in it,' George teased, rejoining Ellie. 'I take it that's your new neighbour's girlfriend?'

'I've no idea,' Ellie replied waspishly. 'I've never seen her before.'

'Quite a cracker, if you don't mind them black.'

For some reason that annoyed Ellie. 'Fancy her, do you?'

'Not me. I was just commenting, that's all.'

Julius glanced over and smiled at Ellie and she returned the smile shyly. Well, it would have been rude not to.

'She must be a Yank as well,' George speculated. He laughed. 'She certainly isn't from around here.'

Ellie watched the woman take out a packet of cigarettes and light up. Even at this distance she could make out that the packet was foreign so that seemed to confirm that the woman was indeed American.

'Probably works at the Embassy with Julius,' Ellie guessed.

'Would make sense.'

The pub had now more or less returned to normal, though

every so often glances were still being thrown at Julius and his friend.

How elegant the woman was, Ellie reflected. She couldn't quite see what her figure was like but had the horrible suspicion it was stunning. She felt dowdy and plain by comparison.

'Good-looking geezer too, your neighbour.' George smiled.

Ellie pretended indifference. 'Is he? I hadn't noticed.'

'Well, I'd say so. And not very African in appearance either. No thick lips and squat nose. Same with her.'

There had to be white blood in the pair of them somewhere along the line, Ellie thought. Not that she knew much about such matters. It just seemed common sense, that's all.

Well, she'd been moaning to herself about the same old faces, and now this. Quite a turn-up for the book.

The black woman shifted position to reveal a long shapely leg projecting through a vent in her coat. George couldn't help but stare at it, in common with most of the other men in the pub.

Ellie was furious. 'You're with me, don't forget,' she snapped.

George immediately brought his attention back to her. 'Sorry.'

She snorted. 'I should think so.'

He reached across the table and laid a hand over one of hers. 'Don't be jealous. There's no need to be.'

'I am nothing of the sort,' she retorted hotly, furious that he should think such a thing, even if it was true. She eased her hand out from under his and picked up her drink.

For the rest of the evening George only took his eyes off her when going to the bar or toilet.

On the way out Ellie managed a good look at Julius's companion, green with envy at what she saw. The black woman was not only gorgeous but dressed in the sort of clothes she could only dream about. And she'd been right, her figure was stunning.

Albert laid his newspaper aside and yawned. It had been a hectic day, four call-outs, one of them major. He was dead beat.

'Would you like a cup of tea?' Jess, sitting opposite, asked him.

'Not for me. You have one though.'

She thought about that, deciding it wasn't worthwhile brewing a pot just for herself. 'Maybe later.'

Albert stretched. 'I won't be late out of my bed, I can tell you. I'm absolutely whacked.'

Jess glanced at the clock on the mantelpiece. Half-past nine, early even by Albert's standards. 'I ran into Polly Hutchins today,' she remarked casually.

'And how's she?'

Polly was someone Jess had known since schooldays. 'Fine. She had her new grandson with her. Lovely little chap.'

Albert frowned. 'Which daughter's had that?'

'Margaret, the youngest. She got married last year to a drayman and this is their first child. When I bumped into her Polly was looking after the baby, taking it for an outing in its pram.'

'That's nice,' Albert commented, not really all that interested.

'Lovely little chap,' Jess repeated. 'Seeing him took me back a bit. When I picked him up and gave him a cuddle I came over all broody.'

Albert laughed. 'Well, it certainly wouldn't me. Who'd want to go through all that palaver again?' He shook his head at the very thought.

'Oh come on, it wasn't that awful,' she cajoled. 'And how proud you were when both ours were born. Especially Paul, him being a boy like. The son and heir.'

'True,' Albert admitted.

He wasn't keen, Jess thought with a sinking heart. That was obvious. Despair filled her, for she was now even more convinced she was pregnant. That morning she'd felt distinctly queasy, though hadn't vomited. And she was putting on weight. Only a little so far, but enough to make her skirts feel tight.

'It shouldn't be too long before you're a grandmother as well,'

Albert declared. 'Give Ellie and George a couple of years and Bob's your uncle. Bound to happen.'

Jess smiled thinly, wondering what he'd say if she suddenly came out and told him what she suspected? It would be a bombshell, all right.

Not yet, she cautioned herself. She had to be sure before she did that. Absolutely certain.

Jess stopped outside the doctor's surgery and stared at the door. She didn't have to look at the brass plate to know the surgery was open.

Should she go in, get it over with? Find out one way or the other? That was the sensible thing to do. This torturing herself was unnecessary if it turned out to be a false alarm after all. There again . . .

The door opened and someone she didn't recognise emerged, a woman roughly her own age. The woman didn't even give Jess a glance as she hurried on her way.

Jess took a deep breath, tempted. And then she remembered the time. She should be home cooking Paul and Ellie their dinner, both would be back soon. Ellie from work, Paul from school, expecting to be fed.

That was it then. Another day perhaps. Yes, another day.

'I do believe we're the only people in the street to have a phone,' Beulah declared proudly, the telephone having been installed out of necessity for Julius's work.

'The pub has a phone,' Julius commented drily. 'I saw it when I was there.'

'Well then, apart from the pub.'

'I suppose so,' Julius agreed, having already used it several times to ring the Embassy on business. It had been put in earlier that day.

Beulah glanced at him out the corner of her eye. 'When you seein' that Marybeth again? She sure is one nice young lady.'

Julius couldn't help but smile. Beulah and Marybeth got on

like a house on fire. 'Oh soon. Sometime soon,' he replied off-handedly.

Beulah's expression became one of concern. 'You ain't losin' interest I hope?'

'Mom,' he scolded softly. 'You shouldn't interfere. Even if you do like Marybeth.'

'Interfere, I ain't interferin'!' Beulah protested. 'And even if I was that's a mother's duty. Her job. As your pop would say, damn right if it ain't!'

Julius decided to humour her. 'Probably this Saturday night. There, that satisfy you?'

'Sure does, hon. I was only askin', that's all. I weren't doin' no interferin'.'

That was a lie, Julius thought. And well she knew it. No matter, it wasn't important. And neither was Marybeth, if he was honest. They got on well, she could be fun. But that special something simply wasn't there. Possibly for her it was, but not him.

He changed the subject.

Jess ran into Beulah in Chapel Market, a large, mainly fruit and vegetable, street trading venue situated only minutes away from Florence Street. There were also a few stalls selling household goods and other sundry items.

'Something wrong, Beulah?' Jess inquired, having noted the black woman's exasperated expression.

'I just can't get no chilli peppers. No one seems to have them.'

'Chilli peppers?' Jess queried with a frown. 'I've never heard of those.'

Beulah sighed. 'Neither has anyone else round here it appears.' The exasperated expression vanished and she regarded Jess keenly. 'Now, has you finished your shoppin'?'

'Yes, I have actually.'

'Good, so has I. Why don't you come back to my place and we'll have some coffee and fresh brownies I baked earlier.'

Jess had never heard of brownies either. 'I don't know,' she prevaricated.

'Why, you got something else on?'

Jess shook her head. There was a pile of ironing to be dealt with but that could easily be done later.

'Then I insist. Pee Wee's gone out so we'll have the house to ourselves and can have a good old gossip. Though Lord knows what I'll gossip about as I knows no one round here yet except you and your family.'

Jess instantly took pity on Beulah, and agreed. As they made their way through the milling people Beulah did her best to explain what chilli peppers were.

They were on their third cup of coffee, Beulah chattering away nineteen to the dozen about life in New York City, when Jess's face suddenly contorted and she bent over.

Beulah stared at her in consternation for a moment, then came to her feet and went to take Jess by the shoulders. 'What's wrong, hon?'

'Pain. Terrible pain in my stomach,' Jess gasped.

'What can I do?'

Jess gulped in a deep breath and then sobbed as the pain intensified. It felt as though her insides were being dragged out of her.

'You'd better lie down, Jess. You can use the chesterfield in the other room.' That was an American type of sofa or couch, she explained.

Jess tried to struggle upright but couldn't manage it. She collapsed again onto the chair.

'Oh my God!' she whispered in horror as a bright red stain spread rapidly across the front of her skirt.

Chapter 4

Beulah had been hovering by her front window for the past two hours, now she saw Albert hurriedly striding down the street. She immediately went to her front door and opened it.

'Albert, come in. It was me who telephoned the fire station,' she called out as he drew close.

His face clearly mirrored his anxiety. 'What's wrong, Beulah? Your message said it was urgent and that I had to come home right away. Something to do with Jess.'

She shut the door behind him and ushered him through. 'Jess has had a miscarriage and been taken to hospital,' she explained.

He stared blankly at her. 'What?'

'Jess has had a miscarriage and been taken to hospital,' she repeated.

He stared uncomprehendingly at the fat woman. 'That's impossible,' he said eventually. 'She wasn't expecting.'

'She was, Albert. And lost the baby right there in my kitchen. I saw it with my own eyes.'

Albert staggered where he stood, reaching out to a piece of furniture to help steady himself. This was incredible. Jess pregnant! She'd never said. Unless . . . could it be Jess hadn't known? He'd heard such things were possible.

'How is she?' he croaked.

'As you'd expect. There's no danger though. They've taken her in as a precaution.'

He swallowed hard. 'The kitchen?'

'We were havin' coffee when it happened. One moment she was fine, the next . . . It was all over very quickly. I telephoned the emergency services and then your station. The man I spoke with there said you were on a call-out but would be informed the moment you returned.'

'Christ!' Albert muttered, still finding it difficult to take this in. It was such a bolt from the blue. Jess pregnant! But she'd told him those days were over. Now this.

Beulah had already laid out a bottle of whisky and a glass. She poured Albert a large one and handed it to him. 'Get that down you. It'll help.'

'I must go to her, Beulah. Right away.'

Beulah wished Julius had been there for he'd have taken Albert in his car. But Julius was at work.

'Drink the scotch first.'

'Which hospital?' he demanded after he'd demolished the whisky in one swallow.

'One of the guys with the ambulance said the Whittington.'

Albert nodded. He knew it. He was mildly surprised it wasn't the Royal Free which was closer. 'I'm on my way then,' he declared, setting the now-empty glass aside.

'Aren't you goin' to get changed first?' For he was still in his working gear.

'No time for that.'

Beulah had a sudden thought. 'You might be a while, Albert, so what about Paul and Ellie?'

Albert frowned, he'd forgotten all about them. 'Ellie has a key but Paul will be back from school long before she gets home.'

Beulah placed a hand on his arm. 'Don't worry, I'll see to them. Now, what shall I say?'

He was fidgeting to get going. 'The truth, I suppose. To Ellie anyway. Just tell Paul his mother's been taken ill.'

'I understand. Leave it all to me.'

He hesitated. 'Thanks for this, Beulah. You've been a friend and good neighbour.'

The sincerity of his words touched her. 'We all gotta help one another in this world, Albert. It's the only way.'

He smiled at her, then hurried out of the house and up the road to the nearest bus stop. It never entered his head to take a taxi, he'd never flagged one down in his entire life. Men of his class simply didn't.

'What time are you leaving, Pa?' Ellie asked anxiously. Albert had been to the hospital where he'd learned that Jess had had an operation, or, to be more precise, was actually undergoing some internal repairs while he was there. He'd waited till she was out of theatre and been assured everything was all right before heeding the doctor's advice and returning home. He'd be allowed in to see Jess later when she'd come round from the anaesthetic.

Albert glanced at the clock on the mantelpiece. 'I'll leave shortly.'

Ellie was about to say something when there was a knock on the outside door. 'I'll get it,' she declared, and left Albert staring disconsolately into empty space. He was racked with worry, sick with it.

Ellie returned with Julius. 'I was so sorry to hear the news,' Julius immediately said to Albert.

Albert nodded. 'She's going to be all right. That's what they've told me.'

Julius could see the state Albert was in. Poor guy, he thought. His own pop would have been just the same if it had been Beulah. 'I understand you're going back to the hospital?'

Albert nodded again. 'They've promised to let me see her when I do.'

'Then I'll drive you.'

Albert didn't know quite what to say to that. 'Are you sure?'

'Of course I'm sure. I'm not doing anything else anyway so it's hardly putting me out.'

'That's very kind of you,' Ellie acknowledged.

'Don't mention it.'

She turned to her father. 'I'm coming with you.'

'They said only I could see Jess,' he protested.

'I don't care. I'm still coming with you and that's final.'

Albert had to smile. 'You're as stubborn as your mother. When she digs her heels in that's it. But what about Paul? We can't leave him round with the Postons any longer. That really would be imposing.'

'He's absolutely fine where he is,' Julius said. 'He and Mom are having a heck of a time. Believe me.'

'All right then, Ellie,' Albert capitulated.

They waited another fifteen minutes, Ellie offering to make tea which both Albert and Julius declined. Then they left the house, Albert locking up, and got into Julius's car, Ellie in the back seat as before.

Julius didn't know where the Whittington was so Albert directed him.

'Well, girl, this is a right to-do,' Albert said, standing staring down at a pale-faced Jess.

'Isn't it just,' she replied weakly.

He fought back the tears that threatened to flood his eyes. Bending over he kissed her tenderly on the mouth, then sat on the bedside chair. 'How are you?'

'How do I look?'

'Terrible.'

She smiled. 'That's exactly how I feel.'

They enjoyed that little joke for a few silent seconds. Then, hesitantly, he inquired, 'Are you sore?'

'Just a bit,' she lied.

'That's natural I suppose.'

'I suppose.'

Another few silent seconds ticked by, then Jess suddenly said, a choke in her voice, 'Oh, Albert, hold me. Please hold me.'

A sort of peace descended on Jess as his arms went round her, and the nightmare began to recede. She'd have had him climb into bed alongside if that had been possible.

After a while she started to talk, telling Albert all about it.

While this was going on Ellie and Julius were sitting on a wooden bench outside in the corridor. 'I'm glad Mum's in a single room and not a ward. At least for now,' Ellie commented.

Julius had been thinking how unimpressed he was by the English hospital, the first time he'd ever been in one, so unlike the American hospitals he was used to. It seemed so . . . well, primitive was the word that came to mind. He could only wonder if they were all like this.

'Yes,' he agreed softly.

'I had no idea, you know. None whatever.'

He frowned. 'About what?'

'Mum expecting. She never said anything.'

A nurse bustled past carrying a kidney dish. He did approve of the English nurses' uniforms though, Julius reflected. They were most attractive. Quite sexy really.

'I'm sure she had her reasons,' he replied.

Ellie worried a nail. 'I wish I could go in and see her. Even a minute would be enough.'

Julius regarded her thoughtfully. 'You're very close to your mother, aren't you?'

'We're very close as a family. It might not look that way sometimes, but we are.'

Julius smiled. 'Same with us. That's why I was so pleased when Mom and Pop came over here. She says I missed her cookin', which is true enough. But there's more to it than that. A lot more.'

'It must be awful belonging to a family that don't get on,' Ellie mused. 'Especially if the mother and father are always fighting. I have a couple of friends whose parents are like that. Forever at it like cat and dog. The atmosphere in the house must be terrible.'

Julius's attention had been caught by an elderly doctor who'd appeared at the far end of the corridor, surrounded by a gaggle of younger doctors hanging on his every word. 'I wonder who that old guy is?' he said quietly to Ellie.

She glanced down the corridor. 'That'll be the specialist probably.'

'Specialist? The main guy?'

She smiled at his phraseology. 'You could put it like that.'

'The main guy,' Julius repeated, and came to his feet. 'You stay here. I won't be long.'

She couldn't imagine what he was up to as he sauntered along the corridor. She watched as he broke into the conversation and then drew the specialist to one side.

Julius returned a couple of minutes later, clearly pleased with himself. 'You've got five minutes with your mom after your pop comes out,' he announced, sitting again beside Ellie.

She stared at him in astonishment. 'How did you manage that? The Sister we spoke to earlier was adamant only my father could go in.'

Julius winked. 'It's amazin' what an American accent and State Department, not to mention Embassy, accreditation can do. It impresses most folk.'

'Oh, Julius,' Ellie breathed in delight. Impulsively she kissed him on the cheek. 'Thank you.'

She suddenly blushed realising what she'd done, turning away so he couldn't see her face. Which of course he already had.

'My pleasure, Ellie,' he smiled.

When she turned round again she was quite composed, though her eyes sparkled with gratitude. Before either could speak further Albert emerged from Jess's room.

'Ellie, you go on in and get Paul. I'm going for a pint. I certainly need one.'

'Will you be long?'

'Half an hour, no more. I just need a drink after all that.'

Ellie could well understand, she'd never seen her father so rattled. 'I'll get Paul ready for bed and tonight I think you should take him up yourself. To reassure him like.'

'I'll do that, Ellie. Good idea.'

Julius came to stand beside them having locked the car. 'I'll say goodnight then.'

'I was hoping you'd come in with me,' Albert stated earnestly to him. 'A drink is the least I can do to say thank you.'

Julius could see how eager Albert was for him to agree. 'OK, Mr Sykes. That would be great.'

'Good chap.'

Harry, the publican, was behind the bar when Albert and Julius went into The Florence. There were only a handful of others present, all playing darts.

'Evening, Albert,' Harry greeted him. 'What'll it be?'

'A pint of best and a large whisky.'

Harry raised an eyebrow. 'That's unlike you during the week. I've never known you touch spirits then.'

'It's been a bad day.' Albert turned to Julius. 'What's yours?'

'A pint of the same.'

'Scotch or brandy?'

Julius held up a hand in refusal. 'I'll pass on that if you don't mind, take a rain check. I've got a lot on tomorrow morning.'

'By the way, Harry, have you met Julius Poston, my new neighbour? He's a Yank.'

Harry beamed. 'Pleased to meet you, Julius. I've seen you in here but we've never been introduced.'

The two men shook hands, then Harry went over to the gantry. 'The wife told me there was an ambulance outside your house earlier,' he remarked casually over his shoulder.

'Jess has been taken in,' Albert informed him. 'I've just been to visit her. Julius here very kindly drove Ellie and me there in his car.'

'Nothing serious, I hope?' Harry queried in concern.

Albert decided to be evasive, not wanting the entire street knowing their business. It was too private for that. 'She'll only be in for a short while,' he prevaricated. 'She'll be right as rain after that.'

Harry took the hint. 'Well, give her our regards, will you?'

'Of course.'

Albert lapsed into silence until their drinks had been set before them and Harry had moved off down the bar to watch the darts players, the nucleus of the pub team having a practice.

'Have you ever played darts?' Albert asked.

The question took Julius by surprise. 'No, I haven't,' he confessed. 'Looks fun though.'

'If you like I'll teach you the rudiments of the game one night.'

Julius acknowledged the offer with a nod. 'Thank you. Yeah, that would be great.'

Albert picked up his scotch. 'Cheers!'

'Cheers, Mr Sykes.'

They both drank. 'And I think it's high time we did away with this mister nonsense. The name's Albert. But never Bert. Jess hates that.'

'Albert it is then.'

Julius gazed about him. 'I sure adore English pubs. We've nothin' similar back home. We have so-called taverns, but they're not the same. They lack the ambience and friendliness.'

'Well, you'll be all right in here from now on, that's why I made a point of introducing you. You'll be regarded as a local and regular, one of the lads so to speak. Word will soon get round that you're a friend of mine.' He paused, then added softly, 'And Jess's.'

Julius could see the strain etched deeply into Albert's face and felt sorry for the man. What had happened must have been an awful shock. 'If there's anythin' I can do while Mrs Sykes is in the hospital you just have to say.'

Albert smiled his gratitude. 'Thanks, son. I appreciate that.'

'And I mean anythin'. It's amazing what I can swing with my contacts at the Embassy. So don't be shy in speakin' up.'

Albert nodded that he understood. 'Your ma and pa seem to be settling in all right.'

'They're findin' it strange, but that's only to be expected. So many things are different here. But they're copin', and Pop's sure enjoying playin' with the band. He says it wails, which is jazz talk meaning swingin', or good.'

'Wail,' Albert repeated, and shook his head in amazement. 'How extraordinary.'

'Now can I ask you somethin', Albert?'

'Fire away.'

'Are people roundabout happy to have black folks livin' here?'

Albert considered that. 'It's something of a novelty I must admit. You come across black people down at the docks, but they're mainly Indians, Laskars they're called, which isn't the same thing. Other than that they're something of a rarity. I will say this, the English, generally speaking, are very fair-minded. As long as you try to fit in you'll be accepted, in my opinion.'

'Good,' Julius murmured.

'There's one thing been puzzling me though.'

Julius frowned. 'What's that?'

'Why Islington? I would have thought you'd have arranged accommodation in a better area. You working with your Embassy, I mean.'

'Oh that's easy,' Julius smiled. 'Mom and Pop have always lived in what you would call workin'-class neighbourhoods. Pop might be a great musician but he's never made a lot of money out of playin'. So when they asked me to find them a place I looked for somewhere they'd feel right at home, and Islington was what I came up with.'

Well, that was that mystery solved, Albert thought. 'You must be used to better though?'

'I had an apartment in Kensington before coming here, a real luxury one too paid for by the Embassy. Mom and Pop would have hated it though, not their sort of neighbourhood at all. Far too classy, and I mean no disrespect by that. And there was no way I was going to live apart with Mom and Pop in town. Mom would have thought that downright unnatural, and I guess so would I.'

Albert approved of that. He was rapidly warming to Julius Poston, and even getting used to him being black. It seemed to Albert, now he'd come to know some, that black people weren't all that different to white. He certainly couldn't have asked for better neighbours.

'Good for you, son,' he smiled.

They ended up staying far longer than the half hour Albert had told Ellie he'd be.

Ellie wondered what had woken her, normally she hardly stirred until the alarm went off. And then she heard it, the sound of muffled crying.

Instantly she was out of bed and shrugging into her dressing gown. Barefoot she padded from her bedroom.

The crying stopped when she tapped the door. 'Paul?' she queried quietly.

There was no reply.

'Paul?'

Again no reply.

She opened the door and went inside, moonlight shining through the open curtains. Paul had his bedclothes pulled up over his head.

She sat beside him, squirming a little to make room for herself. 'Come on now, I know you're awake. I heard you,' she gently cajoled.

He appeared from under the bedclothes, his face tear-streaked. He gave a quiet sob.

'There there,' she murmured comfortingly, stroking his forehead. 'Is it Mum?'

'Yes,' he choked.

'Well, there's no need to cry. She's going to be fine.'

'I dreamt she died, Ellie. I dreamt she never came back again from the hospital.'

'It was only a dream,' she crooned. 'That won't happen. I promise you.'

'Pa won't tell me what's wrong with her. He just said she's been taken ill and that's all.'

'It's a woman's problem,' Ellie explained. 'Pa was probably too embarrassed to say.'

The boy's brow furrowed. 'What's a woman's problem?'

She sighed. This was difficult. 'Well you know how men and women are physically different?'

Paul nodded.

'Well, it's to do with the difference.'

He sort of understood. 'Are you sure she won't die?'

Ellie made several quick motions over her chest. 'Cross my heart. She'll be home before you know it and things will be back to normal.'

He took a deep breath. 'It was a horrible dream, Ellie. It frightened me awfully.'

'Dreams that do that are called nightmares. That's what you had. A nasty nightmare. We all get them from time to time.'

'Even you?'

She groped in her dressing-gown pocket for the hanky she knew to be there. Using it she wiped his cheeks and then held it under his nose. 'Blow.'

When he'd done that she put the hanky away again. 'Do you want me to stay with you for a while?'

'Will you, Ellie?' he demanded eagerly, what had been a tear-stained face now shining.

'I've just said I will.'

'Thanks, Ellie. You're not a bad sister really.'

'I'm pleased to hear it,' she joked, tucking him in. 'Now you close your eyes and think nice thoughts.'

'Like sweeties and ice cream?'

That made her smile. 'Like sweeties and ice cream,' she agreed.

Within minutes Paul was fast asleep, nor did he wake again till called in the morning.

* * *

Jess lay staring up at the ward ceiling. She had been moved to a general ward four days previously. She'd been told that morning, all going well, she'd be out of hospital the day after next, the doctors being pleased with her progress.

Glancing down the ward Jess saw the night nurse busy writing at her desk, a single shaded lamp illuminating her work. Jess had nothing but praise for all the Whittington staff; without exception they'd been kindness itself. She couldn't have asked for better treatment.

Despite being tired her mind was churning with thoughts about the baby she'd lost. The feeling of emptiness that had engulfed her afterwards had taken her by surprise. A terrible emptiness.

Despair welled within her, despair as black as a bottomless pit. Her sense of grief was profound.

A boy or girl? She kept speculating about that. She had asked but no one was able to tell her. The foetus had been taken away by the ambulance crew and disposed of, whatever that meant. Now she would never know what she'd been carrying.

Not that it really mattered. The baby, her baby, was dead and gone. Her baby, and Albert's. Now there truly would never be another child for them, not even an accidental one, her operation had seen to that.

Albert had been a brick about the whole thing. Shocked by what had happened of course, but then that was only to be expected when she'd miscarried a baby he'd known nothing about.

One day she'd ask him would he have been pleased had the baby been born, or not? During his daily visits to the hospital he'd given nothing away in that respect. Nothing at all. Not even the slightest hint.

Jess wondered what time it was? It seemed hours ago that the lights had been turned out. There again, perhaps that was only her imagination. Lying here with nothing to do gave full rein to the imagination, as she was only too well aware.

One thing was certain. She'd never be the same again. Not even if she lived to be a hundred. Losing the baby had done that to her. From here on in there would always be a part of her that was missing. A wound that would never heal over, but fester on and on. She was in no doubt about that.

Stop being so self-pitying, she scolded herself harshly. You're not the first woman to lose a baby and will hardly be the last. But the truth of that did nothing whatever to ease the pain. This particular loss was hers and hers alone to bear. A loss she'd carry to the grave.

One of the other patients began to snore, a strangely comforting sound that reminded her of Albert.

And still the night wore endlessly on.

'We're here, missus, let's be having you,' the ambulanceman announced jovially, taking her by the arm. 'Can you manage?'

She was stiff and sore, but able to walk, if somewhat awkwardly. 'I'm all right.'

'I'll give you a hand just the same.'

Jess was surprised when their door opened and Albert appeared – she'd expected Beulah or one of the other neighbours.

Albert's hand replaced the ambulanceman's, whom they both thanked. Then Albert helped Jess inside.

'Have you taken the day off work?' she queried.

He raised an eyebrow. 'You're not complaining, are you?'

'No, no, just . . . well it's so unlike you. I would have coped.'

He kissed her on the cheek. 'It's good to have you back. We've all missed you.'

'It's good to be back,' she replied, feeling as though she'd been away for at least a year.

'Now you're not to worry about anything. Ellie has kept the house just as you'd want, and Beulah has popped in on occasions to see what she could do. But first things first, we must get you up to bed.'

She was more tired than she would have thought. The short journey had sapped what strength she had.

Another surprise awaited her in the bedroom. On her bedside

table was her favourite vase filled with fresh flowers. 'How lovely!' she exclaimed. 'Who are those from?'

'Me.'

She stared at Albert in astonishment. 'You! You've never bought me flowers in your entire life.'

He coloured slightly. 'Well, there's always a first time. Like them?'

She crossed over and smelt the blooms. 'They're gorgeous.'

'Bought them in the market earlier on. I would have brought some to the hospital but I'd have felt a right berk going on a bus with them.'

Jess couldn't have been more touched. 'Oh, Albert,' she whispered. 'Thank you.'

'Now you get into bed and I'll make you a nice cup of tea. How's that?'

She was too choked to reply.

He made to leave, then hesitated. Putting his arms round her he drew her close and kissed her on the mouth. 'I love you, girl, never forget that,' he declared in a cracked voice.

'And I love you, Albert.'

He gave her another kiss, a quick peck this time, after which he left.

Sitting on the bed Jess began silently to cry tears of happiness.

Chapter 5

Julius was frowning deeply as he laid down the latest report to reach his desk. He stared at it for a few seconds.

'Want some coffee?'

He glanced over at Shelby Robbins, who held the same grade as himself, and whom he shared the office with. 'Not for me.'

Shelby went out into the corridor, returning with a paper cup from the vending machine situated there. Sitting again he lit up.

'It's gettin' worse over in Germany,' Julius said slowly. 'They've now confiscated all Jewish property. That's really puttin' the screws on the poor bastards.'

'Thank God I don't live there,' Shelby exhaled in a worried tone.

Julius guessed what he was referring to. 'You mean Phyllis?' Phyllis was Shelby's Jewish wife.

'Yup.'

'If these Nazis keep on as they are, well . . .' He trailed off, and shrugged.

They both thought about that. 'It won't be our concern,' Shelby said at last. 'Roosevelt would never get us involved in another European war. The country wouldn't stand for it. Once was enough.'

Julius also believed that. There again, nothing was ever set in stone. Things could change.

'We know what the Ambassador thinks,' Shelby went on. 'He's said often enough that the British wouldn't stand a chance against the Germans.'

Julius smiled. 'He never has exactly been pro-British though, has he?'

'You can say that again. Deep down I believe he hates them. Hardly surprising as he's of Irish descent. The Irish have no great reason to love the British.'

'True,' Julius agreed.

'One thing's for certain though,' Shelby said.

'What's that?'

'If there is a war it's going to be helluva exciting round here.'

Could there be another war? Julius wondered. He fervently hoped not. But suppose there was and the Ambassador was right, then Britain would be an occupied country which was a horrifying prospect and one that would shift the entire balance of global power. Would Roosevelt really allow that to happen? Faced with the actual threat of the invasion of mainland Britain Roosevelt might feel forced to intervene.

'What do you think of this guy Hitler anyway?' Shelby asked.

'A crazy, pure and simple. But a damned dangerous one. Like one of those mad characters out of the comic books intent on conquerin' the world.'

Shelby laughed. 'That about sums him up I guess. Only we're not living in a comic strip which is what makes it, and him, scary.'

'Real scary,' Julius agreed.

'Changing the subject, are you taking Marybeth to the Ambassador's Ball New Year's Eve? She sure is some piece of ass that lady. Yes sir, I envy you there.'

Julius had to smile. 'Not jealous are you?'

Shelby pretended innocence. 'Not me, buddy. I'm a happily married man with eyes for no other.' He paused, then added impishly, 'Well maybe eyes, but no more than that. A guy can look and imagine, can't he? Hell, there's no harm in that.'

'I haven't asked her yet,' Julius confessed, somewhat amused by this.

'Well, I'd hurry up if I were you before someone else gets in first.'

Julius thought of Marybeth whom he was seeing later. He'd take the opportunity of asking her then. There was certainly no one else he wanted to take and his presence at the Ball, having been invited, was obligatory.

Shelby winked conspiratorially, dropping his voice when he spoke next. 'Tell me, are you and she . . . ?' He trailed off expectantly.

Now it was Julius's turn to pretend innocence. 'What?'

'You know, don't play the dumbass with me.'

Julius regarded his colleague thoughtfully, knowing if he told Shelby anything in so-called confidence it would be round the entire Embassy before he knew it. There wasn't a bigger gossip, and that included the women, in the building.

'The English have a sayin' I rather like,' Julius stated, straight-faced.

'Which is?'

'That's for me to know and you to wonder about.'

Shelby's disappointment clearly showed and he let out an exasperated sigh. 'Going to be that way about it, eh?'

''Fraid so. I could be, there again maybe not. I take the Fifth.'

'I bet you are,' Shelby prompted, trying again.

'Bet all you want. You'll never know whether you've won or lost.'

At that point their conversation was interrupted by Shelby's phone ringing. Julius took the opportunity to escape the office and any further grilling.

Ellie answered the door to find Julius standing there holding an enormous parcel. 'Come in,' she said quickly, for it was bucketing outside.

'I hope I'm not intrudin'?'

'Not at all. How have you been? I haven't seen you in ages.'

He shrugged. 'I've been tied up at work a great deal. Gettin' home late, leavin' early, that sort of thing. Anyway, is your mom home?'

'In the kitchen. So's Pa.'

Julius found Jess up to her elbows in flour baking for the holidays. 'Hi, Mrs Sykes, how're you keepin'?'

She gave him a large smile. 'Just fine, Julius. In the pink.'

'Hello, son,' Albert greeted Julius from his chair. 'To what do we owe the honour?'

Julius placed the parcel on the table. 'I hope you don't take offence at this. I ordered a turkey through the Embassy for our Christmas dinner and instead of one I've been given two. I thought you might care to have the second.'

Jess's eyes gleamed. 'A turkey! We've never had one of those.'

Julius groped in a pocket to produce a jar. 'This is cranberry sauce which we Americans traditionally serve with it.'

Albert was now on his feet. 'How extraordinarily kind of you, Julius.' He eyed the parcel. 'Just look at the size! Are you sure there isn't an ostrich in there?'

Everyone laughed. 'It's a turkey all right. Shall I take it out?'

Jess began wiping the flour from her hands and lower arms. 'I suppose you cook it just like a chicken, only longer, which is what we normally have?'

'That's right.'

Jess gasped when the bird was revealed. It was massive. 'My God in Heaven!'

'Mom would have offered to keep it in her fridge for you but the fridge is full to burstin' as it is. Anyway, Christmas Eve is only the day after tomorrow. Just put it somewhere cool, that'll do.'

Albert spread his hands wide. 'I wish I could offer you a little something but I've nothing in. I'm picking up the Christmas drink tomorrow night.'

'That's OK, Albert, don't you worry about that. Now, I'd better be on my way.'

'I'll see you out,' Ellie volunteered.

They were leaving the kitchen when Julius suddenly stopped and turned. 'Oh, I nearly forgot. Mom says if you've got a chance why don't you drop by for coffee in the morning,' he related to Jess.

Jess forced a smile onto her face. 'I'm rather busy then, but I will if I can.'

That was a lie, for she had no intention whatsoever of going for coffee with Beulah. Or even entering the Postons' house ever again. Not if she could possibly help it anyway.

Albert rejoined Jess, Ellie and George in the pub, having nipped across the street. It was New Year's Eve and The Florence was jam-packed. They'd been lucky to get a table.

'There's no one home,' he declared. 'I rang and rang but no answer.'

Jess shrugged. 'Beulah has probably gone to the club with Pee Wee and Julius is out elsewhere. Pity, it would have been nice to have had them here to join in.'

'Take it easy,' Ellie whispered to George. 'That's your third pint and we've only been here an hour.'

'I'm all right,' George replied earnestly. 'I won't embarrass you. But it is New Year's Eve don't forget.'

'I appreciate that, but nonetheless.'

'Just like an old married couple,' Albert teased and laughed while Ellie blushed.

'Dad!'

'Well, you are.'

Jess spotted old Ma Jenkins sitting at the far side with some of her cronies and gave her a wave, Ma returning the gesture. Jess idly wondered if Ma had been there all along for she hadn't seen her come in.

A group of men burst into loud, raucous laughter, one of them going quite puce and shaking his head, while another slapped the bar with a hand.

'They're a merry bunch,' Albert commented, guessing someone

had told a really filthy joke to get that reaction. Still, it was all harmless fun.

'Are you having a good time?' George asked Ellie. 'It's still not too late to go to the Roxy if you'd prefer that?'

'I am having a good time. And no, I don't want to go to the Roxy, I'm fed up with the place.'

He shrugged. 'Only asking. Being polite like.'

Taffy Roberts, the Welshman, belching as he went, lurched past their table. 'He's had a few,' Albert observed drily to Jess, remembering how Taffy had called Pee Wee a nigger. Obnoxious man.

The pianist, who'd been taking a break during the past ten or so minutes, struck up again, 'I'm Looking Over A Four-Leaf Clover . . .'

Customers began singing, all of them loving and appreciating the old favourites. 'Auld Lang Syne' would be played on the stroke of midnight when all bedlam would break loose.

Behind the bar Harry and Hazel were working flat out. As was their daughter Marje, drafted in especially for the evening. The floor beneath their feet was already awash with spilt beer.

Jess had been happy enough up until then, but suddenly her mood changed and she began to feel depressed and morose. The jollity had for some reason started to irritate her.

'Who's for another?' Albert queried, finishing his pint.

'It's my shout, Mr Sykes,' George quickly replied.

'On you go then. Get them in.'

Jess was the only one who declined a replacement, saying she'd had enough for the moment. Albert didn't take any heed of that, or urge her to the contrary, knowing Jess wasn't a great drinker at the best of times.

It was about half an hour later, the pub now positively heaving, when Jess turned to Albert. 'I'm going to go home, if you don't mind.'

He stared at her in surprise. 'What's wrong?'

'I've developed a thundering headache. The noise in here is just deafening.'

He was obviously disappointed, it was a special occasion after all. A once-a-year event. 'I'll come with you then,' he reluctantly replied.

'No, Albert, I won't hear of it. You stay, I insist. I'll take a couple of aspirin and if the headache clears then I'll come back.' That was a lie, she had absolutely no intention of returning.

'Are you sure, girl?' he frowned.

'Yes, now don't you worry. Stay and enjoy yourself.'

'Will you be all right?' Ellie asked anxiously, as concerned as her father, having overheard the conversation.

'I'll be fine. I just need a bit of quiet, that's all.'

Outside Jess sucked in a deep lungful of chilly air, then hurried across the road. Once in the house she went straight up to their bedroom and, without putting the light on, sat down on the bed.

For a few moments she remained perfectly still, then placed both hands on her stomach. It was the baby of course, that's what was really bothering her. She had suddenly been plunged back into the great, black bottomless pit of agony and despair. The baby she'd lost and who'd forever haunt her.

She began to cry, racking sobs that shook her entire body.

'How do I look?'

Julius had called for Marybeth at her apartment to take her to the Ambassador's Ball. Neither had been that keen to attend so they had agreed to arrive later rather than sooner.

Marybeth was wearing a formal evening gown of crisp rayon taffeta that was shadow-patterned in a brocade effect with a lovely flower design. The bodice was shirred to give a flattering fullness above a pointed set-in girdle which pulled in her waist. Taffeta pleats emphasised the heart-shaped neckline while the sleeves were full puffed. The colour of the gown was blood red which contrasted dramatically with Marybeth's black skin.

Julius swallowed hard. He was impressed, very much so. 'Absolutely stunnin',' he managed to get out at last.

Her face broke into a beaming smile. 'I'm rather pleased with it if I say so myself. I bought it in Bond Street from a very high-class and exclusive store.'

'You're a knockout, kid. A real knockout. Good enough to eat.'

She laughed, then said tantalisingly, 'Perhaps later, if we're in the mood.'

Her meaning wasn't lost on Julius.

'I'll just get my wrap,' she added.

The wrap, a black velvet cape, completed the ensemble.

Ellie was coming out of the toilet when she ran headlong into Taffy Roberts enroute to the gents a little further down the corridor. There was almost a collision which he staved off by catching hold of her shoulders.

'Why, hello, Ellie fach,' he slurred.

She wrenched herself free. 'If you'll just let me past.' The man was obviously horribly drunk.

'Don't you look pretty as a picture. I swear to God you do.'

Compliments from Taffy Roberts were the last thing she wanted, or needed. She tried to edge past him but he blocked her way.

'I tell you what, Ellie,' he said, groping in a pocket. 'I have some mistletoe here, so why don't you give me a kiss? There's a beautiful girl then.'

The thought of kissing Taffy disgusted her. She backed off as he held the mistletoe above his head and leered, his lips bright and shiny with spit.

'I'll do no such thing,' she retorted hotly, though beginning to be scared. 'Now let me by.'

'But it's New Year's Eve! Surely that merits a nice kiss, eh?'

She backed off even more. 'Don't come near me or I'll scream.'

'Oh no you won't!' he replied, and rushed her, swiftly pinioning her with his arms.

Now she really was scared. His hot, foetid breath washed over her, making her stomach heave.

'Just one little kiss,' he cajoled. 'That's all I ask.'

She twisted her head to one side. 'Go away.'

He laughed. 'Oh, I likes it when they struggle. More exciting that way.'

'What in hell's going on here!'

Ellie instantly recognised the voice as George's.

'Fuck off!' Taffy snarled over his shoulder.

'Let her go, Roberts, or so help me I'll deck you.'

Taffy released Ellie, who fell away with a sob, and slowly turned on George. 'Oh you will, will you?'

'That's what I said,' George stated quietly and defiantly, meaning every word.

Taffy opened his mouth to say something further, but instead suddenly gagged. Clapping a hand over his mouth he wheeled round and ran for the gents where he barged inside.

Ellie sagged with relief. 'Oh George,' she whispered, never having been more pleased to see anyone in her entire life. From the gents came the sound of Taffy being violently sick.

'We'd better get back,' George said, taking her by the hand.

She looked into his eyes and smiled gratefully. 'You'd really have fought that brute for me?'

'Damn right. The Welshman doesn't scare me.'

'Well, he did me. I was almost wetting myself.'

George gave a low laugh. 'You're all right, Ellie, that's all that matters.'

Ellie shuddered. 'He's vile. Really vile. He was slobbering all over me. And his breath stank. You wouldn't believe how awful it was.'

'Well, it's over now. Come on.'

She hesitated. 'What were you doing out here anyway?'

'I decided I also needed to go to the khazi. But that can wait now. I'll go later.'

At the door leading into the saloon Ellie stopped. 'Don't say anything about this to Dad. I don't want to spoil his evening.'

'Mum's the word.'

'No, she's gone home.'

It was a silly joke, but they both laughed nonetheless, a release of tension.

'And George?'

'What?'

'Thank you.'

She kissed him, French style, her tongue wriggling frantically against his. In the middle of this the pianist struck up 'Auld Lang Syne'.

'Happy New Year,' George said when the kiss was finally over. 'I hope 1939 is going to be a good one for the pair of us.'

'I'm sure it will be,' she enthused. 'Happy 1939.'

Heart pounding, chest heaving, Julius flopped onto his back to gulp in air. He'd never known Marybeth so wild and frenzied, so incredibly passionate.

'You're supposed to hold me afterwards,' she purred.

'Will in a moment. Let me catch my breath first.'

She came onto an elbow to stare at him, her body now soft and relaxed where only moments before it had been taut with expectation. 'How was it for you, hon?'

'Do you have to ask?'

She gave a throaty chuckle. 'Not really. I just wanted to hear you say.'

He swivelled his head sideways to look at her, noting with satisfaction the sweat running down between her magnificent breasts. His gaze then swept over the curve of one hip. Reaching out he gently touched it. 'I swear the earth really did move. God damn if it didn't.'

Her lips twisted upwards. 'That good, eh?'

'That good,' he assured her. 'The best yet. A man could die happy after that.'

'Well, don't die on me just yet, sugar,' she teased. 'I've got other plans for you.'

'Oh?'

'Yeah.'

'Such as?'

'You'll find out.'

'Why not tell me now?'

'Because,' she leant closer and brushed her lips over his, 'I don't want to.'

He placed a hand on her firm bottom and squeezed, knowing she loved that. He was rewarded with a groan of pleasure. 'I could sure use a drink,' he said.

'Could you now?'

'Bourbon.'

'With ice. The way you like it. You see, I know all the things you like.'

He raised an eyebrow. 'Do you now?'

'Oh yeah. You bet your sweet butt I do. I've made it my business to find out. And you know why?'

He shook his head.

'I want to please you, that's why.' She stared intently at him, her eyes boring into his, then rolled off the bed onto her feet. Gathering up a flimsy see-through negligée she threw it round herself. 'You sure am some stud, hon.'

'Am I?'

'Oh yeah, you'd better believe it. You're a dream come true. At least for me anyway.'

'You're not so bad yourself,' he replied drily, delighted by the compliment. Well, what man wouldn't?

'Thank you, kind sir.'

His gaze lingered on her figure. Stripped, she truly was stunning. She could easily have been a movie star, if Hollywood had allowed black leading ladies that is. 'So come on, give?' he persisted, still wanting to know what her plans were.

'I thought I just had.'

It took a moment for the penny to drop, and then he laughed. 'I wasn't talking about that.'

'Bourbon, wasn't it?'

'Marybeth!'

Smiling, she sashayed, there was no other word for it, from the room.

'Ma, have you seen my pistol?' Paul asked, having searched, as far as he was concerned, everywhere for it.

'That drawer over there,' she replied, pointing.

He went to the drawer and there, sure enough, it was. 'Thanks, Ma.'

'What is it today, cowboys and indians?'

He nodded. He and the rest of his pals were still on their school holidays.

'Well, make sure you wrap up warm, it's cold out there.'

'I will, Ma.'

'Let me see you before you go then.'

She watched him hurry from the kitchen, her heart swelling within her. How emotional she'd become of late, especially where children were concerned, her own in particular. Losing the baby had heightened her awareness of how precious they were.

He returned wearing a belted raincoat that was long past its best, and an equally old Arsenal football team scarf.

'Where are your gloves?' she queried.

His face dropped. 'I don't like wearing them, Ma. They're itchy. Besides, cowboys don't wear gloves.'

That made her smile. 'Why don't you put them in your pocket just the same.'

'I'll do that on the way out.'

'Make sure you do.'

'Can I go now?'

'Yes, of course, and don't be late for your dinner. I don't want it to spoil.'

'All right, Ma, I won't forget.'

The face of a cherub, she thought. Innocence personified. 'Come here first,' she husked.

Frowning, he did.

Jess put her arms round him and hugged him tight.

'Oh, Ma!' he protested, mortified, considering himself far too old for such nonsense. Thankfully no one else was there to see.

'There,' she sniffed, releasing him. 'Be off with you then.'

He fled, intentionally leaving his gloves behind. Amongst the lads it was considered sissy to wear them, especially woollen ones.

Jess used the bottom of her pinny to wipe her nose. Stupid, sentimental cow, she chided herself. But she just hadn't been able to resist.

'He would have fought for you!' Connie Fox breathed. 'How romantic.'

Ellie and Connie had just left the office and Ellie had recounted the story of New Year's Eve, the first chance she'd had of telling Connie.

Yes, it had been romantic, Ellie realised. Why hadn't she thought of that?

'The other chap sounds awful,' Connie went on, eyes wide.

'He was, believe me.'

'Would your George have won, do you think?'

Ellie considered that. 'I heard my da say once that it isn't the size of the man that counts but what's in his head. That's where fights are lost and won. So yes, I believe he might have done.'

They came to the street corner that was the parting of the ways for them. 'He must really love you, Ellie. I'm quite green.'

Her hero, Ellie thought. George was her hero. She didn't say it out loud though, it would have sounded far too soppy. 'I was very proud of him,' she declared instead.

'And so you should. I certainly would have been. Lucky old you, gel, lucky old you.'

'I know that now. I've had my doubts about George in the past, but not any more.'

'He's definitely the one then?'

Ellie nodded.

'Just make sure I get an invite to the wedding, that's all,' Connie laughed.

'You'll be there. That's a promise.'

'I'll keep you to that. Now I'm off, it's freezing out here.'

She *was* lucky, Ellie told herself as she hurried home. And it had been romantic.

Exciting too, in retrospect.

Chapter 6

Albert rose and switched off the wireless. He and Jess had been listening to the very sobering news on the Home Service.

Jess looked at Albert as he sank back into his chair, his expression one of troubled foreboding. 'It's bad, isn't it?' she said quietly.

Albert nodded. 'I don't quite understand why we have to pledge ourselves to defend Poland, but apparently Chamberlain thinks otherwise.' Chamberlain was the Prime Minister.

'And we're to be allied with France in this.'

'According to Arthur Greenwood.' He was the Deputy PM. Albert shook his head in despair. 'It's all brewing up, just like the last time, sheer bloody nonsense.'

'It's not our fault,' Jess reminded him. 'It's the Germans who want to cause trouble. This man Hitler should be taken out and shot.'

Albert couldn't have agreed more.

'At least you won't have to serve, being in a reserved occupation,' Jess pointed out. 'And Paul is only ten. Any war will surely be over and done with before he's of an age for the Forces.'

'Hopefully,' Albert murmured.

Panic gripped Jess. 'Do you mean there is a chance he might have to?'

Albert's eyes clouded in memory. 'At the end of the last war the Jerries were conscripting boys as young as twelve. That's a fact.'

Jess had read that somewhere years ago but had forgotten about it. She glanced up at the ceiling, fearful for Paul upstairs in his bed. 'Dear God,' she whispered.

'He's already gone into Prague,' Albert stated, referring to Hitler. 'So why not Poland?'

'Because we've now said we'll stop him. Us and the French.'

Albert shrugged. 'Hitler might think it's a bluff on our part. It seems to me he's entirely capable of being that stupid.'

'And we're not?'

'No, I wouldn't say so. For all his faults Chamberlain isn't one to bluff. Not at these kind of stakes anyway. Trouble is, and I'm not the only person to think this, the lads down at the station all agree with me, he's not a war leader. Clever politician yes, but no war leader. He's far too soft for that.'

War, the word reverberated through Jess's head making her go cold all over and break out in gooseflesh. Could anything possibly be more awful? If so, she couldn't imagine what. She shuddered. 'It doesn't bear thinking about.'

'No, it doesn't,' Albert agreed softly.

They both lapsed into silence for a few moments, each lost in their own thoughts.

'Still, look on the bright side,' Albert said eventually. 'It may never happen.'

'Please God.'

'But if it does my money's on Winnie to take over as PM. He's got real fire in his belly.'

Jess had been a Conservative all her life but had never liked Churchill. She didn't know why, there was no sound reason, she simply didn't. 'What about Lord Halifax?'

Albert pondered that. 'He's a possibility, and would certainly be better than Chamberlain in my opinion. But Winnie is the chap for me. He's the one would get my vote.'

Jess sighed and got to her feet. All this talk about possible war was so depressing. Not to mention alarming. 'I'll put the kettle on,' she declared.

'Is there any of that cake left?'

She smiled. 'I put a bit by for you before Paul scoffed the lot. He's got the very devil of an appetite that lad!'

'You can say that again. He costs us an absolute fortune in grub.'

Jess frowned. 'You don't begrudge him though, do you? He is a growing lad after all.'

'That's what you always say.' Albert's face softened. 'But no, I don't really begrudge him. You know that.'

All conversation about the war stopped when they heard Ellie arrive home, after an evening out with George.

George, who was just the right age to be called up, Albert reflected grimly as Ellie breezed into the kitchen.

'What are you staring at?'

Julius snapped out of his reverie to find it was Ellie who'd spoken, the pair of them meeting by chance in Upper Street, the closest main thoroughfare to Florence Street.

He indicated a dray from Whitbread's Brewery that was stationary outside a pub where a delivery was taking place. 'That,' he replied. 'It sure is one beautiful sight.'

Ellie regarded the dray thoughtfully thinking, yes it was rather lovely. They were a common enough sight thereabouts, common enough to be simply taken for granted. 'Don't you have anything like them in America?' she asked.

'Sure. But nothin' so fancy or ornate. I mean, look at those absolutely huge horses for a start. See how groomed and handsome they are. And just look at the size of those hooves! Son of a bitch, they're enormous.'

Ellie blushed.

'Sorry, Ellie,' he instantly apologised. 'My big mouth ran away with me there.'

73

'That's all right.'

His gaze went back to the dray and he smiled in admiration. The horses had leather halters round their necks while their manes were plaited and knotted with different coloured ribbons. Big leather straps also hung around their necks covered with gleaming brass ornamental emblems. The wagon itself was brightly coloured and positively screamed of not only being lovingly looked after, but also deeply cherished.

'There are certain things you English do better than anyone else,' Julius commented. 'From your Royalty right down to somethin' like that. No wonder we Yanks can sometimes be in awe of you. You got class as a race, real class which is what we respect and envy more than anythin' else. Yessir.'

Ellie felt proud to hear him speak of England in such a way. 'Why aren't you in your car?' she queried, changing the subject.

He regarded her with amusement. 'I don't always drive, you know. I do have legs and enjoy using them from time to time.'

That flustered her. 'I didn't mean to be rude.'

'You weren't, Ellie. I was just teasin'. Havin' you on.'

'It's just . . . I mean . . .' She broke off and smiled. 'I don't know what I meant. That I usually see you in your car, that's all.'

'Well not today, at least till later.' He glanced again admiringly at the dray and the two leather-aproned draymen unloading more barrels to be rolled, via a ramp, into the pub cellar. 'What are you doin' out here anyway. Shoppin'?'

'No. I'm meeting George actually. My boyfriend.'

'Oh yeah, he and I haven't met yet. No doubt we will sometime. I'd enjoy that.'

Julius turned up the collar of his coat, for it was nippy. 'Now if you'll excuse me.'

'Nice talking to you, Julius.'

He flashed her a set of perfect white teeth. 'And you, Ellie.'

He strode off a few yards, then suddenly turned. 'Look, Ellie, I'm walkin'!' And having said that he laughed.

Ellie blushed, feeling as if she'd made a right fool of herself. Of course Americans walked, daft of her to have commented otherwise.

'Where have you been? You're late.'

George gulped in a deep lungful of air, out of breath from running. 'Sorry, I had something else to do which took longer than I expected.' He pecked her on the cheek. 'Anyway, I'm here now.'

Her feet were frozen but she decided not to mention the fact. He'd said sorry and explained, that was enough. 'So where are we off to?'

'The pub.'

She stared at him in astonishment. 'At this time of day?'

'I want to have a quiet word and where better than there?' He pointed at the pub still taking its delivery. 'We'll try that one.'

Again she was astonished, The Florence being only a few minutes away. This was unusual, George normally such a creature of habit. Something she both liked and disliked about him.

He took her hand and hooked the arm round the inside of his. 'Shall we?'

'There you are, a shandy,' he declared, setting the drink in front of her. His was a pint.

The pub wasn't a particularly popular one which was why George had chosen it. The table they'd decided on was in a corner well out of the way where their conversation wouldn't be overheard.

'So what's this all about?' she frowned. 'I must say you're being rather mysterious.'

'Not really. I just wanted us to be alone, that's all.' He sipped his pint.

'Well?' she queried.

'As you know, I've finished my apprenticeship and am now taking home a full wage packet every week.'

She nodded. They'd celebrated that the week before last.

He looked into his glass, suddenly unsure of himself. It was a tremendous step after all. One of the biggest of his entire life. And what if she refused?

'Go on, George,' Ellie urged softly.

'I thought . . .' He cleared his throat. 'I thought we might get engaged?' That last came out in a rush.

Ellie caught her breath. She'd known this would happen but hadn't imagined it would come so soon. It had completely caught her off guard.

His expression was both pleading and defiant. 'What do you say?'

This was it, she mused. If she committed herself it was wedding bells. Then she remembered the night in The Florence. New Year's Eve, when George had stood up to that dreadful Taffy Roberts on her behalf, ready to fight for her.

'When do you think we'd get married?' she prevaricated, her heart seemingly fluttering in her chest.

'A year at least. Probably more. We'd have to save up first so we can do it all properly.'

She nodded, but didn't reply.

'I've already been to the bank and drawn out my savings,' he went on. 'If you say yes we can go straight from here to the jeweller's and buy a ring. I can't afford a really expensive one, Ellie, but I have enough to get something decent.'

'I see,' she murmured, wondering why she was putting him through this when she already knew what her answer was going to be.

'I love you, Ellie,' he whispered and, reaching across the table, placed a hand over hers.

There it was. She couldn't resist any longer. 'And I love you, George. Of course my answer's yes.'

His face radiated delight. 'Oh, Ellie! I just know we'll be happy together. I just know it. You're everything I've ever wanted in a woman. Truly you are. I realised that not long after we started going out together.'

His confession touched her to the very depths of her being.

'We're engaged then,' she smiled. 'As from right now, this moment, we're engaged.'

'I'll make you a good husband, I swear. You'll never have any worries about me.'

'And I'll do my best to make you a good wife, George.'

He glanced around to ensure no one was watching. Satisfied they weren't he leant across and kissed Ellie on the lips. 'That seals it then.'

'I'll tell you something, George.'

'What's that?'

'This was well worth being kept waiting for.'

They both laughed.

There were tears in Jess's eyes when she finally released George. 'This is the most wonderful news!' she husked. 'I couldn't be more pleased.'

'Thank you, Mrs Sykes. I take it you approve.'

Jess laughed. 'Of course I approve, you silly bugger. And so does Albert. I can't wait to tell him when he gets home from work. He'll be straight over The Florence I'm sure.'

George put an arm round Ellie's waist and drew her to him.

'Now let's see that ring again,' Jess went on.

Ellie held out her left hand. Jess took it and moved it first one way then another so that the stones sparkled. 'It's a beauty,' she declared. 'Very tasteful too.'

'It was Ellie's choice,' George explained, somewhat unnecessarily. For who else's would it have been?

Jess released Ellie's hand and took a deep breath. 'I'll have to sit down for a minute, my legs have gone all wobbly.'

'Shall I put the kettle on, Ma?'

'You do that, Ellie, and make sure you brew a good strong cuppa. I need that.'

'We're not staying long, Mrs Sykes. We want to go and tell my parents after this.'

'Of course, of course,' Jess nodded. 'And so you should. I'm just pleased you came and told me first.'

Her Ellie engaged, she was thrilled to bits. And George such a nice and steady chap too. Ellie couldn't have done better. Albert was going to be so excited.

'Now, what are your plans?' Jess queried, settling back in her usual chair. Like Ellie, she'd been fully expecting this, but also, like Ellie, not quite so soon.

Not that it mattered. Not in the least.

Albert switched off the light and lay back in bed. As Jess had predicted he'd gone over to The Florence for a few after being told of Ellie and George's engagement.

'Happy?' Jess asked in the darkness.

'About Ellie? Very much so. I approve of that young man. He'll do Ellie proud. You mark my words.'

Ellie a married woman before too long! Jess smiled. It seemed like only yesterday she was changing the girl's nappies. How time flies.

'Did George mention where they might live? Around here I hope. Possibly even in the street if there's something going.'

'I don't think they've thought that far ahead yet,' Jess replied. 'It could be George will want to be near his parents in Highbury.'

Albert grunted, hoping that wouldn't be the case. But if it was, well Highbury wasn't that far away. Just up the road really. No distance at all.

'It's going to cost us,' Jess said. 'Ellie will expect the full works, church wedding, reception after. Won't be cheap.'

'I won't let her down,' Albert replied. 'We'll have morning suits for the men and Paul can be a pageboy.'

Jess laughed. 'He might not like that. You know Paul.'

'He'll do as he's told,' Albert declared darkly. 'Or he'll have me to contend with.'

'Do you think we'll be able to go up West for the dress?' Jess queried. 'Anything bought locally wouldn't be half so good.'

Albert considered that, turning the pros and cons over in his mind.

'There again, we could have it made. That might be an idea. It would certainly be a lot cheaper than Oxford Street and the like.'

Albert started making mental calculations. They did have some money put by, but not a lot. It was difficult to save on what he earned which was sufficient for the upkeep of the family but not much else. But he'd manage. It would just mean a bit of belt tightening for a while, that's all. Perhaps he could even get a part-time job to earn extra, though with his hours that would be difficult.

'Goodnight, love,' Jess whispered when she didn't get a reply.

Albert shifted and turned on his side to face her. Reaching out he slipped a hand up her nightdress, stopping when he felt Jess tense.

'I'm sorry, Albert,' she whispered. 'I'm just not in the mood.'

With a sigh he withdrew his hand. 'That's all right. I understand.'

'I really am sorry. I know this is hard for you, but it's just the way things are at the moment.'

He rolled onto his back. She didn't always refuse him since coming home from the hospital, but did more often than not. And when she did comply he guessed she was simply going through the motions for his sake. He could only wonder if that side of their life, which had always been so good, was more or less gone for ever. He didn't know how he'd cope if it had.

Albert didn't consider himself particularly highly sexed, but he was normal, and still at an age where he had regular urges. 'Is there anything I can do?' he asked quietly.

'Be patient. That's all I ask. All I can ask.'

'I'll try, Jess.' He had to, he told himself. There was nothing else for it. He certainly wasn't going to force himself on her as some men might have done. That was definitely out of the question as it would have gone completely against his nature.

'I still love you, Albert. Never doubt that. It would break my heart if you did.'

'It's just a temporary thing, Jess, it'll pass in time.' He wished he believed that, but it was hope more than anything.

'There is something, Albert.'

'What's that?'

'Will you cuddle me? That would be lovely. Just a cuddle, that's all.'

He took her into his arms and held her close. Like babes in the wood, he thought, remembering the children's story. Like babes in the wood.

They were still entwined when they fell asleep.

Connie Fox was the first to notice Ellie's ring when they turned up for work on the Monday morning. They were coming out of the ladies, which doubled as a cloakroom, when she spotted it. Connie squealed and grabbed Ellie's hand.

'An engagement ring! You've gone and got engaged, you lucky sod.'

Ellie grinned as the other girls in their department came crowding round. 'Let's have a look! Let's have a look!' several cried in unison.

The ring had a small central stone surrounded by chips. It hadn't been the cheapest in the shop but not far off. Despite that Ellie was as pleased as punch with it. Besides, it was on a par with the sort of ring any of the other girls would have expected to receive.

'It's a smasher!' Connie declared, bright-eyed with delight for her friend. Delight and, she'd have been the first to admit it, more than a tinge of jealousy.

'When did it happen?' Agnes Short queried. 'Let's have all the details.'

'Saturday afternoon. George proposed in a pub.'

'Did he go down on a bended knee?' another girl asked, and giggled.

'Don't be daft. Of course he didn't. It wasn't like that at all. It was romantic though, if I say so myself.' The latter wasn't exactly true, but why should she tell the others that.

'He's such a handsome bugger too,' Connie beamed. 'You are jammy. Knowing me I'll probably end up with the hunchback of Notre Dame.'

Everyone, including Ellie, laughed when Connie said that. 'Who'll also have a squint,' Connie added for good measure.

'It is lovely,' Elaine McIntosh, the senior typist, commented. 'Good for you, Ellie.'

'What's the cause of this commotion!'

They all froze when Miss Oates' voice cut through their banter. It was Connie who answered. 'Miss Sykes has just got engaged, Miss Oates, and we're admiring the ring.'

For a fraction of a second Miss Oates' stern expression softened, then hardened again. 'Be that as it may, it's no excuse for all this noise and general kerfuffle. You can admire Miss Sykes' ring later I'm sure.' Adding meaningfully, 'Out of work time. Now get about your duties. All of you.'

'Yes, Miss Oates,' was chorused in reply.

'Rotten old bat,' Connie whispered to Ellie as they turned away.

'Did you say something, Miss Fox?'

Connie was innocence personified, looking as though butter wouldn't melt in her mouth. 'I said it was so cold this morning I wished I'd worn a hat,' she lied.

Miss Oates sniffed, clearly not believing a word of that. 'Get on with it then.'

To Ellie's utter amazement Miss Oates later stopped by her desk. 'Congratulations, Miss Sykes,' Miss Oates said in a low voice, and briefly smiled before sweeping regally on her way.

Ellie was left dumbstruck.

Shelby Robbins hung up his coat and hat and greeted Julius who was already in the office and hard at work. 'Guess what Phyllis and I did last night?' he said.

Julius was concentrating, the report he was drafting proving a tricky one.

'Not the obvious I hope,' he replied drily.

Shelby laughed. 'Well we did actually, but that was later. No, we went and saw your old man. He sure is a great player. We just adored the band.'

Julius glanced up with a frown. 'I didn't know you liked jazz?'

'Hell, yeah. I got stacks of records at home that I brought over from the States. Muggsy Spannier, Art Tatum, Lester Young, Teagarden, all those famous guys. But last night was the first time I'd ever heard your old man. I sure was impressed.'

'What did you make of the club?'

'The Chicory House? It was OK. Nothing special, but OK. Good atmosphere. And hey, those English audiences sure appreciate their jazz. That surprised me. They're usually so buttoned up about everything.'

Julius smiled. 'That's what Pop says. They can be fantastic accordin' to him.'

Shelby pointed a finger at Julius. 'You take my word for it, boy, halfway through the evening . . .' He trailed off when he saw the sudden look in Julius's eyes. They were shooting daggers at him. 'What's wrong?'

Julius counted to ten before replying. 'Do me a favour, Shelby, never call me boy again. I find it insultin'.'

'Oh shit,' Shelby apologised. 'I didn't mean nothing by it. It's an expression, that's all.'

'It's more than an expression if you're a negro. As I said, it's insultin'. And I do mean it when I told you never to call me that again.'

Julius didn't need to elaborate on the threat, Shelby had got the message loud and clear. 'Sorry, truly I am. I'll remember.'

'Do that.' Julius's tone was as cold as ice.

He returned to his report while Shelby beat a hasty, and wise, retreat to the vending machine in the corridor outside.

Julius's eyes flickered upwards as Shelby left the room. There was one thing he would never allow himself to be called, and that was boy. The connotations, and history behind it, made his blood boil.

* * *

Jess put the last dish away and threw down the tea towel. Ellie had already gone out as she was meeting George, and Paul was spending the night at a pal's whose father was taking them fishing early in the morning.

'Finished?' Albert queried from his chair.

Jess nodded. 'All done.'

Albert glanced at the clock on the mantelpiece. 'Then get your things, I'm taking you to the pictures. A Ronald Colman film, I believe.'

For a moment Jess thought she'd misheard. 'The pictures?'

'That's right. Just you and I, the pair of us. And when we come out we'll have fish and chips just like we used to in our courting days.'

Somewhat in a daze Jess took off her pinny. Albert suggesting the pictures, it was unheard of! Usually it took a great deal of persuading on her part for him to go along. Now here he was actually suggesting it.

'Some sort of mushy nonsense according to Ellie,' he went on. 'You're bound to enjoy yourself.'

Jess laughed, this was incredible. 'You'll be proposing we sit in the back row next?'

'And why not!' he retorted, pretending indignation. 'We may be older but we're not decrepit. There's nothing wrong with a couple canoodling, even at our age.'

What a wonderful man he was, she thought, guessing correctly why he was doing this.

'And you can have a box of chocolates before we go in,' he further added. 'As long as you don't scoff the lot and I get one or two.'

Chocolates, pictures, fish and chips! 'What about the pub?' she queried. 'You usually go there on a Friday night when you're not on duty.'

'I can miss the pub for once. And who knows, we might even get back in time for last knockings providing there isn't too long a queue at the fish and chip shop.'

She dropped her gaze for a moment, a great warmth for

Albert bubbling inside her. Then she looked up again, straight into his eyes. 'Thanks, darling. A night out is just the ticket.'

'Then you'd best get ready.'

A little make-up, she thought, and a change of dress. Suddenly she felt like a young girl again. And a courting one at that.

She pecked Albert on the cheek before hurrying upstairs, leaving him with the broadest of smiles on his face.

Chapter 7

It was baking hot in the scullery where Jess was doing her weekly wash. A scullery that always smelt, at least so Ellie claimed, of Sunlight soap and boiled beetroot.

Jess removed the lid from the copper where the wash was coming along nicely and took out the dolly blue. When the wash was finally done it would come out of the boiler, whose fire now blazed underneath, and be put, piece by piece, through the large manually operated mangle situated to one side.

Jess was thinking about Beulah who'd yet again asked her in for coffee, and whom she'd yet again refused with a made-up excuse. This time it had been different though, the hurt of rejection clearly showing in Beulah's soulful eyes.

This couldn't go on, Jess told herself. The Postons had been kindness itself to her and her family and her response was continually to snub them when invited in.

Jess wiped away wisps of damp hair that had fallen across her face, tucking them neatly behind one ear.

She was being unfair by not explaining to Beulah; surely that was the least she could do. Better still, explain and force herself to go into that kitchen of terrible memory.

Except, she couldn't bring herself to do either, for that would mean talking about what had happened, going through the whole damn thing all over again, which would be torment.

Stupid woman, she thought. That's what she was, a stupid woman. What had happened had happened, she'd come to terms with that fact, even found herself living more easily with it, as Albert could testify thanks to their intimate life getting back more or less to normal. She simply hadn't been able to shut Albert out in that way for ever, her love for him being too strong to keep denying him.

Of course the wound would never properly heal, it went far too deep for that. And the great black hole remained and always would. She'd known that right from the start. But she was coping with it better now, not falling into it nearly as much.

'Buggeration,' she swore. She just wasn't being fair where Beulah was concerned. Not fair at all. And that wasn't like her. It went completely against her principles.

Jess glanced out the small, open scullery window to check the weather. Earlier she'd feared it might rain but that threat had cleared away which meant she'd be able to peg out as she'd intended.

God, her hands, she thought. They always looked so awful on wash day, all red and horrible, as if they'd been boiled along with the wash. And she was fresh out of hand cream too! She'd meant to buy some earlier but had forgotten after being in a conversation with old Ma Jenkins whom she'd bumped into.

She brought her mind back to Beulah, knowing she had to do something.

Beulah opened the door to find Jess standing there. 'Why, hi!' she exclaimed in surprise.

Jess was holding a box from the bakery which she now indicated. 'I've got six French Fancies here which I imagine will go well with that wonderful coffee you make. Can I come in?'

'Of course, hon. Of course.'

Jess took a deep breath and forced herself to step forward. Her heart was hammering nineteen to the dozen as she moved into the Postons' hallway.

'I can't remember the last time you were here,' Beulah said affably.

Ouch! Jess thought. She could, only too damn well. The occasion was burnt into her soul. 'I know. That's why I've called by. To explain to you. Can we . . . can we . . .' Jess steeled herself. 'Go into the kitchen?'

'Sure. Or we could use the other room.'

'No, the *kitchen*,' Jess declared emphatically. 'I have a reason for that.'

'Oh?'

Jess followed Beulah, the larger woman leading the way. In other circumstances Jess might have been amused by the ancient, heavily embroidered and garish slippers Beulah was wearing. But she didn't even notice them.

She started to tremble as they approached the kitchen, the trembling increasing as they went through the door. The first thing she saw was the chair she'd been sitting in when she'd miscarried.

'Oh my God!' she croaked, and dropped the bakery box.

Beulah had listened in sympathetic silence as Jess had recounted why she'd been avoiding the house, and kitchen in particular, berating herself for not realising what the problem had been. Now it made perfect sense.

'So that's it,' Jess concluded quietly. 'And I do apologise if I caused you any upset.'

'Oh, honey,' Beulah breathed. 'I been so bone-headed. It just never crossed my mind you'd feel that way.'

Jess picked up her cup and sipped her coffee which had started to go cold during the time she'd been speaking. 'I simply had to get a grip of myself, face the situation. That's why I made myself come. That and because I was so ashamed of appearing to slight you.'

'You ain't never done that, honey. I just couldn't figure why you always turned down my invitations. And yet when I stopped by your place you were always welcomin'. Plain as the nose on your face of course, except I didn't see it.' Beulah studied Jess. 'You OK now?'

Jess glanced around. 'I think so.'

'Still want to stay here, there's always the other room?'

'I'd prefer to stay here.' Jess hesitated. 'There's a question I want to ask you.'

'Shoot.'

'Did you . . .' She paused to draw in a breath. 'Did you happen to notice if it was a boy or girl?'

Beulah shook her head. 'I didn't. It was all happenin' so fast, and I was so worried.'

'I understand.' Jess swallowed back her disappointment. Now she'd never know. But maybe it was better that way.

'Besides, hon, it was . . .' Beulah decided referring to it as an 'it' wasn't exactly tactful. 'The child was too little, hardly formed at all. Even if I'd looked I don't know if I could have seen what the child was. That's the honest truth.'

Jess placed her cup back in its saucer. 'Am I forgiven, Beulah?'

'Of course you is, Jess. There's nothin' to forgive anyway. You was havin' a real bad dose of the blues, understandably so. That's all. Now . . .' She clapped her meaty hands together. 'How about those French Fancy jobs you brought, why don't we try them out?'

Jess reached for the box. 'I hope they're not too bashed.'

'Don't matter if they are. Won't spoil the taste. And I could sure do with somethin' sweet right now. Though Pee Wee always tells me I'm sweet enough. Lyin' hound dog that he is.'

They both laughed.

A little later as Jess was saying goodbye, Beulah queried quietly, 'Will you be back?'

'Any time I'm asked, Beulah. Any time.'

'That's good. That's real good. I'm pleased. And hey, I won't be mentionin' this to anyone, includin' that husband of mine. It's strictly between you and me. OK?'

'OK,' Jess agreed.

She felt buoyant, and definitely freer, as she turned towards her own house.

That particular demon had been vanquished.

'Where have you been?' Jess demanded as Ellie entered the kitchen. 'We were getting all set to start without you. I thought maybe you'd been offered overtime and taken it.'

'I'm starving,' Paul complained.

'You're always starving,' Jess retorted without even bothering to look at him.

'I've been over in The Florence,' Ellie explained.

Albert frowned. 'Drinking at this time of the evening?'

'No, Dad, I wanted a word with the Cliffords before they got busy.' The Cliffords were Harry, the landlord, and his wife Hazel. 'I had the idea at work that a part-time job would be useful to help George and me save up for the wedding. I'll be doing Friday and Saturday nights to start with. Possibly more if I get on well.'

'Can you all sit down and I'll dish out,' Jess requested. 'It's stew and dumplings with boiled tats.'

Albert wasn't at all sure what he made of Ellie's news. His initial reaction wasn't to be all that keen on the prospect.

'Well, Dad?'

'The extra money would certainly help, I'll give you that. But . . . well, all those men?'

'I'll be safe enough, Dad. It's our local, for goodness sake. I know almost everyone who goes in there, and they me. Besides, neither Harry or Hazel would let me come to any harm. Or any of the regulars come to that. I'll be safe as houses.'

That was a point, Albert reflected. 'What do you think, Jess?'

Jess shrugged. 'As you say, the money would certainly come in handy for Ellie. We can't dispute that.'

Paul's eyes gleamed as Jess filled his plate. Three dumplings! He usually only got two. He immediately fell to eating.

'Can't you wait?' Ellie reprimanded him sharply.

'And don't reply with your mouth full,' Jess warned when she saw that's what he was about to do. Honestly, you'd think the boy had never been taught manners.

'I'll enjoy it,' Ellie said to her parents. 'It should be fun. A good laugh.'

'Have you discussed this with George?' Jess queried.

'I told you, Ma, I only had the idea earlier. There hasn't been a chance yet.'

'Well, I think you should have done that before applying at The Florence. George might be dead against it.'

'If he is I'll talk him round,' Ellie replied confidently.

'Hmmh!' Jess snorted, indicating they could now start on the meal.

'Do you begin this Friday?' Albert asked.

'To be there prompt at opening time.'

'What about your tea?' Jess queried in alarm. 'You can't not eat first.'

'I've to have something there. It's part of the arrangement.'

'Well, that's all right then,' Jess reluctantly conceded. She preferred to feed her own family, knowing they'd have good wholesome food and not the muck some folks ate.

'I'll go and see George straight after this,' Ellie declared. 'He should be home.'

Paul speared another potato with his fork and wondered if there was any more stew in the pot when he finished what was on his plate.

George was appalled. 'A *barmaid*?'

Ellie had walked up to Highbury and his parents' house to find that they'd gone out leaving George alone. 'That's right. Think of the help the money will be.'

His face clouded over. He didn't like this one little bit. 'I don't know,' he said grudgingly.

'What's to know? I'm doing it for us, George, to make things easier. What's wrong with that?'

'How much will you get per shift?' he asked.

She told him. 'And that'll soon add up if I put it by every week, believe me.'

He certainly couldn't disagree, it would make quite a difference to their savings. Make things a lot easier as she'd said. He broke away, his brow furrowed in thought.

'George?'

'I can't pretend I like it, Ellie. God knows what you'll have to contend with. When men have been drinking they can come out with all sorts. Be downright crude. You've heard it yourself.'

She sighed. 'I'm grown up, George. There's not a lot will bother me.'

'You hate swearing for a start,' he reminded her.

'Then I'll just have to develop a thicker skin, that's all. Let it wash over my head. Anyway, there isn't much swearing when Hazel or Harry are about, they don't appreciate it either.'

'Well, what about our Friday and Saturday nights together? What happens to those?'

Ellie had already thought of an answer to that. 'We'll go out more during the week instead. It won't be a problem.'

'But Fridays and Saturdays are *the* nights to go out. It won't be the same during the week.'

She went to him and curled an arm round his neck. 'We'll be together. Surely that's what's important?'

'Just the same.'

'I want to do this, George. Please don't be angry?'

'I'm not angry. I . . . just disapprove, I suppose.'

Pulling his head down she blew gently into his ear, knowing how much he adored that. 'Please don't. It'll mean we can get married sooner than we otherwise might have done. Live together under the one roof, spend our nights together in the same bed and all that entails.'

He closed his eyes for a brief second, imagining himself and Ellie in bed. How desperately he wanted that.

She kissed him on the side of the mouth. 'So you agree then?'

He tentatively lifted a hand and brushed it over the swell of her breast which sent what felt like an electric shock coursing through him. 'Oh, Ellie,' he whispered.

'It'll work out, George. You'll see.'

He was about to kiss her full on the lips when, from out in the hallway, came the banging shut of the door announcing that his folks had returned.

'Damn,' said George, smiling ruefully.

Neither of them mentioned the pub job to George's parents, thinking it wisest that way.

Julius ran a hand over his forehead. It had been a long, tiring day and he was thoroughly bushed. He wished he hadn't arranged to meet Marybeth later in town. He could have done without that now.

'What's new?' Pee Wee asked, having been playing music inside his head, working out various variations for a jam session scheduled for that evening.

Julius flopped wearily onto a chair.

'Hi, son!' Beulah greeted him from the stove where she was cooking chicken jambalaya.

'I've got to go away for a few weeks,' he informed them.

Beulah stopped what she was doing to stare at him. 'Where to?'

'Paris. Probably two weeks, no more than three.'

'You mean Paris, *France*?'

He smiled at her excited expression. 'Uh-huh!'

'Hey, that's great.'

'For the Embassy I take it?' Pee Wee queried.

'Yeah. And don't ask what it's about. I can't say. Except that it's routine, nothin' more.'

'Must be important "routine" to send you all that way?' Pee Wee commented shrewdly.

Actually it was very important. He was taking over a number of high-level documents plus a letter from his own Ambassador to the Ambassador in France. There was also a message to be delivered orally.

'Now, Pop, don't try and pry. You know it won't get you anywhere,' Julius teased.

'When are you leavin'?'

'Day after tomorrow.'

'I'll pack your bag, son.'

'I can do that, Mom,' he protested.

Her expression became defiant. 'When you is in this house
that's my job, and don't you forget it. So if there's anythin' special you want to take then make sure you tell me beforehand.'

He sighed in defeat. 'OK, Mom, you win.'

'Darned tootin' I do. Just like always. That so, Pee Wee?'

'Just like always,' he smiled in agreement.

Julius closed his eyes, thinking about the forthcoming trip.
When he'd mentioned it to Marybeth she'd asked if she could
come with him. All she needed, she'd said, were the dates and
name of the hotel he'd be staying at. She'd make her own
arrangements and join him there. As she'd said, she had some
vacation due and had never been to France. And he wouldn't be
working all the time, now would he?

It should be an interesting trip, Julius thought to himself.
Between one thing and another.

As luck would have it, Ellie's first customer was Taffy
Roberts. Her heart sank when she saw him come through the
door.

He stared at her in surprise. 'What are you doing there?' he
demanded.

'Growing tomatoes, what does it look like?'

He laughed. 'Lippy cow, eh? Mine's a large rum and black
and a pint of mild. I take it you can pull a pint?'

'Oh, I think I can just about manage,' she replied offhandedly, having had some instruction on arrival from Harry who'd
also taken her through the prices.

Taffy pulled out a filthy hanky and hawked into it. He then
used the hanky to wipe his nose. 'When did you start?'

'Tonight.'

He grinned, thinking there might be some sport here. 'You won't last. I'd bet on it.'

She placed his rum before him and stared him straight in the eye. 'I'll last just as long as I want to. You'd better believe that.'

Harry reappeared after having popped out the back for a few moments. 'All right, Ellie?'

'Fine, thank you.'

She was aware of Taffy watching her closely as she drew his pint. Thankfully she didn't make a hash of it. Now she had the till to contend with, but that was easy.

Without uttering another word she put the Welshman's change in front of him, then moved on to another customer who'd wandered in meanwhile.

Soon the bar was busy.

'How was it?' Jess demanded eagerly.

'Exhausting. My feet are killing me. I shan't wear heels tomorrow night, that was an obvious mistake.'

Jess nodded her sympathy as Ellie slipped off her shoes. 'Would you like a cup of tea?'

'Just the ticket. I'm parched.'

'Any trouble?' Albert asked casually.

She shook her head. 'Taffy Roberts was a bit mouthy to begin with, but he didn't stay long. Ignorant man. That laugh of his is absolutely horrendous. I swear he sounds like a braying donkey.'

'You didn't mind me popping in?'

'Not in the least, Dad. You usually do on a Friday night and there's no reason to stop that just because I'm there.'

Ellie reached down and massaged her feet. They really were sore. Still, she'd probably get used to it.

'I sat with George who wasn't too happy about you being behind the bar,' Albert remarked.

'I gave him a piece of my mind when he walked me home. Honestly, he sat there glaring at me the entire time. I can't put up with that.'

'He's only concerned, Ellie. Give him a while to get used to the idea.'

She'd actually felt quite sorry for George who'd looked like a fish out of water without her being with him. In a way it was complimentary though, if irritating. Afterwards she'd told him straight she wasn't going to put up with him glaring at her night after night. It was off-putting to say the least.

'What did you get to eat?' Jess asked anxiously.

'Shepherd's pie and veg, Ma. Same as the Cliffords had. It was very nice.'

'I was worried you'd get fobbed off with a Scotch egg or something. No real goodness in that at all.'

How caring her mother was, Ellie reflected. As was her father. She was very fortunate to have parents like them, a fact she appreciated.

'And did you enjoy yourself?' Albert queried.

'Thoroughly. Once the pub got busy the hours just whizzed by. Some of the regulars can be very funny when you're serving them. They sort of flirt with you, but you know they don't really mean it. It's just a game where they're concerned.'

'And you're back there again tomorrow night,' Albert stated, already knowing that to be so.

'At opening time sharp. I'm looking forward to it.' Far better, and more exciting, than the Poxy Roxy, she thought to herself. Just as she'd expected, it had been a right good laugh.

'What do you notice about the people?' Julius asked Marybeth, as they sat at a table outside a rather chic café. Marybeth had arrived in that morning while Julius was at the Embassy.

Marybeth shook her head. 'Nothin' in particular. They seem perfectly normal to me.'

'Their faces,' Julius said slowly and thoughtfully. 'Everyone looks strained, worried sick. No one is laughin' or jokin', they're all so grave.'

Marybeth could now see that was so. 'You're right.'

'And you know why?'

'Do you mean the Germans?'

Julius nodded. 'I don't blame them. I'd be worried too. France could well be next on the list for Hitler to invade.'

Despite the July heat Marybeth shivered, wondering if it had been such a good idea after all to come over and join Julius. There again, she might never get another chance to visit Paris.

'Another thing,' Julius went on. 'It's rare to come across a black person in London, but here they're not uncommon. I like that.'

He glanced over at Marybeth who was wearing a pretty summer dress which showed off her superb figure to the full. Made of rayon jersey, the dress was sleek, smooth-fitting and boasted a floral print on a cream background. It had a cross-over bodice with a modified peg-top skirt that had curved, set-in pockets. Round her waist was a self belt.

Marybeth sipped her Pernod, wrinkling her nose as she did.

'What's wrong?'

'This stuff is crap. It tastes like swamp water.'

Julius laughed. 'It's a typical French aperitif.'

'I don't care if it's typical or not. It's still crap. Can I have somethin' else?'

'Sure.'

'Scotch on the rocks.'

Julius was still laughing as he beckoned the waiter over.

'My God, that was the best yet,' Marybeth sighed, giving Julius a satisfied, feline smile. 'You sure are some lover, honey. You ring my ting-a-ling every time.'

When they'd returned to the Georges Cinq where they were staying in individual rooms for propriety's sake, they'd gone to hers and popped the bottle of champagne Julius had brought along. Within minutes they'd both stripped off and tumbled into bed, Marybeth, never shy to say the least, immediately taking the lead.

'I'm glad you came,' Julius smiled in return.

'I sure did. The full bazooka!'

His eyes twinkled. 'I didn't mean that. I meant come to Paris.'

'You're joshin' me now,' she pretended to scold, wagging a finger at him.

'More champagne?'

'Please.'

She watched the wine bubble and froth into her glass. 'I wish this could go on for ever,' she purred.

'Do you?'

'Oh yeah. And in a way it could.'

'How's that?' He sat back on the bed, supporting himself with pillows.

'You know.'

He shook his head. 'No, I don't actually.'

'Well, let me put it this way, lover, you and I could have beautiful babies together.'

There it was, the plans she had for him. Marriage and a family. He should have guessed.

'What do you think?'

He could see she was being light-hearted, but underneath deadly serious about this. Marybeth wasn't joking.

'Children, beautiful or not, don't figure on my agenda, Marybeth. At least not in the foreseeable future.'

She didn't reply to that, instead dropped her gaze to stare at the bed. 'OK, so kids are out for now,' she eventually whispered.

Christ, Julius thought. That still left marriage.

'Why don't we talk about this another time?' he suggested. 'The way things are who knows what could happen. Everythin's so uncertain right now.'

Instinct told her not to push the matter, even if she desperately wanted to do so.

Marybeth swung herself off the bed. 'I'm goin' to have a hot tub. Won't be long.'

Despite the smile on her face he could hear the hurt in her voice. And that hurt him too.

Chapter 8

Julius arrived home to find Beulah and Pee Wee had gone out. Thirsty after his journey he decided to nip across the road and have a drink of English beer which, despite being warm and not at all what he'd been used to back in the States, he was becoming increasingly fond of. He pulled up in astonishment when he saw Ellie behind the bar.

'Hi! When did this happen?' he asked when it was his turn to be served.

'A few weeks ago. I'm only part-time, Friday and Saturday nights.'

'Well, good for you, kid.'

It irritated her to be called that, but she didn't comment. 'What'll it be?'

'A pint of your best.'

'How was France?' she queried as she was pouring it.

'How did you know I was there?'

'Your ma told my ma who mentioned it. Whereabouts were you?'

'Paris.'

Her eyes widened. 'I hear it's a marvellous place and that the women are really elegant.'

'They're certainly that.' What he didn't say was that they

made their English counterparts look absolutely dowdy by comparison. It wasn't only the way they dressed, they had an indefinable something that set them apart, made even the oldest of them look truly glamorous. Marybeth had been so taken with the clothes and fashions she'd bought a whole bunch of stuff to bring back with her.

'I envy you,' Ellie admitted. 'I'd give my eye teeth to go there.'

'Maybe someday,' he smiled.

'Fat chance of that. There's no more likelihood of my going to France than there is of me flying to the moon.'

She placed his pint in front of him. 'You must tell me all about it sometime when you get the chance.'

'Sure. I'd be pleased to.'

She glanced round the bar to see she wasn't needed elsewhere. 'I've heard the food's awful though. Is it true they actually eat horses and snails?'

He nodded. 'It's true.'

She pulled a face. 'Uck! How disgusting.'

Julius was trying not to laugh. 'And they use lots of garlic. Do you know what that is?'

'I read about it in a book once. It makes your breath stink.' Her expression was one of total revulsion. 'How can they eat something that makes your breath stink? It doesn't make sense.'

'Tastes nice though,' he teased.

'You mean you actually ate it?' She was incredulous.

'Sure thing. We use garlic in the US as well. Apart from givin' the food flavour it's supposed to be good for you.'

'Flavour!' she exclaimed in derision. 'If food is fresh it doesn't need any fancy flavouring added. That sort of thing is to disguise poor-quality meat and the like. Everyone knows that.'

'Except obviously in France,' he commented drily, still teasing.

'Are you serving, Ellie?'

'Excuse me,' she apologised and hurried away to attend to the customer who'd called.

Julius took out a pack of cigarettes and lit up. Ellie had rather a neat little figure, he noted absent-mindedly. Curiously he'd never been aware of it before. Nothing to compare with Marybeth's of course. Marybeth's figure was a completely different ball game.

Marybeth, he reflected. Their time together had been a success, the sex mind-blowing. Well, it certainly had been for him and she'd assured him it had been the same for her.

She'd never mentioned babies or marriage again, which had been a relief, though on several occasions he'd thought she was about to.

He could do a lot worse than have Marybeth for a wife, he mused, she was certainly a class act. Rich too, at least her folks were. Or so he'd been led to believe, though what her father's occupation was he had no idea.

Lots of guys would have jumped at the chance of Marybeth plus money, so what was stopping him? He simply wasn't ready for marriage, he guessed. The thought of being tied down, coming home to the same woman night after night didn't appeal at all.

On the positive side, she'd be a definite asset in his career. The Department favoured married guys, believing it made them more stable. And Marybeth being an ex-member of the Department – he presumed she'd give up work if they tied the knot – could only be helpful too. All in all a very attractive package.

One thing was certain, he needed to give this a lot of careful thinking before reaching a final decision. It would be stupid not to. Damn stupid. And whatever else he considered himself to be it wasn't that. No sirree.

'I didn't know you smoked?'

He snapped out of his reverie to find Ellie had returned and was starting to wash glasses in the sink situated directly beneath where he was standing.

'Only occasionally, and usually cigars,' he replied. 'My preference is Havanas. They're the best.'

'Cigars, oh my!' She was impressed. 'Winston Churchill smokes those. I've seen him on Pathé News at the cinema. Huge ones.' She studied Julius speculatively for a moment. 'Do you know who Winston Churchill is?'

He thought the naïveté of that endearing. 'Sure do. I met him a while back at a reception we had at the Embassy.'

Ellie was stunned. 'You've actually *met* him? What's he like?'

Julius considered that. 'I thought him very funny to tell the truth. Extremely humorous. Though obviously, goes without sayin', there's a far deeper side to him.'

'How long did you speak to him for?' She was agog.

Julius tried to remember. 'A couple of minutes I guess. And yes, he was smokin' a cigar at the time. A large one, as you said.'

'What did you talk about?'

'This and that, nothin' of consequence. I'm not high enough up the totem pole to be doing that.'

If she'd been impressed to learn Julius smoked cigars, this had impressed her a hundred times more. He'd actually met and spoken to Winston Churchill! It was incredible.

Nice skin, Julius noted. But then most English girls had. Not so American women, their skins paled by comparison. Especially in the mid- and far west where the sun could, and invariably did, do a lot of damage.

Ellie had finished the washing up and now began drying the glasses and putting them away.

Any further conversation was halted when the door swung open and a half-dozen or so men came crowding in, quickly followed by another group.

When Ellie found time to look at where Julius had been she discovered he'd gone. Smiling ruefully she got on with the job, thinking how much she'd enjoyed their chat. She couldn't get over the fact he'd not only met Winston Churchill but actually spoken to the great man.

'I want to talk to the pair of you,' Julius stated, stirring sugar into his coffee.

'What about, son?' Beulah asked. She and Pee Wee had just returned from the West End where they'd had a splendid lunch in a little Bohemian Soho restaurant Pee Wee had discovered.

'I think the pair of you should consider goin' back to New York. Preferably quite soon.'

Pee Wee glanced up at Julius. 'Why's that?'

'You must have read the recent newspapers. The situation in Europe has deteriorated dramatically during the past few weeks. If, and so far it's only that, Hitler invades France, then England could be next. The last thing I want is for you two to be caught up in a war.'

'We'll be safe enough,' Pee Wee replied slowly. 'We're American citizens, the Germans wouldn't dare lay a finger on us. Uncle Sam would have somethin' to say if they tried.'

Beulah's eyes were flicking from one man to the other. This was serious.

'What if the Nazis were to bomb London? A droppin' bomb can't distinguish between an Englishman and an American,' Julius pointed out.

'Do you really think he will invade England?' Beulah queried in a frightened voice.

A large part of the reason Julius had been sent to Paris was to hear first-hand reports from agents coming out of the rest of Europe. He'd personally interrogated, and debriefed, several of them. Of course he couldn't tell his parents that. 'It's a distinct possibility in my opinion.'

'What does our Ambassador say?' Pee Wee frowned.

Julius made a pyramid with his hands. 'How shall I put this? The Ambassador doesn't have great faith in England, or its Empire. He believes the German war machine would simply roll right over this country.'

'Holy shit,' Pee Wee muttered.

'Do you agree with him?' Beulah queried.

'To be honest, Mom, I just don't know. What I do know is I'd be a lot happier if you two were on a boat steamin' Stateside. Then I wouldn't have to worry about you.'

'I see,' Pee Wee murmured.

'Would you come with us?' Beulah asked.

Julius shook his head. 'Can't do that, Mom. London is where I'm posted and here I stay until either the Department, or Ambassador, say otherwise. That's how it is.'

'I wonder what the other guys in the band will do?' Pee Wee mused. 'One thing's certain, they're goin' to be awfully disappointed if we do leave, the band that is. We're all havin' a ball here. The English audiences sure do love our music. They're some of the most appreciative cornflakes I've ever come across.' The latter was a jazz term referring to the general public. 'And ain't that the truth.'

'I can fix up passage for you anytime you like,' Julius went on. 'All you have to do is say and I'll get you on an American liner sailin' out of Southampton.'

'Well, I ain't makin' no decision right here and now,' Pee Wee declared. 'I got to think this through.'

Beulah gazed around her, reflecting on how fond she'd become of this house, and Islington. She'd miss both dreadfully if they were to go.

'You think on it then,' Julius said to Pee Wee. 'But it would be better, and perhaps safer, if you reached that decision sooner rather than later.'

'I got you, son.'

Julius rose from his chair. 'Won't be a second. I brought you both somethin' from Paris.'

The 'something' transpired to be perfume for Beulah and a fancy vest, waistcoat that is, for Pee Wee which he'd known he would love.

He wasn't wrong – his parents were delighted with their gifts.

When Pee Wee got home in the early hours Beulah was in bed, but wide awake. 'I been waitin' for you,' she explained.

He kissed her on the forehead. 'Is it what Julius said?'

'Yeah.'

'Thought it might be.'

He quickly undressed and slipped in alongside her. 'So what do you reckon?'

'I ain't leavin', Pee Wee. I'm stayin' right here.'

'What about the Germans?'

'Screw them. All I know is that Julius has to stay so I is too. I ain't skedaddlin' off leavin' my only son in danger. Shit no. I stays put and that's an end of it.'

He slid an arm round her considerable bulk, enjoying the warm, musky smell of her body. A feeling of sublime content-ment swept through him as it sometimes did when he and Beulah were in bed, snuggled up together. 'Then that's how we'll play it,' he agreed.

'You sure, Pee Wee?'

'Well, I ain't gettin' on no boat without you. What kind of man do you take me for?'

She smiled. 'The lovin' kind.'

'Same with you, hon. Same with you. Now put that light out and let's get some shuteye.'

When the light was out she gathered his head into the full-ness of her ample bosom.

'Julius ain't goin' to take kindly to this,' Pee Wee murmured.

'You just leave him to me. I'll sort that out.'

She would too, Pee Wee thought dreamily. His Beulah could sort anything out.

God bless her.

A grim-faced Albert switched off the wireless to turn and stare at Jess whose expression was one of shock. 'So there we are,' he said. 'We're at war.'

Jess couldn't think of a suitable reply, so instead just shook her head.

They'd been listening to the Prime Minister, Mr Chamberlain, making the dreaded announcement. The formal declaration of war had been issued at 11 a.m. when Britain's ultimatum to Germany had expired. The Germans had not suspended hostili-ties in Poland and so Britain was at war with Hitler's Reich.

Albert felt sick inside. How many young men were going to be killed as a result of this madness? Legions of them, just like the last time when the flower of the nation's youth had been decimated.

'I need a drink,' Albert declared. 'Badly.'

Jess was thinking of Paul who was playing out in the street somewhere, and shuddered. Tears rolled down her cheeks.

'I'd hoped . . . I'd prayed . . .' She trailed off, overcome with emotion.

'There there, girl, we'll be all right. You'll see.' He wished he felt as confident as he was trying to sound.

'Oh, Albert!' she husked, and went to him. He wrapped his arms round her. 'When do you think it'll start?'

'I've no idea. That depends on all sorts of things I should imagine.'

They stood like that in silence for a little while, then Jess broke away to dab at her nose with the end of her pinny. 'I'll put the kettle on.'

'Not for me, pet. I'm going over to the pub. Want to come?'

'No, tea's fine. On you go then. Just don't be late for dinner. It's chicken.'

'I won't be late,' he assured her. 'Are you certain you don't mind me going out?'

Jess shook her head.

'You'll be all right?'

'Of course I will. Now stop fussing. And if you see Paul tell him I want him.'

Hazel, behind the bar, took one look at Albert's face. 'You've heard the news then?'

'On the wireless.'

He glanced around. People were sitting in small groups, huddled together, as if for protection, and talking quietly. The atmosphere was funereal.

'So what are you having?'

'A large scotch and a pint of the usual.'

'It's terrible, don't you think?'

'Oh yes,' he agreed softly.

As Hazel moved off to get his order, Albert ran a hand over his face. Although he'd had a lie-in that morning, it being his weekend off, he felt bone weary. The PM's statement on the wireless had sapped the strength right out of him.

'Those are on the house,' Hazel declared, setting down his drinks. 'All the regulars get a free one this morning. Two in your case. Harry said it was the least we could do in the circumstances.'

'Thanks.'

Hazel lit a cigarette. 'I suppose we all knew it was coming. Nonetheless it was a shock when it actually did.'

Albert knew exactly what she meant.

'You'll be all right though,' she went on. 'Being a fireman I mean. You'll be exempt.

'We've got a couple of nephews, lovely lads, living in Coventry. Just the right age to join, or be called, up,' she added. 'My sister will be beside herself. Poor mare. I feel so sorry for her.'

Albert smiled his sympathy, thinking of Paul whom he hadn't come across on his way over.

Harry appeared from out back. 'Some to-do, eh, Albert?'

'To be honest, it hasn't fully sunk in yet. But I suppose it will soon enough. Thanks for the drinks by the way.'

'You're welcome.'

Harry sighed. 'Bloody Germans. I hate those bastards, I truly do. I hope they all fry in hell.' He shook his head. 'I feel I should be doing something, except I don't know what. I'm all at sixes and sevens.'

Albert was about to reply to that when an air-raid siren suddenly began wailing, causing everyone to look up in alarm.

'Oh my God!' Hazel exclaimed. 'They're bombing us already.'

As if by common consent the entire pub, including Harry and Hazel, made a beeline for the door. Once outside they all, some of the regulars still holding their pints, stared up at the sky. Residents from the houses round about were emerging to do the same.

'See anything?' someone asked.

Dozens of pairs of eyes were scanning the heavens, but there wasn't a single plane, German or otherwise, to be seen.

'Must be a false alarm,' a woman declared hopefully.

After about five minutes, during which nothing happened, people started drifting back to where they'd come from.

'That was scary,' Hazel said when she was again behind the bar.

Whereas the pub had been quiet before, now it was buzzing with excited conversation, everyone talking animatedly.

Albert saw off his scotch and ordered another, wishing he could shake off the feeling of terrible dread and foreboding that had taken hold of him.

Julius had simply never known a Sunday at the Embassy like it. The place, from top to bottom, was a veritable madhouse, every phone in the building seemingly ringing non-stop.

Being a Sunday, most of the staff had been off duty. Without being told they'd all returned to work knowing their presence would be required. The Ambassador was closeted in a meeting with his closest advisors.

'Want a coffee?' Shelby Robbins asked Julius, looking as harassed as Julius felt.

'Not at the moment.'

'OK.'

Shelby hurried from the office to the vending machine in the corridor where he found a queue.

Marybeth came into the room. 'How're you doin'?'

'Same as everyone else. Up to my ass in it.'

She laughed. 'Me too. Ever since I got here I been runnin' around like a headless chicken.'

'So what can I do for you?'

'I was thinkin', why don't you come by tonight? I'll fix us a little somethin' to eat and you can stay over if you want.'

Julius considered that. 'I'm tempted, Marybeth. But I really should get back to my folks. It's not every day a war's declared after all. Mom especially will want me there.'

Marybeth shrugged. 'I understand. It was only a thought.'

'Maybe tomorrow night, huh?'

'Yeah, sure.'

She smiled weakly at him, then abruptly left, hurrying, as everyone in the building appeared to be doing, on her way.

He could always return home first and then go on to Marybeth's, Julius reflected. That would be OK. As long as he saw and spent some time with his mom and pop.

In the event it was after ten when he finally arrived at Florence Street, which ruled that right out of the question.

Ellie didn't know whether to laugh or cry at what George had just told her. 'But what about our engagement?' she protested.

'We'll still be engaged. That won't change.'

'But you . . . you won't be here for most of the time. You'll be at sea. And why the Merchant Navy anyway?'

'Listen,' Jess interjected, who was in the kitchen with them. 'I'll leave the pair of you to it. I've got things to do upstairs.'

George turned pleading eyes to her. '*You* understand, Mrs Sykes, don't you?'

She sighed. 'I suppose so, George, if that's any consolation. There are going to be an awful lot of young men go off before long. That's as inevitable as day following night. It's war for you.'

'So, why the Merchant Navy?' Ellie demanded again when her mother had gone, her thoughts in turmoil. This had come like a bolt from the blue. And a most unwelcome bolt at that.

'If I wait to be conscripted it'll be the Army, Ellie, and I don't want that. If I have to do something, and I will, then my preference is the Merchant Navy. I'm an engineer by trade after all, they'll be crying out for chaps like me. And the way I see it, life with them will be a lot easier than with the Royal Navy. I'd hate all that rigid discipline, it goes totally against the grain.'

Despite herself, Ellie could see the sense in that. It was just so soon after war being declared. It could have been months yet if he'd waited for conscription.

George took her into his arms. 'I'm going to miss you like buggery, Ellie.'

'I'll miss you too,' she husked in reply.

'It won't be so bad. You'll see.'

She wished she could believe that, but couldn't. 'When do you leave?' she asked.

'I don't know. As soon as I've signed the necessary papers I presume. Certainly not long afterwards.'

Her mind, which had been in turmoil, had now gone numb. Within the space of a few short minutes her world had been turned on its head.

'I'll write whenever I get the chance,' he promised.

'Me too.' She took a deep breath. 'Have you spoken to your parents about this?'

'Not yet. I wanted you to be the first to know.'

She appreciated that. For some reason it meant an awful lot to her.

'Can you stay for a bit? Have a cup of tea?'

'Of course. But not too long. The parents, I want to get that over and done with.'

'Right then.'

There were tears in her eyes as she filled the kettle.

'This is a right pain in the ass,' Beulah complained to Jess who'd come round to help her put up the black-out curtains which every house had now been ordered to have at every window.

Jess slipped another hook into place. The curtains were crude affairs hastily run up from cheap, but heavy, material currently being sold in a number of the local shops. 'We may be thankful for them before long,' she replied.

Beulah paused to stare fearfully at Jess, knowing that she

meant should bombing start, as everyone believed it soon would. 'Did I tell you that Julius wanted Pee Wee and myself to go back to the States?' she said.

Jess glanced at her friend. 'Seems good advice to me. This isn't your war after all.'

Beulah's expression became one of defiance. 'I ain't leavin' my baby behind. No sirree! I ain't doin' that. He says he has to stay, and as I's here with him then I stays too.'

Jess nodded that she understood, thinking of Ellie and Paul. If she'd been in Beulah's position she'd have done the same. Black or white, she further reflected, colour didn't matter when it came to your family. The same bond was there irregardless.

'I wonder how long it will be before they introduce rationing?' she mused.

'They likely to do so?'

'It's almost certain. Don't forget we're an island, Beulah. A great deal of what we use has to be imported by sea. That's bound to be disrupted which will lead to inevitable rationing.'

'I never thought of that,' Beulah frowned. 'I'm used to the States where we grow, or manufacture, everythin' we want or need.'

'Well, we're not so lucky I'm afraid. And if rationing does come in then it's going to make life a lot more difficult. Belts will have to be tightened all round.'

Beulah completed her section of curtain and heaved herself down off the chair she'd been standing on. 'I doubt it'll affect us too much, Julius will see to that. They ain't goin' to be sinkin' no American ships comin' in, that's for sure. We'll get what we need through the Embassy.'

'Lucky you,' Jess muttered, though not unkindly.

A huge smile lit up Beulah's face. 'Don't you fret none, Jess, I'll make sure some of what we gets comes to you. That's what friends are for, ain't it?'

Jess smiled her gratitude. 'You're very kind, Beulah. But if you take my advice don't tell anyone else about you getting supplies from the Embassy. It could easily lead to a lot of bad feeling. And you don't want that.'

'I hears you, lady. I hears you loud and clear.'

Jess hoped she had. And wouldn't forget.

Chapter 9

Connie Fox hastily lit a cigarette and took a deep drag. 'Christ! I needed that,' she exhaled. 'Miss Oates, the bitch, has been getting at me all bloody morning. If I thought I'd get away with it I'd strangle her.' Then, as an afterthought, 'Very slowly so I could watch her eyes pop.'

'You don't really mean that,' admonished Agnes Short, who was with Connie and Ellie in the toilet having their tea break, that being where they had to have it.

'I damn well do,' Connie hissed. 'The woman's a menace. And to pick on me today of all days too.'

Ellie frowned. 'What's different about today?'

Connie had another puff on her cigarette, her expression showing she was thoroughly relishing it. 'My chap told me last night he'd had his conscription papers. He's to report in next Monday.'

'Oh, Connie,' Ellie sympathised.

Agnes Short sniffed. She was a plain girl who'd never had a single boyfriend in her entire nineteen years. She couldn't help but be jealous of Connie, even if Connie's lad was off to the war.

'It's a sod, isn't it?' Connie said.

Ellie thought of George who'd been gone a fortnight now.

True to his word he'd written, twice. And then the letters had stopped as he'd gone to sea. 'Don't I know it.'

'Of course!' Connie exclaimed softly. 'Your George. I'd forgotten. You've been through the same thing.'

'Excuse me,' muttered Agnes, and vanished into a cubicle.

Connie finished her tea and rinsed her cup at the sink. 'We're going to be like a couple of old maids, you and I,' she commented.

Agnes, on hearing that, felt terrible. She was convinced that was to be her fate in life. An old maid like Miss Oates.

'Can I try one of your fags?'

Connie stared at Ellie in surprise. 'But you don't smoke?'

'And I've never tried. I'd like to now though.'

Connie produced a packet of Players and offered it to Ellie. 'What's brought this on?'

Ellie thought about that. 'I suppose I'm so fed up with everything. At least trying a cigarette is different and exciting.'

Ellie put the cigarette between her lips, then bent towards the match Connie had struck. Next moment she was furiously coughing.

Connie laughed. 'That happened to me first time too. You just have to persevere. You soon get used to it.'

'Dear God,' Ellie gasped when she at last managed to catch her breath. 'You actually enjoy that? It's terrible.'

'As I said, you have to persevere. Then you get to like it.'

Ellie took a second, tentative draw, and this time she didn't cough or choke.

'It rather suits you,' Connie pronounced.

'What, smoking?'

'Having a cigarette in your hand. Makes you look very sophisticated.'

Sophisticated? Ellie hardly thought of herself as that. She began to warm to the idea of being a smoker.

A toilet flushed and Agnes emerged from the cubicle. 'That's a mug's game,' she commented, nodding at Ellie's cigarette.

'Sez you,' a sarcastic Connie replied.

'You wouldn't get me spending my hard-earned money on fags,' Agnes declared, starting to wash her hands.

'I don't suppose you drink either,' Connie retorted cuttingly.

'Occasionally. But not often.'

'And I'll bet you it's sherry too.'

An amused Ellie watched this exchange, thinking it served Agnes right for being so judgemental.

Agnes blushed, for the sherry jibe was true. 'Excuse me, it's time to get back to work.' With that she brushed past Connie and Ellie and out of the toilet.

'Can't bear her, the sanctimonious cow,' Connie declared disapprovingly. 'If she'd been a Catholic she'd have ended up a nun. You know? None of this, and none of that. And none of the other either.'

Both girls laughed, Ellie thinking that very funny. None of the other! As if any of them did that.

'She's right about the time though,' Connie went on. 'Have another drag then nip it for later.'

Ellie had the drag, this one leaving her slightly light-headed which wasn't an entirely unpleasant sensation.

'Here, I'll do it for you,' Connie said and, taking the cigarette from Ellie, nipped the end off into the sink where she flicked it down the plughole.

'Put that in your pocket,' she instructed, handing back the remainder.

Miss Oates was watching the clock when they returned to their desks, but couldn't say anything as they were dead on time, having had their allotted fifteen minutes almost to the second.

Albert arrived home in a particularly good humour for it had been one of those rare shifts when there hadn't been a single call-out. His good humour vanished the moment he saw Jess's anguished expression. 'What's wrong?' he demanded.

Without replying she came over and handed him a letter, Paul standing by the sideboard watching this interplay.

Albert began to read the letter which was from the school and it soon became apparent why Jess was in such a state. The school was closing and the pupils were being evacuated into the country.

'I'm not going,' Paul declared stubbornly, having already been through this a number of times with his mother. 'I'm staying here. I'm just not going.'

'Albert?' Jess's eyes were wide and staring.

'It would be for his own good, Jess. Who knows what it'll be like round here when the bombing starts, as it's bound to sooner or later.'

Jess stumbled to her chair and sank into it. 'I couldn't bear being parted from him, Albert. Please say he can't go.'

Christ, Albert thought. This was difficult. He didn't want Paul to be evacuated either.

'We must think of the boy, Jess. It's his welfare that's at stake. If something happened we'd never forgive ourselves for keeping him behind.'

Jess sobbed and dropped her face into her hands, her chest and shoulders heaving.

'You can't make me go,' a thoroughly frightened Paul declared in a quavering voice.

'I'm your father and you'll do as I say,' Albert told him sternly.

Paul ran to Jess and threw his arms round her. By now he too was crying.

Albert crossed to the mantelpiece and leant against it. This, although it hadn't been mentioned between them, wasn't entirely unexpected. Children were being evacuated from all over London. Now it appeared to be St Margaret's turn, Paul's school.

Jess wrapped Paul against her bosom, hugging him for dear life. The thought of him being sent off somewhere to live amongst strangers was total anathema to her. Unthinkable.

Albert could only watch helplessly, feeling utterly wretched. What on earth was he to do?

* * *

Jess shrugged into her dark green candlewick dressing gown and sat on the end of their bed. It had taken her hours to get an almost hysterical Paul off to sleep.

'Am I wrong about this?'

Albert stopped undressing to stare at her, noting yet again her red-rimmed eyes. He sighed. 'Yes, I think you are. I'm not saying it's an easy decision to take, far from it, but one, in my opinion, that has to be. As I said earlier, it's for his own good, Jess. We have to put the lad's safety first and foremost.'

That was the last thing she wanted to hear. Yet, in her heart of hearts, she knew Albert to be right.

'We both love him, Jess,' Albert went on softly. 'And that's why he has to go. Not easy for any of us, I admit. In fact downright bloody difficult. But there we are.'

Jess stayed silent, trying to get her mind to think straight through all the emotion that was churning inside her.

'Why don't I speak to him tomorrow night? Try and make him see sense. Just he and I, the pair of us. A man to man so to speak. How about that, eh?'

'He'd be with strangers, Albert. What if they're not very nice?'

'I'm sure whoever he gets boarded with will be. And, after a few weeks for him to settle in, you can go and visit to make certain everything's all right.'

Jess brightened at the prospect of that, realising she was coming to accept the situation. 'What will you say to him?'

'Explain the good points, that it isn't the end of the world. That in actual fact it's probably going to be a huge adventure which he'll thoroughly enjoy.' Albert laughed. 'And let's hope it's not too enjoyable an adventure or he might not want to come home again when the time comes.'

He went to Jess and took a hand in his, squeezing it reassuringly. 'Leave it to me. Agreed?'

She looked up into his face, loving every inch of him, appreciative of how good a man he was and how lucky she was to have him. 'Agreed.'

* * *

'I thought you only worked here Friday and Saturday nights?' Julius queried of Ellie who was behind the bar at The Florence.

'Hazel's down with the flu and Harry asked me to do some extra shifts to help out,' Ellie explained.

'There's a lot of flu about,' Julius replied. Shelby Robbins at the Embassy was one of the number off with it.

'So what can I get you?'

'A pint of best.'

'Coming right up.'

It was funny, she reflected as she pulled the pump. She was beginning not to even notice that Julius was black. Well, of course he was, that was obvious. But now she was beginning to see him as just a man and not a black man.

'Quiet tonight,' Julius commented, making conversation.

'I prefer it busy. Time passes more quickly that way.

'There you are,' she declared, putting his pint in front of him. 'That's ten pence ha' penny.'

He slid a shilling across the bar. 'You know, even after all this while I still have trouble with English money. It's so complicated! Give me good old dollars and cents any day.'

She rang the ten pence ha' penny up on the till. 'I suppose it must be difficult for a foreigner. I hadn't really thought of that.'

'Threepennies, sixpennies, florins, half-crowns, farthings, ha' pennies . . .' He trailed off and shook his head. 'It just goes on and on. You almost need a college degree to understand it all.'

That amused her. 'Did you go to college?'

'Sure. University of Wisconsin, that's in the mid-west. Milwaukee is the town. Famous for making beer and steel. Schlitz! The beer that made Milwaukee famous, as their ads go. Then there's Pabst, Blatz, Miller, all good beers.' He corrected himself. 'Or I should say, lagers. That's what you call that type of beer over here.'

Ellie was fascinated. 'Why didn't you go to college in New York?'

A cynical smile twitched his lips upwards. 'How shall I put

this? A lot of colleges in the east, the good ones anyway, don't accommodate coloured folk – unless you're an outstandin' football or basketball player that is. Then they make exceptions. But I wasn't particularly talented at either, so I went where they'd have me.'

Ellie thought that awful. 'Did you have to pay for college?'

'Sure did. Doesn't come free. At nights I worked in a big food store called A&P. Sometimes I stacked shelves, other times I packed sacks at the check-outs.'

'What's a sack and a check-out?' Ellie frowned.

'A sack is what you'd call a paper bag, the sort you put your groceries into. And a check-out is where you take your cart – you'd call it a trolley – to pay.'

Ellie couldn't imagine a trolley in a food shop. How bizarre! It was all beyond her. Sounded fascinating though. There again, she reminded herself, if she went to America wouldn't she find it just as bewildering as an American coming to England.

'That paid for my college, my keep and to run my car,' he further explained.

'You had a car even as a student?' She was astounded.

'Needed it to get around. Nothin' fancy, mind you, an old jalop Chevy. But it did me.'

Jalop and Chevy? He'd lost her again. It was a different language. 'Does everyone there have a car?'

Julius shook his head. 'Nearly everyone, except the very poor. And before you ask, yes we do have poor in the States same as everywhere else. It isn't quite the land of milk and honey that you English think. Though it's still God's own country, and ain't that the truth.'

'You must miss it?'

He smiled at her, showing off his perfect white teeth. 'Like crazy sometimes. But that's just how the cookie crumbles. I chose my job and have no regrets.'

He produced a packet of cigarettes and lit up.

'Can I have one of those?'

That surprised him. 'I've never seen you smoke?'

'I only started recently. And those look fun.' She took the unfamiliar, soft pack which he'd placed on the bar, looking at one side, then the other. 'These are American I presume?'

'As apple pie, babe. Help yourself.'

The taste was different to English cigarettes. A sort of toasted flavour, she decided.

'What do you think?' he asked.

'They're nice. I think I prefer them to the English variety.'

That pleased him. 'Tell you what, why don't I get you a carton?'

'A carton?' What was that?

'Yeah, ten packs. Two hundred.'

Ellie gulped. 'I couldn't possibly afford so many. But it's kind of you to offer.'

He waved a dismissive hand. 'I wasn't meanin' for you to pay. A gift, from me to you.'

'I couldn't possibly, Julius. It would be far too expensive.'

'I get them through the Embassy, Ellie. Believe me, the cost is peanuts. So what do you say?'

What else could she say? 'Thank you very much.'

'It's a deal then. I'll pick them up tomorrow and drop them by your house.' He had a thought. 'Are you in the pub again tomorrow night?'

She nodded.

'Then I'll bring them here. A good excuse to have another beer, eh?'

What a lovely smile he had, she reflected. Quite a bobby dazzler. 'It's a deal, to use your words.'

Julius hadn't meant to stop long, but in fact stayed well over an hour chatting to Ellie, The Florence remaining quiet.

Ellie was on her way home for dinner when she halted, her attention caught by a poster. It was an appeal on behalf of the London Auxiliary Ambulance Service who wanted new members, full training given.

The germ of an idea was born in her mind, something she'd

have to give a lot of thought to. Ambulances and crew were going to be desperately needed once the bombing started, which had to be a far more exciting, and worthwhile, job than she now had.

She rather fancied the idea of whizzing round the streets in an ambulance with its bell clanging. Now that would be exhilarating! Doing her bit, as people were now calling service to their country in any form of war effort.

As she walked away she wondered what the uniform was like.

'So what do your pals at school think about this evacuation?' Albert queried off-handedly. Jess had left them only minutes before, saying she was popping round to see Beulah. He knew she wouldn't be back for at least an hour.

A sullen-faced Paul shrugged.

'It must have been mentioned?' Albert tried again.

Paul muttered something inaudible.

'It's terrible getting old,' Albert joked. 'I'm going deaf.'

Paul shot his father a withering look, having realised during the meal that something was up. Now he knew what. Albert was going to have one of his 'little talks'. 'None of them want to go.'

'None at all?'

Paul shrugged again.

This was going to be tough going, Albert thought. But then he'd expected as much. 'I find that odd.'

'Well, speccy Watson is keen, but he's strange.'

Albert hid his smile. 'How is he strange?'

'He swots.'

'Oh!' Well, that explained it then. A lad, in Paul's book anyway, who swotted had to be strange. If not from another planet altogether.

'Pity, the others are going to miss all the fun.'

Paul showed a flicker of interest. 'What fun?'

'Bound to be lots of that. A bunch of pals away from their parents, out in the country where things are so different. I have to say, if I'd still been at school I'd have jumped at the chance to live in the country for a while.'

Paul frowned. 'Why?'

'All the animals for a start. You don't see many cows, sheep and saddle horses in Islington, do you now?'

'Saddle horses,' he repeated slowly. 'You mean like cowboys and indians have. That sort?'

'Oh yes. Folk in the country ride, as well you know. They dress up in red coats and go chasing foxes all over the place. It's called a hunt.'

Paul tried to imagine that. 'Many people?'

'Dozens and dozens, I believe. Riding over fields, jumping hedges, wading streams. That's what they do sometimes.'

Paul's attention had now been well and truly caught. 'What happens to the foxes when they get them?'

'The dogs kill the fox. Hounds they're known as. A great pack of them, and when they finally catch the poor beast they rip it to shreds with their teeth. Then the head huntsman cuts off its tail.'

'Cuts off its tail?'

'As a trophy. So I read anyway. They say the chase, all those horses, people and hounds in full flight, is a sight to behold.'

Doubt entered Paul's mind; it seemed too good to be true. 'Are you telling fibs, Dad?'

Albert made a sign across his chest. 'Cross my heart and hope to die, every word is the gospel.'

Paul imagined himself, wielding a large knife, cutting off a fox's tail. That appealed.

Albert could see he was getting through to the lad. 'Then there are the trees and woods where you can go exploring. You could play Robin Hood there.'

'We've got trees in Islington,' Paul replied stoutly.

'So we have, but not many. I'm talking about an entire wood full. Hundreds and hundreds of them, all sorts, shapes and sizes. Trees where you could tie a rope and make a swing for example. And no one to tell you off either. Nobody else in sight at all, just you and your pals getting up to whatever.'

Albert paused, thinking he was beginning to enjoy this. Paul was certainly starting to show enthusiasm. 'Then there are the streams and ponds where you can go swimming,' he went on. 'When the weather's good of course. Just strip off and in you go. Just like Tarzan, only there won't be any crocodiles to worry about.'

'Could we fish there?' Paul asked eagerly.

'Probably. I don't see why not. Unless it's private and then you'd need permission.' He suddenly had a brainwave, recalling an old fishing rod in a local pawnbroker's. The damn thing had to be dirt cheap as it had been in the window for years.

'And I know where I can lay my hands on a rod too,' he declared enticingly.

'You do?'

'Not that you'll need one as you aren't going. But if you were I could always get it for you. That would make you popular with the other lads. Make them jealous too.'

Paul had really enjoyed the time he'd gone fishing with a pal and his dad. A country stream or pond would be far better than the dirty old canal any day. His mouth almost watered at the prospect.

Albert decided to play his trump card. 'The food in the country is absolutely wonderful. Home-made butter and jam, milk straight from the cow. Enormous breakfasts, huge joints at the weekend. Stacks and stacks of grub, as much as any grown man can eat at any meal. Those people in the country certainly know how to live. Why, if you want a fresh egg you simply go out and pick one up, probably newly laid only moments before. The taste of those is unbelievable.'

Although he'd just had tea, Paul's stomach rumbled. What his dad was describing was sheer heaven.

'While country folk are gorging themselves at every opportunity we townies are going to be having it hard. It's only a matter of time, weeks possibly, before rationing is declared. We're all going to have to pull our belts in then all right.'

He glanced sideways at Paul hanging on his every word.

'Naturally rationing won't apply in the country. Well, stands to reason when you think about it, they grow and produce the stuff right there. It's all on their doorstep so to speak.'

He shook his head. 'No, they won't be going short, lucky sods.'

Paul's stomach rumbled again, louder than before.

Albert knew then he had him. In fishing terms, hook, line and sinker.

'Another couple of waffles, Pee Wee? Plenty of batter left.'

'I's full, Beulah, and that's the truth. I couldn't manage another mouthful.' He leant back in his chair and stared at her. 'Three of the guys in the band announced last night that they're goin' home. Say they don't want no part of no war.'

'Who are they?'

Pee Wee told her.

'So what happens now?'

'We spoke to Lord Fitzaran who naturally was disappointed, but wants to continue on with the three of us remainin'. If we agree, that is.'

'And did you?'

Pee Wee nodded. 'It won't be the same without those guys, all we'll have left is a trio. But we'll be OK.'

Beulah dropped her gaze, knowing Pee Wee was only staying because of her. No doubt the other two who'd also agreed to stay had their reasons.

'Thanks, honey,' she said softly.

Pee Wee took a deep breath. 'Now how about another cup of coffee? I could sure use me one.'

Beulah came to her feet and hurried over to the pot.

'Let's have a look at you,' Jess said. She and Paul were in Paddington Station where they'd joined the others from St Margaret's waiting to be evacuated. There were hundreds of children and parents milling about, from a number of schools, all for the same reason.

She straightened his tie, which didn't need straightening, fighting back the tears that threatened to engulf her. With his best raincoat, schoolclothes and cap, he looked very smart indeed, she thought. Well turned out. His small suitcase was by his side.

'Hello, Eddy!' Paul called out, and waved. Eddy was in his class.

'Now you'll remember to write as soon as you can,' she reminded him. 'Everything you need for that, including stamps, are in your case.'

'I won't forget, Ma,' he replied wearily, wishing she'd stop making such a fuss. Honestly, you'd think he was still a baby!

Jess grabbed the sleeve of one of the teachers walking by. 'Do you know where they're going yet, Mr Bailey?' she queried.

He shook his head. 'Nothing definite. Only that it's supposedly in the West Country. That's all I can tell you.'

Jess's face clearly reflected her disappointment. It was bad enough that Paul was going off, but to not even know where!

'They're starting to board now,' Mr Bailey declared. 'You'd better get Paul in line.'

She wouldn't cry, she told herself. She mustn't. Not until he'd gone.

Paul could see her distress. 'I'll be all right, Ma. You mustn't worry.'

'I'll try not to, son,' she promised, knowing full well she would, like buggery.

He protested when she suddenly hugged him to her. 'Watch my fishing rod, Ma. You might break it!' He held the rod he was clutching, his pride and joy, slightly away from her. He was also mortified at being publicly hugged. How embarrassing!

Jess released him. 'Let's get you into line then.'

It was another twenty minutes before Paul was safely aboard, and the last door banged shut. The platform was crowded with parents, mainly women. A sort of collective groan went up as the guard blew his whistle and waved his green flag. Jess could just make Paul out at the far end of the carriage he was in.

The train creaked and clanked, then began to move, a long brown serpent snaking its way out of the station.

'Oh Paul!' Jess sobbed, voice clogged with emotion.

Finally, at long last, she allowed the tears to come.

Chapter 10

'God, I hate this black-out!' Ellie complained. 'It doesn't half make life difficult.' She glanced at Connie Fox walking alongside, the pair of them having just completed their day's work and now on their way home. Connie didn't reply or comment.

Ellie frowned. 'What's wrong with you today? You've hardly said a word and you've been going round like you'd lost a pound and found sixpence.'

'I've got a lot on my mind.'

'Oh?'

Connie came up short to stare at her friend. 'Can you keep a secret?'

'Of course.'

'No, I really mean it. If I say what's bothering me then you must swear not to tell another soul.'

Ellie was intrigued. 'I promise, Connie. I swear.'

Connie took a deep breath. 'I think I'm in the pudding club.'

Ellie's hand flew to her mouth. This was terrible! Worse, a catastrophe. 'How?'

Connie gave a cynical laugh. 'How the hell do you think? The usual way. I let Barry do it the night before he had to report to the Army.' Barry was the name of her chap.

'Oh Connie,' Ellie sympathised.

'Just my bloody luck to be caught out. The only time I've ever gone all the way too. My parents are going to kill me.'

Ellie had no doubts about that. The shame this would bring on the family. The humiliation! Not to mention the stain on Connie's character. 'Didn't you use a . . . well, froggy?'

Connie nodded. 'That's the joke. I insisted, wouldn't have done it otherwise. But the damn thing came off. We didn't realise until it was over and then I found it by fishing around inside.'

How horrible, Ellie thought. And disgusting too. She hoped Connie hadn't done that in front of this Barry. But she didn't ask.

'Talk about a pantomime,' Connie went on bitterly. 'Farce more like. Barry kept saying afterwards everything would be all right, that the chances of anything happening were one in a million. Well, he was wrong. Couldn't have been more so.'

Ellie shivered, for it was a freezing December evening. 'Let's walk on,' she said.

They continued for a little way in silence. 'How . . . how far gone are you?'

'Only the month.'

'Then perhaps your period is just late?'

Connie shook her head. 'If it is it's the first time ever. I'm regular as clockwork. Always have been. So there's very little likelihood I'm late or skipped a month. I'm up the duff, have to be.'

Ellie wished she could think of something constructive to say, but couldn't. 'So what are you going to do?'

'Write to Barry I suppose. Maybe he'll get compassionate leave and we can get married. If he does the right thing by me, that is.'

Ellie doubted the Army would let him away so soon, no matter what the reason. In peacetime yes, but not with a war on. There again, if there hadn't been a war on he wouldn't have been conscripted in the first place, and this wouldn't have happened.

'Failing that,' Connie continued, 'there is a woman I've heard of over the Caledonian Road way who helps girls like me. Gets them out of their spot of bother.'

Ellie abruptly halted, utterly appalled. 'Surely you wouldn't do that, go to an abortionist? That's . . .' She swallowed hard. 'That's murder. And downright dangerous as far as you're concerned.'

Connie sighed. 'I wish I could think straight. One moment I'm thinking this, the next that. I'm so confused.'

Ellie took Connie's hand in hers. 'Just promise me you won't go to an abortionist, please?'

Connie stared her friend straight in the eyes. 'It isn't you who's pregnant, so you can't ask that.'

'I'm only thinking of you.'

'So am I,' Connie replied softly. 'So am I.'

What a mess, Ellie thought. Thank God she hadn't been tempted before George went off. If she had she might have ended up in the same predicament.

They arrived at the spot where they always parted. 'I'll keep your secret, Connie. It's safe with me.'

'Thanks. I know that.'

Ellie hesitated. 'There is something . . .' She trailed off.

'What?'

'I've . . .' Thankfully it was dark, she thought, for her face was flaming. 'I've always wondered. What was it like?'

Connie laughed. 'A disappointment really.'

Ellie frowned. 'In what way?'

'It was all over so quickly. Hardly any time at all. I thought it was supposed to last a while, but not in our case. We'd hardly started before it was finished. I was disappointed all right.'

'Did you . . . did it feel good?'

'What there was of it. Quite pleasant actually. But not the huge experience I always thought it would be. I felt terribly let down afterwards. If that's all there is to it then it's awfully over-rated in my opinion.'

Ellie was fascinated, but didn't feel she could continue the conversation any further. Perhaps another time. She wanted to learn more about the great mystery.

'Write to Barry tonight,' she advised. 'That's what I would do. The sooner he knows about this the sooner he can maybe do something about it.'

'I'll do that,' Connie nodded. 'And listen, thanks for being a pal.'

'Anything I can do, you only have to ask.'

Connie appreciated that, fear flickering again inside her that if the worst came to the worst she might have to tell her parents without having Barry to stand by her. She offered up a silent prayer he would.

It was when she was walking down Florence Street that it dawned on Ellie that the word love had never been mentioned. Not once.

She found that incredibly sad.

Mrs Selly laid down a cup of tea on Paul's bedside table, then lit the candle standing there. 'Paul! Paul!' she said, shaking him by the shoulder.

'Don't want to get up,' he moaned. 'Still tired.'

'It's four thirty, Paul. Time to be up and doing. There's jobs to be done before school.'

He came groggily awake to gaze up at the middle-aged woman hovering over him. In the few short weeks he'd been there he'd come to hate life in High Barton. 'It's freezing,' he complained.

'Don't be so soft, lad. Get thae clothes on and come downstairs for first breakfast. There's a good lad.' And with that Mrs Selly left the room.

Four thirty in the morning! he thought in despair. He'd never been up at that time in his life before arriving at the farm. Now it was every morning, seven days a week.

He couldn't say the Sellys were cruel, they merely expected him to fit in with things. To help with the chores as their own son would have done, if they'd had one. To them, what he was expected to do was quite normal.

Cows first, milk those along with Mr Selly. Then feed the

pigs, hens after that. On and on till it was time for second breakfast after which he had to trudge the two miles to school.

On arriving back again he'd have to work till supper. Even when that was over there would be no respite. There was always something to do, some job to be done.

How he wished he'd never left Florence Street. His dad had been right about the food, there was plenty of that, lashings of it. But so far that was the only thing his dad had been right about.

'Are you up, lad?' Mrs Selly called from downstairs.

Gritting his teeth, Paul swung out of bed and literally threw on his clothes, as fast as he possibly could. Thankfully the wood stove would be burning in the kitchen, he'd soon get warm in front of that.

A warmth that wouldn't last long, only until he had to leave the house.

'Son of a bitch!' Julius yelped. 'That's painful.'

Marybeth treated him to one of her catlike smiles. 'It's meant to be.'

He put a hand to his back which came away streaked with red. 'You've drawn blood.'

She pretended innocence. 'Have I?'

'You goddamn well have. As you intended.'

Marybeth laughed and lay back on the bed from where she studied him. 'I thought you might enjoy it,' she purred.

'Well, I didn't.' His face screwed up in a grimace; what she'd done had really hurt. And still did.

Marybeth's nostrils dilated and her breath started coming in short, sharp pants. Slowly, provocatively, she opened her legs. 'I'm ready for you now, hon. Real ready.'

Julius stared at Marybeth, aware of blood running down his back. This was a side of her he'd never seen before, and not one he was certain he liked.

He decided a few words were in order.

* * *

Ellie stopped beside Connie's desk. 'Heard anything yet?' she asked in a whisper, not wanting to be overheard.

Connie shook her head.

'And are you still . . . ?' She trailed off, not completing the sentence.

Connie nodded.

Ellie made a sympathetic face, and continued on to her own desk. It was early days, she reminded herself. Barry's reply was probably even now in the post.

She hadn't failed to notice how haunted and fearful Connie's eyes were.

'I very nearly fell asleep in class,' Eddy Ackworth, Paul's schoolchum, confided in him. Like Paul, Eddy had been billeted on a farm, the only difference being that his farm was closer to the village of Talyton, where the school was located, than Paul's, which meant he didn't have to walk so far there and back again.

The St Margaret's pupils were being taught in the village hall, the tiny Talyton school just not being large enough to accommodate the evacuees, so they were separated from the village children, none of whom impressed the Islingtonians one little bit.

Paul yawned. 'Me too. I'll never get used to being here. Never.'

Eddy morosely stuck his hands into his trousers' pockets. 'If I knew how I'd do a bunk home.'

Paul had also thought of that. 'It's too far, Eddy. We'd have to get to Clyst Binkleigh first to catch a train, and that's over ten miles away. And if we did get there what would we use for the train fare? I don't have any money. Have you?'

'Not a sausage.'

'Well then. We're stuck here and there's nothing we can do about it.'

Eddy's shoulders slumped. 'They say this war could last for years. Years and years.'

'I know,' Paul replied, wishing with all his heart he'd never been talked into coming here.

'I'm not sure I can stand that. It's not only the work, it's the smell. Everything round the farm stinks.'

Paul nodded his agreement. Animal muck everywhere it seemed to him, and no way of getting away from it. If he'd known the word he'd have said it hung over the Sellys' farm like a miasma.

'And I never get out to play any more,' Eddy went on miserably. 'Even if I did there's no one to play with.'

Paul reflected it was exactly the same with him. He couldn't remember the last time he had any fun.

'Have you been able to use that fishing rod of yours yet?' Eddy queried. He'd thought it smashing when he'd first seen it and had made Paul promise to let him have a go of it sometime. Fat chance of that now.

Paul shook his head. 'And I don't think I ever will. It was a waste of time bringing it with me.'

Their conversation was cut short by the handbell being rung for their return to class.

Both boys slouched hang-doggedly back into the hall.

'Something's wrong, I just know it,' Jess declared to Albert who'd just arrived in off the night shift. She brandished the latest letter from Paul. 'He's not saying there is, but I know better. Call it a mother's intuition if you like.'

Albert sighed. It had been a long, hard night centred round a major call-out in a local mattress manufacturers. Beside anything else, he had a splitting headache thanks to some smoke inhalation.

Albert sat at the table. 'Let me see it.'

Jess handed him the letter then busied herself with his breakfast, fried egg with bread and dripping.

Albert had to screw up his eyes, thanks to the headache, in order to focus. It certainly wasn't a long letter, no more than a dozen lines. He read it through, shaking his head as he laid it aside. 'He seems fine to me.'

'It's what he's not saying that's worrying. As if he's holding something back. I know Paul, I should do, I'm his mother after all. The boy's not happy.'

'He's just taking a while to settle in, that's all,' Albert argued. 'It can't be easy.'

Jess snorted. 'There's more to it than that.'

Could she be right? he wondered. He had a lot of respect for his wife's judgement, it didn't often let her down. But in this particular instance he suspected she was simply being over-protective.

Ellie gazed about the pub, thinking how quiet it was for Christmas Eve. The previous year it had been positively heaving by this time.

'Are you thinking what I'm thinking?'

She turned to find Hazel beside her. 'How quiet it is?'

Hazel nodded. 'There again, it is the first Christmas of the war, people might not be feeling like celebrating. And don't forget, an awful lot of young men are away who were here last year. Including your George. How is he by the way?'

'Fine. I had a letter from Canada, a place called Halifax. He's enjoying himself apparently, though keen to get home again.'

'Any news of that?'

'No. Nothing. He had no idea.'

'But he's safe, that's the main thing,' Hazel pointed out.

Ellie rubbed her hand. She'd developed a rash around her fingers which could itch terribly. She'd been to the doctor who'd given her some cream for it.

'We might get busy later,' Hazel said hopefully. 'Are your parents coming in?'

Ellie shook her head. 'Dad's working. But he will have New Year off. They'll definitely be in then.'

Hazel glanced over at the decorations – paper rings and paper bells, the latter hanging from the lights. The tree had all sorts of sparkly bits on it while little balls of cotton wool represented snow. Even the decorations seemed lacklustre this year, she thought. As if they too were aware there was a war on.

'Give me a shout if we get a sudden rush,' she declared, and left Ellie to it.

What a miserable Christmas Eve, Ellie reflected as she got ready for bed. Business had been steady later on, but no more than that. There certainly hadn't been any fizz about the occasion. Harry had pronounced the evening a flop when they'd been having their staff drink afterwards.

Ellie picked up and examined the small bottle of scent that Harry and Hazel had given her as a present. How kind that had been of them, she thought, as she unscrewed the top. It smelt gorgeous, reminding her of a garden in summer. She dabbed a little behind her ears and then on a few other pulse points.

She'd half expected Julius to have popped in. If only for a quickie, but he hadn't appeared. He must have gone to a party or function, she decided. Oh well, he may drop by next day. As could Beulah and Pee Wee, the pair of them having been to his club in Soho that night.

Dad would be at work Christmas Day, but she might suggest to Jess that she come on over with the Postons. That might cheer her up a bit. Jess had been somewhat down since Paul went off. She herself would be behind the bar.

A few moments later she froze in horror on realising that her engagement ring was missing from her finger. 'Stupid mare!' she berated herself, knowing full well what had happened. Because of the rash she'd taken it off later in the session while washing up, and clearly forgotten to put it back on again.

A quick glance at her bedside clock confirmed that it was too late to return to the pub, Harry and Hazel would be in bed by now. Anyway, even if they weren't they were hardly likely to answer a knock at this time of the morning on the presumption it was some drunk wanting another drink.

Ellie took a deep breath and told herself not to panic. The ring was bound to be where she'd left it, and would still be there at opening time. She'd get it back then.

The last thing she did before getting into bed was to put some more cream on her hands to soothe the irritating itching.

'It was there, right there,' Ellie declared, pointing to a corner of the draining board. Only it wasn't any more.

'Well, I never picked it up,' Hazel replied. 'But perhaps Harry did, though he never mentioned it which I'm sure he would have done. I'll go and fetch him.'

Ellie kept hunting while Hazel was out back. Where was the damn thing? It couldn't be far away. She went all round the draining board and then beyond, first to the left and then the right. There was no sign of her ring.

Harry appeared with Hazel in tow, both wearing concerned expressions. 'Have you found it yet?' he demanded.

She shook her head, aware that she was close to tears. How could she have been so stupid and forgetful!

'Are you certain that's where you left it?'

'Absolutely, Harry. I quite clearly remember laying it down.'

'Then let's have these glasses off this bottom shelf and see if it's somehow dropped down there.'

'I'll do that with Ellie while you open up,' Hazel instructed.

They had ten minutes before the first customer appeared during which they scoured the entire bar area, to no avail.

'I've already put out last night's empties,' Harry said as Hazel served. 'It might be amongst that lot, though how it could have got in the bin is beyond me.'

'What about the sink itself?' Ellie suggested. 'What if it's fallen down the plughole?'

That was another possibility, Harry mused. And a good one at that. Luckily there was a trap at the bottom of the waste pipe before it ran off.

'Give me a couple of minutes,' he said, and hurried away to find a pair of suitable pliers.

Ellie served and watched anxiously as Harry got to work on the trap when he returned. Thankfully it was still quiet just like the previous evening.

With a grunt Harry freed and removed the trap, water spilling onto the floor when he did. A quick examination found it to be empty apart from a silver threepenny bit and a kirby grip.

'Sorry, Ellie,' he apologised. 'No joy.'

Ellie was frantic, what was she going to say to George if it didn't turn up? It was her engagement ring after all, something far more precious than what it had actually cost. And that was enough, considering they were working-class people.

'I'll start on the empties,' Harry declared, coming to his feet, the trap securely back in place. 'Give me a shout though if I'm needed here.'

'We'll find it,' Hazel assured Ellie, patting her arm. 'It has to be around somewhere. It certainly couldn't have been stolen, not from behind the bar.'

True, Ellie thought. Except, where was the bloody thing!

'What am I going to do, Mum?' Ellie asked Jess in despair when they'd returned home. As Ellie had suggested, Jess had come over to the pub with the Postons where Ellie had quickly informed her that the ring wasn't to be found. Jess had returned at closing time to help when they'd all looked for the ring again. And again, to no avail. It had simply vanished.

Jess shook her head. 'I honestly don't know, love. I suppose all you can do is hope that it will eventually turn up.'

Ellie couldn't believe this had happened. All her own fault too, there was no one to blame but herself. 'And what if it doesn't?'

Jess thought about that. 'You could go back to the shop and buy a replacement, one exactly the same. That way George need never know.'

Ellie rubbed her temples. A splitting headache had come on halfway through the session and was still there even though she'd taken a couple of aspirins. She had no doubt that the headache had been brought on by anxiety.

'Was the ring expensive?' Jess queried.

'More than I can lay my hands on right now. I'd have to save up. Money that was supposed to be for the wedding.'

Jess sighed. Life could be so cruel at times. She didn't blame Ellie for removing her ring, it was quite natural in the circumstances. She might have put it somewhere safer though.

Ellie slumped into a chair. What a mess to get herself into. And at Christmas too! Christmas was ruined as far as she was concerned. Well and truly.

'Buck up,' Jess smiled. 'I'll put the kettle on. Dad will be awake and down for his dinner soon. There's that to look forward to.'

Jess checked the chicken she'd left in the oven – it was coming on a treat. The potatoes and vegetables were all prepared and just needed putting on which she'd do as soon as she heard movement upstairs announcing Albert was out of bed.

She wondered what sort of Christmas Paul was having, and wished with all her heart he was with them. Christmas wouldn't be the same without him.

When Albert appeared he was told the bad news that the ring was missing and he couldn't have been more sympathetic, for a man that is. But that didn't console Ellie any.

'Christ, Marybeth! How did you get yourself into such a state?' They'd been to a departmental drinks party at the Embassy and were now on their way to Florence Street for a late Christmas lunch.

Marybeth giggled. 'Too many martinis, honey. I should've counted.'

Julius was furious for two reasons. One, he hated drunk women, it was so unfeminine and undignified. Secondly, how could he take her to his parents like this?

Marybeth suddenly croaked, 'Stop the car! Stop the car!'

Julius immediately drew alongside the pavement and hastily opened her door moments before she was violently ill.

That was it, he thought grimly. He was taking her home and leaving her there. Goddamn her!

When it was over Marybeth fell back into her seat where she used the back of her hand to wipe her mouth. 'Sorry, hon,' she slurred.

Julius almost gagged at the stench wafting in. It was stomach-turningly horrendous.

Marybeth closed her eyes and was almost instantly asleep.

Paul had never known such an awful Christmas. If he'd imagined he was going to get a break from working then he'd been wrong. The animals don't take the day off, Mr Selly had explained. They still had to be looked after no matter what day it was. He'd been roused as usual at four thirty.

The food had been good, Paul couldn't deny that. And lots of it. But that was about all he could say. There had been no fun, or presents. Nothing at all. Not even a cracker. After the meal it had been back to work again.

He should write and tell his parents how unhappy he was, Paul thought. How desperately unhappy. Maybe they'd be able to do something if he did.

The truth was, what if they couldn't? Then they'd be as unhappy as he. Which he didn't want. And there wasn't anything really to complain about, except the work and the fact the Sellys were such a miserable, joyless pair. Their intentions were good, he knew that. What it all boiled down to, he supposed, was the fact he missed his pals. Seeing them at school wasn't enough, not the same. They were in class most of the time. He missed his pals and Islington.

But most of all he missed his mum. Heart-breakingly so. It was terrible feeling so utterly alone.

Chapter 11

'What's wrong with you, you look dreadful?' Ellie asked Connie Fox as they went into the toilet for their morning tea break. She'd been worried about her friend ever since arriving at work, but this was the first chance she'd had to have a word.

'I've finally had a reply from Barry,' Connie replied, voice brittle and crackling at the edges.

'And?'

Before Connie could explain, Agnes Short and Elaine McIntosh joined them which halted that line of conversation.

Connie shook her head. 'I'll tell you when we leave at dinner-time,' she said quietly.

Ellie pulled out a packet of cigarettes. 'Here, have one of these.'

'More Yankee ones?' Connie commented.

'I told you, it's my next-door neighbour. He gets them for me. Refuses to take payment either.'

'Lucky you,' Connie said, lighting up.

'Isn't he the black chap?' Agnes smirked her disapproval.

'So what?'

'Nothing, nothing at all. I just don't think I'd like black

people staying so close. My father says they lower the tone.'

That angered Ellie, who thought Agnes a right bitch. 'He's obviously never met any then. The whole family's lovely.' Then, cuttingly, 'I must say I'd rather have them next door than some I could name.'

Agnes bridled, knowing Ellie meant her. 'Just what do you mean by that?'

Ellie's eyes hardened, she was in no mood to take any nonsense from Agnes. Casually, she too lit a cigarette, then proceeded to blow smoke in Agnes's direction. 'Probably what you think it means.'

If Connie hadn't been so distraught she'd have laughed. 'I'd shut up if I were you,' she told Agnes.

Elaine McIntosh moved away and sipped her tea. She wanted none of this. She'd never said, being a quiet girl, but she too didn't have much time for Agnes.

'Don't talk to me like that!' Agnes snapped back.

'I'll talk to you any fucking way I choose, you nasty little snot.'

Agnes gasped in indignation, her face going bright red.

That was telling her, Ellie smiled inwardly, though she was shocked to hear Connie use *that* word. She certainly didn't approve, thinking it even worse to have been uttered by a woman. It just showed how upset Connie was.

Ellie couldn't wait for dinner-time when she returned to her desk, dying to know what Barry had said in his letter. From the looks of things it wasn't promising for Connie.

Ellie was outraged. 'He said *what!*'

'How could he be sure that he was the only one and the child was his,' Connie repeated, tears glinting in her eyes.

'The rotten sod,' Ellie hissed. No wonder Connie had been so distressed all morning. What an accusation. It was beyond belief.

'He won't be applying for compassionate leave or coming home. He more or less told me to sling my hook.'

Even though they were in the street Ellie took Connie into her arms and hugged her tight. 'I'm so sorry.'

Connie sobbed, overcome with emotion. How she'd managed to get into work that morning she didn't know. It had taken every ounce of her willpower.

'If that's his attitude then you're well rid of him,' Ellie declared.

'Maybe so,' Connie choked. 'But there's still the baby. What am I to do about that?'

'There is only one thing to do,' Ellie stated quietly. 'Tell your parents and have it.'

Connie closed her eyes, thinking of the explosion that was going to cause. Not only fury but terrible hurt. Her parents would be beside themselves with shame and humiliation. Their lives ruined, or so they would claim.

As for her, no one would ever marry her now. Not with an illegitimate child in tow. A bastard.

When they finally parted Connie didn't go home as usual, instead she went into a pub. She needed time by herself to think. To try to come to terms with the situation.

In her heart of hearts she'd been certain Barry would stand by her, do the right thing.

How wrong could you be.

Albert came into the kitchen to find Jess poring over a map. 'What are you doing?' he queried in surprise.

'It's Devon and Cornwall,' she explained. 'I got it from the garage.'

'Are you trying to find Talyton?'

Jess nodded, not sure what his reaction was going to be.

'I see,' he murmured. 'Any luck?'

'Not so far, Albert. It must be terribly small, or else I'm just missing it.'

He joined her at the table. 'Here, let me have a shufti.'

He knew it was somewhere near Exeter, but had no idea if it was north, south, east or west of there. Using a finger he began to trace an ever-widening circle.

It was five minutes before he found it. 'There we are!' he declared triumphantly.

Jess peered at the indicated spot on the map. 'It is small,' she observed.

And seemingly right in the middle of nowhere, Albert thought. He studied the map again to locate the nearest railway station, all of which were marked.

He soon found that as well. 'Clyst Binkleigh,' he pointed out to her. 'Some sort of branch line ending in Exeter itself. So, it can't be reached direct. You have to go to Exeter first, and then change. All in all quite a journey by my reckoning.'

'How far between this Clyst place and Talyton?' she queried.

Albert made a face. 'Maps aren't exactly my strong suit, but a fair old distance I'd say.'

'Then there must be a bus?'

Albert was only too well aware of what this was leading up to, nor was he all that surprised. Jess had never come to terms with Paul's evacuation and had convinced herself something was wrong with the lad. Which he doubted very much.

'Probably,' he replied slowly. 'Though how often they run is something else. It's not like here, you know, one along every few minutes or so. Country buses may only run once or twice a day. Especially in such remote areas.'

'What about taxis?'

He almost laughed out loud at the ludicrousness of that. 'It's hardly likely judging by the size of the place. You could maybe hire a horse and cart if you're lucky.'

Jess bit back her disappointment.

'Why don't you put the kettle on? I could use a cuppa,' he said, hoping to change the conversation.

Jess hesitated. 'Albert?'

Here it was. 'Uh-huh?'

'We did agree I could go and visit Paul sometime. I thought, well, maybe next week?'

He had agreed, dammit. It might even have been his own suggestion, he couldn't remember. 'I don't see how you can actually get there, Jess. It seems downright impossible to me.'

She glanced again at the map, realising the difficulties of reaching Talyton. Why, oh why, did it have to be so out of the way!

'Besides,' Albert went on. 'Paul still hasn't settled in, we know that from his letters. If you turn up don't you think it's only going to make matters worse?'

'It's more than unsettled, Albert. I'm convinced of that.'

He regarded her steadily. 'You believe that because it's what you want to believe, girl. Paul's fine. A little homesick perhaps, but fine nonetheless. He just needs a while longer to find his feet and get into the swing of things. You'll see.'

Jess remained unconvinced, every fibre of her being urging her to go to her son.

'He has his pals around him,' Albert continued. 'So he's hardly lonely. It's not as if he's been sent somewhere he didn't know anyone. You're worrying unnecessarily, Jess, take my word for it.'

He began filling the kettle at the sink. 'Now let's drop this. All right?'

There was no reply. And when he turned round again it was to discover he was the only one in the room. Jess had gone.

Connie sat brooding, staring at her parents. Her father was engrossed in the daily crossword puzzle, which he did every night, while her mother was knitting. It was a scene of perfect domestic tranquillity.

How could she tell them? she asked herself for the umpteenth time. How could she possibly?

'Things are getting hard to come by in the shops,' Minnie Fox commented quietly.

'Oh?' Her husband Dick didn't bother to look up.

'Mainly food. I had terrible trouble getting those chops we had for supper. In fact I had quite an argument with the butcher before he'd sell them to me.'

Dick sighed. 'I suppose it'll only get worse before it gets better.'

'At least rationing hasn't come in yet. Though that could happen any time according to what you hear.'

Connie's eyes flicked from one to the other. She loved her parents in a deeply satisfying way. As parents went they were comfortable to be with, easy-going really. Understanding, patient, most of the time. But if she dropped her bombshell . . .! She could well imagine the shock, tears, and everything else that would go with those. It would quite simply be the end of their world as they'd known it and she the culprit, the perpetrator of the terrible deed . . . It made her feel sick to the very pit of her stomach.

'Whatever happens, we'll be all right for coal. I'll see to that,' Dick replied, writing in an answer. He was a clerk in a local coalyard.

'Well, that's something at least,' Minnie nodded, her knitting needles clacking nineteen to the dozen.

Dick closed his eyes. 'Now what's a six-letter word for . . .'

Connie decided to go to bed. She couldn't tell them, she just couldn't.

Not yet anyway.

Marybeth caught up with Julius in the corridor leading to Acquisitions. 'Hi, stranger!'

His heart sank on hearing her voice, for he'd been avoiding her since Christmas Day. 'Hi!' he smiled back.

'Where have you been?'

He shrugged. 'Busy, I guess. You know how it is.'

Using an index finger she stroked his cheek. 'Am I forgiven yet?'

'Sure.'

'Truly, hon?'

'Well, it was a tad inconvenient. And I had to lie, I don't like doing that to my folks. I said you'd developed a migraine.'

She smiled, her expression one of enticement and promise. 'I'm missin' you.'

'As I said, I've been busy. There's a war on, remember? That makes things kinda hectic to say the least.'

'You can't be workin' all the time, hon. A little R'n'R is required as well.' That meant rest and recreation.

'If you don't mind, I'll take a rain check for now, Marybeth. I'll call when I can. That's a promise.'

She could see he wasn't going to commit himself. 'I'll hold you to that now.'

'I'll call.'

For a moment he thought she was going to kiss him, then she was walking away, her hips swaying provocatively.

He *was* missing her, he realised. But only where bed was concerned. He'd never known anyone like her between the sheets. She was pure dynamite.

As for Marybeth herself? That was something else. He didn't appreciate women who got drunk, far less drunk to the point of vomiting.

That really put him off.

Connie had found the street without difficulty having looked it up first in the *A to Z*. The house whose number she'd been given was exactly the same as all the rest. It had seen better days.

She took a deep breath, steeling herself to go through with this, which wasn't easy. The thought of what lay beyond the door she was now staring at made her flesh creep.

This was only to find out what was what, she reminded herself. She wasn't committing herself to anything. There was no need for that yet. And if she wasn't happy she could just walk away and never return. Nobody was going to pounce on her the moment she walked through that door.

She was horribly aware she was covered in goose bumps and her teeth were chattering. The latter because it was such a cold night, she tried to reassure herself, knowing it to be nonsense. She was plain scared through and through, to the point where she wouldn't have been surprised if she'd wet herself.

Slowly she mounted the steps to the door and, taking another deep breath, rang the electric bell.

She forced a smile onto her face when the door opened.

'Get your back stuck into it, boy, we got a lot to shift before supper,' Mr Selly urged Paul, as they forked hay down from the upper level of the barn. The next job was shovelling out muck from the pig pen, a task which Paul absolutely loathed.

Mr Selly shook his head in despair. 'You're willing, boy, I'll give 'ee that, but you townies just don't know how to graft. You're soft now, but I'll soon harden you up. Make a man of you.'

Paul didn't reply to that, knowing better. Mr Selly didn't like being answered back. Giving cheek, as he called it.

Paul strained to do better.

Jess came breezing into the kitchen. 'Someone here to see you, Ellie.'

It was Connie. 'I hope you don't mind me barging in?'

'Not at all,' Ellie replied quickly, wondering what this was all about. 'Mum, this is Connie Fox who works with me.'

'Pleased to meet you, Connie,' Jess beamed and shook Connie's hand.

That was the only introduction necessary as Albert was out, Ellie didn't know where.

'Can I have a word?' Connie asked, trying not to let her anxiety show.

'Of course. Go ahead.'

Connie looked faintly embarrassed. 'In private I meant.'

Ellie knew that Jess was about to get on with a pile of ironing that she'd been putting off. 'Let's go to my room,' she suggested.

'Shall I bring up a cup of tea?' Jess offered.

'No, no, but thanks all the same,' Connie answered. 'I won't be here long.'

Ellie led the way upstairs, closing her bedroom door behind

the pair of them. Connie glanced about, noting that the bed-room was bigger than hers. Quite a bit bigger actually. She envied Ellie the space.

'So what is it?' Ellie queried.

Connie sat on the edge of the bed. 'You're not going to like this. I know you'll disapprove. But I've decided to go to the woman just off the Cally Road. In fact I've already seen her and made an appointment.'

Ellie was aghast. 'Oh Connie, how could you?'

Connie dropped her gaze. 'There's no other way, honestly. And I'm not just being selfish either. If I tell my folks it'll ruin their lives, and I don't want to do that to them. Can't, Ellie.'

Ellie could understand that, though she was certain, after all Connie was only human, that the excuse about not being self-ish wasn't entirely true. Connie was thinking of herself as well.

'I see,' Ellie murmured. 'When's the appointment for?'

'Next Monday night at eight. It's to cost a tenner.'

A lot of money, Ellie thought. 'Have you got that much?'

Connie nodded. 'I can scrape it up.' She looked beseeching-ly at Ellie. 'Can I have one of your fags? I've run out.'

Ellie produced a packet and they both lit up. 'So why are you here to tell me this?' she queried.

'I don't want to go on my own, Ellie. I need a friend to be with me.'

Ellie swallowed hard. The friend was obviously her.

'Will you do it?' Connie pleaded. 'Please?'

Ellie didn't see how she could refuse. A friend in need, as the saying went. 'I'll go with you,' she agreed. 'Though on the strict understanding I don't approve.'

Connie relaxed slightly. 'Thanks. You're a pal.'

Ellie was curious. 'This woman, what's she like?'

Connie considered that. 'Pretty ordinary really. You'd cer-tainly never give her a second look in the street. Like someone's nan I suppose. Elderly, grey-haired, with a nice, kindly manner about her. Her name's Mrs Smith.'

Ellie laughed. 'I'll bet!'

'No, that's what it is. At least that was the name on the door.'

'Did she say . . .' Ellie hesitated. 'How . . .?'

'She didn't and I never asked,' Connie interjected swiftly. 'I didn't want to know.'

Ellie couldn't blame her. In similar circumstances she didn't think she'd want to know either. It simply didn't bear thinking about. 'Are you sure about this?' she asked.

'Absolutely. Get it over and done with, that's the best thing. Put it behind me so to speak.' She paused, then went on, 'You know what really hurts?'

'What?'

'Barry's letter and his saying how could he be sure he's been the only one. I hope now the bastard gets shot.'

'Connie!' Ellie exclaimed in horror. 'You don't mean that.'

'Yes I do, I bloody well do. Serve him right, the rotten, insinuating swine.'

She was very upset, that was all, Ellie thought. She couldn't believe Connie would have wished such a thing otherwise. And Connie had a right to be deeply upset after such an insulting letter. But not to the extent of wishing this Barry dead.

They agreed where and when they'd meet up on the Monday night. Ellie was dreading it. But undoubtedly nowhere near as much as Connie.

She must be terrified out of her head.

'When are you going to see that nice Marybeth again, Julius?' Beulah asked.

Julius inwardly groaned. Here we go again, he thought. 'No idea, Mom,' he replied offhandedly.

'Thin's OK between the pair of you, I take it?'

'Sure.'

'You don't sound too convincin'.'

He didn't reply to that.

'Julius?'

He produced a cigar and trimmed the end. He didn't answer

until he'd puffed it alight. 'Mom, why don't you stop meddlin'?'

That flustered Beulah. 'I ain't meddlin'. No sirree! I ain't no meddler. I's just askin', that's all. Bein' polite. Besides, she sure is one pretty gal.'

'So you keep sayin',' he replied sarcastically.

Beulah gave him a baleful look. 'I take it you's tellin' me to mind my own business?'

'That's right, Mom.'

'Huh!'

He could see how peeved she was, and wished he hadn't been quite so abrupt. But it had been a long hard day at the Embassy and he was bone tired. 'Marybeth is very busy at the moment,' he explained, which was true enough. 'Like me. There isn't much time left for socialisin'.'

'Then why didn't you just say that in the first place,' Beulah replied waspishly. 'Instead of accusin' me of being a meddler.'

'Well you are,' he smiled. 'Being a typical mom I suppose. It's simply that you've got to remember I'm grown up now. I make my own decisions.'

'I knows you grown up. Like I said, I was just bein' polite. Showin' interest, that's all.'

'OK then.'

'OK.'

They stared at one another. Then, simultaneously, both burst out laughing.

But the point had been made. Beulah had got the message.

'Goin' home?'

Shelby Robbins shrugged. 'If it was up to me I'd stay. But there's Phyllis and the kids to consider. Even if they have political immunity I don't want them here when the Krauts arrive.'

'*When?*' Julius repeated. 'You seem certain about that.'

'That's what the Ambassador thinks, it's only a matter of time. Shit, Julius, you know that.'

Julius sat on the edge of his desk and smiled thinly. 'The

Ambassador could be wrong. The English might fight off the Germans. And, in my opinion, they probably will. They're tough cookies, Shelby. Real hard-asses.'

'We ship out next week,' Shelby replied. 'We've got till then to get everything packed and ready.'

'Anyone else chickenin' out?'

Shelby winced. 'That's not fair, Julius. You don't have kids so it's easy for you to sit in judgement. Hell, man, I've got responsibilities.'

'So why not just send the family Stateside and you remain here?'

Shelby turned away so Julius couldn't see his face. The truth was, he was as anxious to leave as his wife, not wanting to end up in the middle of a shooting war. The English might get beaten but they wouldn't give up easily. Julius was right, they were tough cookies. Stubborn too.

'Well, Shell?'

Shelby sighed. 'Phyllis has forced my hand on the matter. Won't hear of me staying when the offer's there to get out.'

True, but not the full truth, Julius thought. He knew Shelby Robbins to be a coward of the first water; the family was simply an excuse to get his butt out the firing line.

'I hope you have a good trip,' Julius said. 'And don't get sunk enroute.'

'Sunk!' Shelby exclaimed in alarm.

'It's just come in from our people in Berlin. U-boat commanders have been ordered to attack all neutral shipping as well as Allied vessels.'

'Jesus,' Shelby breathed. He hadn't counted on that. 'You sure?'

'Uh-huh. The signal arrived about an hour ago.'

Shelby swallowed, then swallowed again. 'I've gotta get some coffee,' he said and hurried off to the vending machine.

That had been nasty of him, Julius reflected. But he had enjoyed it. He'd never liked Shelby anyway. And the news was true.

Sitting at his desk he got on with work. Shelby did not reappear in the office for the rest of that day.

It was a real pea-souper with visibility reduced to only a couple of yards. That, combined with the black-out, was making it extremely difficult for Ellie and Connie to find their way in what was relatively unfamiliar territory, this part of Islington not being particularly well known to either of them. They were walking arm in arm for support, with mainly Ellie supporting Connie.

'How do you feel?' Ellie asked.

'Terrible.'

Ellie wasn't at all surprised.

'I hope we're not going to be late,' Connie said.

Ellie glanced at her friend's face in the dark. Even through the fog she could see Connie was as white as a sheet.

'Here we are,' Connie announced a little later and they turned into the street where Mrs Smith lived.

On arriving outside the door Connie stopped and gulped. This was it, she thought. This was bloody it.

'All right?'

Connie nodded.

'Up we go then.'

They climbed the steps and halted in front of the door, Connie closer to the electric bell. Ellie waited for her to push it.

Instead Connie closed her eyes. Then gave a sudden whimper.

'Connie?'

Clickety clack, clickety clack. In her mind's eye Connie was watching her mother knitting, the needles going nineteen to the dozen. What if it was a knitting needle Mrs Smith used? She'd heard tales, blood-curdling tales. The thought of one of those inside her, probing, prodding, made her almost scream out loud.

'I can't, Ellie. I can't,' she whimpered, the vision of her mother's knitting needles still clearly before her. She shuddered from head to foot.

Ellie let out a huge sigh of relief. 'Let's go to my local and have a drink,' she suggested.

Connie needed no additional prompting. Both girls turned away and stumbled back into the fog and black-out.

Chapter 12

Ellie's jaw dropped in surprise when she opened the door to find George smiling at her.

'Hello, angel!'

'George!' She flew into his arms and the pair of them, not caring what the neighbours might say or think, kissed deeply.

'What are you doing here?' she gasped when the kiss was finally over.

'We docked in the Pool a few hours ago and I've got three whole days before we're off again.' The Pool referred to was the Pool of London.

This was marvellous. 'You might have written and warned me,' she chided.

'I didn't know our destination till we were at sea. Then, of course, it was too late.'

'Well, you're here, that's the main thing. Now come inside, I can't have you standing on the doorstep.'

He laughed as she pulled him into the hall. 'It's so good to see you again, Ellie. I can't tell you how much.'

'And for me to see you.'

Albert and Jess were also delighted at George's unexpected appearance and made much of him, Albert producing a bottle of whisky, or what was left of it anyway, that he had put by. George was only too happy to accept the offered scotch.

'I thought we might go to The Florence,' George suggested to Ellie. For there they could find a quiet corner and be more or less alone which was impossible with Albert and Jess at home.

'I'll only take a tick to get ready,' Ellie beamed and hurried off upstairs to her bedroom.

'So how has it been?' Albert asked, watching George closely. To date a lot of merchant shipping had been sunk, lost mainly to German U-boats.

George shrugged. 'It's difficult to explain, Albert. Monotonous most of the time, incredibly exciting at others.'

'Do you mean the U-boats?'

'Partly. It certainly makes you think when you know they're in the area. But so far, thank God, we've been lucky.'

'Let's hope you stay that way,' Jess commented.

'And the other exciting things?' Albert prompted.

'Some of the places I've been ashore. New York was the best. We had a terrific time there. New York followed by Maracaibo. Now that was exotic to say the least.'

'Maracaibo,' Albert repeated, eyes gleaming. He'd always wanted to travel but never had. 'You certainly have been getting around.'

George was thinner than the last time she'd seen him, Jess noted. And somehow older too, which showed in his face and the set of his mouth. There was a new-found confidence about him.

Ellie surpassed herself and was back down again in just over ten minutes, George frowning ever so slightly when he saw her.

'That was quick,' he acknowledged.

'Shall we go then?'

'Enjoy yourselves,' Jess told them as she and Albert watched them leave.

* * *

As George had hoped The Florence was quiet and they managed to find a suitable corner. He went up to the bar while Ellie settled herself at the table.

It was Hazel who was serving and she made a big fuss of him, declaring that the first round was on the house in celebration of his safe homecoming. They had a bit of a chat before George picked up the drinks and rejoined Ellie.

'This is new,' he observed as he sat.

'What is?'

'You smoking.'

She sensed, rather than heard, the disapproval in his voice. 'Do you mind?'

He shrugged. 'Not really. It's your choice if you enjoy it.'

'I'm told it makes me more sophisticated,' she declared earnestly.

He laughed. 'I don't know about that.' He glanced at the packet she'd laid on the table. 'Aren't those American?'

She explained about Julius and his getting them for her and not charging. 'Isn't that kind of him?'

George wasn't sure what to make of that. What he wasn't going to say to Ellie was that he didn't like women smoking, thinking it made them look tarty.

'I suppose,' he said slowly, and took a deep drink of his beer. Good old English draught, so much better than the bottled stuff they got on board or the foreign muck you found abroad.

'They really are good neighbours,' Ellie bubbled on, still not over the shock of George turning up out of the blue.

'You've changed your hair,' he stated quietly.

'Had it cut short. It's all the rage at the moment. Everyone is having it done.'

'It's very nice,' he lied. He preferred it long, especially when, occasionally, she had done it up in a French pleat. Now that had been attractive.

'I'm glad you like it.'

She was also wearing more make-up than she'd used to, he

thought. That didn't do her any favours either in his opinion. Like smoking, he considered it tarty.

George glanced about him. 'At least this place hasn't changed. It's just as I remember it.'

Ellie didn't catch the inference. 'Now tell me everything that's happened to you,' she urged.

Well, there were certainly some things he couldn't relate, he thought. The girl in New York most definitely being one. He was about to begin recounting what he could when he suddenly noticed Ellie wasn't wearing his engagement ring.

Ellie went bright red when he mentioned the fact, hastily telling him what had happened and ending the explanation with a profuse apology.

'I'm going to replace it when I get the money,' she declared. 'One exactly the same if the jeweller can match it.'

Her losing the ring had made him angry and saddened him too. This wasn't turning out at all as he'd expected and hoped. It was all a bit of an anti-climax. Ellie had changed so much and, he hated to admit it, was actually irritating him. The evening, as far as he was concerned, was proving something of a disaster. Where was the girl he'd left behind? She certainly wasn't sitting opposite.

'Well?' she demanded.

'Accidents happen.' He couldn't help but feel that her losing the ring was somehow an omen.

'I know, but it was my own stupid fault. I should have put it somewhere safer.'

He had a swallow of beer to save himself from having to reply to that, and, changing the subject, started telling her about Maracaibo instead.

'Now, what about here, the Home Front?' he asked when he'd finished.

'You'd hardly know there was a war on,' Ellie answered. 'Rationing has been brought in at long last, but that's about it so far.'

'No bombing?'

'We were expecting a lot of that, except it just hasn't happened. According to the Evening News the occasional German plane has flown over London, but only the occasional one. Nothing to worry about.'

George nodded as he digested that. It more or less tied in with what he'd already heard. 'Then you're lucky.'

'That's what we think. Some people are beginning to believe we might escape bombing altogether, though that's doubtful according to Dad. He says it's only a matter of time. In the meanwhile we're all thankful for the respite.'

George was about to comment further when someone came bursting into the pub immediately capturing Ellie's attention. 'It's Connie!' she exclaimed. 'A pal who works with me.'

Connie waved and hurried straight over. 'Your mum said you were here,' she explained. Then, to George, 'I'm sorry to burst in like this, but I must have a word with Ellie.'

Not bad, George thought. A bit of a cracker. He rose to his feet and shook Connie's hand as Ellie introduced them.

Ellie was furious. What on earth could be so important for Connie to break in on them as she'd done? George's first night home too.

'Let me get you a drink while you have that word,' he smiled to Connie.

'Are you sure? I've got money.'

'I wouldn't hear of it,' George replied gallantly, not at all fazed by this intrusion. In fact he rather welcomed it. 'Now, what'll it be?'

'Gin and orange please.'

'Large?'

'If you can stretch that far.'

He laughed. 'I can.' And with that he left them, crossing to the bar.

'What's this all about?' Ellie demanded.

'I had to tell you. Just had to. Guess what?'

Ellie shook her head.

'I came on when I got back from work this evening.'

It took a moment for that to sink in. 'You mean . . .?'

Connie nodded vigorously, her eyes ablaze with excitement. 'I wasn't pregnant after all. Don't ask me how I missed a couple of periods when I've never missed a single one before, or even been late.'

'Oh Connie,' Ellie breathed, delighted for her friend. 'What a relief.'

'You can say that again. You can understand now why I just had to rush here and tell you. I'm over the moon. Ecstatic!'

Ellie suddenly frowned. 'Didn't Mrs Smith examine you when you went to see her?'

'She did, and confirmed I was up the duff. All I can think is the rotten old cow was going to pretend to do the business and then charge me as if she had.'

Ellie thought that appalling. Truly despicable. 'Anyway, it doesn't matter now. You're in the clear.'

Connie shook her head. 'Thank God I've been putting off telling my parents. Now they need never know anything about my scare.'

'And Barry was shown up in his true light. You're well rid of the swine, believe me.'

'Can I have one of those?' Connie requested, pointing at Ellie's cigarettes.

'Of course.'

Both girls lit up. 'I'm so pleased for you,' Ellie declared.

'You can imagine how *I* feel. It's as if I was due up for execution and then given a reprieve at the last moment. Hallelujah!'

George reappeared at the table. 'Finished with whatever, or shall I go away again?'

'Quite finished,' Ellie stated.

George glanced from face to face. 'Good news I take it?'

'The best,' Connie replied. 'But don't ask what. I can't say.'

'Girlie stuff,' Ellie explained.

'Oh!'

'I must go and leave you two to it,' Connie declared a little later when her glass was empty.

George was disappointed; he'd thought her fun. 'No need to leave on our account.' Ellie shot him a look which he chose to ignore. 'Now how about another all round?'

Ellie wasn't best pleased, wanting George to herself. But what could she say?

Nothing.

'Would you like to come in for a cuppa?' Ellie asked when they finally left the pub, having arranged with Hazel to have the next two nights, a Friday and Saturday, off. 'Dad's on early so he and Mum are bound to have gone to bed by now.'

George didn't find that proposition attractive in the least. He was amazed at how much he'd cooled on Ellie in such a short space of time. It was as if she'd become a different person entirely during his absence. There again, maybe he was the one who'd changed.

'I won't, Ellie. I've been on the go for over eighteen hours now and I'm about collapsing,' he lied. 'Do you mind?'

She forced a smile onto her face. 'No, of course not. It would just have been nice, that's all.'

'I'll pick you up tomorrow evening, say about half past seven. Or would eight be better?'

'Seven thirty's fine, George.'

He kissed her, but not the passionate kiss she'd been expecting. 'See you then, Ellie.'

'I'll be ready and waiting.'

She watched him disappear into the black-out, disappointment heavy within her. She'd been hoping for a nice bit of canoodling to round things off. To sort of cement their being back together again.

Oh well, she thought philosophically. There was always tomorrow night.

* * *

Paul lay in his bed listening to the wind howl and roar and rattle at his window. How he'd come to hate High Barton, particularly the smells and hard work that went with it.

If only there was someone else his own age around, if not to play with at least to talk to. But there wasn't. There were times, like now, when the loneliness made him want to cry. And sometimes did.

He wished with all his heart he'd never let his father talk him into being evacuated. That had been a terrible mistake on his part.

He pulled the bedclothes up until they were just under his chin, thankful at least that the bed was warm and cosy. After a storm like this there was bound to be a lot of clearing up to do in the morning, a morning that would start at half past four as usual. He groaned inwardly at the thought.

Closing his eyes he waited to get back to sleep, hoping the wind wouldn't wake him again.

His window continued to rattle furiously.

'You're a sly one. He's gorgeous,' Connie whispered to Ellie, Miss Oates not in evidence for the moment.

Ellie smiled. 'You mean George?'

'Who else! He's a real dreamboat. Lucky you.'

Ellie had never considered George to be a dreamboat, far less gorgeous. But who was she to argue with her friend's opinion. 'How are you feeling today?'

'You can imagine. Simply wonderful. What a load that was lifted from my shoulders.' She hesitated. 'I'm sorry again for barging in on you like I did. I really shouldn't have.'

'It's all right,' Ellie reassured her. 'Forget it.'

'Are you seeing him again tonight?'

Ellie nodded.

'Where are you going?'

'No idea. The flicks maybe. Or perhaps up West. It all depends on what George wants to do.'

'Well whatever, I'm sure you'll have a smashing time.'

Ellie failed to detect the jealousy reflected in Connie's eyes and tone of voice. Connie had been serious when she'd declared George a dreamboat. She'd have cut off her arm for a bloke like him.

'I'm sure we will.'

Connie leant even closer. 'Just don't make the same mistake I did with Barry. I don't want to be escorting *you* round to Mrs Smith's.'

'There's no likelihood of that,' Ellie stated firmly. 'The wedding night and not before. War or not.'

Connie found herself wondering what George would be like with his clothes off?

The picture she conjured up made her smile.

Julius killed his car engine and sat back to stare up at Marybeth's apartment. Because of the black-out he couldn't tell whether or not she was at home.

He sighed. It was months now since the incident at Christmas during which he hadn't taken her out again or visited her. She'd come to accept the situation, even if she had done so with bad grace.

Truth was, he missed her. No he didn't, he corrected himself. It was their lovemaking he missed. Sometimes thinking about it, remembering, brought him out in a sweat and made him jumpy as hell.

Should he go up or not? There was part of him desperately wanted to, the ultimate male part that is. It wanted to very much indeed.

'Damn!' he muttered and reached for the ignition key. This wasn't doing him any favours. He should get out of there. Go home. Have a drink, relax. Take a hot tub. Put Marybeth right out of his mind.

Except, he couldn't. His urges were too strong for that. They were tearing him apart.

If only she hadn't been so good in bed, had such an incredible body. Hadn't . . .

Julius took a deep breath. 'Son of a bitch!' he exclaimed softly. Just thinking about her had made him excited.

He removed the key from the ignition and reached for the door handle. Maybe she wasn't at home in which case it was that drink and hot tub.

As it transpired, she was.

The number came to an end and they both applauded. 'Fancy a breather?' George queried.

Ellie nodded, but didn't reply. Of all places to bring her to, the bloody Poxy Roxy!

It had been George's suggestion, he saying how much he'd thought about the dancehall while he'd been away, and how he'd love to go there that evening. She'd felt there was nothing else she could do but fall in with the idea, even though it was the last place she wanted to be.

'The band's great,' George enthused as they left the floor.

Ellie didn't think them great at all, indifferent more like. And that was being kind.

'I adore the name. Doctor Crock And His Crackpots! That's funny.'

Their name was far better than their music, Ellie reflected. Then mentally chided herself for being such a misery guts. She was with George, that was all that mattered. And he was enjoying himself, so the least she could do was give the impression she was too.

'Why, hello again, I thought I saw you up.'

It was Connie who'd materialised beside them, smiling hesitantly. 'Hello, Connie,' George enthused. 'Where did you spring from?'

'Are you with someone?' Ellie inquired.

Connie shook her head. 'I came by my lonesome to eye up the talent. Well, there's precious little of that around. I suppose most of the chaps who'd normally be here are in the Forces.' She pulled a face. 'Just my luck.'

'No matter, you've found us to talk to now,' George replied, pleased to see the blonde whose company he'd enjoyed the previous evening.

She could have done without this, Ellie thought in despair. Would she never get George to herself? It seemed not.

'Great band, eh?' George smiled to Connie.

'Terrific. Especially when they do their novelty numbers. Those are a right laugh.'

George eyed Connie up and down. 'Lovely dress.' The dress in question was a young whirl-skirt frock in fine rayon crepe romaine. The elongated bodice and lowered waistline gave it a chic, longer look. Its figure-moulding drapery was released from shoulder shirring to be caught up into a solid shirred triangle at the waist. The colour was cadet blue.

'This old thing!' Connie laughed dismissively. 'I've had it for ages. Trouble is, it's so difficult to buy anything new nowadays with a war on. Almost impossible. Isn't that right, Ellie?'

Ellie, feeling quite drab by comparison, nodded. She thought Connie looked stunning, especially with her long hair brushed into a Veronica Lake peekaboo.

'Have you danced yet?' George asked Connie.

'Not so far.'

He turned to Ellie. 'Do you mind? Can't have your pal being a wallflower after all.'

Ellie forced a smile onto her face, wishing Connie far away. 'No, we can't have that. Go ahead, give her a twirl. I'll be here when you get back.'

'Are you sure?' Connie frowned at Ellie.

'Course I am, be my guest. Just watch his feet, that's all. He's got two left ones.'

'That's not true!' George protested.

Ellie smiled sweetly, a smile that hid the fact she was seething.

It was.

'Ellie!'

She glanced round in surprise as George came hurrying

across the street. It was Saturday afternoon and she'd just left work.

'This is nice,' she declared as he came up beside her. Taking him by the arm she continued on her way, hoping that Connie, who hadn't yet emerged, wouldn't try to catch up with them. She'd had quite enough of Connie sticking her nose in the previous evening.

George's expression was one of concern. 'It's bad news, I'm afraid.'

'Oh?'

'There's been a change of plan and I have to report back to the ship right away. We're sailing in a few hours.

'I'm sorry,' he added when he saw her stricken face.

'Why's that?' she managed at last to ask.

He shrugged. 'No idea, angel. I'm not exactly privy to the whys and wherefores. I had a telegram earlier on saying we sail at six and to be on board as soon as possible.'

His whole leave had been a disaster right from the word go, she thought miserably. Now this. 'Do you know when you'll be home again?'

He shook his head. 'Who's to say! I really am sorry, Ellie. Truly I am.'

'Isn't there even time for a coffee or something?'

'I've hung on long enough waiting for you to get out of work as it is. I really must make tracks. There's a lot to do before we leave.'

'So that's it for now then,' she stated leadenly.

'I'm afraid so.'

'You will take care?'

'I'll certainly be doing my best.' He suddenly pointed. 'Look, there's my bus. I'll write. That's a promise.'

'But, George . . .' Her protestations were cut short by a hurried kiss. Then he was gone, sprinting back across the street. He turned and waved before jumping on board.

Easy as pie, George congratulated himself, settling into a seat. What he'd told her was a load of nonsense, he wasn't due back to the ship till the following late afternoon. He glanced back to see Ellie walking dejectedly along the pavement. How he'd been looking forward to coming home and being with her again, only the reality hadn't been at all as he'd anticipated.

Maybe the fault was his, perhaps visiting foreign countries had widened and altered his outlook. He just didn't know. What he did know was that Ellie wasn't for him any more. She somehow irritated him, made him want to be elsewhere, preferably with another woman. Whatever spark, chemistry, had been between them had disappeared. Gone, puff! In a cloud of smoke.

He certainly didn't feel proud about lying to her, far from it. But he simply couldn't face another night in her company, which he found really sad.

He already knew how he'd spend that evening, his last ashore, which should have been with her. It would be the dockside pubs with any of his mates who were around. A right good piss-up and laugh, that's what he'd have. And there were bound to be gash females about, there always were in dockside pubs, the sort you certainly wouldn't take home to Mother.

He thought of the girl in New York City. What a cracker, a real bobby dazzler. He'd be looking her up again if he ever returned that way. No doubt about it.

Lily was her name, Lily Gomez. A dark-haired beauty with flashing eyes and a figure to die for. The two of them had got on like a house on fire. Her Limey, she'd called him. Her London Limey. He smiled in recollection.

He would write to Ellie, he'd keep that promise. But it wouldn't be the sort of letter she'd be hoping for. One last letter, and that would be it.

The losing of her engagement ring *had* been an omen, he thought. Very much so.

He put Ellie out of his mind.

Paul arrived at school having braved torrential rain to get there. He went straight inside, although the bell was not due to be rung for another five minutes yet, to look for Eddy.

'Have you seen Eddy Ackworth?' he asked Sylvia Hebden who sat next to Eddy.

Her eyes widened. 'Haven't you heard?'

'Heard what?'

'About last night?'

She was being annoying, he thought. 'How could I? I've just got here, dope.'

'There's no need to be rude,' she snapped.

'All right, go on. What's happened?'

He felt sick after she'd told him.

Chapter 13

'You can't go out like that, Julius, your shirt's all wrinkled,' Beulah chided.

He quickly glanced down his front. 'It's OK, Mom. It'll do.'

Beulah snorted in indignation. 'No son of mine's going out in a shirt like that. Whatever will folks think?'

'I can't change it, Mom. It's the only one of this colour in my closet.'

'Then get it off and I'll do it here and now.' She held up a meaty palm. 'No arguments either. You ain't steppin' over no door of mine unless you's right and proper. Now get it off. Pressin' it will only take a few minutes.'

Julius sighed, knowing further argument was useless. Beulah would have her way come what may.

Shrugging out of the shirt he handed it over. 'There you are.'

Her eyebrows shot up as he moved away. 'How did you do that, son?'

Frowning, he turned to her. 'What are you talkin' about?'

'Your back's all scratched.'

Shit, Julius thought. He'd been with Marybeth the previous night, clearly the scratches were her doing. He inwardly cursed her, and himself for not realising at the time that she was marking him. 'Is it?' he replied, pretending surprise.

Beulah was no fool, it didn't take a genius to put two and two together. 'How's that Marybeth by the way?'

He couldn't look his mother in the eye. This was embarrassing in the extreme. He felt like a little boy who'd been caught in a naughty act. He grunted something unintelligible.

Beulah gave a low, throaty laugh. 'She must be a wild thing all right. Hot diggety!'

'Mom!' he cringed.

'So you two's together again. You never said. But then you never tell your poor old momma nothin'. I swears you don't.'

'Mom, leave it be, eh?'

'If she does that then I just wonders what else she does to you,' Beulah teased, thoroughly enjoying his discomfiture. 'But I suppose I can imagine.'

Thoroughly flustered, Julius fled the room, Beulah's knowing laugh echoing in his ears.

Albert frowned when he entered the kitchen, for Jess was sitting staring distractedly into space, and there was no sign of breakfast. 'What's wrong?' he demanded.

Jess held up a letter. 'This came in the morning post. It's from Paul. It says . . .' She broke off and took a deep breath. When she spoke again there was a choke in her voice. 'His friend Eddy Ackworth is seriously ill in hospital after being bitten by rats.'

'Rats!' Albert exclaimed, knowing full well what a rat bite could lead to.

'It seems the boy was forking hay in a barn when the attack took place. Paul says he's got menilitis as a result.'

Menilitis? 'You mean meningitis?'

Jess shrugged. 'Paul's handwriting. Spelling or whatever.'

The lad could easily die, Albert thought grimly. He knew the father, but only to nod to.

'If he can get bitten then so can Paul,' Jess stated, staring directly at Albert. 'According to this he too forks hay in a barn.'

Albert sighed and leant against the mantelpiece, aware of what was coming next.

'We sent Paul away because we thought there would be bombing,' Jess went on. 'Well, that hasn't happened.'

Albert nodded. 'But it will eventually. Take my word for it.'

'You've been saying that for months, Albert, and still no bombs. What if you're wrong?'

He was certain he wasn't, but how was he going to convince Jess of that. 'Paul's safe where he is.'

'Not when his pal gets bitten by rats he isn't!' Jess retorted, hysteria creeping into her voice. She shuddered. 'Rats are filthy animals who carry all sorts of horrible diseases. You told me that yourself once when one of your mates at work got bitten.'

Albert remembered the incident clearly. Rats in a frenzy running from a burning warehouse. Sandy Bass had been unlucky to have got in the way of a whole demented stream of them. Sandy had nearly lost his leg as a result.

'I'm sure Paul's having a whale of a time,' Albert said doggedly.

'Then how come he never mentions that? Not once in all his letters has he ever said he's enjoying himself. You've read them, you know that to be true.'

Albert didn't reply.

'Well?'

'So what do you propose we do?' he asked softly.

'Bring him home of course. What if it was Paul who was in hospital, what then? You'd be the one blaming yourself because you'd sent him away.'

'We can't,' he said, equally softly.

'Why the hell not?'

He turned to face her, hurting at the anguish he saw deeply etched into her face. 'We looked at the map together, Jess, where Paul is staying is completely out of the way. I'm not even sure, with the best will in the world, we could get there.'

Her shoulders slumped, for what Albert said was true enough. 'I only know I want him home,' she sobbed.

'There there, girl.' He swiftly went to her and took her into his arms. 'Don't go on so.'

Ellie, who'd come downstairs, was standing in the doorway staring at them, wondering what on earth this was all about. Something had clearly upset her parents.

'Oh Albert,' Jess further sobbed. 'I just want my son home again. It's not right that he's living with strangers, it's tearing me apart.'

Albert racked his brains. How to actually get to Talyton, that was the problem. 'Let me think about this,' he crooned.

Eyes glistening with tears looked beseechingly into his. 'Does that mean you agree?'

'If it's what you really want, Jess.'

'Oh I do. More than anything.'

Albert was still convinced the country was the safest place for Paul, and yet this rat business had sown doubts in his mind. And who was to say, perhaps he *was* wrong about the bombing? It was seven months now since war had been declared and everything remained, rationing and shortages apart, more or less exactly as it had been before.

Maybe he was being too cautious, his job taught him to be that way. Caution above all else. It saved lives.

'I'll come up with something,' he promised.

Ellie came into the room and put the kettle on. Her mother was going to need a cup of tea when she calmed down. By now she'd gathered something of what the upset was about.

They might fight like cat and dog at times, but she too was missing her brother. He was a decent soul really.

'What's wrong with you?' Albert asked Ellie later that evening. They were alone, Jess upstairs resting.

Ellie shook her head.

Albert laid his paper aside having been catching up on the latest regarding the war. The news wasn't good, Hitler had invaded Norway, Denmark already overrun after showing little resistance. The outlook was bleak for Britain.

'Come on, what is it?' he prompted, feeling incredibly weary.
It had been a hard day with five call-outs, one of them major.
Not to mention the business with Jess that morning.

'It's George and me,' Ellie replied in a quiet voice.

'What about the pair of you?'

She glanced over at her father, and smiled. What a comfort
he was, always solid as a rock. A great surge of affection for him
welled through her.

'Something's not right between us, I can tell.'

Albert remained silent, waiting for her to go on.

Ellie lit a cigarette, inhaling the smoke deep into her lungs.
'I think he might have lost interest.'

'Did he say that?'

'No, but then it's what he didn't say that's the problem. It was
as though . . .' She groped for the right words. 'He was uneasy
with me. As if he almost didn't want to be in my company.'

Albert wasn't sure what to reply to that. 'Are you certain?'

'Oh yes. He didn't really like it when we were alone and only
brightened up when someone else joined us.'

Albert studied his daughter. The girl was no fool, far from it;
if she thought something was amiss then it probably was. 'You
mustn't forget George has been away, in daily danger. That
must affect a man.'

Ellie could understand that. 'But that wouldn't necessarily
mean he'd go off me, would it?'

Albert had to agree. 'No,' he admitted.

'It just wasn't the same, Dad. I realised that the first night he
was home. He'd changed towards me, become distant.'

'And you? How did you feel about him?'

'The same as before he went off. I hadn't changed, but he
had. Noticeably so.'

Bending over, Albert picked up the poker and attended to
the fire. He'd give it a little longer before putting on more coal,
that being another thing that was becoming in short supply.
'Any idea when he's back again?'

Ellie ran a hand over her face. She had the beginnings of a

headache, whether or not it was brought on by her worries she didn't know. She only hoped it didn't worsen. 'No. None at all.'

'Well, I suppose all you can do is wait and see. I can't offer any better advice than that I'm afraid. Lame advice though it might be.'

Her father was right, she thought. That's all she could do. 'Thanks, Dad.'

'Why don't you pop over to the pub and have a drink? That might cheer you up.'

She considered that, and decided against it. She didn't want to be surrounded by people, preferring the peace and quiet of where she was. 'I'd rather not.'

'Short of a bob?'

'I have money. I just don't want to go.'

They both lapsed into silence, Ellie thinking about George, Albert about Paul and wondering how they could get to Talyton.

A silence disturbed only by the steady ticking of the clock on the mantelpiece.

'I was hopin' to find you in,' Beulah said. 'I got you somethin' here. Somethin' real nice.'

Beulah laid a cardboard box on the table while a puzzled Jess looked on. 'If you's like most women I know then you loves candy,' Beulah declared.

'Candy? Do you mean candyfloss?'

Beulah laughed. 'Naw, that's our word for . . .' She hesitated, searching her memory. 'I believe you folks call them sweeties.' She laughed again, pleased with herself and her new-found knowledge of colloquial English.

'I certainly do. Particularly chocolate.'

'Ah!' Beulah's face lit up. 'I'm glad about that, Jess, because that's what I got here. All kinds of chocolate bars.'

Beulah delved into the box and produced several dozen gaily wrapped bars, all obviously American. 'It's my Julius, he brought me back a whole mess of these. And I thought, I's sure

Jess would like some. And so here you are. From me to you.'

'How kind,' Jess murmured, quite touched. 'This is enough to last us for months, particularly with Paul not about to guzzle them.'

'And how is that little son-of-a-gun?'

Jess's face immediately crumpled. 'Oh, Beulah!'

Pee Wee stared out of their back window, watching the council workers erecting an Anderson shelter. The shelter was comprised of two curved sections of corrugated steel bolted together at the top and sunk three feet into the ground, with an entrance protected by a steel shield and earth embankment. The recommendation was that the householder should cover the roof with at least eighteen inches of soil, the assurance then being that the shelter would survive anything other than a direct hit. All Pee Wee could think was how uncomfortable an overnight stay would be in there.

'How those guys comin' along?' Beulah queried.

'Nearly finished I reckon.'

Beulah joined him in staring out the window. 'Spooky, eh?'

'Yup,' he agreed. 'We'll be like a couple of jack rabbits down a hole in there.'

Beulah laughed at that idea. 'Sure enough. All snuggled up, comfortable as can be. My ass! I tell you, Pee Wee, just goin' in that thing will play merry hell with my rheumatism.'

He put an arm round her. 'That ain't bad at the moment, is it? You ain't said nothin'.'

'Not at the moment, but this English climate sure don't help none.'

'It's the goddamn' damp,' Pee Wee sympathised. ''Tain't cold like we's used to back in New York, but it sure is damp. Gets into your bones too. Why, even I's beginnin' to creak a bit.'

As if to emphasise the point, it started to rain. And it quickly turned into a downpour.

'I'll fix some coffee for those poor guys out there,' Beulah said, the workmen showing no sign of stopping or taking cover.

When the coffee was ready she called the two workmen to the back door and gave it to them. They were extremely grateful but declined her offer to come inside until the rain stopped. They had a quota to fulfil, they explained, and the rain could continue on for God knows how long.

Returning to the kitchen Beulah discovered Julius was home from the Embassy, busy complaining about having got wet while dashing from his car to the house.

'I want to talk to you, Julius,' she declared sombrely.

He stared at Beulah, having noted her tone. 'Sounds serious, Mom?'

She nodded. It was.

'Are you quite sure?' a very much taken-aback Jess queried. This was the last thing she'd expected.

'Yeah, the weekend after next. I suggest we leave early on the Saturday morning which should give us plenty of time to reach Talyton.'

Jess could have kissed Julius; here was the answer to their problem. She really didn't know what to say.

'What about petrol?' the ever-practical Albert asked, he too most appreciative of this kind offer.

'There's no shortage of gas at the Embassy,' Julius replied with a broad smile that showed off his perfect white teeth. 'I'll simply fill up on the Friday night and put a couple of full jerry cans in the trunk. That should be more than enough.'

'We're in your debt,' Ellie smiled at him.

Julius made a dismissive gesture. 'It's my pleasure to help you folks. I'm sure you'd do the same for us if it was the other way round.'

Albert nodded. Yes, he would have done. 'We seem to be taking all the time from your family and giving nothing in return,' he commented with a frown.

'Baloney! You're good neighbours, made us feel right at home the moment we moved in. That goes a long way as far as I'm concerned. Anyway, I haven't seen anythin' of England outside

London. It'll be like a short vacation for me. I'll enjoy it.'

'I'm working that weekend,' Albert mused. 'It might be difficult for me to get a switch of duty.'

'You don't need to come along,' Jess told him. 'I'll be fine on my own with Julius. Isn't that right, Julius?'

'Hope so, ma'am.'

Jess crossed over and sank into a chair. 'I can't tell you what a relief this is. I've been worried sick since that letter arrived.'

'And before,' Albert quietly reminded her.

'It's a date then,' Julius declared. 'Saturday after next. We'll finalise arrangements closer to the time.'

'It's a date,' Jess agreed, enjoying saying the strange expression.

Albert saw Julius out, thanking him profusely at the door, explaining unnecessarily, for Beulah had already done so, how important this was to Jess.

'I'm just pleased I can be of help,' Julius replied and then hurried to his car, for he was meeting Marybeth and was already late.

Ellie laid her letter aside. Like Paul's to Jess, hers had also come in the morning post. Her face had gone deathly white and drawn while reading it.

'From George?' Jess asked casually, having already recognised the handwriting when she'd brought the letter through.

Ellie nodded, but didn't reply.

'How is he then?'

Ellie picked up her cup of tea, and sipped it. Very carefully she replaced the cup on its saucer. 'He doesn't say.'

'Oh?'

'He's in Liverpool it seems. Or was when he posted this. He expected to sail at any moment.'

Jess sat at the table and took Ellie's hand in hers. 'What is it, poppet?'

Ellie looked her mother straight in the eye. 'He's broken off our engagement.'

Jess had feared the worst on seeing Ellie's reaction to the letter. 'Does he say why?'

'According to him he's realised he made a mistake and that it just wouldn't work out between us.'

'I see,' Jess murmured.

Ellie took a deep breath. 'I knew this was coming. I told Dad he'd lost interest and I was right.'

Jess squeezed Ellie's hand in sympathy. 'How do you feel?'

'How do you think?'

Jess smiled thinly. 'Stupid question, I suppose. Awful, I should imagine.'

She wouldn't cry, Ellie told herself. She was damned if she would, even if her whole world had just collapsed around her. 'I really fell for him that night in the pub when he was willing to fight Taffy Roberts in my defence,' she said quietly. 'Up until then I wasn't sure. But that night made my mind up for me. Now this.'

Jess's heart went out to her daughter; what a dreadful thing to have happened. How painful it must be for Ellie. She wished she had a magic spell to take at least some of the pain away.

'Look at it this way,' Jess said. 'Better this to have happened now than after the wedding. That really would be a tragedy.'

Ellie frowned. 'How do you mean?'

Jess told herself she must try and put this delicately. 'Better to fall out of love before marriage than afterwards. This way no lasting harm has been done. And you must remember, no matter what you're feeling right now, there are always plenty more fish in the sea.'

'I suppose so,' Ellie murmured.

'Now can I make a suggestion?'

'What?'

'Why not take the day off from the office. Do something different, go for a walk or whatever. That's what I would do.'

Ellie could see the sense in that. She certainly wasn't in the mood for putting up with Miss Oates. 'All right, Mum, I will.'

'Good girl. Now, is there anything I can get you?'

Ellie shook her head.

'If there is later on just say.'

Ellie smiled her appreciation, a smile that came out all lop-sided and crooked.

After a few minutes she picked up the letter again and slow-ly tore it into tiny pieces.

Ellie returned from her long walk along the canal to find her father waiting for her when he should have been upstairs in bed, since he was on the night shift.

'Your mum told me,' he stated quietly. 'I'm so sorry.'

Ellie shrugged. 'It's happened, and that's all there is to it.'

'You're being very brave.'

She almost laughed to hear that. She didn't feel brave, far from it. What she did feel was a terrible humiliation, and loss. For she had loved George, even if it wasn't the grand passion you some-times read about in novels. She would have made him a good and loyal wife, and hopefully a good mother to their children.

Again, for the umpteenth time, she fought back tears. 'If you don't mind, Dad, I'd rather not talk about it any more.'

He nodded his understanding. 'If that's what you want.'

She went to him and kissed him on the cheek. 'Thanks for waiting up, I appreciate it. Now you'd better get off to bed where you belong at this time.'

He started to turn away, then stopped. 'Life's full of knocks, Ellie, for everyone. We just have to learn to put up, and deal, with them, no matter how hard they are.'

'I know that,' she whispered.

Albert left her to it, he'd done what he could for now. He'd be there for her if she needed him. As she was well aware.

'I must say I'm impressed with the countryside round here. It really is quite beautiful,' Julius commented to Jess. They'd been on the road for a long time but were now nearing their destination.

Jess gazed out over the rolling, lush fields, some dotted with cows, others sheep. She couldn't think of a bigger contrast to Islington than this. The air was wine compared to the soot-laden atmosphere she was used to.

'It is lovely,' she agreed, thinking she must be wrong about Paul. Surely he was happy in these idyllic surroundings?

'I hope Paul's around when we get there,' Julius said, navigating a nasty bend in the lane they were travelling along.

'As it's Saturday he might be out playing football with his pals,' Jess replied. 'But don't worry, we'll find him.'

'After all this way I certainly hope we do,' Julius commented drily. A joke on his part.

They'd stopped once to have a picnic, Jess having brought along sandwiches and a flask each of tea and coffee. There was more than enough left for the return journey.

Julius stopped the car a little further on, and pointed up at a road sign. 'High Barton, that's the place isn't it?'

'That's it,' Jess confirmed, excitement bubbling up in her at the thought of seeing Paul again.

Ten minutes later they entered a yard in front of a typical thatched Devon farmhouse that Julius thought to be rather run-down.

'Here we are,' he declared.

Several chickens ran away squawking, as Jess got out of the car. She thought that was delightful.

Julius strode towards the main door with the intention of knocking on it when he spotted a man and boy busy in some sort of pen. He gestured towards the pen and he and Jess made their way over.

Paul's face was a picture when he saw her, his mouth dropping open in amazement. 'Mum!' he yelled and, quickly scaling one side of the pen, flew at her.

She held out her arms. 'Oh, my darling!'

Mr Selly was standing gawping at Julius as though Julius was the very Devil incarnate. This was the first black person he'd ever seen. Without realising what he was doing, and albeit he was Church of England, he crossed himself.

'Take me home, Mum, take me home,' Paul sobbed when he was in Jess's embrace. 'I hate it here.'

She couldn't believe the smell of him, he stank to high heaven! He was covered in what she didn't know to be pig muck, having been mucking out the pig pens.

A tear-stained face peered up into hers. 'Will you take me home, Mum, please? Please?'

Jess was rattled to say the least. She hadn't known what to expect, but it wasn't this. Something was clearly wrong.

Mrs Selly appeared to also gawp at Julius, her expression one of fright. She went swiftly to her husband and muttered, 'Don't ask 'em in, for pity's sake.'

Mr Selly had no intention of doing that. All he wanted was this black fella off his land as soon as possible.

Jess knelt in front of Paul and, using a hanky she'd had in her pocket, wiped his face and nose. 'Now what's this all about, Paul?'

It all came tumbling out. The time he had to get up every morning, the hard work he had to do on the farm, a lot of it back-breaking, the loneliness, only seeing other children when at school. So on and so forth.

It didn't take Jess long to ascertain the full story. As Paul had admitted, the Sellys hadn't been cruel, merely expected him to work all hours when not at school.

'Pack your things, son,' she said at last, he immediately scampering off to the house.

The Sellys backed away when she and Julius approached. 'Get him to stay where he is!' Mr Selly said in a quavering voice.

Smiling, Julius hung back.

Jess spoke to the Sellys for almost quarter of an hour, establishing the truth of what Paul had told her. They were clearly puzzled that Paul should have objected to their treatment of him, seeing nothing unusual in it.

Jess thanked them for looking after Paul, but it was obvious he just wasn't suited to country life.

Paul was waiting for her, suitcase by his side, when she and

Julius returned to the car. She and Paul got into the rear where Paul immediately cuddled up to her.

As they drove off Julius rolled down his window wishing Paul had had time for a bath before they'd left.

It had been a long drive down. It was going to seem an even longer one back.

Chapter 14

Albert and the rest of his shift sat grouped round the station's wireless set listening to Churchill delivering a pep talk to the nation, Churchill having now been Prime Minister since the previous May when Neville Chamberlain had resigned. What Churchill called the Battle of Britain was now at its height, raging in the skies over southern England.

'Never in the field of human conflict,' he declared, 'was so much owed by so many to so few . . .'

Albert listened in rapt admiration as the great man's words boomed out. Thank God Churchill was now Prime Minister, he thought. What confidence Churchill exuded, what inspiration. He was certainly the leader the country needed in this terrible time of crisis.

When the speech was finally over Danny McGiver switched off the set, each man in the shift looking from one to the other.

'That voice,' Henry Leway said, shaking his head in admiration. 'It's just amazing.'

Albert couldn't have agreed more.

'At least London isn't affected so far,' Percy Noble commented, raising a laugh when he held out a hand and crossed two fingers.

Any further discussion was interrupted by the alarm bell ringing for a call-out.

The entire shift immediately erupted into action.

Julius was the first into the pub when Ellie opened the door for the evening session. 'You must be thirsty,' she joked as he headed for the bar.

'Not so much thirsty as angry. I want to cool off a bit before going into the house.'

'The usual?'

'Uh-huh.'

She went to the pump and began pulling his pint. 'Want to talk about it?'

He smiled and shook his head. 'Can't.'

'You mean won't?' she teased.

'That's right. It's to do with the Embassy.'

He took out a packet of cigarettes and lit up, laying the packet on the bar. 'Help yourself.'

'Thank you. I will.'

He studied her through a haze of smoke. 'How are you off for tabs?'

She now knew what he was referring to having heard him use the expression before. 'I'm a bit low, to tell the truth.'

'Then I'll get you another couple of cartons.'

'Please let me pay this time?' she pleaded as she set his pint in front of him.

'Now, Ellie, don't start that again. It's my little gift, OK? Besides, I enjoy givin' them to you.'

'Well if you insist,' she replied reluctantly.

'I do. Now that's an end of it.'

She touched his hand. 'You're a real sweetie, Julius. Thank you.' And with that she moved away to serve another customer who'd just come in.

How different English girls were to their American counterparts, Julius reflected. They were so much easier and relaxing to be with, not having the aggressiveness, and abrasiveness, of

American women. Even their accents, once you got used and attuned to them, were far more pleasant, less harsh, on the ear.

He'd heard about George breaking off their engagement, but had never mentioned the fact thinking it best, and less embarrassing for her, that way. Personally, he thought George a fool. Ellie was a right good-looking gal, a fact he was noticing more and more. Bright too, with a lovely personality.

'How's Paul?' he asked when Ellie returned to his part of the bar.

'Fine. Still thrilled to be home again. For the first week he hardly left Mum's side, it was as though they were attached to one another. But that's stopped now, which I'm sure Mum is delighted about. It must have been wearing for her with him shadowing her everywhere except into the toilet.'

Julius laughed at that.

'Much to his annoyance he's started school again. Quite a few of the St Margaret's lot have also come back, their complaints the same as Paul's, so the school has re-opened to accommodate them. The authorities aren't best pleased after the trouble they went to in the first place, but there we are. Once Paul had gone I believe there was almost a revolt with the others demanding to return home. Only a few have stayed on I understand.'

'Can I have a large scotch as well?' Julius asked, admiring Ellie's bottom when she turned to the gantry. Larger than Marybeth's, and a different shape. What the English called pear. But delicious all the same.

Ellie quickly delved under the bar when she saw him reach for his cigarette packet. 'Here, have one of my fags this time.'

Julius couldn't help but laugh again. The English usage of that word never ceased to amuse him.

'What's so funny?'

His eyes twinkled. 'Don't ask.'

'Is it me?' She glanced down her front. 'Is there something wrong?' She checked her slip to make sure that wasn't showing.

'It isn't you,' he assured her.

'Then what? It must be something for you to laugh like that.'

He was about to reply when two more customers came in claiming Ellie's attention. He waited patiently, smiling all the while, for her to return.

'Well?' she queried a few minutes later. The fact he was still smiling annoyed her. She'd already peered in the mirror behind the bar to make sure there wasn't something wrong with her face, like a bogey hanging from her nose.

'In my country fag has a different meanin' altogether.'

She raised an eyebrow, waiting for the explanation.

'You certain you want to hear this, Ellie, you might think it rude?'

'I want to hear,' she stated emphatically, flushing furiously when he told her.

'Well, I never,' she managed to say at last, not daring to match his gaze.

'Now you understand why I laughed. It always tickles me pink when I hear you English refer to a cigarette as that.'

'I can well imagine.'

Clearing her throat she began energetically wiping down the bar, even though it didn't need wiping down.

Julius stayed a little longer, then left, Ellie having avoided him during this time.

Beulah roared when he recounted that part of their conversation.

Julius arrived in his office to find a new guy installed behind what had been Shelby's desk.

'Hi! You must be Julius Poston,' the man said, rising and extending a hand. 'I'm Walter Zwicke. I've taken over from Robbins.'

Zwicke was short and slim with a foxy face topped by thinning red hair brushed straight back. Julius took an instant dislike to him.

'Pleased to meet you,' Julius declared as they shook. 'Just got to England?'

'Yeah, from Toronto. I've been there the past five years. Great place Toronto, if you know your way around.'

Julius wondered what he meant by that. 'You must know Marybeth Emerson then? She was stationed in Toronto before bein' posted here.'

The foxy look became even foxier. 'Sure do. One helluva gal! I'll look forward to seeing her again.' He paused, then made a funny little movement with his head. 'Hot damn! Pretty girl that Marybeth. A real snake.'

Julius wasn't at all sure he liked Marybeth being called a snake. He'd always considered that a derogatory expression. 'You fixed up with an apartment yet?'

'Yeah, I've already moved in. Nice number, if not as classy as the one I had in Toronto. That was just off Yonge Street.'

'Sorry, Walter, I don't know Toronto.'

Zwicke shrugged. 'No matter. Now, if you'll excuse me, I'll get on and try to clear up some of this mess Robbins left behind.'

That astonished Julius who simply couldn't imagine Shelby leaving a mess behind, Shelby having been the most diligent of people. 'That so?'

'Yeah. But I'll soon fix it. No sweat.'

Now Julius was certain he didn't like Walter Zwicke. The guy was a creep.

'So why are you so smug today?' Agnes Short demanded during the morning tea break. 'You've been staring into space and mooning ever since you arrived.'

'Have I?' Connie replied innocently.

'I'm only surprised Miss Oates didn't come down on you like a ton of bricks for wasting company time.'

'I noticed her staring into space as well,' Elaine McIntosh piped up.

Ellie, who was also present, hadn't. But then she'd spent most of the morning downstairs in the basement filing.

Connie had a sip of tea. 'I'm sure I don't know what you're

talking about,' she prevaricated, wishing they'd change the subject. This could be embarrassing.

Agnes suddenly smiled. 'Do you have a new beau? Is that it? Is there a new man in your life?'

Damn! Connie thought.

'Is there?' Ellie queried, wanting to know all about him if there was.

''Fraid not.'

Agnes wagged a finger at her. 'I think you're telling porkies, Connie Fox.'

'This is ridiculous,' Connie blustered. 'I wasn't even aware of staring into space far less anything else. What a load of nonsense. Utter rubbish.'

Ellie was intrigued; why was Connie over-reacting like this? For she most certainly was, she knew Connie only too well.

Connie resolved her immediate dilemma by laying down her cup and saying, 'Excuse me.'

And with that she vanished into a cubicle and didn't come out again until it was time to resume work.

'*Have* you met someone?' Ellie asked as they hurried home for dinner.

Connie sighed. 'Now don't *you* start. Agnes is just trying to mix it, that's all. Cause trouble. You know what that bitch is like?'

Ellie dropped it, but kept on wondering why Connie had over-reacted as she had.

A married chap perhaps? She wouldn't put it past Connie to do that sort of thing.

He'd never get used to this bloody black-out, Albert thought as he stepped out of The Florence into the pitch dark. Well not quite pitch, for the moon was up.

He halted abruptly when he saw the fight taking place on the opposite pavement. He could just make out three figures laying into a fourth who was down on the ground.

'Fucking nigger!' one of the assailants yelled.

'Black cunt!' shouted another.

Their Geordie accents gave them away as the three squaddies who'd also been in the pub, nasty pieces of work. Loud, boisterous and clearly looking for trouble. Harry, the landlord, had had to speak to them several times and come within an inch of throwing them out.

The person on the pavement had to be either Pee Wee or Julius, Albert grimly deduced, they being the only black blokes living thereabouts.

He was across the street like a flash to grab the nearest squaddie by the shoulders and spin him round. He might be an older man but he was strong and, thanks to his job, tremendously fit. His first punch, which connected squarely with the squaddie's chin, knocked the man senseless.

Julius, for it was he on the ground, grabbed another squaddie's foot, but the squaddie kicked himself free and took to his heels. Albert was about to pounce on the remaining one when he also ran off. Quickly Albert knelt beside Julius. 'Are you all right, son?'

Julius groaned. 'They took me completely by surprise. There was no reason. They just jumped me.'

'Can you get up?'

'Ahhhh!' Julius grunted when he tried.

Albert glanced at the squaddie he'd knocked out who showed no signs of moving. 'Wait here,' he said tersely, and hurried to the Postons' front door.

Beulah's eyes flew open when he told her what had happened. Brushing past him, not caring about the black-out, she rushed to Julius.

As luck would have it Jess was visiting. 'Call the police on their telephone,' Albert instructed her when she appeared. 'Tell them there's been an attack and we have one of those involved. We also need an ambulance.'

Without uttering another word Albert hastily returned to Julius and Beulah who was cradling him and crying uncontrollably.

Oh Christ! Albert suddenly thought when he saw the squad-die still hadn't stirred. Had he killed the sod? A feel of the neck pulse reassured him that wasn't so.

'How are you now?' he asked Julius anxiously.

'Pain in my chest, bad pain. I think some ribs might be bro-ken.'

Beulah's crying became an hysterical wail.

Another customer emerged from The Florence. 'Who's that?' Albert called over.

'Mike Pratt.'

'Mike, can you get a couple of the lads out here? We've had a bit of trouble.'

'Okey-dokey, Albert.' Mike vanished back into the pub, re-emerging shortly with two others plus Harry, the landlord.

The squaddie on the ground was beginning to come round, Albert watching as he pulled himself into a sitting position.

Quickly Albert explained to Mike, Harry and the others what had happened. 'I knew they were no good,' Harry declared, shaking his head.

Jess appeared at Albert's side. 'The police and an ambulance are on their way.'

The squaddie stared up at those surrounding him, realising he wouldn't get very far if he tried to make a bolt for it. 'You hit me,' he accused Albert.

Albert laughed, thinking that funny. 'Of course I hit you. You and your mates were knocking ten bells out of Julius there.'

'Let me go?' the squaddie pleaded. 'He isn't worth anything. He's only a coon. The scum of the earth.'

Albert fought back his anger. 'That man happens to be a good friend of mine. And it's you who's the scum of the earth, certainly not him.'

'Arsehole,' the squaddie muttered venomously.

Albert was sorely tempted to haul the squaddie to his feet and give him another smack.

'All right, lads, what's to do?'

The speaker, whom nobody had heard approach, was PC

McKechnie, the local bobby. McKechnie was a giant of a man who came from the Highlands of Scotland. This had been his beat for years.

Again Albert explained what had happened. He and McKechnie knew each other well, the latter often being present at fires Albert and his crew were attending.

'I see,' McKechnie said when Albert had finished. 'I'll just escort this wee chappie back to the station where we'll telephone the Military Police. They'll soon find out who his mates were, and take the matter from there.'

He pointed his truncheon at the squaddie. 'Get up and put your hands behind you.'

The squaddie, who looked a midget alongside the giant Highlander, yelped as the handcuffs were clicked shut.

'That hurt?' McKechnie queried.

'Yes.'

McKechnie smiled. 'Good.'

An ambulance, its lights reduced by tape to mere pinpricks, rounded the corner to halt beside them. Jess was kneeling alongside Beulah, trying to console her, Beulah's wailing having given way to deep sobs.

McKechnie had a word with the ambulance people and Julius was soon put on a stretcher and lifted into the vehicle.

'I'll keep Beulah company,' Albert said quietly to Jess. 'She can't go on her own.'

'No you won't,' Jess replied firmly. 'You're on early tomorrow and need your sleep. Besides, what Beulah needs is another woman along. You see to things here and I'll be back when I can.'

'All right.' That was a relief. Concerned as he was, Albert didn't really fancy a hospital visit.

Beulah was helped aboard the ambulance where Jess joined her. The doors were closed and moments later they were on their way.

'Now,' said McKechnie, prodding the squaddie with his truncheon. 'Let's be having you.'

McKechnie and the squaddie disappeared up the street leaving Albert and the others standing outside the pub.

'Want another drink?' Harry asked Albert. 'On the house.'

Albert decided he would. 'I'll just lock up and then I'll be back over,' he replied.

'Right.'

Albert hoped Julius was going to be all right, the lad had taken quite a beating before he'd intervened. A kicking could lead to all manner of internal injuries.

'Bastards,' he muttered, referring to the squaddies. They deserved all they got at the far from tender mercies of the MPs.

'I'll fix us some coffee,' Beulah declared, she and Jess having just returned from the Royal Free Hospital where Julius had been taken. Julius had been correct in thinking he had broken ribs, but apart from that, plus a pretty bruised and cut face, he'd escaped further injury. He was being kept in overnight with the promise of being allowed home the next day.

Jess sat and watched Beulah fill the kettle, feeling terribly sorry for the fat woman. Tonight must have been such a shock, not to mention worry.

'I'm sorry about all this,' Jess stated quietly. 'And ashamed that it happened here.'

Beulah glanced over at her. 'Yo's no need to feel ashamed, hon, 'tain't your fault in any way.' Beulah's eyes flicked to the clock. 'Pee Wee will be home soon. He's going to be real upset when he hears. Lord knows he will. He'll take it bad.' Beulah sighed. 'I wondered what it would be like for black folk in England. Now I know. Just the same as everywhere else, I guess.'

Jess had no answer to that.

'Hungry, hon?'

Jess shook her head.

'I got chocolate cake. That not tempt you?'

'No, Beulah, but thanks anyway.'

'It don't tempt me neither,' Beulah admitted. 'Now that's a

thing. Dear God if it 'tain't. I swear it's almost unheard of.'

Despite herself, Jess had to smile.

Beulah sat, her ample buttocks overflowing the wooden chair. 'I got such a fright tonight, Jess. I can't tell you.'

'I can well imagine.'

'No, you can't, hon. It always scares me when whites turn on us black folks. My pappy's pappy came from the south you know, Georgia that is. Some Klan members got hold of him one time, tortured the poor son-of-a-bitch and then strung him up. No reason for that either, he just happened to be a black man in the wrong place at the wrong time. It was after that the family packed its bags and headed north.'

'Klan?' Jess frowned.

'Ku Klux Klan, honey. They's real mean white folk. Mean as hell. Why, in the old days they killed a black just for sport, like they did my grandpappy. 'Twasn't nothin' to them. We ain't human in their eyes, see?' Then vehemently, 'But we *is*! As human as anyone else, no matter what colour they are. And that's a fact.'

Jess thought the story of Beulah's grandfather a truly appalling one.

'As for womenfolk,' Beulah went on. 'If you was pretty and caught some white man's eye it was common to be raped. And no one would ever do anythin' about it afterwards, no sirree. The woman was just meat to be used.'

'How awful,' Jess murmured, horrified.

''Twas no use goin' to the sheriff, he'd just laugh in your face and tell you to get your black ass out of there.'

Beulah fell silent, only rousing herself again when the kettle started to boil. 'Ain't life wonderful,' she commented caustically, heaving her huge frame aloft.

Ellie paused when she heard voices coming from Julius's bedroom. Beulah hadn't mentioned that he already had a visitor.

'Come in!' Julius called out when she knocked.

The other visitor was Marybeth, sitting on the edge of Julius's bed and holding his hand. Marybeth frowned when she saw the new arrival.

'I'm sorry,' Ellie apologised. 'I'll come back another time.'

'Not at all, join us,' Julius insisted, removing his hand from Marybeth's.

What a truly beautiful woman, Ellie reflected, wishing she had a figure as stunning. 'I'm only here for a minute,' she said. 'I just wanted to see how you were.'

'Pretty sore I guess.' He indicated his chest. 'I'm all trussed up like a chicken here. Now, you haven't met Marybeth yet.' He proceeded to introduce the two.

'Your poor face,' Ellie sympathised when that was over. It was indeed a sight, all puffed and swollen with nasty-looking abrasions in places, while a section of his left cheek had been stitched.

'Looks worse than it is,' Julius assured her. 'Though the stitches do smart a tad.'

'I think he's bein' terribly brave,' Marybeth purred in a silky voice, eyes boring into Ellie's to the point it made Ellie feel decidedly uncomfortable.

'Bullshit, I'm being nothin' of the sort,' Julius protested.

'Oh but you are,' Marybeth insisted. 'At least I think so.'

Ellie wished now she hadn't come, but how had she been to know Marybeth would be here.

'I'll be round to thank your dad when I'm on my feet again,' Julius declared. 'I could have ended up really hurt if he hadn't shown up. I owe that guy.'

'It's just lucky he left the pub when he did,' Ellie replied.

'It certainly was for me.'

'I'm on my way over there now,' Ellie smiled. 'I'm working tonight.'

'Of course, it's Friday,' Julius nodded.

'A *barmaid*, how sweet,' Marybeth declared with just a hint of condescension in her voice, knowing that to be the English equivalent of what she would normally have called a cocktail waitress.

The hint was enough for Ellie to pick it up, colouring slightly. 'It's only part-time. I have a proper job during the day.'

'And what's that, honey?'

Ellie told the American woman.

'Interesting,' Marybeth murmured, giving Ellie the impression she found it quite the opposite. A position of little consequence.

'Ellie, go over to that drawer and open it will you?' Julius requested, pointing.

She crossed to a chest of drawers and indicated. 'This one?'

'That's it.'

She found two cartons of cigarettes inside which she took out.

'I've been meanin' to drop them by for days but never found the time,' Julius explained.

Ellie glanced at Marybeth whose expression had become inscrutable, with the exception of the eyes which had hardened. Oh God! she thought. Why oh why did Julius have to give her these now?

'Thank you,' she smiled at him.

'My pleasure, as always.'

Ellie's feeling of being uncomfortable had deepened even further. For the life of her she couldn't think why Marybeth was being so antagonistic, she hadn't done or said anything untoward after all. 'I suppose I'd better get along,' she murmured.

Julius was genuinely sorry to see her go and would have asked her to hang on if Marybeth hadn't been there. 'Give my thanks to Harry and the others who came out last night.'

She nodded. 'I will. They'll want to know how you are.'

She hesitated at the door. 'Goodbye, Marybeth. Nice to meet you.'

'And you, Annie.'

'It's *Ellie*,' Julius quickly corrected her.

'Oh, sorry. My fault.'

The misnaming had been quite intentional, Ellie was certain of that. She gave a last smile, and then was gone.

'Sweet child,' Marybeth said, picking up Julius's hand again. 'Seems fond of you.'

Marybeth's bitchiness hadn't been lost on Julius who wondered why on earth she'd behaved as she had. Then it dawned; she was jealous!

He found that highly amusing. Amusing, and surprising.

Chapter 15

'I wonder if I could have a word in private, Miss Oates?' Agnes Short requested.

Miss Oates halted, having been hurrying past. 'Can't it be said here, girl? I am rather busy.'

'I'd prefer in private if you don't mind.'

Miss Oates sighed, what now? 'All right, come with me.'

Agnes rose from her desk and dutifully followed the older woman to another part of the building where they could be alone.

Ellie glanced over at Connie who pulled a face and shook her head, indicating she had no idea what that was all about. Ellie then shook hers, indicating the same.

How mysterious, Ellie thought.

Ellie was first in the toilet at morning tea break, immediately lighting up which she'd been looking forward to for the past hour. Connie was next, also lighting up immediately.

Agnes was last to appear, the others speculating amongst themselves as to why she'd wanted to speak to Miss Oates.

'Come on, Agnes, give,' Connie demanded the moment the door was shut behind the girl.

'You mean Miss Oates?'

'Of course.'

Agnes smiled, but didn't instantly reply, enjoying being the centre of attention for once. 'I'm leaving,' she finally announced.

'Leaving!' exclaimed Elaine McIntosh. She hadn't thought of that possibility.

'Why?' Ellie frowned.

'I'm joining the WRNS.'

The others were completely taken aback. 'Bloody Nora!' Connie murmured. This was a complete surprise.

'Everybody is talking about doing their bit nowadays,' Agnes explained. 'So I thought I should too. Anyway, it has to be better than working here which bores the backside off me.'

'The WRNS?' Ellie mused. The female branch of the Navy. Pretty uniform too. She'd seen it.

'When do you go?' Elaine inquired.

'I'm not sure, but soon. I've had the interviews and been accepted. Next thing will be a letter in the post telling me where, and when, to report. It could be any time.'

Agnes was right, Ellie reflected. 'Doing your bit' was a favourite topic of conversation of late. Agnes's action in joining up gave her pause for thought.

'How did Miss Oates take the news?' Connie queried.

'There wasn't much she could say or object to. There is a war on, after all. What she did do was wish me all the very best, and to say pop in any time in future when I was passing.'

'Well,' murmured Elaine. Who would have thought the old bat would have suggested that.

Connie was tempted to remark that Agnes might land herself a boyfriend at long last, but didn't. That would have been too catty, given the circumstances.

'Tell us about the interviews?' Ellie prompted.

Agnes's news was the sole topic of conversation during the entire tea break.

'I tell you, Churchill isn't the man for the job,' Percy Noble declared with the air of someone who's convinced he's right.

So far it had been a quiet day at the fire station, the only call-out having been earlier to a chip pan that had caught alight. Albert had often said if he had a pound for every chip-pan fire he'd attended he'd be a millionaire. An exaggeration of course.

'So who would you have as PM?' Danny McGiver queried.

'Halifax. He's the obvious one.'

Albert, being a great fan of Churchill's, was fuming. 'Nonsense,' he retorted.

'Look at Churchill's history,' Percy persisted. 'One balls-up after another. India for instance, and what about Gallipoli? An awful lot of people lost their lives because of Gallipoli. It was a complete cock-up right from the word go, and all Churchill's doing. It was his idea to send the troops in there.'

Albert's expression became grim, knowing that to be true. 'Everyone makes mistakes,' he replied rather lamely.

'Not on that scale they don't.'

'I don't like or trust any politician,' Henry Leway stated. 'As far as I'm concerned they're all a bunch of shysters. Grumbles every last one.'

'Isn't that a bit harsh?' Danny smiled, knowing his Cockney slang.

'I don't think so.'

'Churchill was lucky about Dunkirk,' Percy Noble said. 'I doubt he would have survived as PM if that miracle hadn't taken place. And believe me, a miracle it was. The Germans made a blunder and let our boys off the hook. Thank God.'

They all paused for a few moments to reflect on that. No one knew for certain what would have happened next if the entire BEF, British Expeditionary Force, had been killed or captured; it certainly would have been a blow of staggering enormity and consequence.

'Yes, Churchill would have been kicked out of office and we'd have sued for peace,' Percy went on.

The others stared at him in disbelief. 'Sued for peace?' Danny choked.

Percy shrugged. 'What else could we have done, you tell me? It would have been the only logical thing to do.'

'Bugger logic,' Albert hissed. 'We'd never have surrendered, never!'

'I didn't say surrender, I said sue for peace. There's a difference.'

'Like hell there is,' Albert riposted sharply. 'It's simply playing with words.'

'Well, that's what I think would have happened,' Percy insisted doggedly.

Danny decided this had gone far enough. The last thing they needed was a falling-out amongst themselves. Apart from anything else, that could be dangerous when out on the job.

'Let's not allow this to get out of hand,' he said in a placatory tone.' I suggest we stop this argument and listen to the wireless instead. Agreed?'

Even Albert could see the sense in that, though he remained utterly convinced Percy and Henry were wrong about Churchill. There were various mutterings of agreement, including his.

The wireless set was already tuned to the Home Service on which the announcer was relaying the war news.

It made depressing listening.

It was Julius's first day back at the Embassy and pleased he was to be there having become extremely restless languishing at home. He was still trussed up, and sore, but his ribs were well on the mend according to the doctor whose instructions were to take it easy and not exert himself in any way.

He was about to turn into his office when he spotted Walter Zwicke and Marybeth further down the corridor, the pair of them laughing together.

Sharing reminiscences no doubt, he thought, and went inside.

'Yuck!' exclaimed Paul, screwing up his face. 'This tastes terrible, Mum.'

Albert gave his wife a sympathetic look. 'He's right, Jess. It's not very nice.'

Ellie sat in silence, not making a comment.

'It's powdered egg,' Jess explained. 'And before you say anything further that's all I could get. There isn't a fresh egg to be had in any of the shops.'

'Powdered egg,' Albert mused. 'Whatever next?'

'Spam.'

He stared at her in amazement. 'Never heard of it.'

'It's something new. Don't ask me what's in it, a sort of mishmash I believe. But that's what the butcher's selling now in place of what we're used to.'

'Sounds revolting,' Albert muttered.

'I don't know, but we'll soon find out if that's all that becomes available.'

Paul thought fondly of the wonderful meals he'd enjoyed at High Barton, his mouth watering at the memory. Not only wonderful but as much as you could eat at every sitting. Then he scowled, that was the only good memory he had of the place. Nothing, not even the temptations to be found in such abundance, would have got him back there. He'd loathed High Barton and his life there.

'Can I say something?' Ellie asked quietly.

Jess glanced at her, expecting another complaint about the powdered egg which she too found horrid. 'Of course.'

Ellie cleared her throat, not quite sure how her parents were going to take this. Well, she hoped.

'I've decided to join the ambulance service.'

'Ambulance service?' Albert queried with a frown. 'What's brought this on?'

'One of the girls at the office has joined the Wrens to do her bit for the war effort. And that set me thinking I should do something as well. I considered the Wrens and the WRAC, but realised that would mean me being away from home which I didn't want. Then I remembered a poster I saw a while back about the ambulance service and decided that was ideal.'

She stopped and stared from her mother to her father and back again. 'What do you think?'

Jess smiled. 'It's a tremendous idea, Ellie. I'm proud of you.'

'Have you applied yet?' Albert queried.

'No, I wanted to speak to you both first. I didn't want you thinking I'd gone behind your backs.'

Albert nodded his approval. 'I agree with your mum, it is a tremendous idea. You'll certainly be contributing a lot more than you do in that office of yours.'

A warm glow spread through Ellie, who was excited at the prospect of what lay ahead. And the best bit was, no more Miss Oates! 'It's settled then. I'll go along this evening and make inquiries.'

She hesitated, then said, 'One more thing.'

'What's that?' Jess queried.

'This powdered egg, it really does taste disgusting.'

They all laughed, Ellie hugely relieved that her parents were in favour of her plan.

'Good God, look at what just walked in,' Hazel whispered to Ellie, the pair of them behind the bar.

Taffy Roberts, resplendent in a brand-new army uniform, swaggered over. 'A pint of best,' he declared.

'Joined up I see,' Hazel observed.

'That's right, me beauty. They didn't have to conscript me neither. In I went and put me monicker on the dotted line. King and Country, eh?'

'I wondered why we hadn't seen you for a while,' Hazel remarked.

'Training on Salisbury Plain. Putting me and a lot of others through our paces. Now I'm a fully fledged fighting man.' He puffed out his chest. 'Bring on those German boyos. I'll show them what a Welshman can do. Oh yes indeed.'

Ellie was trying her best not to laugh. For some inexplicable reason the uniform made Taffy look ridiculous. Well, it didn't fit properly for a start, being at least one size too large. But it was more than that, though for the life of her she couldn't say what. It simply made him look ridiculous, that was all.

'That one's free for joining up,' Hazel declared, placing a pint in front of him. 'Everyone who does that gets one on the house.'

Taffy beamed. 'Why thank you, missus. I appreciate that.'

Picking up his drink he swaggered away. What he'd told Hazel and Ellie was a lie. He hadn't joined up at all, he *had* been conscripted, and it had taken a visit from PC McKechnie, plus the threat of jail, to get him to comply.

Deputy Section Officer D'Arcy was a woman in her mid-fifties with a nononsense look about her. She ran an experienced gaze over the six latest recruits for training. At first glance anyway, they seemed a likely bunch.

Ellie had reported at eight o'clock sharp to Lawn Road, Hampstead, not quite knowing what to expect. She was both excited and nervous, desperately hoping she'd fit in all right. There hadn't been much time to get acquainted with the other trainees, but they appeared to be friendly enough.

'You'll be here for two weeks,' D'Arcy informed them, having first introduced herself. 'And I have two words of advice. The first is, pay attention at all times, the second, if you don't understand something don't be frightened to say so. Is that clear?'

There was a chorus of yeses and nods.

'Does anyone know anything about first aid?'

No one did.

Pity, D'Arcy mused. It would have made things a bit easier. 'Can any of you drive?'

Again the answer was no all round.

This was the fifth lot of trainees and not a driver amongst them, D'Arcy thought in dismay, the service being chronically short of drivers.

Ellie had applied to join the London Ambulance Service, but instead had been assigned to the auxiliaries, known as the

London Auxiliary Ambulance Service, an adjunct of the regular service.

'Well, we're going to have to do something about that,' D'Arcy went on. 'So on top of the usual training you'll also be taught to drive a vehicle. Any objections?

'Good,' D'Arcy smiled when there weren't any. 'Now if you'll follow me into the building we'll make a start.'

Pee Wee arrived home to find Beulah sitting staring morosely into the fire. 'Hello, hon.'

She glanced over at him and smiled. 'You're even later than usual.'

'Had trouble findin' a cab. Waited ages before I could get hold of one.'

'You want somethin' to eat?'

Pee Wee shook his head. 'Just a drink, that's all. How about you?'

'I'm fine.'

He went to where the liquor was kept and poured himself a large bourbon. 'We were full again tonight. Lot of military people present.'

'Uh-huh.'

'We played good. Better than usual with a lot of jammin'. Lord Fitzaran was there with a Lady Hermione somethin' or other. You should have heard her talk, all fancy lah-di-dah. But pleasant enough.'

Beulah nodded, continuing to stare into the fire.

Pee Wee crossed over and sat opposite. 'You OK, hon?'

'Yeah, sure. I just . . .' She trailed off and bit her lip.

'You just what?' he prompted softly.

'It don't make sense. It's crazy. But I got this feelin' that's real peculiar.'

He was suddenly alarmed. 'You ain't sick, are you?'

'Not that kind of feelin', Pee Wee. Not the sick sort.' She snorted. 'I guess it's just my imagination, that's all.'

'Come on, Beulah, spill it.'

She glanced over at him. 'I believe it's called a premonition.'

He had a deep swallow of bourbon. 'Yeah? What sort of pre-monition?'

'That somethin' real bad is about to happen. And I mean *real* bad. The worst kind of bad. The kind that makes your skin go all creepy.'

Pee Wee wasn't sure what to reply to that. He'd never before known Beulah to have a premonition, if indeed that's what it was. 'Is it just a general thing, hon, or anythin' specific?'

'General, I guess. I ain't seein' no visions if that's what you mean.'

They sat in silence for a few seconds. 'Well, we gotta remember there's a war on here,' he said eventually. 'It could be to do with that.'

'Could be,' she agreed.

Pee Wee didn't like this, not at all. It made him distinctly uneasy. Spooked even.

'I just hope and pray it don't involve Julius,' Beulah muttered. Please God, not him. Her only son.

Pee Wee gulped down the remainder of his bourbon and shuddered. That had also crossed his mind, though he hadn't said. 'I'm sure it don't,' he declared, trying to reassure her. 'Hell!' he laughed. 'You been starin' into that fire for too long. It flickerin' and dancin'. It's got you hypnotised, that's what. Hypnotised into seein' things that ain't there.'

She forced a smile onto her face, well aware of what he was trying to do. 'You's probably right, Pee Wee. And you know somethin'?'

'What?'

'I think I will have a drink after all.'

'That's my girl!' he enthused, coming to his feet. 'Now don't you go worryin' no more, hear?'

'I hear, lover boy.'

He kissed her tenderly on the cheek. 'Three fingers or two?' Those were colloquial American measures of spirits.

Her reply made him roar.

* * *

Corporal Mann of the Transport Corps grimaced as Ellie ground the gears of the Vauxhall Cadet VX she was attempting to drive.

'Sorry,' Ellie apologised.

Patience, Corporal Mann told himself. Patience. Remember she's a woman and don't swear or yell her out.

'It's the clutch,' Ellie went on. 'That's what's giving me trouble.'

That and everything else, Corporal Mann thought. Christ, but she was clueless. 'Down into third now,' he instructed, wincing as she ground the gears yet again.

This was impossible.

'How long you been seeing Marybeth for?' Walter Zwicke casually asked Julius. 'I only found out the other day that you two were romancing one another.'

That surprised Julius. 'Hasn't Marybeth mentioned it?'

Zwicke stuck the end of a pencil into his mouth and shook his head.

'I'd thought she would have done.'

'We don't bump into one another very often. I suppose it's just never crossed her mind.' Zwicke's eyes glittered mischievously as he watched Julius.

'Oh I don't know. A good while I guess,' Julius returned to Walter's original question.

'Is it serious?'

Julius was careful how he answered that. For all he knew Zwicke and Marybeth might have been, and still were, good friends. 'You know how these things are? We rub along OK I suppose.'

Julius's evasiveness wasn't lost on Zwicke. 'Just wondered, that's all.'

Taking the pencil from his mouth he resumed work.

Julius thought about Marybeth and Zwicke. He had mentioned Zwicke to her shortly after he'd taken over Shelby's desk, her reply being, yeah, she remembered Zwicke, and that had been about it. Neither enthusiastic or unenthusiastic, non-committal rather, which surely meant they hadn't been good friends, simply colleagues.

Zwicke was simply being polite, showing interest, nothing more, he decided.

His first impression of the man hadn't changed. He still didn't like the guy.

Julius slammed his car door shut and locked it.

'Hello, Julius.'

The moon was up and there were many stars out so he was able to recognise her standing on the pavement at the other side of his car. 'Hi!'

'Just back from the Embassy?'

'You got it.'

He walked round and joined her. 'How's the ambulance service doing?'

'Oh, it's doing fine, but I'm not. Far from it.'

He frowned. 'What's the problem?'

She pointed at the car. 'These things. Try as I might I just can't seem to get the hang of driving. The army corporal trying to teach me, although he hasn't said, is at his wits' end I think.'

'I'm sorry to hear that, Ellie. It's a bitch,' he sympathised.

'Having been given the opportunity I do want to drive, and drive well. But I don't think it's going to be. Part of the trouble is I've only got a fortnight to learn, and there's only so much time in a day when there's all sorts of other things to learn as well.'

Julius could see her point, it must be difficult. Then he had an idea. 'What are you doing after you've eaten?'

She failed to see the relevance of that. 'Nothing. Why?'

'I could take you out in my car if you want?' He glanced about. 'The black-out doesn't make the best of conditions, but if we go around the back streets we shouldn't run into much traffic. If any at all. What do you say?'

Ellie was thrilled. 'That would be wonderful!'

'OK, you got yourself a date. Knock on our door when you're ready.'

What a lovely man, she thought, not for the first time. This was exceptionally kind of him. 'I'll do that.'

He smiled, his white teeth gleaming in the darkness. 'See you then.'

As Ellie went inside she was already mapping out in her mind what route they'd take, one that should be the quietest.

'Easy on that clutch, baby, easy. Don't stab with your foot, be more fluid,' Julius advised softly.

They were crawling along, but then that was the only safe way to drive under these conditions. The limited light from his taped-up headlights gave only a minimum of illumination.

Ellie for her part felt far more relaxed than she did with Corporal Mann. When Julius spoke to her there was no criticism, or exasperation, in his voice, which boosted her confidence.

'That's it,' he crooned. 'It's just a case of gettin' the right rhythm.'

'Like music?' she smiled.

'Yeah, like music. Think of the clutch and gears as instruments that you're playin'. Get to have a feel for them like they were an extension of yourself. Understand?'

'I think so.'

'You're doin' good, Ellie. Honestly. No BS.'

That puzzled her. 'What's BS?'

Julius laughed. 'Bullshit. An American expression. It means I'm not joshin' you.'

'Lying to me?'

'Exactly.'

Ellie was at a loss to see how bullshit equated with lying, but there you are. The American usage of English could be quite bizarre; at times it almost seemed a different language altogether.

'Now change down to turn this corner,' Julius instructed.

Ellie managed to do so without grinding the gears, which pleased her enormously. When she moved back up it again went smoothly.

'See, you can do it. Easy as pie,' Julius grinned.

Ellie's stomach contracted when his leg accidentally brushed against hers. She found she was holding her breath.

Julius had also been aware of the touch, enjoying it as well. Sitting this close to Ellie he could smell her, a smell he liked a lot. It certainly appealed.

They drove in silence for a little bit, so far having been lucky in not having encountered any other traffic. There again, no one in their right mind drove in the black-out unless they had to.

'You can start headin' for home now I reckon,' Julius said. 'I think that's enough for one night.'

'All right.'

'I thought I might have a beer at The Florence after this,' he declared casually. 'Care to join me?'

Ellie didn't have to be asked twice. 'I'd love to. Learning to drive is thirsty work.'

He laughed, a deep rumbling sound. 'If you say so, kid.'

'Ellie please. I don't like being called kid.'

That amused him. 'OK, *Ellie.*'

'That's better.'

He was enjoying this, her company, he truly was. 'We can have another lesson tomorrow night if you wish?'

'Are you sure, Julius? I don't want to take up too much of your time. That wouldn't be fair.'

'I'm free, so it's up to you.'

'Then it's a date, as you would put it.'

'A date,' he agreed.

'Well, I don't know how you've managed it but you pass,' Corporal Mann declared.

Ellie beamed. 'Thank you.'

'You've certainly improved over the past few days. Quite incredible really.'

All down to Julius, Ellie thought. He was a terrific teacher, and great fun to be with. Not to mention a handsome sod who was charming with it.

Later that day, Ellie's fortnight completed, Deputy Section Officer D'Arcy posted her to the station in Pentonville Road, the closest to Florence Street.

Chapter 16

'You sure are one vocal lady,' a sweat-slicked Julius commented, staring in admiration at Marybeth's naked body. It was as slicked as his own.

She took that as a compliment. 'Surely some of your past lovers have been just as noisy?' she teased, probing at the same time.

He cocked an eyebrow. 'What sort of question is that?'

'A fairly straightforward one, I should think.'

'Oh really?'

'Yes really.'

He gently stroked a silky thigh, appreciating the length and shape of her legs. 'I was brought up never to discuss bedroom matters other than with the person involved. I was taught that was manners.'

'Oh really?'

He laughed. 'Yes really.'

'You're probably right,' she admitted. 'I was just curious, that's all. I mean, I don't know how other women behave, never havin' been to bed with one.'

'I should hope not.'

Marybeth was lying, she had once years previously while at college. Enjoyable it had been too, but not really for her. She preferred the real thing. The hardness of a man's body, the male penetration. The differences between the genders.

'You want a drink?'

He shook his head.

Marybeth considered having one herself, then decided against it. 'What are you thinkin' about?'

He hadn't been thinking anything. 'You,' he lied, knowing that was the answer expected.

'Nice thoughts I hope?'

'How could they be otherwise with you involved?' She adored flattery and he was quite capable of laying it on thick when he felt like it. But not too often, that would have spoilt her.

'You are sweet, baby.'

There was a look in her eyes which told him their lovemaking wasn't finished, that this was merely a breath-catcher between bouts. His eyes flickered to the top of her legs. 'Not as sweet as some things I could name.'

Marybeth sighed, feeling that urgent urge returning. Not yet though, she told herself. Give him time to recover. She moved her bottom sensuously against the sheet beneath her, as Julius had so recently been.

Julius smiled as he watched. 'You certainly know how to get to a guy, don't you?'

'If you say so,' she purred huskily.

He turned away. 'Mind if I have a butt?'

That annoyed her slightly, as he'd hoped it would. 'Do you have to?'

He came to his feet and reached for his cigarettes. She wasn't the only one who could play games. 'I'll have to go soon,' he replied, lighting up.

He enjoyed the uncertainty and irritation that flashed across her face. 'I thought you were stayin' the night?'

He shrugged. 'I got a bunch of work in the car that needs doin'.'

'Then do it here,' she urged.

Of course there wasn't any work, he was just playing. 'That wouldn't happen, Marybeth. You're far too great a temptation,' he answered, changing tack, flattering her again.

She preened. 'I'll promise to leave you alone for a while till you're finished.'

'Is that a real promise?'

'Sure is, honey. On my life.'

Yeah, he thought. And he was the President of the United States.

Marybeth also came to her feet and shrugged herself into a rose-coloured cotton wrap that she'd bought in France. A favourite of Julius's. Going to him she kissed him on the cheek. 'Can't I make you change your mind?'

He simply smiled.

'Can't I?'

'I don't know,' he prevaricated, pretending to consider the matter. Of course he was going to stay, as he'd intended all along. But why let her have things all her own way?

She ran a hand across his chest, her breathing becoming shallower to the level he recognised only too well. Slowly she sank to her knees in front of him.

A moment later, before anything further could happen, an air-raid siren close by began to wail.

Christ! he thought, tensing as he always did whenever a siren went off.

'It's only another false alarm,' Marybeth said, looking up at him. 'That's the third this week.'

He was about to reply when from off in the distance came the sound of what could only be bombs exploding. 'Holy shit!' he exclaimed; this wasn't a false alarm at all, but an actual raid.

'Put out the lights,' he instructed her, and hurried to the nearest window. When she'd done that he threw back the drapes and opened the window.

The explosions were louder now, although he couldn't see where they were impacting. He became aware of Marybeth holding tightly onto his arm.

'It's finally happened,' he said. 'The Krauts are hittin' London.'

Marybeth shivered, which had nothing whatsoever to do with the cold. Somewhere out there people were being killed and maimed. God alone knew how many. Standing there listening to that excited her in a way she'd never been excited before.

Suddenly there was a massive explosion, far louder than any of the others, which caused the glass to rattle in its panes.

Julius quickly shut the window again and pulled the drapes back into place. There could be no doubt about it, London itself was under attack. And a very heavy attack at that.

'Is there a shelter here?' Julian asked.

'We've been told to use the basement.'

'Then get dressed and we'll go down there.'

She clutched even more tightly onto his arm. 'Not yet, Julius. Not yet.'

'We could get killed standin' here, for Christ's sake!'

Her entire body was alive, throbbing with need. To her ears it seemed the mass bombing was getting closer.

'Come to bed,' she husked, voice choking with desire.

'Marybeth . . .'

His protest was stifled when her lips fastened onto his, her tongue a red-hot snake stabbing into his mouth, her hands everywhere, pleading with him to do as she wanted.

'Julius, please? Please?'

He groaned when a hand fastened onto him and began urgently to move. He was only flesh and blood after all.

Within minutes Marybeth was screaming like some animal being slaughtered in an abattoir. If Julius had thought her loud before then that was nothing compared to this.

And all the while there was the sound of exploding bombs and the rattle of ack-ack fire.

'I have to go back on duty, Mum, I might be needed,' Ellie declared to Jess, the pair of them trying to come to terms with what was happening, that at last the long-expected bombing was now actually taking place.

'You can't go out in that!' Jess exclaimed in horror.

A white-faced Paul watched them in mute terror, having come downstairs from his bedroom after the noise woke him.

'I have to, Mum. It's my duty.'

'But . . . but . . .' Jess trailed off impotently, every fibre of her being wanting her to protect her children, keep them safe from harm.

'I'll be all right. You'll see.'

Tears welled in Jess's eyes. This was terrible. She wished with all her heart Albert was here and not at work. 'You will take care?'

'Of course I will. Now you and Paul get out to that shelter. Tuck yourselves up in there.'

Jess followed Ellie into the hall where Ellie quickly slipped on her coat. It wasn't a long walk to Pentonville Road, she'd be there in ten or so minutes.

Ellie pecked Jess's cheek, and then was gone, the door slamming shut behind her.

Jess bowed her head, her lips moving in a muttered prayer.

'There must be hundreds of the bastards,' Percy Noble observed in awe, every member of the station outside staring up at the sky.

Albert could make out the shadowy outlines of the German planes, the occasional one being picked up by searchlights. Long lines of tracers seared heavenwards reminding him of a firework display he'd once seen in Highbury Fields.

Suddenly there was the sight of a plane being hit, its entire tail section disintegrating to leave fire streaming from where that had been.

A cheer went up as the stricken plane spiralled towards the ground to vanish somewhere in Clerkenwell.

'I hope they roasted all the way down,' Danny McGiver declared vehemently, meaning every word of that. He truly did.

Albert turned to face the fiery inferno that lit up the horizon. It might have been the very gate to hell itself, he thought grimly. There was no doubt where the Jerries were targeting, the Docks, obviously their main attack point.

'I wouldn't like to be in the middle of that,' Henry Leway commented, joining Albert to stare at the orange and crimson conflagration lighting up the night sky.

'No,' Albert agreed softly.

The ack-ack gunners hit another plane, this one knocked sideways and then dropping like a stone. 'That's going to land in our manor,' Danny McGiver judged.

The section trooped back into the station waiting for the call-out which duly came ten mintues later.

An exhausted and still frightened Pee Wee arrived home about six in the morning. He called out Beulah's name, then Julius's. When he didn't get a reply to either he went out to the shelter in the back from which came the sound of Beulah snoring.

That made him smile as he poked his head into the entrance. 'Beulah, wake up, hon. Wake up.'

She did so with a grunt. 'That you, Pee Wee?'

'Sure is.'

'What's the time?'

He glanced at his wristwatch and told her. 'You OK?'

'Yeah yeah,' she replied dismissively. 'Is Julius with you?'

'He ain't in the house so he must have hung on wherever he was when the raid started. He'll probably call or be along soon.'

Beulah crawled out of the shelter, Pee Wee helping her to her feet. 'Oohhh!' she groaned.

'What's wrong?'

'My rheumatism. It's damp in there.' She made to move, and stumbled, Pee Wee quickly catching her.

'I's stiff all over and my back aches like hell,' she complained. 'What I need is a good hot tub.'

'I'll fix one for you,' he offered.

Beulah stared up at the sky. 'That sure was one son-of-a-bitchin' clambake last night,' she declared. 'I was so scared I nearly peed my pants.'

Pee Wee ran a hand over his face; he was dog tired. 'I had to walk back,' he said. 'Couldn't get a cab no way.'

'You must be bushed?'

'I am. Bushed as can be.'

Beulah glanced over at their house, and then next door to where the Sykeses lived. There was no apparent damage to either that she could make out. In the confusion of the night before, and shut up in the shelter, it had been difficult to know where the bombs were landing.

'Let's get some coffee,' she said.

'There's nothin shamin' in changin' your mind you know,' Pee Wee declared over their second cup.

Beulah stared blankly at him. 'What you talkin' about?'

'Stayin' on here. In London that is. It wouldn't be no sweat for Julius to arrange a boat for us. We could be back in the good ole US of A before the month is out.'

She regarded him steadily. 'That what you want, Pee Wee?'

'Want? I told you before, hon, it ain't what I want. It's what you want that matters.'

Beulah would never have admitted it, but during the height of the raid she actually had considered returning. 'I'm stayin' put,' she declared stubbornly. 'As long as Julius is here then I stays with him.'

Pee Wee sighed, he'd thought that's what she'd say. 'That's OK by me then.'

'You sure? I won't take offence if . . .'

'I said it's OK by me, Beulah,' he interjected. 'And I means it. Sheet! We been married too long for me to go off leavin' you now. What kinda man you take me for?'

She gave him a broad, loving smile. 'The best kind, Pee Wee. But then I've always known that. The very best kind.'

Reaching across he took hold of her hand and squeezed it. 'You too, hon. A lady of the first water.'

At which point their conversation was interrupted by a call from Julius to tell them he was safe, and how were they?

'I'll fix you that tub,' Pee Wee said to Beulah when, much relieved, she came off the telephone. 'Then I gotta hit the sack before I falls over.'

'You want me to come with you? I could use some more sleep. It sure was uncomfortable in that shelter, and that's a fact.'

'I couldn't think of anythin' nicer.'

'Hell no,' she agreed, and they both laughed.

What they'd just experienced was the first night of what was to become known as the Blitz.

'That was only the start you know,' Albert said wearily, sinking into a chair, having just come off shift.

'Was it bad for you?'

He shook his head. 'But it must have been for the poor buggers who do the Docks area. They took a real pounding. The figures are unofficial, but I'm told there are hundreds dead. Between three and four by all accounts. And that's only the dead, not the injured.'

A great feeling of sadness settled over Jess. All those lives! 'Would you like some breakfast?'

'What have you got?'

'Powdered egg.'

He groaned. 'Better than nothing I suppose.'

'I'll put the kettle on.'

Jess was in the middle of cooking, wishing she had some bacon to go with the egg but that wasn't to be had for love nor money, when Ellie arrived in. 'I could use some of that tea, Mum. I'm dry as a bone.'

Jess set out a fresh cup and saucer. 'How did your night go?'

'Not too bad, considering. A stray stick of bombs fell over the Cally Road way, but luckily landed mostly on waste ground. There were only a few casualties, and none of them serious.'

Albert glanced around. 'Paul gone to school?'

'He went and hasn't come back, so it must be open,' Jess replied.

'How's he?'

'Very frightened at the start of the raid, then we went into the shelter and he thought that was a great adventure. Said it was just like camping.'

Albert laughed. 'Trust him.'

'Egg for you, Ellie?'

'It's powdered,' Albert informed his daughter, screwing up his face.

'I'm not really that hungry, Mum. Toast will do. Is there any jam?'

Jess shook her head. 'It's finished and we won't get our next allocation till Friday. So you'll have to do without I'm afraid.'

Ellie shrugged; they were getting used to having to do without thanks to the severe rationing in place. 'The last lot wasn't all that nice anyway. Tasted funny.'

Jess had heard the rumour going round that jam was now being made out of turnips and swede instead of fruit, but decided not to mention that. They griped enough about powdered egg and the ubiquitous Spam.

Albert glanced at the mantelpiece clock. 'Let's hear the news and what they have to say about last night. Ellie, you're closest.'

Ellie switched on the wireless set, the news predictably dominated by the air raid.

It had been a frantic morning for Julius, his phone ringing seemingly non-stop. He absent-mindedly stroked his chin where he'd nicked it when using Marybeth's unfamiliar razor.

After their lovemaking they'd gone down to the basement where they'd spent the duration of the raid with other inhabitants of the apartment block. At one point, when there had been something of a lull in the bombing, he'd nipped back upstairs for bedding which he and Marybeth had wrapped round themselves before finally going to sleep sitting propped up against a wall.

Julius smiled to himself. On arriving at the Embassy the word had been that the Ambassador had decamped for safety reasons to a house in Windsor. The majority of staff had thought that funny, if cynically so. Wasn't it just like Joe Kennedy to hightail it at the first sign of danger with scant regard for those he'd left behind in the hot seat?

Julius sat back in his chair and closed his eyes. Christ, but he was tired. Between Marybeth and the raid he hadn't gotten much sleep, a couple of hours at most, if that.

Walter Zwicke frowned as Julius lit a cigarette. 'Do you have to do that in here?' he asked waspishly.

That surprised Julius, for Zwicke had never previously complained about his smoking. 'You got a problem with it, Walter?'

'I've never mentioned, but I do suffer from asthma. Not badly, but I'm a sufferer nonetheless.'

Anyone else and Julius would have immediately put out his cigarette, but not with Zwicke. His aversion to the man grew with almost every passing day. The guy was a slimeball. A real jerkoff.

'You married, Walter?' he queried, evading the subject of smoking.

Zwicke blinked. 'As a matter of fact I'm not.'

'It's just, that's something else you've never mentioned. I reckoned you probably weren't.'

'I guess the right little lady has never happened along. Leastways, not so far,' Zwicke smiled.

Zwicke was lying about being asthmatic, Julius just knew that to be so. He probably simply didn't like being round smokers, that's all. Well, tough shit.

'So why London during a war?' Julius probed. 'Were you posted here?'

Zwicke shook his head. 'It was volunteers only. I reckoned it would be a great help to being promoted. Hell, it must look good on your record, don't you think?'

Julius had to agree with that. 'And you're ambitious?'

'You got it. I want to go straight to the top. Be a main man. How about you?'

Julius considered that. 'Yes and no I suppose. If it happens, fine. If not, well I can live with that. I'm not the pushy sort if that's what you mean.'

Zwicke frowned, being pushy was second nature to him. Julius made it sound as if it was wrong. A fault of some kind.

Julius took a deep drag on his cigarette, then slowly exhaled, enjoying Zwick's look of irritation.

'How's Marybeth?' Zwicke suddenly inquired.

'Jim Dandy.'

'As I said before, she sure is some good-looking dame. You're to be envied.'

Julius couldn't stop himself, Zwicke was beginning to show an overkeen interest in Marybeth. 'By you?'

Zwicke laughed. 'By any red-blooded guy I'd imagine.'

Neatly dodged, Julius thought. A politician's answer. 'Yeah, I guess you're right.'

'Wonderful ass.'

That jolted Julius, finding it insulting. It was Zwicke's tone of voice, a combination of licentiousness and sleaze that made the so-called compliment sound dirty.

Julius didn't reply.

Zwicke glanced at his wristwatch. 'Hey, look at the time! I got a meeting. Catch you again later.'

Julius watched Zwicke hurry from the office, wondering about the man.

Wondering.

It was bedlam in the Casualty Department, wounded people sitting and lying absolutely everywhere. The atmosphere was one of pain coupled with despair.

'Set her down,' Ellie instructed Josie Farnham who was

partnering her in the makeshift ambulance she'd been given to drive. Gingerly they laid the stretcher they were carrying, and the patient on it, on the floor.

A Nursing Sister walked briskly over. 'How many have you got?' she demanded brusquely.

'Four, including this one,' Ellie replied. 'The other three can walk but need help to get in here.'

Sister nodded and glanced down at the young woman on the stretcher who was unconscious and groaning piteously. Both legs had been blown away at the knee, the wounds temporarily bandaged by Ellie herself.

Sister squatted and made a hasty examination. She knew from experience, and because all the available doctors were already working flat out, that the woman hadn't a hope of surviving.

Standing, she glanced around. 'Find a space somewhere and put her there,' she instructed. 'Then bring in the others.'

For a brief moment a look of terrible hopelessness crossed Sister's face, then it was gone, her professional, no-nonsense expression back in place.

'Right,' she said, and left them.

'You heard her,' Ellie nodded to Josie. Picking up the stretcher again they carried it to the first available space where they made the young woman as comfortable as they could.

Ellie stared at the still groaning young girl, wishing there was more she could do. But there wasn't. At least the woman was unconscious, which was something of a blessing.

When the three walking wounded had been brought in and deposited Ellie whispered to Josie that she had to go to the bathroom. She'd be out in a minute or two.

On entering the bathroom she locked herself in a cubicle and, leaning over the bowl, threw up.

Somewhere someone was shrieking in agony.

Hazel was taken aback as Ellie came into the pub next morning when they'd only been open ten minutes.

'I need a drink,' Ellie declared, slumping onto a bar stool. 'Large gin and orange please.'

'At this time?'

Ellie nodded. 'I've just come off duty. My first night at the sharp end.' She shuddered, then said in a whisper, 'It was terrible. Ghastly. You've no idea.'

Hazel poured the drink and placed it in front of Ellie who immediately had a swallow. 'Do you know Mackenzie Road?'

'Of course.'

'Well, it isn't there any more. The whole street was flattened. We think the Jerries must have been after the power station there. Well, they got it.'

Ellie took another swig. 'There were bodies everywhere, Hazel. And bits of bodies, arms, legs.' She halted for a second, then croaked, 'I saw a decapitated head. It was just lying on the pavement, eyes open, the expression one of surprise. He'd been an old man with white hair.'

Ellie finished her drink and fumbled for her cigarettes. Her hands were shaking as she lit up.

'Another?'

'Please.'

Hazel was doing that when she remembered. 'I found something of yours,' she said.

'Oh?'

Hazel gave Ellie her drink, then went to a drawer. 'Your engagement ring,' she declared, laying it beside Ellie's glass.

Ellie had forgotten all about the lost ring. 'Where was it?'

'On one of the shelves. God knows how it got there or wasn't found when we were searching. But you've got it back now.'

Ellie stared at the ring, remembering, thinking of George.

'It's a keepsake if nothing else,' Hazel sympathised. 'And worth a bob or two if you want to sell it.'

'Yes,' Ellie agreed dully. It was both of these things.

'Do you want to talk some more about last night?'

Ellie shook her head.

'Be alone?'

'Not really. But I'd better get back, Mum will be worried.'

Hazel patted Ellie on the hand and then turned away to get on with things.

Outside again, Ellie took the ring from her coat pocket and crossed to the nearest drain. The diamonds twinkled briefly in the harsh morning light before vanishing into the depths below.

Chapter 17

Try as he might Julius just couldn't get comfortable, the platform at Victoria tube station unyielding beneath his backside. He reckoned he was one of several hundred spending the night on that particular platform.

The air was hot, and smelly, some of the latter from the tube itself, but mainly arising from the heavy concentration of bodies.

Earlier in the day he'd been sent to Windsor with several highly classified documents for the Ambassador. Having delivered them safely he'd started back, only to break down close to the station after nightfall.

He knew what was wrong with his car and could easily have fixed it himself, but when he'd opened the hood, and switched on his flashlight, an irate ARP Warden had materialised seemingly out of nowhere screaming, 'Put that light out!'

Explanation, even argument and showing his diplomatic credentials, had been useless. The Warden had insisted the flashlight stay off, and if he disregarded that the police would be summoned.

Not wishing to be involved in a police incident, which would be embarrassing, Julius had been left with two choices. Either try to walk home, which would have been a total nightmare in the black-out, or else spend the night in the tube and fix his car come daylight. He'd decided on the tube as the sensible thing.

He spotted a young girl staring at him, and guessed it was because he was black, the girl quickly turning away when he smiled.

Marybeth was going to be wondering what had happened when he didn't show, having arranged to take her out. Wondering? She'd probably be livid thinking he'd deliberately stood her up. Marybeth could be very unreasonable at times and had a ferocious temper.

He thought about the documents he'd delivered to the Ambassador skulking out at Windsor away from the dangers of the Blitz. He didn't know why, but he'd gotten the distinct impression something was wrong, and that the documents were closely related to whatever it was. The atmosphere in the Ambassador's residence had been unusual to say the least.

How incredibily resilient these people were, Julius reflected, gazing about him. None of them seemed in the least way put out at having to spend their night like this. He knew from the newspapers that this was a common occurrence for many of them, and not a one-off as it was for him. You simply had to admire their fortitude and ability to just get on with things no matter what. He couldn't imagine Americans being the same way. But then the English prided themselves in being called the bulldog breed, he could see now how apt that nickname was.

And then he spotted them, his jaw almost dropping open in amazement. A young couple, covered by a blanket so that only their heads remained visible, were, and there was no doubt about it, actually having sex, their bodies moving slowly and rhythmically together.

'Holy shit!' he swore softly, unable to believe his eyes. How could they, surrounded as they were by so many other people, in full view of all, actually do that, the act of utmost intimacy. It was mind-boggling.

Julius shook his head in bewilderment. Where was the famous English reserve he'd heard so much about before leaving the States? Another casualty of war perhaps, if it had indeed ever existed at all.

He tore his eyes away to look elsewhere, that being the least he could do, the decent thing.

'Holy shit,' he repeated, stunned.

He couldn't wait to tell Marybeth. She'd scream with laughter.

And she did.

Jess groped for the candle she'd extinguished several hours previously and the box of matches beside it. Moments later the candle flickered into life lighting up the inside of the shelter. An eerie interior where shadows danced with every movement she made.

She couldn't sleep; try as she might she just hadn't been able to drop off. Not helped by the far-off crump of exploding bombs and the rattle of incessant ack-ack fire.

Paul, tucked up warmly, was gently snoring. His innocent face might have been that of a cherub fallen to earth.

Reaching across she gently ran a hand over his hair, smiling to think of how much she loved this darling son of hers. How like his father in looks he was fast becoming. The spit, a chip off the old block. She must mention that to Albert when he got home off shift.

Her own face clouded over to think of Albert and Ellie out there in the middle of what was going on. What a worry it was, a sick pain that gnawed at her insides and stretched her nerves almost to breaking point.

She'd developed the art of not showing too much concern when they arrived back from work; they'd had enough to deal with without her adding to the problem. But they both knew what she went through, of course they did. Especially Albert.

She glanced at the wind-up bedside clock she always brought into the shelter with her. Twenty past three, hours to go yet before the nightly ordeal would be over and they could return to the house.

She shivered for, despite having several cardigans on, she was still cold. This wouldn't have been so bad in summertime, but it was mid November and the weather that went with that. Perhaps she could lay her hands on a small paraffin stove somewhere. Though getting the paraffin would be difficult. It, like everything else, was scarce. And undoubtedly horrendously expensive if she did find some.

There was always the black market of course, but Albert wouldn't allow her to buy from that, he being dead against it. Every spiv dealing in the black market should be taken out and shot, he'd declared more than once. There again, he wasn't the one having to endure this damn shelter night after night. God bless him.

Outside the bombs continued to fall and the ack-ack rattle.

Albert had never seen anything like it. From where he was standing it seemed as if all of London was ablaze. The sweat was running off him in rivers.

The Islington Fire Service had been called in to help the City of London Fire Service. His understanding was that Moorgate, Aldgate, Cannon Street and Old Street were taking the full brunt of what was the heaviest attack yet. Building after building, whole streets of them, had already been devastated. And still the conflagrations raged despite the Herculean efforts being made to bring them under control.

In front of Albert and the others was a wall of flame, a great beast intent on devouring all in its path. More fires, none of them small, burned fiercely all around.

'Parachute mines!' someone shouted. And there they were, serenely floating downwards, all with a lethal load of explosives attached.

From overhead came the drone of the German planes, their pilots being guided from afar by the extent and ferocity of the blaze.

Danny McGiver cursed volubly as the hose he was holding and directing at the fire suddenly ran dry, the water source having been used up.

'Look out!' Henry Leway screamed at Albert as a nearby office block buckled and began to crash earthwards, great chunks of masonry flying and bouncing in all directions.

Percy Noble was running to help Danny when the ground opened up beneath his feet and, with a yell, he disappeared from sight. A sheet of flame roared up from the hole into which Percy had fallen.

Jess was a bag of nerves, Albert and Ellie should have been home hours ago and still there wasn't any sign of them. She worried a nail, a habit she'd recently got into.

She started a little later at the sound of the front door opening, then closing again. It was Ellie who entered the kitchen.

'You're late,' Jess declared unnecessarily.

Ellie sank into a chair where she ran a hand over her soot-blackened face.

'And where's your dad? That's what I want to know,' Jess went on, a tremble in her voice.

'He's probably still down at Moorgate,' Ellie replied. 'I saw him there earlier.'

Jess frowned. 'Moorgate?'

Ellie explained what had happened, words failing her when she tried to describe the sheer immensity of the fires that had been raging there and elsewhere.

'Dear God,' Jess whispered, horror-struck.

'I've been to-ing and fro-ing to the hospitals all night long,' Ellie said. 'The casualties were never-ending.'

'Many killed?'

Ellie nodded. 'Hundreds from what I could gather. And I presume those are just the ones we know about.'

Jess took a few moments to digest that. 'But your father's safe?'

'He was when I saw him. I don't think he noticed me though. He was too busy at the time.'

Jess's expression became sympathetic. 'You look dead beat.'

Ellie yawned. 'I am. All I want to do is crawl into bed and sleep for a week at least.'

Jess could understand that. 'Would you like something to eat?'

Ellie shook her head. 'The mobile canteens were out in force with cups of tea and sandwiches for whoever wanted them. I had a bite before my last run to a hospital. That'll do for now.'

'Then up you go to bed. And wash your face first. It's filthy.'

'I'm not surprised,' Ellie muttered, thinking she didn't give a toss what she looked like. All she craved was sleep, and hoped she didn't have nightmares about what she'd just been through and witnessed, knowing some of the scenes from the previous night would stay vividly etched in her mind till her own dying day.

Ellie had been in bed for nearly an hour before Albert arrived home to slump into the same chair she had.

'Ellie told me about it,' Jess said. 'She saw you earlier.'

Albert glanced up at her, his face strained and haggard. 'We lost Percy Noble. Poor bastard.'

Jess had met Percy on several occasions but couldn't say she knew him well. 'He was married, wasn't he?'

Albert slowly nodded. 'Wife and four kids. The youngest only a nipper.'

'Would you like a cup of tea?' she asked grimly.

'Please. That would be lovely.'

She filled the kettle and put it on. 'I take it you're not hurt in any way?'

'No. Danny McGiver got a bit burnt though. Nothing serious.'

That was a relief. 'Do you want to go to bed right away, or stay up for a while?'

He sighed, a sigh that seemed to come from the very depths of his being. 'No bed for me. I'm due back in two hours, so I'll just have a doze in this chair.'

'Two hours! But you've only just come off,' she protested.

He was only too well aware of that. 'Fires are still burning, Jess. We have to return and assist those still at the scene.'

What could she say? Nothing. It was his job and he had to do what had to be done. 'Was it really as awful as Ellie described?' she asked softly.

Albert's eyes momentarily clouded over in memory. 'It was . . . it was . . .' He broke off and shook his head. 'Monumental,' he said at last. 'An ocean of flame stretching as far as the eye could see. I honestly don't think London can take another night like it.'

Jess went to him and kissed him on the forehead. 'I'm sorry about Percy. He seemed a decent man to me.'

'He was. I trusted him with my life, and have done on occasion. He'll be sorely missed at the station.'

Jess busied herself with the tea things. 'How about some breakfast?' she asked over her shoulder as the tea was mashing.

There was no reply.

Turning she found Albert was already fast asleep, his head lolling to one side.

She was tempted not to, but knew he'd be furious if she didn't, so she woke him when it was time to go back to the station.

Josie Farnham glanced at her watch, and frowned. Twenty past ten and no bombing yet, what was going on? 'Do you think it's possible they're not coming tonight?' she queried hopefully of Ellie.

There were eight of them present, four playing rummy, two others immersed in books.

Ellie shrugged. 'Search me. I don't know.'

'It's beginning to look like it.'

Ellie thought about that. 'Maybe it's bad weather over the Channel?'

'Could be.'

'There again, perhaps they're on their way even now. Changing tactics by coming later than usual.

Ellie hesitated, then said slowly, 'I wonder . . .'

'What?'

'According to the papers and news broadcasts our boys have been giving them a right pasting when they reach the coast. Maybe they've halted for a while to regroup, or assemble new planes to replace the many they've lost.'

'If that's true,' Josie mused. 'Who knows what's true any more? If the figures put out are right then we've already shot down the entire Luftwaffe twice over.'

Ellie laughed. 'Maybe somebody can't count?'

Josie also laughed. 'Maybe that's so.'

Josie settled into a chair and picked up her knitting. She was making a pullover for her brother in the Army, though since the Blitz had started she'd hardly made any progress with it.

When midnight came and went the general agreement was it was going to be a raid-free night. For which they were all profoundly grateful.

'I'm not going!' Paul declared, his face screwed up in defiance. 'You can't make me. I'll run away if you do.'

'Enough of your cheek,' Albert growled. 'I won't have you speaking to us like that. We're your parents, don't forget.'

Paul sobbed and, running to Jess, buried his face in her skirt.

The cause of all this was the letter they'd received from Paul's school. Many of the children originally evacuated had returned home and now the authorities wanted to re-evacuate them. This time, which they hadn't been informed before, the children's destination was to be Lincolnshire.

'There there, don't get yourself into such a state,' Jess crooned, stroking Paul's hair. She didn't want him to go either. That was the last thing she wanted after his experience with the Sellys.

'Albert?'

He was at a loss what to do for the best. It was over a week now since the bombing had stopped, and life had more or less returned to normal. Well, normal for wartime that is. For the time being at least, London was relatively safe again.

Albert could plainly see how distressed Paul was at the thought of going away again, and he could hardly blame him after the Sellys. That had been awful for the lad and it had made him extremely angry when Jess had told him about it. The boy had been treated virtually like slave labour. On the other hand, as Jess had pointed out, that was the way of things for young-sters in the country.

'I don't know,' he said at last.

'Please, Dad?' Paul whimpered, his face now tear-streaked.

'What do you think, Jess?'

She felt Paul's grip tightening on her skirt. 'It's so difficult, Albert.'

He couldn't have agreed more. The trouble was, he firmly believed this was only a temporary lull in the bombing and that it would soon start again. But he might be wrong.

'It was horrible in Devon,' an anguished Paul choked. 'And I missed you both so much. I was promised cowboys and indi-ans, and all sorts, but it was only hard work.'

Albert listened to that with a sinking feeling in the pit of his stomach. He remembered only too well the rosy picture of life in Devon that he'd painted for Paul to persuade him to go. A rosy picture that couldn't have been more untrue. Who was to say things would be any different in Lincolnshire, another rural community.

Albert took a deep breath. All his instincts told him Paul should leave the city, but what effect would that have on the boy, not to mention Jess, after what had gone on before? 'I just don't know what to do,' he confessed.

'Then let him stay,' Jess said quietly.

Paul sobbed again, this time in relief.

'Are you sure, Jess?'

She looked down at her son, then again at Albert. 'It'll break my heart if he goes. Truly it will.'

Moments ticked by while Albert and Jess stared at one anoth-er. He knew she meant what she said, literally. He couldn't do that to Jess, not in a million years.

'All right,' he agreed.

Jess quickly knelt and gathered Paul into her arms. And now it was she who cried.

Albert prayed they weren't making a mistake.

Marybeth came into Julius's office and closed the door behind her. 'Where's Zwicke?' she queried, Julius being alone.

'Gone to a meeting with one of the Russian attachés. Why?'

She crossed over and sat on the edge of his desk. 'Heard the latest scuttlebutt?'

'Which is?'

'Kennedy is bein' recalled to Washington.'

'Aaahhh!' Julius exhaled, and laid down his pen. Now this was news. 'Are you sure?'

She shrugged. 'I said scuttlebutt, nothing's official yet. But I'm told it came from an impeccable source in the British Government.'

Who would be well pleased, Julius thought, Kennedy being no friend of theirs. He couldn't help but wonder if Churchill himself was behind Kennedy being recalled, *if* it was true. 'Any idea who the new guy might be?'

Marybeth shook her head. 'Nothin' on that so far. Though the appointment must have been made by now.'

Julius couldn't say he was sorry to see the back of Kennedy, who hadn't been popular with many of the staff, especially those, and he was one of them, who liked England and the English.

Julius then remembered the documents he'd taken out to Windsor and the unusual atmosphere he'd encountered. Could it be one of them was the actual document informing Kennedy he was being recalled? It was certainly a possibility.

'I wonder who it will be?' Marybeth mused. 'The new guy I mean.'

Julius had no answer to that. Any name he might come up with would be sheer speculation. He only hoped whoever it was would be better-suited to the post, by which he meant more sympathetic to the English, than Kennedy had been. However, they were getting beyond themselves here. They didn't know for certain Kennedy was going. So far it was only rumour.

'I was thinkin' about you earlier,' Marybeth smiled at Julius. 'Which is the real reason I'm here.'

'Oh?'

'Why don't we go away for a weekend together? Get out of London and into the countryside. I thought we could book into one of those quaint old English taverns with a thatched roof and crazy beams everywhere. What do you say?'

Julius sat back in his chair and studied Marybeth. She was becoming even more clinging of late, even more demanding of his time. Nonetheless, the idea appealed. 'Anywhere specific in mind?'

'Not really. I'll leave that up to you. You're the guy after all. You make the arrangements. Just one thing though, we register as Mr and Mrs Poston. I'm not havin' any of that shit with separate bedrooms, the English bein' so prudish and all.'

'You'll have to wear a weddin' ring to pull that off,' he pointed out.

'Don't worry, hon. That'll be my department. When we leave I'll be wearin' a gold band. Bet your sweet butt I will.'

He continued to study her, noting the amused glint in her eyes. Why, oh why, did he feel there was some secret agenda here?

Imagination, he decided, shrugging off the notion. And he certainly could use the break. 'Any weekend?' he queried.

She nodded. 'Just say the word and off we toddle.'

'I'll get onto it then.'

Bending over she kissed him on the lips. 'You do that.'

After she'd gone he made a note in his diary before resuming the work she'd interrupted.

'Gosh!' Paul exclaimed, eyes popping. 'Are you sure they're real?'

Eddy Ackworth, long since having recovered from his

meningitis, and also returned to Islington, nodded vigorously. 'Cannon shells from a Jerry fighter.' He pointed. 'Look, you can see the Jerry writing.'

A well-impressed Paul could indeed see the strange, Gothic lettering. 'Where did you get them?'

'Found them of course. They were lying in the road close to a bombed-out house. I searched all around but couldn't find any more.'

Paul gazed at the shells in awe.

'Mickey Silver has a parachute from a mine that was dropped that never went off. The soldiers who defused the mine left it behind.'

Paul was green with envy, desperately wanting a souvenir for himself.

Eddy put the shells away in his pocket. 'What do you want to play at?'

Paul shrugged.

'Shall we get the tyres out?'

Paul thought that was a good idea. 'All right.'

The tyres in question were old ones from cars which they played with by propelling them along the road using the palm of a hand. Sometimes they used a stick instead of their hand. It just depended.

'Let's go then.'

The tyres were kept in a shed at the rear of Eddy's house which was four streets away. All the way there, and for the rest of that morning, Paul couldn't help thinking enviously of the shells and parachute.

A laughing Marybeth collapsed onto the large antique bed that dominated their bedroom. An amused Julius came and sat beside her. 'What's brought this on?'

'I don't know. I'm just enjoyin' myself, I guess. Today's been fun.'

'For me too,' he smiled.

'Those English lanes are wonderful to walk along and the

olde worlde decor of this place just blows my mind.' Then, seductively, 'But most of all I'm enjoyin' just bein' with you.'

'And I with you,' he further smiled, standing up. 'Let me put some more logs on the fire and then we'll turn in. OK?'

'Oh yes,' she breathed, a voice filled with sexual promise.

'You use the bathroom first then. Sorry it's along the corridor, but that's how it is.'

Marybeth collected what she needed and left him attending to the fire.

She'd do what she intended when it was his turn in the bathroom.

Marybeth was already in bed when he returned, her smile catlike and full of anticipation. She'd turned off all the lights except the bedside one. The fire, with the guard securely in place, crackled merrily.

She watched him undress, admiring the lean and taut body that she knew so well. She squeezed her thighs together, eager for what was coming next.

'Shit,' Julius exclaimed softly a few moments later, rummaging through his bag.

'What's wrong, hon?'

'I can't find the rubbers. I'm sure I packed them.'

Of course he wouldn't find them, she gloated. She'd already removed them and hidden them in her own bag. 'If you packed them they must be there,' she declared disingenuously.

He kept on rummaging, to no avail. 'Son of a bitch,' he swore.

'No luck?'

Making a face, he looked at her and shook his head. 'I'm certain I packed them. I can remember doing it.'

'Well, you're obviously mistaken.'

'Sorry, hon,' he said, going to the bed and getting in.

'That's all right. It doesn't matter.'

'Honest?'

'Honest,' she lied.

She switched off the bedside light and snuggled up close. 'Why don't you kiss me?'

As their lips met she ran a finger down the crack of his buttocks, delighted at the reaction it had when she felt a nudge on her leg. He'd always been quick like that.

'No, hon, sorry,' Julius apologised, drawing slightly apart. 'I hate disappointin' you but I can't without a rubber.'

'Of course you can,' she husked, fondling him.

He was tempted, sweet Jesus he was. But common sense managed to override that. 'What if somethin' should happen?'

'It won't,' she replied glibly.

'But it could.'

Her hands were now moving everywhere, urging, caressing, stroking, everything she could think of to make him throw caution to the wind, her own need growing with every passing second.

Julius groaned; if only he could have bought some more rubbers, but that was impossible this time of night, especially in the deepest countryside. And tomorrow was Sunday, everything would be shut.

'We can't stop now, hon. We can't,' she pleaded.

It took every ounce of his willpower, but he managed it. With a muffled exclamation he rolled out of bed and onto his feet. 'I said no, Marybeth, and I mean it. Now you cool down a bit and I'll do the same. We just can't take the risk and that's all there is to it.'

She knew there was no persuading him, the moment having come and gone.

She was absolutely livid. Her plan had failed.

Chapter 18

'We've had terrible rows about it,' Beulah declared. 'But I'm just not sleepin' in that damn shelter any more. It wasn't built for someone my size anyway.'

Jess nodded her sympathy, having dropped by for a chat as she hadn't seen Beulah for several days.

'It's also playin' murder with my rheumatism being out there where it's hellish damp. So I told Pee Wee, that's it. My fat ass stays in here at night-time and if I get blown to kingdom come, then so be it, goddamn it.'

Jess had to smile at Beulah's colourful language, even if she didn't approve of it. But that was Beulah for you and her friend was American so you had to make allowances for the cultural differences.

'What about you, Jess, doesn't it bother you?'

'Our shelter isn't that damp,' Jess replied truthfully. 'Not that you'd really notice it. And I can't say I have all that much trouble getting in and out.'

Beulah sighed. 'That's because you're a stick compared to me, honey. You don't know how much I envy you that. There was a time you know, yeah, there was a time. But Pee Wee swears he likes me as I am, so who am I to argue?'

'It is a lot safer out there, don't forget,' Jess tentatively pointed out.

'That's what Pee Wee says. But then I remind him he don't have no rheumatism. Fit as a fiddle that man. Yes sir. And another thing I remind him, his ass ain't as humongous as mine. Why, when I'm in there I feel that if I stood up I'd take the whole goddamn shelter with me. And what if I get stuck with no Pee Wee to help, what then?'

'He does come home every morning, he'd find you,' Jess smiled.

'I don't want him to find me stuck like that. It would be humiliatin', that's what. Humiliatin'.'

Jess had a sudden thought. 'What about Julius? Where does he sleep then?'

'He keeps real weird hours. Ain't home most of the time. And if he is home night-time he sleeps in his own bed because he knows there really ain't room in the shelter for the pair of us.'

Jess could understand that. Without being cruel, Beulah was an extremely large lady, more than built for comfort. 'How about Pee Wee's band, are they still getting good audiences?' Jess asked, changing the subject.

'Sure am. Even durin' all that bombin' the band played on and the audiences stayed right in their seats. There again, there ain't been no bombs fallen on Soho yet, so probably that's a factor.'

'And he's still enjoying it?'

'Loves every moment. Loves English audiences. Thinks they're wonderful.'

'That's good,' Jess nodded.

'Don't even get homesick, which surprises the hell out of me. I know I do. Sometimes real bad. Nothin' to do with you English or England, it's simply there ain't no place like home as the sayin' goes.'

Jess could well understand that. She couldn't imagine living abroad, in someone else's country. Nor would she want to live in another part of the country. She was a Londoner through and through and an Islingtonian first and foremost.

'Hey, you want a cup of chocolate? I got that,' Beulah asked.

Jess's face lit up. 'Oh Beulah, have you really?'

'Sure have.'

'There hasn't been drinking chocolate in the shops for months. Plus lots of other things.'

Beulah winked. 'That Julius of mine comes in real handy at times. I don't think there's nothin' he can't get out the Embassy. Which reminds me.'

She went to a cupboard and opened it. 'For you, hon.'

Jess gasped as a large tin of ham was placed in front of her. It was her entire family meat ration for two months at least. Maybe longer. 'I can't take that, Beulah!'

'You sure can, sweetie pie. You don't want to upset me none, do you?'

Jess shook her head.

'Then you take it.' She returned to the cupboard to produce more tinned foodstuffs. 'And these.'

There were apricots, raspberries, carrots, potatoes, all sorts. 'Oh Beulah!'

Beulah filled the kettle and put it on. 'And I know Julius is gettin' some more cigarettes for Ellie, so you can tell her that.'

'How can I thank you. How can *we* thank you?'

'Don't need no thanks. We're friends, Jess, that's all that matters.'

Jess watched Beulah spoon two large measures of chocolate into cups, her mouth watering at the prospect of this unexpected treat. 'There's something I've been meaning to ask you for a while, it's been puzzling me.'

'Shoot.'

'Pee Wee means small, is that right?'

Beulah nodded.

'But he isn't. I mean, he's not exactly tall, but he's not small either.'

An amused glint came into Beulah's eyes. 'It's a joke, hon,

given him by members of a band he belonged to years ago.'

Jess was still mystified. 'Oh?'

'You see, it's just the opposite. He ain't small, but real big. And I mean *real* big. Where it counts.'

It took a moment for the penny to drop, then Jess's face flamed scarlet.

Beulah burst into cackling laughter.

'Hi, stranger!'

Ellie, standing at the bar of The Florence, found a smiling Julius beside her. 'Why hello. I haven't seen you in ages.'

'Been busy. You know how it is?'

She did indeed.

'Can I buy you a drink?'

'It's me who should buy you one, Julius, as a thank you for those cigarettes you dropped off at the house.'

'Another time, Ellie, the drinks are on me tonight. I'm celebratin'.'

He gestured Harry over and ordered a repeat screwdriver for Ellie, large he insisted, and a double scotch for himself plus a pint of best.

'Can I ask what you're celebrating?'

His expression immediately became coy. 'It's Embassy stuff, Ellie.'

She nodded. 'I see. So you can't tell me.'

He considered that. 'Maybe I can. It's going to be in the newspapers tomorrow anyhow. A new Ambassador has taken over from the old one who leaves tonight for the States. The new guy's called Winant. John G. Winant.'

She regarded him keenly. 'Do I take it you didn't like the old one then?'

Julius took out a cigar case, extracted one and then clipped it. 'It wasn't that exactly. I just didn't think him the right man for this particular job. Hopefully Winant will be better.'

Their drinks arrived which he paid for. 'Want to sit down?'

She had no objections to that, pleased Julius had turned up.

She always enjoyed his company, he was so easy and relaxing to be with.

'Talkin' of jobs, how's the ambulance business?' he queried.

Ellie lit a cigarette. 'Not too busy at the moment, I'm happy to say. Nothing like when the bombing was going on. That was horrendous.'

'Yeah, I guess.' She looked older, he reflected. Somehow more mature. And there was a new depth in her eyes that hadn't been there before, the result of her recent experiences he presumed. He felt himself in the presence of a woman as opposed to a young lady.

'And the drivin'?'

She laughed. 'Oh that's come on by leaps and bounds. I'm quite the expert nowadays.'

'And modest with it,' he teased drily.

'Of course.'

A neighbour came into the pub and waved to Ellie. She waved back. 'I'm driving an American vehicle at the moment,' she informed Julius.

That interested him. 'Really?'

'A Buick eight that's been converted into what's referred to as a regulation multi-purpose box van mode. The only trouble is it's a left-hand drive, but I've learned to cope with that. God alone knows where the car came from in the first place, but I've been landed with it.'

'Good cars Buicks,' Julius commented. He'd driven one himself for a while in the States.

'How about you?' she asked. 'Is it this change over of Ambassador that's making you so busy?'

'Partly.'

She could see he didn't want to elaborate on that. 'How's the girlfriend?'

'You mean Marybeth? Fine, I guess.' He frowned, thinking of the weekend they'd had away together. What a disaster that had been. All day Sunday she'd been cold as ice to him.

'Why the furrowed brow? Is it to do with Marybeth?'

He took his time in replying. 'Yeah, she and I don't see eye to eye on certain things.'

'Oh?'

He wasn't sure he wanted to explain this to Ellie, then decided he would confide in her. 'It's simple really. She wants to get married and have kids. I don't.'

Ellie had a sip of her drink, followed by a puff on her cigarette. 'Is that because you don't want to get married in general,' she asked slowly. 'Or because of Marybeth herself?'

Julius glanced at Ellie, then away again. 'The truth is, I don't know,' he replied honestly.

'Do you love her?'

This was beginning to make him feel uncomfortable. Did he love her? Marybeth loved him, but did he love her? He'd said he did on several occasions, but had he meant it?

'Well?' Ellie prompted.

'Again, I don't know.'

'Then you don't.'

That harsh judgement startled him. 'Why do you say that?'

'Because if you did you'd know it. According to my mum anyway, she says love's unmistakable. Anything else just isn't the real thing.'

He smiled. 'Surely that's a bit black and white?'

Ellie couldn't resist the joke. 'Like you and me?'

He laughed, and so too did she. 'Sorry, I hope that wasn't offensive? It wasn't meant to be.'

'Not in the least,' he assured her. 'Yeah, like you and me.'

'So you don't love her.'

'I never said so.'

'Then you do?'

'I never said that either,' he protested.

It amused Ellie that he was floundering. 'In this country we call it sitting on the fence. Neither one thing or the other.'

'Do you indeed?'

'Yes we do.'

Julius took a deep breath. 'I certainly don't want kids. Not for now anyway. I want to be a bit older before I commit to those.'

Ellie didn't reply to that.

'The trouble is . . .' He hesitated.

'Go on.'

'Marybeth keeps tryin' to push me into marriage. Why, only recently she tried to trick me into, hopefully on her part, gettin' her pregnant.'

That shocked Ellie a little. Not everyone had her morals, she reminded herself. Connie Fox for one, Julius, it would seem, for another. 'You're sleeping with her then?'

Julius nodded. 'Have been for a long time.' He studied her face. 'You don't approve, do you?'

Ellie shrugged. 'It's none of my business.'

'But you don't approve?'

Ellie dropped her gaze to stare into her drink. 'I believe that act should be kept for the wedding night, or at least the honeymoon,' she stated quietly. 'It's how I was brought up.'

'So you didn't with George, even though you were engaged?'

She shook her head. 'There were times when he wanted to, but I wouldn't allow it. Just as well too, considering what happened. If I had I'd have felt ever so cheap when he broke it off. Cheap and degraded having squandered something that rightfully belongs to the man I presume I will marry one day.'

Julius was impressed. What a difference between Ellie and Marybeth, a difference that had absolutely nothing whatsoever to do with colour. 'Maybe you're right,' he declared.

'I am for me anyway,' she replied.

They sat for a little while in silence, each smoking and drinking, Julius contemplating his relationship with Marybeth. He and she got on well enough, most of the time anyway. And she was fabulous in bed, not to mention stunningly good-looking. But was that enough? Perhaps he was in love with her and too stubborn to admit it to himself? On the other hand, perhaps not.

'Just one thing,' Ellie said at last.

'What's that?'

'Whatever you do, don't make a mistake. You could regret it for the rest of your life.'

True, he thought. Very true. 'Another drink?' Ellie had now finished hers.

'No, I'd better be getting along. But thank you all the same.'

'My pleasure, Ellie. Any time.'

She rose from her seat. 'I'll be seeing you.'

He rose also, out of manners. 'Thanks for listenin' to me. You've been a friend.'

She smiled. 'Goodnight, Julius.'

'Goodnight, Ellie.'

He watched her walk from the pub, uneasy, and thoughtful, after their conversation. She was right of course. Did he or did he not love Marybeth?

That was the question. But one he couldn't answer.

Julius discovered it to be snowing when he left the Embassy. Shivering, he turned up the collar of his coat. Ambassador Winant had thrown a party to introduce himself to the staff, personally going round and shaking every single individual by the hand and having a few words. Julius had taken to the man right away, which he never had with Kennedy.

What had further impressed him was that Winant had refused to go and live in Windsor, setting up in an apartment adjoining the Embassy instead where his wife, still Stateside, would shortly be joining him. No bolt hole for Winant.

Julius glanced at his watch to note it was still relatively early. The arrangement was he'd go to Marybeth's place where they'd meet up later, she being detained at the Embassy with some unfinished work to do before calling it a day.

On a whim Julius decided to stop in at a little local pub that the Embassy staff used. The canapés he'd had at the party had left him with a thirst to which beer seemed the more enjoyable answer than water.

The King's Head was small and somewhat dingy, but the atmosphere was friendly enough. It also had the reputation for

selling a wonderful pint of Bass which Julius had recently developed a fondness for.

Once inside he ordered and then lit a cigarette while his pint
was being poured. He looked round in surprise when a hand
descended on his shoulder.

'All alone?' Walter Zwicke asked.

Son of a bitch, Julius inwardly cursed. Running into Zwicke
was the last thing he wanted. 'Yeah.'

'Come on over then. I got a table all to myself.'

The guy was drunk, Julius observed. 'I'm not stayin' long.'

'Don't matter,' Zwicke slurred. 'Join me anyway. You and I
should have socialised before now, sharing an office as we do.
So come on over, good buddy.'

Julius winced, loathing being called that by Zwicke. 'OK,
sure. Only for a couple of minutes though.'

'I'll have a large scotch to go with the pint,' he informed the
barmaid when she placed his Bass in front of him. He'd need
that to put up with Zwicke.

'Sorry, sir. There's none left.'

He stared at her. 'Brandy?'

She shook her head. 'We're all out of spirits and don't know
when we'll have more in. That's how it is. Sorry.'

The war of course, Julius thought. At least he wouldn't go
short, there always being plenty available at the Embassy. He
paid for his Bass and then reluctantly made his way across to
Zwicke.

'Sure love these English pubs,' Zwicke declared as Julius sat.
'They beat the hell out of the taverns we have back home.'

Julius nodded his agreement.

'Boring party I thought,' Zwicke went on. 'I made my escape
right after meeting Winant. Came in here instead.'

Julius didn't know what to say to Zwicke, doubting they had
anything in common. Apart from the job that is. And he certainly didn't want to talk about that.

'So how you doing?' Zwicke demanded.

'OK.'

'I saw Marybeth at the party. She sure is some broad that woman. Yes sir.'

'As you keep mentionin',' Julius replied evenly.

'Lovely ass.'

Julius fought back the impulse to hit Zwicke. The guy really was a chromium-plated, one-hundred-per-cent creep.

Zwicke winked salaciously. 'But then I'm not telling you anything you don't already know. Isn't that right, good buddy?'

Again Julius didn't reply, instead taking several deep swallows of his pint, desperate to get out of there as soon as he could.

Zwicke sat back and sighed. 'She was missed when she left Toronto, though not by some of the wives. No sir.'

That jolted Julius. 'What do you mean?'

Zwicke was suddenly having trouble focusing his eyes. 'What does what mean?' he hiccuped.

'Marybeth wasn't missed by some of the wives.'

'You know?'

'No, I don't.'

Zwicke shook his head. 'Shouldn't say any more. It's the liquor talking.'

Julius smiled disarmingly. 'You can tell me, in confidence of course. I'm your good buddy, remember?'

'Yeah.'

'So?' Julius pressed.

Zwicke had a mouthful from his pint. 'Sure is strong this English beer. Far stronger than back home.'

'It sure is,' Julius agreed. And Zwicke clearly hadn't gotten used to it yet. 'Marybeth?' he prompted quietly.

'Real popular she was. And friendly too. Hell, half the guys must have had a piece of her tail. More than half. Young and old.'

Julius, still smiling disarmingly, went cold all over. 'That popular, eh?'

'A floozie through and through. High-class I have to admit, but a born floozie nonetheless.'

'Married guys as well?'

'She wasn't particular about whether or not the guy was married. If she was of a mind, he got laid.'

Julius swallowed hard. 'You too?'

'Nah! I tried, Jesus I tried. But she just never took a shine to me. Couldn't understand it. Still don't. I mean, what's wrong with me? I'm no different to some of those guys.'

Julius was in a daze. He'd realised Marybeth wasn't a virgin the first time he'd slept with her, but this! It made him feel sick to his stomach.

'Even the Ambassador himself had her,' Zwicke went on. 'It was after that she got posted here. He probably wanted her out of the way. Know what I mean?'

'Yes,' Julius replied in a voice that was little more than a whisper.

'I heard she was real good too. Quite a performer. Gives one helluva blowjob.'

Julius couldn't take any more. He had to get out of there, and fast, before he lost control and beat the living shit out of Zwicke. Without uttering another word he rose and strode from the pub.

'Hey, Julius, where you going? Where you going, good buddy? You've left your beer.'

Julius didn't go to Marybeth's as they'd arranged, instead he drove straight home.

What was it Ellie had said during their conversation in The Florence? Don't make a mistake you might regret for the rest of your life.

Jesus!

It wasn't fair, it just wasn't fair at all, Paul thought bitterly as he started putting on his pyjamas. His pal Eddy Ackworth now not only had the Jerry cannon shells but a piece of Perspex, given to Eddy by his father, from the cockpit of a downed Jerry plane as well. And he didn't have one, not one, souvenir to boast about and show off.

This resentment was still churning in his mind long after Jess had kissed him goodnight and switched off the light.

It was three days now since the Ambassador's party during which Julius had succeeded in avoiding Marybeth, having lied on the telephone that feeling sick was his reason for not going to her apartment that night. Now he was there, determined to break it off for good between them.

Marybeth's face crumpled when he finished speaking, and she turned away from him. Her shoulders began to heave.

'It's all lies,' she finally croaked.

'No it isn't,' he replied patiently. 'I checked. I sent a wire to a guy I know in the Toronto Embassy and he confirmed all that Zwicke said.'

'Who was that?'

'Orin Bates. Remember him?'

She did, only too well.

'So I guess that's it.'

Marybeth crossed to a decanter of scotch and poured herself one, her hands shaking violently. When she drank some of the liquor ran down her chin.

'Don't go, please, Julius?' she pleaded.

He shook his head. 'Zwicke called you a floozie, and you've certainly acted like one. Hell, I don't want to sound self-righteous here, I'm not exactly as pure as the driven myself. I certainly have no objections to a girl havin' had a bit of experience in her past, that's only to be expected, but I'm not datin' what amounts to a goddamn amateur whore.'

Marybeth's expression was stricken, her entire body now starting to shake. 'It wasn't like that, Julius. I swear.'

'Then what was it like?'

She had another gulp of scotch. 'I was young, wild. None of it mattered, not to me anyhow. I was simply havin' a good time, enjoyin' myself.'

'Enjoyin' yourself?' He laughed cynically. 'More than that, Marybeth, far more. Half the guys in the Embassy I'm told,

young and old, includin' the Ambassador. That's not enjoyin'
yourself, that's bein' the easiest lay around. A piece of goodtime
meat for whoever happens along.'

He paused to draw breath, his emotions a combination of
anger and total contempt. 'And I want none of you.'

The tears were now freely flowing down Marybeth's face, her
body continuing to shake. 'I love you, Julius. I swear to God I
do. I want to marry you, settle down and have your children.'

He'd always thought Marybeth beautiful, but at that
moment she was as ugly as sin. Loathing rose up inside him as
he thought, pictured, what she'd been up to before they'd met.
That was something he'd never, could never, forget. 'Goodbye,'
he stated abruptly.

She gasped when he said that, then flew across the room to
grab his arm. 'Please don't go. Forgive me. Please forgive me!'

He tried to push her off but she clung tenaciously on, all the
while making gobbling sounds similar to those made by
turkeys. It was horrible.

Marybeth slid down him to latch onto a leg, wrapping her
arms tightly round it. 'Please, please,' she whimpered.

'Let go, Marybeth. Let go.'

'I love you, Julius. I love you so.'

'Well, I don't love you. Now let go, for Christsake! Keep a
little dignity.'

He somehow reached the door, although she continued to
cling fiercely onto him. He hadn't known what to expect on
coming to her apartment, but certainly not this.

He managed to open the door then attempted yet again to
prise himself free. In the end there was nothing else for it. Using
the palm of his hand he smacked her hard across the face.

Taken by surprise, and reeling from the force of the blow,
Marybeth tumbled backwards to measure her length on the
floor. Seizing his chance Julius fled, slamming the door shut
behind him.

A great agonised wail went up from her apartment as he hurried for the stairs, not daring to wait for the lift.

Only when he was back in the street did he stop and take a deep breath. That had been awful, simply awful. Pitiful too.

He had just reached his car when the air-raid sirens, silent for the past few weeks, began to howl. Moments later the first of hundreds of German planes roared overhead, ack-ack guns simultaneously bursting into action, their fiery tracers lancing skywards.

The Blitz had resumed.

Chapter 19

'Is that you, Julius?'

He looked round the kitchen, wondering where his mother's voice was coming from. 'Where are you?'

'Under the table.'

He smothered a laugh to see Beulah's large and rotund posterior protruding upwards, she on all fours with her hands over her head. 'What are you doin'?' he demanded.

'What does it look like, stupid? There are bombs fallin' out there.'

'Then why not go to the shelter if you're so worried?'

'Don't give me none of your sass now. I ain't goin' to no shelter, and that's the end of it.'

The house shook as a bomb fell relatively nearby. 'Holy shit!' Beulah exclaimed. 'That son of a bitch was real close.'

A grim-faced Julius sat in a chair from where he could see Beulah's face. From outside came the crackle of ack-ack fire.

'You go to the shelter,' Beulah said.

He didn't reply to that, having no intention of doing so. Nor was he prepared to argue about it. Leaning backwards he lit a cigarette. He wasn't being particularly brave, it was simply that he believed if your number was up then that was it no matter what.

'You drive home through the bombin'?' Beulah demanded.

'Sure did.'

'You're crazy, real crazy. Why didn't you stop somewhere and get under cover?'

'I'm under cover now,' he pointed out.

Beulah pulled a face. 'There you go, sassin' me again. You know what I mean.'

He sighed. 'I wasn't in the mood to spend the night with strangers, Mom. Not in the mood at all.'

'Why's that?'

He drew in a deep lungful of smoke, then slowly exhaled. 'I broke up with Marybeth tonight, permanently, that's why.'

Beulah studied him. 'You did, huh?'

He nodded.

'Why you do that, boy? She's a good woman, that Marybeth. Good-lookin' too. I like her.'

Julius took his time in replying. 'I've mentioned the guy I share an office with, Walter Zwicke?'

'A few times. You don't care for him, do you?'

'He's a creep. A total slimeball. But that's not the point. He told me somethin' the other night, all about Marybeth's past, when she was in Toronto.'

'I take it from the tone of your voice it wasn't good?'

He closed his eyes for a moment, wondering how much longer this raid would go on for. 'No, it wasn't,' he confirmed.

Beulah waited and waited. 'Well, are you goin' to tell me?' she finally queried.

'It'll disillusion you about her.'

'That bad, eh?'

'That bad, Mom.'

'Holy sheeet!' Beulah exclaimed as another bomb exploded, this time even closer. The lights flickered, then went out, leaving them in darkness apart from the glow off the fire.

'I nearly wet my pants there,' Beulah confessed.

That made him smile, despite the danger they were in.

Slowly, he began to repeat his conversation with Zwicke followed by what had taken place in Marybeth's apartment.

Ellie pulled the Buick alongside the kerb when they came across the burning wreckage of one of their station's own vehicles. 'Christ!' Ellie exclaimed. 'That's Molly Davis and Pat Halfpenny's car.'

Ellie and Josie Farnham scrambled out of the Buick and cautiously approached the wreckage. To their horror, Molly and Pat were clearly visible in the front seats, both dead, their bodies flaming torches.

'Oh!' Josie choked, and turned away, wondering if her colleagues had died instantly, or had been trapped alive to be burned to death. She prayed it was the former.

'We'd better get back in case it explodes,' Ellie advised sensibly.

'There's nothing we can do anyway.'

'No,' Ellie agreed, thinking, poor bloody cows.

'Pat owed me ten bob,' Ellie said huskily as they drove off down the street. 'That's one debt she won't be repaying.'

Behind them the makeshift ambulance that was now a funeral pyre continued to burn.

The Chicory House was jam-packed, mostly with uniforms. Nor were they all British. Numbered amongst them were Free French, Polish, Czech and Belgian service men and women, all thoroughly enjoying themselves, spellbound by the music Pee Wee and the band were playing.

They were in the middle of 'I'm A Ding Dong Daddy' when suddenly the scream of a descending bomb could be heard, seemingly right above them. Fear clutched at Pee Wee's heart, and his fingers momentarily faltered.

Several members of the audience rose and dashed for the exits, others sat as though paralysed, looking upwards.

This was it, Pee Wee thought. His time had come.

It was only a few seconds, but it seemed an eternity, before the bomb exploded not far away. Dust rained down from the ceiling while glasses and tables were knocked over, some of the glasses tinkling to the floor.

'I think I'll get my ass out of here,' John Parlour whispered to Pee Wee, the band having stopped playing.

'Yeah,' agreed Muggsy Young, the other member of the trio.

Pee Wee took a deep breath. 'Hell no,' he stated firmly. Holding up a hand he addressed the audience. 'Listen, folks, I ain't lettin' no Germans spoil my session, and we doin' real good too. So if you'll just stay right where you are me and the boys here will get on with it. God bless Winston Churchill and the President of the United States!'

A great cheer greeted that, followed by tumultuous applause. One or two of those who'd dashed for the exits returned, rather shame-faced, to their seats.

'How about a jazzed-up version of "Rule Britannia"?' Pee Wee suggested.

John Parlour laughed. 'You're crazy, man. But I love it.'

Dust was still floating down from the ceiling as they swung into the new number.

Despite the bombardment Jess had managed to fall asleep, albeit a fitful one. She now came awake feeling something was wrong.

Reaching out she groped for Paul who should have been sleeping beside her, only he wasn't there. With a muffled oath she threw off her blankets and came onto her knees.

Paul glanced round from the side of the entrance to the shelter where he'd been sitting watching the raid. 'It's all right, Mum, I'm here,' he called to her.

'Get back inside this instant,' she commanded.

'Aw, Mum!'

'Get in!'

The moment he obeyed she clapped him round the ear. 'What do you think you're doing?' she scolded, voice shrill with fright. 'Do you want to get yourself killed?'

Paul clapped a hand over his ear, taken aback, for it was rare that either Jess or Albert hit him. 'That's sore,' he complained.

'Your backside will be a lot more so if I tell your dad what you did. You stupid child.'

'I wasn't in any harm, Mum. And you should see it out there. The sky's all lit up.'

Her fury began to subside. He was safe again, that was all that mattered. 'I don't care what the sky looks like. All I know is it's full of German planes and you were in danger.'

Paul was upset because he'd upset Jess. 'I'm sorry,' he mumbled, genuinely contrite.

'And so you should be.'

Suddenly she swept him into her arms and hugged him tight. 'Oh darling,' she whispered, eyes filling with tears. 'I couldn't bear to lose you. It would break my heart.'

He didn't reply to that. He didn't think he'd been in danger, but wisely didn't push the point. He was deeply touched by this show of affection from Jess, the love he felt for her swelling within him.

Jess released Paul and wiped her eyes. 'Now you get back into bed and never do that again. Understand?'

'Yes, Mum.'

'Good.'

She fussed with his blankets, making sure he was nicely tucked in. Bending, she pecked him on the forehead.

Jess didn't get another wink of sleep for the rest of that night, her anxiety staying with her and keeping her awake. For the first time in a long while she thought about the baby she'd lost, which had caused her so much pain.

'If this blows we've all had it,' Danny McGiver said to Albert through gritted teeth, the pair of them in charge of a hosepipe pumping water into a small distillery situated in the City Road, a distillery containing huge amounts of alcohol. It had been hit by several incendiaries and was burning fiercely.

In a loud clamour of noise more fire engines appeared to

assist, their personnel quickly swinging into action. Elsewhere the police and ARP wardens were busily evacuating the surrounding streets.

There was a great whoof of flame from the top of the building that shot a good thirty feet into the air, sparks flying in every direction.

Albert winced as a falling red-hot cinder neatly sliced his cheek, blood immediately starting to flow.

'You all right?' Danny asked, having seen what had happened.

Albert nodded.

'Want to go off and get it attended to?'

'Don't be daft, Danny. It's only a scratch.'

Danny grinned wolfishly, that having been a joke. He knew Albert far better than that.

The heat was pummelling Albert, his skin glowing with sweat underneath his tunic and protective gear, his eyes gritty and sore from continued staring into the inferno. He, like Danny and the others from their station, had been on duty for almost eighteen hours. To say they were totally exhausted would have been an understatement.

Henry Leway came hurrying over. 'Water supplies are getting low. We're trying to tap into another source but having difficulty as the main access points are buried beneath rubble.'

'Christ,' Albert muttered. If they ran out of water now the building and contents would surely go up, causing utter devastation over God knew how large an area. The chances were they would also go up with it.

'Who wants to live for ever anyway?' Henry Leway said, and burst out laughing. He was known for his black sense of humour.

Albert thought of Jess, Paul and Ellie, then put them quickly out of his mind. He mustn't worry about what-ifs, but continue concentrating on the job in hand.

Julius stood at his office window staring out over London, or what was left of it anyway. Miraculously the Embassy hadn't been hit so far, though many of the buildings round about had.

Smoke from a great many smouldering fires was rising sky-wards, the result of the previous night's raid, the heaviest of the war to date according to what was being said. He couldn't help but wonder if there would be anything left at all of London when this was finally over.

Down below people were hurrying to and fro, going about their business as if nothing had happened. You had to admire them, he thought, you just had to. What indomitable spirit.

Turning he glanced at the neighbouring empty desk, and smiled. A word in the right place, he'd been in this particular Embassy far longer than Zwicke after all, and Zwicke had been transferred to another office, without a murmur of complaint or resistance, Zwicke correctly guessing the reason why. On reflection it had probably suited Zwicke just as much as him.

As for Marybeth, several times she'd attempted to accost him, re-plead her case, but in each instance he'd cut her short. Hopefully she'd now give up and leave him alone.

Half the guys, and more, in the Toronto Embassy! He shook his head in disbelief. And to think he'd actually considered mar-rying her, a born floozie of the first water. That had been one very narrow escape for which he was most grateful.

As he'd said to her, he'd expected a bit of 'history' in a woman's past, that was only natural, at least to his mind it was, but what she'd been up to was just out-and-out promiscuity. And he didn't believe leopards ever changed their spots, no mat-ter what promises and assurances were made.

His thoughts were interrupted by the telephone ringing.

Jess, Beulah and others were gathered outside the house of old Ma Jenkins who, it appeared, had suffered a heart attack during the raid. As chance would have it, it was Ellie's ambulance that had been despatched to take her to hospital.

'How is she?' Jess inquired anxiously when Ellie and Josie appeared carrying Ma on a stretcher. Ma's eyes were closed, her skin a muddy green colour.

'Not too clever I'm afraid,' Ellie replied, manoeuvring the stretcher round the back of the ambulance. Moments later the stretcher had been slid aboard and Josie had gone in with it.

Ellie closed the rear doors, then wiped hair that had come astray off her face. She was dead beat.

'Dad back yet?'

Jess shook her head. 'What about you, when can I expect you home?'

Ellie shrugged wearily. 'When I appear I suppose. That's all I can say.'

Jess understood.

Jess's heart sank when she saw Albert's face which was grey, sunk in on itself, and haggard. Almost stumbling to his chair he collapsed into it.

'I heard you were round at the station asking after me,' he said.

'I was worried, Albert.'

He attempted a smile. 'In case I was hurt?'

Or worse, she thought, giving a shrug. 'Your cheek has been cut.'

He explained what had happened, and then told her about the distillery which they'd managed eventually to bring under control without it blowing up.

'I'll put something on that cut,' she declared.

'Don't fuss, woman. I'm fine.'

'But it might get infected. Just let me wash it with antiseptic.'

He sighed. 'On you go then, if it'll keep you happy.'

She crossed over to the cupboard where the antiseptic and cotton wool were kept, both usually employed on Paul's various scrapes and bruises. Albert grimaced a little when she dabbed his wound.

'Are you hungry?'

'No, we ate from the mobile canteens. All I want is a wash, change of clothes, and then over to The Florence for a few pints. After that it's bed for a couple of hours, I'm on again later.'

'You'd better have a shave as well,' she advised him. 'You're as bristly as an old broom.'

Somehow he managed to laugh. 'I'd forgotten about that.'

She threw the used cotton wool onto the fire. 'Just how bad was it?'

He thought about that. 'As bad as it's been, maybe worse. But we didn't lose anyone, nor was anyone injured. Thank God.'

'I saw Ellie earlier on, old Ma Jenkins has been taken into hospital with a suspected heart attack. They sent Ellie's ambulance for her.'

'Sorry to hear that about Ma,' he sympathised. 'Ellie all right?'

'Tired, same as you.'

Albert rubbed his forehead – tired wasn't the word for it. 'And Paul?'

'Out somewhere. Well, with the school shut I can hardly keep him indoors all day. He'll be enjoying himself with his pals, probably playing a game of some sort. They're safe enough during the day when there aren't any planes about, or bombs going off.'

'Fair enough,' Albert murmured.

Jess eyed him anxiously. 'Are you sure you don't want to go straight to bed?'

He took a deep breath, then hauled himself aloft. 'Nope. I want those couple of pints. Would you like to come with me?'

Jess considered his invitation. 'I'd better not. I should be here when Ellie gets in. And for Paul when he turns up.'

Going to Albert she kissed his unscathed cheek. 'You've earned your drink. Get yourself ready and on over there.'

Fifteen minutes later he was propping up the bar at The Florence exchanging banter with Hazel.

'You *must* return to the States, Mom, it's far too dangerous for you here.'

A look of defiance came over Beulah's face. 'Are you goin'?'

'You know I can't,' Julius protested. 'My job's in London.'

'Then I stays put, you hear? Me and Pee Wee ain't goin' nowhere if it means leavin' you behind.' She crossed her arms stubbornly across her massive bosom.

'But the air raids, Mom, the bombin'?'

'Hell, I ain't worried none about those. Sheet no! It takes more than a mess of German planes to scare Beulah Poston.'

Julius had to smile. 'Is that why you hide under the table when an attack's takin' place?'

She disregarded that jibe. 'I ain't goin', Julius. And that's that.'

He'd known before speaking to her this would be the case, but had felt compelled to try to talk some sense into her. 'There's a boat leavin' for Boston in three days, first-class accommodation. I can even arrange for you to sit at the Captain's table?'

Beulah snorted. 'Ain't tempted. Not even a little bit. Where you is, I is. OK?'

He went to her and took her into his arms. 'You're incorrigible, Mom.'

'I is?'

'Yes you are.'

She thought about that. 'Is you joshin' me in some way because I don't know what that means?'

What a star, he smiled, as he explained it to her.

'Thanks,' Ellie said, accepting a cup of tea from Josie. 'I'm ready for this.'

'Me too.'

Ellie glanced at the clock as it chimed, and frowned. Ten o'clock and no raid so far. 'They're late,' she commented.

'Who?'

'Who do you think? The Jerries, of course.'

Josie, who'd developed pronounced dark bags under her eyes, also glanced at the clock. Before joining the auxiliaries she'd been a shop assistant in the Co-op. 'Maybe they're not coming tonight?'

Ellie sincerely hoped that to be the case. It had been five nights on the trot now since the last time they'd failed to appear due to awful weather conditions over the Channel.

Josie yawned. 'I'd love to get my head down.'

'Then why don't you?'

There were a number of camp beds laid out at one end of the room where the girls sometimes kipped. They weren't in the least bit comfortable but no one cared a jot about that. The alternative was to doze in one of the available chairs.

'I think I will when I finish my tea.'

Two new girls had joined them as replacements for Molly Davis and Pat Halfpenny, taking their predecessors' places in the nightly card game that went on when they weren't out on call. There hadn't been many games played of late.

Ellie lit a cigarette, thinking she too might have a turn on one of the camp beds later on. She was about to say so to Josie when outside the sirens began to wail.

'Oh well,' Josie sighed resignedly. 'No rest for the wicked.'

'Chance would be a fine thing,' Ellie retorted, and they both grinned.

Quarter of an hour later the phone rang, the first request that shift for an ambulance.

'It's only bread and dripping I'm afraid,' Jess apologised to Paul waiting expectantly at the table.

His face fell in disappointment. 'But I'm starving, Mum!'

'I'm hungry too so you're not alone,' she snapped in reply, ashamed that was all she could give the boy for his tea. Between rationing, and the price of food going through the roof, she was at her wits' end.

'My stomach's rumbling,' he complained.

She was beginning to get angry now, as much with herself as him. She could always have gone next door to see if she could scrounge something from Beulah, but her pride wouldn't let her do that. If it was offered, well that was one thing, but to ask quite another. She was enough in the black woman's debt as it was. Thank God Albert and Ellie were able to get something from the mobile canteens when they were on call.

She placed two slices of bread and dripping in front of Paul. 'There you are.'

He eyed it with distaste, not really liking bread and dripping as his mother knew only too well. 'Are you sure there's nothing else?' he asked in a small voice.

She fixed him with a beady glare. 'No, there isn't. And just be thankful there's that, me lad.'

He bowed his head. 'Yes, Mum.'

What Jess didn't tell Paul was that those were the last two slices of bread in the house. She was having to do without.

Jess, clad only in her underwear, stared at herself in the wardrobe mirror. If she'd ever moaned on about carrying too much weight, then she certainly wasn't now. She was skinny as a rake, her ribs protruding in places. Her breasts, which Albert loved so much, were reduced to half the size they'd been. It filled her with despair.

'What are you doing?' Albert queried groggily from the bed, having just woken.

She picked up and slipped on her dressing gown. 'Nothing.'

'You were gawping at yourself in the mirror. That's most unlike you.'

She went over and sat beside him on the bed. 'I really shouldn't say anything, you and Ellie are the ones at the sharp end of all this, but I've been awfully down recently, Albert. It just seems to be getting on top of me. The bombing, the food situation, the incessant worry.'

'Oh Jess,' he whispered, reaching out and taking her hand.

'I see so little of you nowadays. You're nearly always on duty, and when you are home you're invariably asleep.'

She attempted a brave smile at seeing the concern on his face. 'I'm sorry, I shouldn't have said that. You've got enough on your plate as it is.'

He pulled himself into a sitting position and drew her to

him. 'This can't last for ever, Jess, it must end one day. And when that happens we'll get back to normal, things will be just as they were. I promise you.'

How safe she felt in his arms, she thought. A warm sense of peace started to steal over her.

Albert began to gently rock her to and fro, wishing with all his heart he didn't have to shortly return to work. But he had to, there was a war on and he was needed.

'This is nice,' she whispered.

He stroked her hair, she closing her eyes in appreciation. 'I'm glad I married you, Albert Sykes. They don't come any better.'

'And I'm glad I married you. We've both been lucky.'

She couldn't have agreed more.

'Why don't you come under the sheets and we'll cuddle up?' he suggested.

She didn't need any urging, moments later they were wrapped around one another. Just like Hansel and Gretel, she thought dreamily, lost in the woods, but having each other.

They remained like that until it was time for Albert to get up and go back to the station.

Paul couldn't believe his eyes. What had been a warehouse was now in ruins, but there, right in the middle of what remained of the building, clearly visible, was part of the fuselage from a downed German plane. And on the remnant of fuselage, small enough for him to pick up and carry, were Luftwaffe markings.

Wait till he showed this to Eddy and the others, they'd be green with envy. Spitting with it. He laughed aloud as he hurriedly made for what would be a prize souvenir, far better than anything any of the other lads possessed.

There were clumps of smouldering debris everywhere, and in places small fires that had started up again after the initial blaze had been put out. Paul paid no attention to any of this as he made straight for the coveted section of fuselage.

Reaching the fuselage he attempted to pick it up, having to struggle as it was heavier than he'd anticipated. He was still struggling with it when live cannon shells from the stricken plane, lying buried in the smouldering and burning debris, went off.

Three of the exploding shells hit Paul squarely in the back.

Chapter 20

'That's the last one gone,' Albert declared, rejoining Jess and Ellie in their kitchen. Paul had been buried several hours earlier in Highgate Cemetery, many friends, neighbours and school chums of Paul's there to pay their respects. Afterwards quite a few of them had come back to the house.

Albert now poured himself the last of the scotch, two bottles of which had been donated by Julius. Everyone had rallied round in this time of shortages; margarine, meat and cakes, not to mention bread, donated so that the wake could be done properly. The Postons' contribution was the largest of all thanks to their Embassy connection.

Jess was sitting staring blankly into space, her face red raw from crying, Ellie in another chair, curled up in a foetal ball.

Albert bit his lip, unsure of what to do or say next. He was in just as much shock as Jess and Ellie, but was handling it better.

It had been PC McKechnie who'd broken the news, assuring Jess, in that kindly way of his, that Paul had been killed outright and wouldn't have felt a thing. That had been some consolation at least.

Jess shook her head. 'I still can't really take it on board,' she husked, her voice cracked and shredded from the outpourings of grief. 'I keep expecting him to walk through that door asking what's to eat as he's starving. He was always that.'

Ellie sobbed and buried a clenched fist in her mouth.

'I got angry with him the day before because all I had for his tea was bread and dripping and he complained, but it was all we had. I'll never forgive myself for that. Never. His last full day on earth and I got angry with him.'

'Stop it, Jess,' Albert said, a choke now in his own voice.

Jess looked at him, her eyes terrible to see. 'He was a lovely lad, wasn't he, Albert?'

Albert nodded.

'I was so proud of him. A little scamp at times, but so proud of him. Since it happened I keep wondering what he would have been if he'd grown up?'

Albert swallowed the contents of his glass, shuddering as it went down.

'He wanted to be an engine driver,' Ellie suddenly stated. 'He told me that once.'

Albert smiled wryly. 'Most boys his age want to be that. It's one of those things.'

'I also keep wondering what his wife and children would have been like?' Jess said dully. 'Now I'll never know.'

Ellie stood up, she couldn't bear any more of this. 'I'm going to my room,' she declared.

'Are you all right?' Albert queried.

Of course she wasn't. She kept remembering all the times she'd been horrible to her brother. Downright nasty on occasion. Though, she reminded herself, caring and loving on others. He'd been such an irritating little sod sometimes, especially where food was concerned. No angel either, considering some of the things he'd done to her.

'I just want to be on my own for a while, Dad. Today's been . . .' She groped for a suitable word. 'Draining.'

'On you go then.'

'Don't call me for anything. I'll come back down when I'm ready.'

He wished there was more scotch, gallons of the stuff. 'Right, we won't.'

Jess took out a handkerchief that was already sodden and wiped her nose. She'd never been so mentally battered and bruised in her entire life, not even after losing the baby. She hadn't known the baby, whereas she'd given birth to Paul, brought him up, been through all the trials and tribulations of childhood with him. Loved him as you can only love your own flesh and blood.

'Would you like a cup of tea?' Albert asked. 'There's bound to be some left in the pot.'

Jess shook her head. 'I'm awash with tea as it is.'

'Can I get you anything else then?'

She looked at him, the tears having returned. 'Can you bring my son back to me?'

Albert had no answer to that. None at all.

'What was it like?' Hazel asked Julius as he came up to the bar.

His brown eyes were soulful. 'Awful, Hazel. Simply awful.'

'How are Jess and Albert?'

He shrugged. 'As you'd expect, I guess. The pair of them must be going through absolute hell.'

She made a sympathetic face. 'Pint?'

'Any Bass?'

'Sorry, we're out.'

'Then a pint of whatever.'

Hazel picked up a glass and began to pour. 'Was it a good turn-out at the service?'

'Certainly lots of people there.'

'I would have imagined there would be,' Hazel replied. 'Albert and Jess are very popular round here, highly thought of. The sort who'd always be there for you if you needed them. The salt of the earth. No offence meant, but real locals too. Both born and bred Islingtonians.'

Julius thought of Ellie, what a state she'd been in. There had been times when he'd wanted to put his arm round her, reassure her. Though what he could reassure her about he didn't know. Just be a friend, he supposed.

'Are you going back to work?' Hazel inquired, making conversation.

'No, I've taken the day off. Thought that best.'

'There you are,' Hazel declared, placing his drink in front of him. 'The way things are going there might not be any beer left come the end of the week. It's that bad.'

At which point they were interrupted by PC McKechnie coming into the pub. 'Hello, Haze, how are you?'

'Tiptop, Dougal, and yourself?'

'Looking for someone. Taffy Roberts hasn't been in, has he?'

Hazel shook her head. ''Fraid not. Why?'

McKechnie laid his helmet on the bar and ran fingers through his sandy-coloured hair. 'He's done a runner from the Army. Gone AWOL.'

Hazel laughed. 'Well, there's a surprise! I was amazed he joined in the first place.'

'He didn't join,' McKechnie corrected her. 'He was conscripted. And then only after I had a word with him and threatened jail if he didn't report in.'

'Lying bastard,' Hazel said contemptuously. 'Not you, Dougal, Taffy. He told everyone here he'd joined up. Made a big thing about it too. Was strutting all round the bar in his uniform.'

McKechnie nodded to Julius. 'How are you?'

'Fine, officer, thank you.'

'At the funeral?'

'Yes, I was.'

'How did it go?'

'As funerals do. A lot of sadness, a lot of cryin'. A lot of pain and grief.'

McKechnie sighed. 'Rotten business. It was me who broke the news to Jess.' He paused for a brief second. 'You know, no matter how long I'm in this job that sort of thing never gets any easier, especially when you know the people involved. It's even worse when it's a child.'

Julius could well imagine.

'So much death about nowadays,' McKechnie went on. 'It's everywhere, round every corner. Did you know old Ma Jenkins has gone? Passed away yesterday.'

'I heard,' Hazel nodded. 'Grand old woman. She's another who'll be missed.'

'Aye,' McKechnie agreed softly. 'I used to call in on her from time to time to see she was all right. Never left without having had a cup of tea and piece of cake. Made lovely Dundee cake too, my favourite.'

He cleared his throat. 'There's a new family moving into her house from up Canonbury way. They've been bombed out so the Council has given them Ma's place.'

'That wasn't empty long,' Hazel commented cynically.

'It's the times we live in, Haze. The times we live in.'

Hazel looked at Julius, then back at McKechnie. 'Will you have a dram while you're here, Dougal?'

That surprised Julius, spirits hadn't been available in the pub for weeks now.

'How kind of you, Haze. I will.'

'You just wait there then.' And with that she hurried away.

'Had any more trouble recently?' McKechnie inquired of Julius, referring to the incident when Julius had been attacked by the three squaddies.

'None at all, I'm happy to say.'

McKechnie grunted. 'That's good. You and your family are a bit of a rarity round here, you understand. Though it wasn't the locals who gave you bother. If any do, or try to, they'll hear from me quickly enough. I'm a foreigner here myself don't forget, I understand these things.'

Julius was impressed to hear that. 'Thank you, officer.'

Hazel reappeared carrying a huge glass of scotch. 'Get that down you, Dougal, it'll warm the cockles.'

He eyed the drink appreciatively. 'It will indeed, Haze. God bless you. *Slàinte!*'

They made small talk for a while longer, McKechnie finally

leaving with the promise that either Hazel or Harry would be in touch if Taffy was spotted in the neighbourhood or came into the pub.

'You never saw that,' Hazel stated emphatically when McKechnie had gone.

Julius feigned innocence. 'Saw what? I've no idea what you're talkin' about.'

Hazel smiled. 'That's the idea. It's best to keep the police sweet, a good rule for any landlord and landlady. And in case you're wondering, we do have a few bottles of spirits on the premises. But for private consumption only. Not to be sold. Understand?'

'Perfectly.'

'Right then, another pint?'

He drained his glass. 'I'd better before you run out of beer too.'

'Let's pray it doesn't come to that.'

'Amen,' Julius concurred.

While Julius was in the pub Beulah and Pee Wee were discussing the situation with the Sykeses. 'I think I'll go round and see Jess later,' Beulah said. 'Maybe I can be of further help.'

'I wouldn't do that, hon,' Pee Wee counselled. 'Let them be, for today anyway. I'm sure they don't want no outsiders, no matter how well-meanin', buttin' in right now. They'll want to be by themselves.'

'Reckon?'

He nodded. 'We done everythin' we can for now. If they wants somethin' more they'll come knockin'. At least that's how I sees it.'

Beulah thought that was probably good advice. She'd call round next morning and find out what was what. 'He was such a nice kid too,' she mused. 'Damn shame.'

Pee Wee recalled Albert and Jess's faces at the graveside, two broken people if ever there were. He'd later spoken briefly to Albert, but what could you really say? Nothing. Words were empty at a time like that, but better spoken nonetheless.

'I keep thinkin' . . .' Beulah trailed off, her expression stricken.

'What, hon?'

'Julius and Diane and baby Bradley. What I'd be like if any-thin' ever happened to one of them.' Diane was Julius's elder sister, Bradley her son.

'Yeah,' Pee Wee agreed softly. It didn't bear thinking about.

When Julius returned from the pub he couldn't understand why Beulah made such a fuss of him, and continued doing so for the rest of that day.

Jess's visits to the graveside had become a daily ritual. Every morning she caught the bus to Highgate, returning usually just before noon.

She was there now, staring at Paul's grave, the flowers adorning it withered and dead as he was. She knew she should remove the flowers and put them in the bin provided, but couldn't bring herself to do so.

Albert didn't approve of these visits, saying she was only torturing herself. And maybe she was, but come she had to.

She blamed herself for Paul's death. If only she'd left him in Devon with the Sellys he'd still be alive. But no, she'd had to go and bring him home.

It was no use reminding herself how unhappy he'd been at High Barton, that was hardly relevant now. An unhappy Paul far better than a dead one.

Jess groped for her handkerchief, and wiped her eyes. She'd already been standing there half an hour during which it had rained twice, but that didn't matter. It could have been a thunder or snow storm for all she cared. What was important was that she was with her son, her beloved boy, whom she missed so much it was mentally crucifying her.

Not only had she brought him back from Devon but had been against it when the authorities had wished to re-evacuate him, wanting to keep him with her.

Selfish, that's what she'd been, utterly selfish. And this was the result. A dead child and she with her heart broken.

If only she could turn the clock back. If only she'd never gone to Devon. If only she'd insisted he be re-evacuated.

For her, the two most painful and agonising words in the world right then.

If only . . .

Jess got wearily out of her chair when the sirens sounded, the ninth night in a row they'd wailed their warning that yet another raid was about to take place. Would it never end?

Crossing to the fireplace she picked up the small, framed photograph of Paul, the only one she possessed. For a moment she held it to her bosom and closed her eyes, then gathered up the rest of the things she'd be taking to the shelter.

'Ellie?'

'Hello, Julius.'

'I thought that was you.'

He got out of the car and closed his door. 'It's so difficult to see anything, or anyone, in this black-out. People are just shapes moving in the darkness.'

She laughed. 'Spooky, isn't it?'

He turned up the collar of his coat, for it was wild and blustery. 'Shouldn't you be on duty at this time?' he queried with a frown.

'I'm on days for the next fortnight. I think they thought I needed a bit of a rest after . . .' She trailed off and bit her lip.

'Paul?'

She nodded.

'How are your mom and dad? I haven't seen either of them for a while.'

Ellie shrugged. 'Trying to cope. Getting on with it. It isn't easy for them.'

'Or you,' he added softly.

'No,' she agreed. 'But it's worse for them, particularly Mum. She really took it badly.'

Julius glanced at the sky. 'I hope this weather keeps up. It's been over a week now since the last raid.'

'A welcome respite,' she smiled. 'The forecast is awful I'm happy to say.'

He had a sudden thought. 'Listen, what are you doin' after you've eaten?'

She wondered why he'd asked that. 'Nothing much. Listen to the wireless I suppose. Do some ironing for Mum.'

'Well, I've got a better idea. Why don't we go to The Florence for a drink? Far more excitin', don't you think?'

She couldn't disagree. It would be good to get out and enjoy herself for a bit, have a break. 'All right.'

'Fine then. It's a date.'

For some reason those words sent a thrill through her. Of course it wasn't a date in that sense, she knew that. It was only his way of saying meeting up. 'What time?'

Then he remembered the state of affairs at The Florence, no spirits. 'I've had a better thought,' he declared. 'Instead of the pub why don't you come to our house? At least there I can offer you some gin.'

She couldn't see why not. It was better than drinking beer which she didn't really like. 'As I said, what time?'

He thought about that. 'Eight?'

'Suits me.'

'That gives you time to eat and get sorted out. Me too.'

'Eight then.'

Julius found himself whistling as he went inside. He was looking forward to this.

'I'm afraid Mom's out,' he declared, ushering Ellie into the lounge. 'She decided to take advantage of the raids being stopped and go into the club with Dad. I hope you don't mind that there's only the two of us.'

'Not in the least.' She nearly said, I presume I will be safe? But decided not to. It would only have been a tease anyway. Of course she was safe. Julius had no interest in her that way.

'By the by, there's somethin' for you on that chair there,' he said, pointing.

Ellie went to the chair and picked up the carton of cigarettes lying on it. 'You really are terribly good to me, Julius. Thank you.'

'Only bein' neighbourly.'

She'd been a little tense before knocking on the door, but somehow he'd almost instantly put her at her ease. She now felt completely relaxed.

Julius waggled a glass in her direction. 'I've already started so you've got some catchin' up to do. Now make yourself comfortable while I pour you a drink.'

She sank into the chair the cigarettes had been on and gazed around. She hadn't been in this room since the Postons had arrived and invited the family in for a meal. That seemed a lifetime ago considering all that had happened since.

'Tonic water as well!' she laughed. 'You are organised. All mod cons, I must say.'

'As usual, compliments of the Embassy. Uncle Sam looks after his own.'

'Hmmh!' she grunted in appreciation on tasting the G&T he handed her. 'This is strong.'

'Complainin'?'

She shook her head. 'Don't be daft. It's wonderful.'

Julius went to the sofa, kicked off his loafers and sat with his legs along the cushions. 'So, how'ya been?'

'If you mean work, not too hectic. It'll liven up once the bombing starts again as it's bound to.'

He indicated. 'There's an ashtray there if you want to smoke.'

'What about you?'

'In a minute or two.'

What large feet he had, she noticed. Then flushed, remembering something she'd heard about men with large feet.

'What's wrong?'

'Nothing.'

'Sure? You went kind of pink all of a sudden.'

She couldn't meet his gaze. 'There's no reason,' she lied. It had been Connie Fox who'd told her about men with large feet. Connie whom she hadn't seen since joining the auxiliaries. She made a mental note to try to get in touch.

'What's the latest between you and your girlfriend?' Ellie asked. 'The last time we spoke properly she was trying to get you to marry her.'

The smile vanished from Julius's face. 'We broke up. I don't take her out any more.'

'Oh?'

He wondered if he should tell Ellie the reason why he'd broken with Marybeth, then thought the better of it. That was a bit too personal.

'I just decided to call it quits while I was ahead,' he said instead.

That pleased Ellie, though she couldn't think why. It was none of her business. 'Do you miss her?'

He considered his answer before replying. 'Some aspects of our relationship. But generally speakin', no.'

Ellie understood what he meant by that. He missed going to bed with Marybeth. How like a man, she thought a trifle prudishly. 'So is there anyone new?'

'What is this, Ellie, the Spanish Inquisition?'

This time she went bright red. 'Sorry. I wasn't being nosey. I'm genuinely interested. As a friend.'

He had a long, satisfying gulp of bourbon. 'Well, there isn't. I'm a free agent again. What about you?'

She laughed. 'When do I have a chance to meet anyone? I'm either at work or home, with nothing in-between.'

'There must be guys in the ambulance station?'

That amused her. 'Two of them, both retired. Somewhere in their late sixties I should imagine. We're auxiliaries, don't forget.'

He could understand her amusement. 'A little old for you, eh?'

'Just a little,' she agreed.

'Too bad,' he said. 'A good-lookin' doll like you shouldn't be without a gentleman caller.'

Doll! She'd never been called that before. As for 'gentleman caller', how quaint. It gave her a warm glow to think he considered her good-looking. Unless he was merely being polite of course. She couldn't tell from his expression whether or not that was the case.

She recrossed her legs, feeling one of them catch something on the chair as she did. 'Damn!' she swore when a quick examination revealed she'd snagged a stocking causing a ladder.

'What's wrong?'

She explained. 'And it's the last pair I've got too. They're not to be had in the shops for love nor money.'

Julius came over and had a look at the offending chair, a small nail that had partially worked loose being the culprit. 'I'll fix that right away,' he declared, and hurried from the room, returning almost immediately with a hammer. A couple of taps did the trick.

'Sorry about that,' he apologised.

Ellie made a face. 'Hardly your fault. It was an accident.'

'Caused by our chair,' he pointed out. 'At least let me make amends. A dozen or so pair of nylons should be adequate compensation, wouldn't you say?'

Ellie gasped. 'Nylons! A dozen pairs!' Her eyes were shining. 'Can you really manage that?'

'Sure. It's not a problem. I'll have them for you as soon as I can.'

'Oh Julius!' she breathed. 'That would be fantastic. I'm not exaggerating when I told you they're like gold dust round here. And nylons are absolutely impossible to get hold of. If you do get lucky the stockings are lisle like I'm wearing. Horrid things really.'

It pleased him to see how delighted she was; he made a mental note to sort out the nylons first thing in the morning on arrival at the Embassy. 'Let me freshen your glass, it's empty,' he declared.

'Not too much. I don't want to get tiddly.'

When he'd refilled her glass, and his own, he produced a cigar, one of a new batch recently arrived from Cuba, clipped it and lit up. 'Would you like to hear some music?' he asked. 'We have a Victrola and a great many records. Some of them featuring my dad.'

'That would be lovely,' she exclaimed, realising that a Victrola was what she knew as a gramophone.

Julius replaced the needle before winding up the machine and putting on the first record. 'Let's try this for size, eh? It's one of my dad's called "Moonlit Eyes".'

The alcohol was beginning to take effect, she thought, as the music, a ballad, wafted dreamily over her.

'What do you think, Ellie?'

'I like it, very much.'

He beamed approval.

How much better than the music played at the Poxy Roxy, she reflected. No comparison at all.

'Care to dance?'

She'd closed her eyes for a few moments in appreciation, now she opened them again. 'I'm not very good,' she confessed, suddenly all shy and coy.

'Neither am I, so that makes us even.'

He lifted the arm of the Victrola and placed it back at the beginning of the record. 'Shall we?'

It didn't take her long to realise he'd been lying to be kind, he could dance all right, beautifully so. He reminded her of a big black panther, she thought, as they moved round the carpet, she drinking in the smell of the cologne he was wearing, unused to men who used such a thing.

When the record was finished she asked if it could be played again, she liked it so much.

A smiling Julius complied.

Ellie found Jess asleep in the kitchen with a blanket draped over her lap. She was holding the photograph of Paul clutched in both hands.

Ellie stared at her mother who looked so settled and comfortable. Wake her or leave her as she was? In the end Ellie decided to leave her.

Going upstairs she thought about what a wonderful evening she'd had with Julius, it couldn't have gone better. They'd talked about all sorts, her life, his life, experiences they'd had, a whole range of topics.

They'd also drunk a lot – too much really, she hoped she wouldn't regret it in the morning – laughed, danced and told jokes. The time had simply flown past.

'Moonlit Eyes,' she murmured as she undressed, and smiled. None of the other records he'd played had been a patch on that. Somehow its haunting melody was special.

Just like the evening itself.

Chapter 21

Albert laid aside the book he'd been reading, and yawned. So far the shift had been uneventful and he hoped it continued that way. The recent air raids had been sporadic, sometimes the Luftwaffe came, sometimes not. There was no distinguishable pattern to it.

'I've been meaning to ask,' Danny McGiver, sitting opposite, said. 'How's Jess?'

Albert stared at his friend and colleague, thinking about his answer. 'Not so good I'm afraid,' he eventually replied.

Danny nodded. 'Understandable I suppose. It must be a terrible thing to lose a child.' Adding when he saw the look that came over Albert's face, 'For both of you.'

'Yes,' Albert agreed softly. 'At least I have my work to keep me busy, take my mind off it. Jess just sits at home and constantly broods. I know she tries to hide the fact, but she cries a lot when Ellie and I aren't there. And every morning it's the same, a trip to the cemetery to visit the grave.'

'Poor cow,' Danny whispered.

'The trouble is she blames herself for Paul's death. I've told her that's nonsense but she'll have none of it. She's convinced she's at fault and that's that.'

'Can't the doctor do something? Give her pills or whatever?'

'He might if she'd go and see him, but she won't. She says the doctor can't help what's wrong with her.'

Albert sighed. 'If it wasn't for the war I'd take her away on holiday. A week in Brighton perhaps, that might buck her up somewhat.' He smiled cynically. 'There again, if it wasn't for the war Paul would still be alive and the holiday wouldn't be necessary.'

Danny shook his head. 'I sometimes think this is going to go on for ever, that it'll never end. But of course it will, one way or the other, eventually. Has to.'

'She's also losing weight,' Albert went on. 'Well we all are, what with rationing and shortages, but Jess more than others. She's skin and bone, which breaks my heart.'

'She had a lovely figure too,' Danny sympathised. 'I always admired her for that. A real bobby dazzler.'

Albert smiled in memory. 'You should have seen her when I married her, Danny, a stunner if ever there was. I was the envy of nearly every bloke I knew. Now she's more like a scarecrow than anything else.'

'Christ, I'm sorry,' Danny murmured.

'Her face has gone quite haggard and lined, pasty with it. I swear she looks ten or fifteen years older than she did.'

Danny was lost for words, he simply didn't know what to reply to that.

Albert thought of his own grief, the hurt almost unbearable at times. Again and again pictures of Paul would flash through his mind. Paul playing, laughing, Paul as a baby with Jess changing his nappies, having him at the breast. He loved Ellie of course, but Paul had been different in that Paul had been his son. Nor would there ever be another boy child to replace Paul.

'How about a cup of tea?' Danny queried, and winked. 'I've got a couple of digestives in my box, so we can have one each.'

'Grand,' Albert tried to enthuse. A biscuit, and sort, was a treat nowadays.

'Shan't be long,' Danny declared, rising from his chair.

Albert watched Danny's retreating back, but in his mind he was still thinking about, and remembering, Paul.

His son.

The fire had been extensive, but was now under control. This was the sixth trip Ellie and Josie Farnham had made to the scene, currently waiting to ensure the last of the casualties had been removed, at which point they'd return to the station to be in readiness for any further call-outs.

Ellie had spotted the mobile canteen earlier during one of her previous visits, and now decided to avail herself of it while she had the time.

'I'll catch up with you in a few moments,' Josie replied when Ellie told her what she intended. 'I have to find somewhere for a crafty pee. I'm bursting.'

Ellie smiled. 'You do that.'

The canteen was manned by the WVS, the Women's Voluntary Service, a solitary member now serving. When she arrived Ellie found herself to be the only one waiting.

'A cup of tea and something to eat please,' she asked the woman who had her back to her.

Ellie had a shock when the woman turned round. Dear God, she thought.

'Hello, Miss Sykes, how are you?' Miss Oates asked, the face as stern as ever.

Ellie was further taken aback that Miss Oates had recognised her so easily as she was in full protective gear with her face filthy and dirt-streaked.

As though reading her mind Miss Oates said, 'Your voice, Miss Sykes, I never forget a voice.'

Ellie swallowed hard, quite thrown to suddenly find herself in the company of her old boss and enemy. 'I'm fine, thank you.'

Miss Oates regarded her keenly. 'Well, you don't look fine. I'd say you were totally knackered.'

Ellie's jaw literally fell open to hear Miss Oates use such language. It was beyond belief. 'I suppose I am,' she eventually mumbled.

'Not surprised in that job. I admire you for doing it, Miss Sykes. Yes indeed.'

Was there no end of surprises? Ellie watched as Miss Oates poured her a cuppa and then placed a sandwich and bun on a plate. 'These buns are fresh baked this morning. They're nice and tasty, couldn't have made better myself,' Miss Oates declared, placing the tea and plate on the canteen counter.

'Thank you.'

Ellie blew on the tea which was scalding hot, then started on the sandwich, wolfing it down as she was ravenously hungry.

'I ran into a friend of yours the other day,' Miss Oates informed her.

'Oh?'

'Miss Fox. She left the office shortly after you, but you probably know that.'

Ellie shook her head. 'I didn't.'

'There's hardly anyone there now,' Miss Oates stated. 'Reduced to a skeleton staff. Just enough to keep business ticking over. The others are all off doing war work. In Miss Fox's case she's taken over a milk round she said.'

'A milk round?' Ellie found that incredible, unable to imagine Connie driving a horse and cart.

'Releases a man for the Forces you see. Told me she was enjoying it. Loves being out in the fresh air.'

'So how is she?' Ellie asked.

'Happy as a pig in the proverbial. Took up with a new chap just before she left and, according to her, the pair of them are getting along famously. A seaman, I believe. Well, good luck to them I say. I hope it works out.'

Ellie vaguely remembered something about Connie possibly having a new boyfriend just before she herself had left the office, but as she recalled Connie had denied it at the time. She guessed Connie had done so because she and this seaman had only recently met up and she hadn't wanted to look foolish if it hadn't lasted, been a flash in the pan so to speak. She could well understand that.

Ellie tried her tea again which was now drinkable, and then had a bite of her bun. As Miss Oates had said, it was delicious.

A middle-aged ARP warden came strolling over. 'Evening, Beryl, how are tricks?'

The stern expression vanished to be replaced by a broad smile. 'Hello, Stanley. Wondered if you'd be around.'

'Here I am, in all me glory.'

Beryl? Ellie had never known what Miss Oates' Christian name was, and would certainly never have guessed something as common as Beryl. In other circumstances she would have laughed.

'Tea and two sugars is it?' Miss Oates queried winsomely.

Bloody hell! Ellie thought. Miss Oates was actually flirting with this Stanley. She simply couldn't believe it.

'That's right, ducks. Two sugars it is. If you can spare that amount.'

Miss Oates winked. 'Anything for you, Stanley. You know that.'

Stanley laughed, then turned to Ellie. 'Do you belong to that vehicle over there?' he inquired, pointing.

A stunned Ellie nodded.

'Well, you've got the all clear. No more casualties, that's been confirmed now.'

'Thank you.'

Ellie finished her bun and tea while Miss Oates and Stanley chatted, then, having said goodbye, went in search of Josie who she presumed was having difficulty finding a secluded spot.

Talk about a turn-up for the book! *Beryl*, she thought, and this time did laugh.

'Ah, there you are. Please sit down,' Station Officer Titmuss said, indicating the chair in front of her desk.

Ellie, who'd been summoned to see the SO, was wondering what this was all about. For the life of her she couldn't think of anything she'd done wrong. 'Thank you.'

SO Titmuss regarded Ellie kindly. 'What would you say to a spot of promotion, Ellie? I'd like to make you up to DSO.' That meant Deputy Station Officer.

Ellie was flabbergasted, she'd never imagined this to be on the cards. 'Why me?' she queried.

'Because you're a born leader and all the other girls look up to you. You're a natural choice for the job.'

Ellie tried to digest that, having been completely unaware she was held in such esteem by the others. 'What about DSO Winterbottom?' she asked. Alice Winterbottom was the current DSO.

'Alice is also in for promotion. She's taking over a new station being opened in the Ball's Pond Road. So her post is falling vacant as from the first of the month, and I'd like you to assume her duties. It means a little extra money of course, which always comes in handy.'

Ellie thought about that. It would mean she wouldn't be out in the ambulances as often as before, paperwork being the new priority. And lots of it.

'Well?' SO Titmuss prompted.

Ellie made a decision. Why not? Anyway, she rather fancied the idea of wearing two stripes on her arm. And as the SO said, extra money would be useful, her mother would certainly welcome it. 'Thank you, I accept.'

SO Titmuss beamed. 'Good girl. Well done. Congratulations.' Rising, she came round her desk and shook Ellie warmly by the hand, Ellie having also risen.

Josie Farnham wasn't best pleased when told the news as it meant she'd have a new partner, she and Ellie having become close during their time together. More importantly, they both got on terribly well.

Ellie found herself looking forward to her new duties, even if they wouldn't be quite as exciting as what she now did.

Maybe less exciting, but also less dangerous she reminded herself. Which, if she was honest, was something of a relief.

The date was May 10, 1941, and if Londoners thought they'd been through the worst of the Blitz, that it couldn't possibly get worse than it had been, then that night proved them horribly wrong. Later it would be called the night that nearly took the heart out of London.

The news slowly filtering through to the battling firemen was one of terrible carnage. The Chamber of the House of Commons had been reduced to rubble, the Lords' Chamber having also been hit, as had Big Ben, though that was still standing. The roof of Westminster Hall was ablaze, while the square tower at Westminster Abbey had fallen in. Miraculously, although surrounded by fires, St Paul's remained intact. The number of dead, dying and casualties didn't bear thinking about. All the services, including the Fire Brigade, were stretched to the limit, and beyond.

Henry Leway staggered up to Albert, having to shout to be heard above the roar of flames and crackle of burning buildings. 'We haven't a hope in hell of controlling this lot,' he gasped.

'We'll just have to,' Albert snapped in reply.

Henry shook his head. 'It's impossible, I tell you.'

Albert paused to stare at his colleague. Henry was on the point of breaking he realised. 'Get a grip of yourself, Henry, for Christsake!' he shouted.

To Albert's amazement Henry started to cry, tears rolling down his soot-blackened face. 'I've had enough. Can't take any more. Too much. Too much.'

Albert let go of the hosepipe he was holding and slapped Henry hard causing him to cry out. 'Stop snivelling like a child and get on with it,' Albert bellowed. 'We need every man we've got and you're one of the best. Don't let us down now. Don't let the public down, they're relying on us. All of London is relying on us tonight.' By that he meant the entire Fire Brigade.

Henry blinked several times, then ran a hand across his face.

Taking a deep breath he straightened himself. 'Sorry, Albert,' he apologised. 'I don't know what came over me.'

'Are you all right now?'

Henry nodded.

Albert gripped and squeezed his arm. 'Good chap. Let's just forget this, eh?'

'Thanks.'

Turning, Henry hurried away.

'Gas!' someone yelled a little later. 'Gas escape!'

Oh my God! Albert thought. He couldn't smell anything, but that was hardly likely in the smoke-laden atmosphere that was also heavily polluted by the many combined odours from all manner of burning things.

Seconds later the gas ignited sending a searing ball of flame billowing in all directions. Albert was lifted off his feet and thrown backwards to land with a jarring thump which knocked the breath out of him, leaving him dizzy and dazed.

He slowly became aware of Henry Leway by his side. 'Are you hurt, Albert?'

He gingerly felt himself all over. 'Don't think so.'

'Then try and sit up.'

Albert hesitantly brought himself into an upright position to stare at the roaring gas escape. From the size and intensity of it he guessed a main had been breached. 'That has to be turned off,' he croaked.

'I know.'

'Then get to it. I'll be with you in a moment.'

'Right,' Henry declared, and dashed away.

Albert pulled himself to his feet where he swayed slightly. He had to hold a hand across his face to ward off the intense heat which was already blistering his skin.

'Over here!' someone shouted. 'Unconscious fireman!'

People were milling everywhere, like ants in a heap, all trying to do something specific connected with their job. Albert wondered who the fireman was. One of theirs or from another station?

He made his way over as an ambulance crew appeared carrying

a stretcher between them. Albert's heart sank when he reached the prostrate figure to see it was Danny McGiver.

Instantly he was kneeling alongside Danny feeling for a neck pulse, swearing beneath his breath when he couldn't find one. Before he could try another point the ambulance chaps, regular service and not auxiliaries like Ellie's lot, were also there doing a quick examination.

'Can't tell if he's dead or not,' the older of the two shouted to Albert. 'He a friend of yours?'

Albert nodded.

'We'll get him straight to hospital where he can be dealt with.'

Albert watched numbly as Danny, one arm trailing over the side, was stretchered away.

Not Danny, he thought in despair. Please God, not Danny. Then he turned his attention again to what had to be done.

It was another half an hour before the gas main had been turned off and that particular fire extinguished.

Jess came out of the cemetery gates and crossed over to the bus stop where no one else was waiting. Twenty minutes later a bus still hadn't appeared, which didn't surprise her after the previous night's terrible raid. The buses could hardly be expected to run to schedule after that. She'd been lucky on the way there having caught one almost immediately.

Then the idea came to her. Why not walk home? It was an awful long way, miles, and would take her ages, but the more she thought about it the more determined she became that's what she'd do.

A sort of punishment, she told herself grimly. A small penance for Paul's death which had been all her fault.

She started off knowing it would probably take her a while. But no matter what, no matter how many buses passed her, it was a journey she was going to complete.

A small penance, she thought again.

* * *

Albert knocked on Danny's door. He was done in, almost dropping from exhaustion, having just come off his longest shift ever. On returning to the station it was to be told that Danny wasn't seriously hurt and was now home.

'How is he?' Albert asked Danny's wife Vera when she answered his knock.

'Come in and see for yourself. He's in bed.'

Albert followed Vera through to where Danny was. 'Hello, mate,' Danny whispered by way of greeting.

The upper part of Danny's head was swathed in bandages which ended just above his ears. There was no sign of blood on them, a relieved Albert noted.

'Some people will do anything to skive off,' Albert joked.

Danny attempted a smile, and winced. That hadn't been a good idea. 'As if.'

'He discharged himself, you know,' Vera stated disapprovingly. 'They wanted to keep him in for forty-eight hours for observation.'

'Now don't start again,' Danny chided. 'I explained, they needed the bed for someone worse off than me. Best I was home anyway, you're a far better nurse than any they have at the hospital.'

Vera wagged a finger at him. 'Don't you try and soft-soap me, Danny McGiver. It won't work, you hear?'

'Yes, dear,' he replied meekly, knowing full well, despite what she'd said, Vera would have been delighted to be told that. Anyway, in a way it was true.

'Cup of tea, Albert?' Vera asked.

'Please. Good and strong. The sort you can stand a spoon up in.'

'Coming right away.'

'Hey, what about me?' Danny protested.

'You've already had four since you woke. We are on rationing, don't forget.'

'If you're making a pot for Albert then it'll stretch to me,' Danny pointed out.

'Well all right.' Vera pretended to concede, having been going to give him a cup anyway, and disappeared out of the room.

'She's a gem. Don't know what I'd do without her,' Danny declared, having enjoyed that little bit of banter.

Albert smiled and sat on the edge of the bed. 'You gave me a hell of a fright last night, mate,' he said softly. 'I thought we'd lost you. What's the damage?'

'Concussion, that's all. And a few abrasions. I was lucky.'

'What happened exactly?'

'Don't know, Albert. One moment someone was shouting gas, the next thing I knew I was in an ambulance. I must have been hit on the head by flying debris of some sort. Thank God for my helmet. It might have been curtains if it hadn't been for that.'

Albert was noting how pale and wan Danny was. 'Head sore?'

'More than I'm letting on to Vera. She thinks I'm a mug for discharging myself, but it was the right thing to do. There were casualties everywhere, most in a far worse state than myself.'

Danny closed his eyes for a few seconds, and grimaced. 'Christ!' he swore quietly. 'Sometimes there's a stabbing pain that goes right through my brain like a red-hot poker. Not pleasant, I can tell you. Not pleasant at all.'

Albert could well imagine. 'Well, that'll be you off work for a couple of weeks, jammy blighter.'

'Don't you believe it,' Danny retorted quickly. 'A couple of days more like. There's a war on, me old son, or have you forgotten?'

Albert laughed. 'How could I after last night. That was sheer bloody murder and no mistake. But listen, I think you should reconsider this couple of days bit. Heroics are all very well, but we need you to be fit when you get back, up to the job. You'll only be a liability to the rest of us if you're still crocked.'

Danny hadn't thought of that. Much as he hated to admit it, Albert had a point. 'All right then,' he replied reluctantly.

'Good.'

Danny was beginning to feel tired again, but didn't want to say in case Albert went. He was enjoying the company. 'How about the rest of the chaps, they safe and sound?'

'Our lads are, but a bloke from Clerkenwell got killed. Name of Nick Hastings, ring any bells?'

Danny was about to shake his head, but stopped himself in time. In his present condition that wouldn't have been wise. 'No, it doesn't. How did he get it?'

'The gas explosion. He was close by when it ignited.'

The two men stared at one another, both thinking that might well have been Danny.

'Poor bastard,' Danny whispered.

'Can I come in?' Beulah asked, popping her head round the kitchen door having found the main one ajar.

Jess was sitting with her feet in a basin of hot water. 'Do,' she replied dully.

'Sweet Jesus!' Beulah exclaimed when she got closer. The water in the basin was tinged pink from blood. 'What happened to you?'

'Nothing really.'

'Don't give me that bullshit, Jess Sykes. You's bleedin'.'

Jess spoke slowly and emphatically, explaining her reason for walking back from Highgate, Beulah gazing at her in fear – for Jess – and disbelief.

'How bad are they?' she queried, indicating Jess's feet.

'Bruising mainly, plus a few minor cuts. Nothing to worry about. Honestly.'

Beulah pulled over a chair and sat beside Jess. 'You must stop torturin' yourself like this, girl. It's no good. No good at all.'

Jess hung her head and didn't reply.

'It ain't your fault Paul died . . .'

'It was,' Jess interrupted in a whisper.

Beulah stared at her friend in consternation. 'You did what you thought best and that was bring him home again. I'd have done exactly the same thing in your situation. I swear I would.'

Again Jess didn't reply.

'If you keeps this up you're goin' to have some kind of break-down, girl, and what good is that to anybody? None at all. You have Albert and Ellie still to think about, you must remember that. If you goes all to pieces you's lettin' them down, and they need you, probably more than they's ever done in their entire lives before. You's the rock in this here family, Jess, the one they all rely on. Besides, what would your Paul say to see you like this?'

Jess's chest heaved as she fought back tears. 'I miss him so much,' she said in a cracked voice.

'Of course you do, hon. You was his momma, that's only natural. But now he's gone you must make him proud of you, and don't think he don't know what you's goin' through. He's up there watchin' you grievin', and I'll bet my sweet ass wishin' you'd stop all this and get on with things. I'm sure that would make him happy.'

Jess blinked back a tear. 'Do you really think so?'

'I'm as certain of that as any mortal person can be. You gotta let go, Jess, for his sake as well as your own. You havin' no breakdown ain't goin' to help anythin'.'

Jess swallowed hard. Let go? That was impossible. How could she?

'You hear me, girl?'

'I can't,' she whispered.

'Oh yes you can, and will. All the grievin' in the world ain't goin' to change things, and that's a fact. Shit, he might have died of all kinds of ailments, kids do. Would you have blamed yourself for that too?'

'No,' Jess confessed.

'Well, there you are then. Grievin' is right and proper, but there comes a time when you have to stop and let go. Get on with life.'

'That's easier said than done,' Jess chided softly.

'I knows that. But done it's gotta be. And stop punishin' yourself, for Christsake! You didn't make no mistake, you did your best and no one, I repeat, no one, can do better than that.'

Beulah took a deep breath. 'I'll stop preachin' now. I've had my say. The rest is up to you.'

Jess somehow managed to smile. 'Why don't you put the kettle on while I dry my feet.'

'That's my girl.'

Jess appreciated Beulah's concern, knowing her to be well-meaning. But it wasn't her Julius lying buried up in Highgate, it was Paul.

And the fault *was* hers, despite what Beulah said.

Chapter 22

'I look like a total frump!' Josie Farnham complained, emerging from the ladies wearing one of the new uniforms they'd just been issued. Her navy blue slacks were baggy, while the matching tunic, rather similar to those worn by the RAF, though nowhere near as neatly tailored, hung loosely from her shoulders. The belt at her waist had the effect of making her hips appear twice their normal size. The ensemble was set off with a forage cap plus shirt and tie.

Ellie choked back a smile. Josie was right, she did look terrible. Frump wasn't the word for it.

Josie stared at Ellie in dismay. 'Do we have to wear this?'

Ellie nodded. ''Fraid so.'

Several of the other girls had come crowding round, their combined reaction one of consternation. They'd all been hoping for something smart and attractive that would show off their figures, but this was a disaster.

'I've seen better-dressed scarecrows,' Babette Meadows commented, and laughed.

'It doesn't even begin to fit,' Josie further complained.

Ellie dreaded to think what she was going to look like in her new uniform which she hadn't yet tried on. It remained in her office draped over a chair.

'Don't they have different sizes?' Chris Pannell queried with an anxious frown.

'They have but . . . well, they're simply small, medium and large,' Ellie explained.

Chris groaned.

'Maybe we can do something with them, fiddle around a bit if you know what I mean. A tuck here, a little taken in there,' Babette suggested hopefully.

'Can you dressmake?' Ellie queried.

'I wouldn't go that far. But I do have a sewing machine that I have been known to run up things on.'

Ellie had to admit, the overall impression of the new uniform was pretty ghastly. It made her think enviously of a Wren she'd seen recently. Now *that* uniform had been the bee's knees. A world apart from the monstrosity Josie had on.

'And to think we've been moaning all this time waiting for these to arrive!' Josie said in disgust, shaking her head.

'They are disappointing, I have to admit,' Ellie declared. 'But these are what we've been given so I suppose we'd better make the best of them.'

A little later she tried on her own uniform which was just as badly fitting as Josie's.

'Bloody hell!' was her reaction when she saw herself in a mirror.

Albert stared in distaste at the plate Jess had set in front of him. Spam fritters yet again.

'Before you say anything that's all I could get,' Jess said defensively.

He nodded. 'I understand.' Then, with a heartfelt sigh, 'What I wouldn't give for a nice chop, or steak and kidney pie.'

'There's mock banana trifle to follow,' Jess stated.

Albert eyed her dyspeptically. 'And what exactly is that? I mean, what's mock about the banana?' Bananas hadn't been seen in Britain since the outbreak of war.

'It's really parsnip.'

'Parsnip!'

'A new recipe I'm trying. One put out by the Ministry. It's supposed to taste delicious.'

Albert barked out a cynical laugh. 'I'll bet!'

'Let me put it this way,' Jess said quietly. 'It's better than starving.'

Albert had no reply to that, so started in on his fritters, the first mouthful making him pull a face.

Jess placed her own plate on the table and sat facing him. Ellie would get hers when she came off shift.

It was three weeks now since the last air raid and things had returned to some sense of normality. No one expected this lull in the raids to go on indefinitely, but they were enjoying the respite while they could. The best part for Jess, and no doubt countless others, was that she was once more able to get a good night's uninterrupted sleep in her own bed. Sheer bliss after the discomfort of the shelter.

'I had a letter today,' she announced casually.

'Oh?'

'From the authorities. I've to report for work next Monday morning.'

Albert paused in eating to frown. 'Doing what?'

'The letter didn't say. It just gave me the address of a factory off the City Road and stated attendance was compulsory.'

Albert thought about that, his emotions mixed. It wasn't actually a surprise, more and more married women were being allocated war work, so why should Jess be any different. 'What about the hours?' he queried.

'Didn't tell me those either, so I won't find out until I get there.'

He continued eating his fritters, forcing himself to chew and swallow the horrible things. He had to keep his strength up after all, necessary in his job.

'So there we are,' Jess said, thinking it would be strange working again after all these years. She hadn't done since marrying Albert.

'How do you feel about it?'

Jess shrugged.

'I just hope it isn't too hard. Some women are expected to graft like men these days. I can understand why, but it still isn't right.'

Jess hadn't been sure what to expect from Albert when she told him, he could be extremely protective. There again, he no doubt realised there was no option in the matter. Not to report would have meant a visit from PC McKechnie and the possible threat of jail. She certainly didn't want either.

After a while Albert came to the conclusion he was pleased Jess had to work, it would occupy her mind and hopefully stop her brooding about Paul.

Yes, all in all, it was a good thing. He approved.

Jess tensed as Albert's hand crept over her breast. His breathing had changed during the past few minutes so she knew what was coming next.

'Jess?'

'What?'

'Are you awake?'

'You know I am.'

The hand slid inside her nightdress. 'It's been a long time, Jess. Too long.'

He'd been more than patient, she told herself. Since Paul's death he hadn't made any demands, appreciating that lovemaking was the last thing she wanted. Anyway, during the air raids it had been almost impossible with him on constant night duty, coming home worn out and only wanting to sleep. But that had changed now the raids had temporarily stopped. The old patterns had had time to reassert themselves.

'I love you, Jess,' he whispered.

She smiled to hear the tenderness in his voice. 'And I love you.'

He began caressing her. 'We don't have to,' he further whispered.

A man like Albert had needs, she reminded herself. It would be cruel for her to deny him, she simply couldn't. Not after these many, long months during which he'd shown such consideration and understanding.

Taking the hand from her breast she kissed it, then drew him to her.

It was going to be another warm day, Ellie thought as she let herself out of the house, leaving to go on duty. Somewhere a bird, she had no idea what sort, was singing joyously. An uplifting sound to hear in the middle of war.

As she turned into Upper Street a milk cart was approaching her, a woman driver holding the reins. She recognised Connie Fox immediately.

Connie saw, and recognised, Ellie at the same time, her expression instantly changing. Biting her lower lip she reined in.

'Hello, Connie!' Ellie exclaimed in delight.

'Hello.'

'It's been a long time. How are you?'

Connie regarded Ellie nervously. 'Fine. And you?'

'Mustn't grumble I suppose. I came across Miss Oates some while back, running a mobile canteen for the WVS would you believe. She told me you were doing a milk round nowadays.'

'Really?' Connie replied unenthusiastically. 'Imagine that.'

Ellie frowned. 'I've never seen you on this particular round before?'

'That's because I'm new to it,' Connie explained. 'I was doing another one up in Barnsbury, but they transferred me.'

Something was wrong, Ellie realised, though she couldn't think what. Was it her imagination or was Connie trying to avoid her eyes? 'I must say you're looking well.'

Connie shrugged. 'The outdoor life agrees with me. It's certainly an improvement from being cooped up in a stuffy office all day long.'

'I don't miss that at all. Do you?'

'Not in the least,' Connie agreed.

'When the war's over I shan't be going back to office work. I've had that.'

Connie fiddled with the reins.

'Miss Oates said you were going out with a seaman and that it's all hunky-dory between you,' Ellie prompted, wanting to hear all about it.

'Yes,' Connie rather vaguely replied.

'So?'

'So what?'

Ellie sighed in exasperation. 'Who is he? What's he like? Where did you meet? Come on, I want to hear.'

Connie gave Ellie a rather sickly smile. 'I simply haven't got time to chat right now, Ellie. I wish I did but haven't. I must get on. You know how it is?'

Ellie didn't. Surely Connie could spare a few minutes. Before she could utter, or protest, further, Connie flicked the reins. 'I'll see you again no doubt. Take care.'

'And you!' Ellie called after Connie, the horse and cart having moved forward in the meantime so that now she was addressing Connie's back.

How odd, Ellie reflected as she continued on her way. How extremely strange. Why had Connie been so put out at seeing her? For Connie clearly had. Had something been said in the past that she'd forgotten about, or had she offended Connie in some way?

If it was either she certainly couldn't remember.

It was a new experience for Albert to arrive home after his shift and Jess not be there to greet him. This was going to take a bit of getting used to.

Trouble was, being her first day he had no idea when she would get in. The best thing, he decided, was just to settle down until she appeared which happened three quarters of an hour later.

Albert was instantly on his feet. 'So how did it go?' he demanded.

Jess kissed him briefly on the mouth. God she was tired, not being used to standing all day long. 'A piece of cake,' she declared. 'Couldn't have been easier. The work that is.'

He crossed over and put the kettle on, it having been standing at the ready. 'What kind of firm is it and what exactly are you doing there?'

'It's a small engineering works producing aircraft parts. I run a machine that stamps out some of the bits that then go on to be finished and assembled on to something else. As I said, couldn't be easier. Boring mind you, the same procedure over and over. But the other women are a jolly lot and we all have a good laugh together.'

He could see how tired she was, but there was an excitement in her eyes, an interest perhaps, that hadn't been there since Paul's death. That pleased him enormously.

Jess slumped into a chair. 'I'll have that cup of tea and then get going with the meal.'

Albert couldn't bring himself to ask what that meal was, dreading the answer.

'So, you'll manage all right?' he queried.

'Oh yes. If I have one complaint however, it's the noise. Some of those machines make a terrible racket. I was quite deafened for the first couple of hours. But no other moans apart from that.'

'Good.'

Jess smiled at Albert, trying to remember the last time he'd put the kettle on and made a cup of tea.

She couldn't, which made her appreciate this one all the more.

'I just can't get used to not havin' you round durin' the day, Jess. I feel so goddamn lonely all the time now,' Beulah complained.

Jess regarded her friend with sympathy. 'You have Pee Wee?'

'Ain't the same, hon. I'm talkin' female company here, good old girlie stuff. You know what I mean?'

Jess knew only too well. There was nothing like a proper chinwag with another woman.

'Anyway,' Beulah went on. 'I must say being at work has done wonders for you. I sure is delighted at that.'

Jess smiled. 'It does have its drawbacks though.'

'And what are those?'

Jess dropped her gaze to stare into her coffee, a far superior drink than the ersatz rubbish they now sold in the shops. Brought in by Julius from the Embassy of course. A cup of Beulah's coffee was a real treat.

'The main one is I don't get to the cemetery every morning any more. I miss that dreadfully.'

Now it was Beulah's turn to be sympathetic. 'Maybe that's a good thing,' she replied softly.

Jess didn't answer.

'At least I believe so. You was mopin' and grievin' too much, girl. As I've told you before, you has to get on with your life and leave the past in the past.'

'Maybe,' Jess reluctantly agreed.

'Well, that's how I sees it. And I'm sure I'm right.'

Jess pictured Paul in her mind and a lump rose into her throat. She'd have given anything, anything at all, to have him back.

'It don't mean you forget him, Jess, it don't mean that at all. Sure I know it's hard, but it's happened and that's all there is to it.'

Beulah decided to change the conversation, to try to snap Jess out of the black mood she'd suddenly fallen into. 'How would you like a piece of chocolate cake I baked this morning?' she queried.

Jess's face lit up. 'Have you really got one?'

'You bet your ass I do, hon. As chocolatey as chocolate can be.' Beulah laughed. 'Let's make pigs of ourselves and eat the whole damn thing, eh?'

'Oh I couldn't possibly!' Jess protested. 'I'd be sick.'

'No you won't. And afterwards you'll sure as hell feel a whole lot better, or my name ain't Beulah Poston.'

'It's gorgeous!' Jess declared after the first bite of the gigantic slice Beulah had placed in front of her, her eyes now shining where only minutes before they'd been dull and melancholic.

Beulah laughed again, a deep rumbling sound that came from the very bottom of her huge belly.

As she'd prophesied they did eat the entire cake and neither was sick. Full to the gills with chocolate perhaps, but certainly not sick.

Albert looked across at Ellie who'd just finished helping her mother wash and dry the dishes from their evening meal. He and Ellie were both currently on day shift. Ellie was doing the crossword puzzle that appeared daily in the newspaper they took.

'Stuck?' he queried because she was frowning.

Ellie nodded.

'What's the clue?'

'He cometh on stage. Six letters, the first is I, and the third E.'

'He cometh on stage?' Albert mused. 'Sounds Shakespearean to me.'

'That's what I think.'

Albert thought about it for a few minutes, then shook his head. 'Beats me.'

'Me too,' Ellie sighed in exasperation. Crossword puzzles were a relatively new thing she'd taken up, having found she was usually pretty good at them. That night's was particularly difficult. At least she found it so.

'Ah!' Ellie suddenly exclaimed. 'Iceman.'

'Iceman?' Albert repeated, wondering how that fitted in with Shakespeare.

'It's a play by Eugene O'Neill. *The Iceman Cometh*. Cometh on stage, see?'

'How on earth did you know that?' Jess demanded.

'We did it at school. One of a number of plays we had to study. I thought it terribly depressing.'

Albert watched her write that down. 'It's just dawned on me, tonight's Friday night,' he said slowly.

Ellie glanced across at him. 'So?'

'When was the last time you went out and enjoyed yourself? Since you joined the auxiliaries, and the Blitz started, you haven't been out of the house. At least not that I'm aware of.'

'I agree,' Jess chipped in. 'It's not right that you're home night after night as you've been.'

Ellie stared from one parent to the other, thinking what Albert said was true enough. Since George, apart from The Florence which didn't really count, she hadn't been anywhere.

'High time you had another chap,' Jess declared. 'Do you the world of good.'

Albert nodded his agreement.

'You know what it's been like,' Ellie reminded them. 'There hasn't been time for anything apart from work and sleep.'

'Well, there is now,' Albert retorted.

'But I don't want to go on my own.'

'Then hook up with a pal. One of the girls from the station, say.'

Ellie immediately thought of Josie Farnham who was also single and on the loose. Maybe Josie would fancy the idea? 'I'll think about it,' she prevaricated.

'Take the chance while it's there,' Albert urged. 'Who knows when the raids will start again and then it'll be impossible for who knows how long.'

'You could go to the Roxy,' Jess suggested.

Ellie pulled a face. 'That dump!'

'It's local and it would be best, should you meet someone nice, that he's local too. Easier that way.'

What her mother said made sense, Ellie reflected. A local chap would indeed be easier. If she went up West the chaps there would come from all over London, miles away, which would be a problem at the best of times, far more in the middle of a war when so much was disrupted and out of joint, not least the transport systems.

'Do you have a pal at the station?' Albert asked.

Ellie told them about Josie whom she'd been teamed with and the fact they got on so well together.

'Well, there you are then,' Jess declared. Rounding on Albert she then went on, 'And I'd like a night out at the pictures, Albert Sykes. Ellie isn't the only one who hasn't been anywhere in ages.'

He smiled at her. 'Tomorrow night too soon?'

'Tomorrow night would be absolutely right,' she enthused, delighted with this turn of events.

Albert was delighted too. What a change in Jess since she'd started work, she was a new woman. More like her old self. 'I'm looking forward to it,' he said, voice ringing with sincerity.

'Me too.'

If Ellie hadn't been present she'd have given Albert a kiss.

'Go on tour!' Beulah exclaimed.

'Only for a short spell, hon. Four weeks, hardly anythin'.'

Beulah wasn't pleased at all by this news that had come right out the blue. 'You wanna go?'

Pee Wee shrugged. 'Ain't got much choice in the matter. Besides, it's for a good cause. Playin' the military camps will cheer those guys up. Good for morale was how Lord Fitzaran put it.'

'And what about The Chicory House?'

'Another band will take our place while we're away so it won't shut down or anythin'.' He put on what he hoped was a winning smile. 'Look at it this way, hon, it's a great opportunity for us to see somethin' of England. We'll be goin' all over.'

'Us!' she exploded. 'I ain't goin' nowhere. I toured with you before, man, and it's a pain in the butt. I's too old for that kind of nonsense nowadays. Livin' out of a suitcase, spendin' nights travellin' in an old beat-up bus, always uncomfortable, never a hot tub available when you needs one.' She shook her head. 'You tour if you must, Pee Wee, but count this here chicken out. I'm stayin' right where I am and nothin', or nobody, will make me change my mind.'

'It's only for a month,' he repeated. 'Ain't the end of the world.'

Beulah sighed. 'I suppose if it's to help military morale. But I don't like it none, Pee Wee. I don't like it at all.'

He went to her and took her into his arms. 'I'll be back before you know it, sweetpea.'

She hated being parted from him, absolutely loathed it which was why she'd toured with him in the past. 'Yeah, a month ain't too bad I reckon,' she reluctantly replied. 'Just you see it ain't no more than that.'

'I promise. A month is the deal and that's what it'll be. I swear.'

That mollified her a little. 'When do you leave?'

'Sunday after next. We're to meet up at The Chicory House and go from there.'

'I'll fix you somethin' to eat,' she said, breaking away, still unhappy at all this.

Pee Wee wisely dropped the subject, nor did Beulah refer to it again for the rest of that day.

'Why the long face?'

Ellie came out of her reverie to find Julius standing beside her, she having popped into The Florence for a quick one. 'Sorry, I was thinking,' she explained, indicating the chair beside her. The pub was quiet as it was still early.

'Problem?' he queried, having sat.

'No, not really.'

He pulled out a packet of cigarettes and offered her one, the pair of them then lighting up.

'Want to talk about it?' he asked.

She was pleased to see him, but then always was. 'Mum and Dad think I should get out more. Socialise, that sort of thing.'

'And don't you?'

Ellie shook her head. 'As I reminded them, there's a war on. There just hasn't been the time lately, what with one thing and another.'

'Well, you know what they say, all work and no play makes Jill a dull broad.'

She laughed. Dull broad indeed!

'That's better,' he approved. 'Hot damn if it isn't.' He suddenly became all confidential. 'Shall I tell you a secret?' he whispered.

'What's that?'

He leant closer and whispered again. 'You don't laugh enough. It suits you.'

'Idiot!'

He winked. 'It's called black humour.'

Ellie found that very funny. 'I don't know how you do it, Julius, but you always buck me up. You're a constant tonic.'

'You mean like that stuff they put in gin?'

She wagged a finger at him. 'Now you're just being plain silly.'

'Am I?'

'You know you are.'

He beamed broadly. 'But it's fun. Isn't it?'

She nodded. 'And it's bucked me up. Thank you.'

'My pleasure, Ellie.'

She could smell his cologne which seemed even stronger than usual, a smell she now associated with him. She'd come to like it.

Staring into her face Julius had a sudden idea. One he decided he'd have to give thought to.

Ellie's intended quick drink turned into three before she and Julius finally left the pub. Afterwards it dawned on her it had been as though neither wanted to go, wanting to prolong their time together.

Subconsciously, it had certainly been so in her case.

Chapter 23

'Let's hope there are some decent-looking blokes here and we get asked up to dance,' Josie Farnham said to Ellie as they crowded into the Roxy dancehall. There were certainly plenty of people present, many of the men in uniform.

Ellie was already enjoying herself. She and Josie had stopped off for a couple of drinks on the way there which had set the mood; now they would see what was what.

Ellie didn't recognise the band, a new one since the days when she'd been a regular attender. They were currently playing a waltz, the dance floor jammed with couples dancing to it.

'Do I look all right?' Josie asked anxiously, waving a stray wisp of hair away from her eyes.

'Stop fretting, you look fine.'

Josie dusted imaginary specks of whatever off the front of her dress which had a halter neck and sleeves that ended just above her elbows. Its deep blue colour suited her dark complexion.

Ellie nudged her friend and nodded towards a chap moving in their direction. 'He's gorgeous,' she whispered.

The chap in question had pale blond hair and wore the uniform of an RAF pilot. Ellie wondered if he'd fought in what was now known as the Battle of Britain.

To Ellie's disappointment the pilot brushed past them without giving either a second glance. No luck there, she thought.

The number came to an end and the dancers applauded. Some came off the floor while others remained where they were.

'God, it's hot in here,' Josie commented, for it was stifling. She hoped her carefully applied make-up didn't start to run.

Ten minutes went by and still no one approached them. Then a chap in a lounge suit came over and smiled at Josie. 'Would you care to dance?'

'I'd love to. Thank you.'

The chap, in his late twenties Ellie judged, took Josie by the arm and led her away.

He'd seemed nice enough, Ellie thought, though nowhere near as handsome as the pilot whom she now spotted with a flaming redhead much younger than himself.

Ellie glanced around, wondering idly if she'd bump into anyone she knew. It was entirely possible being the local dancehall.

'Excuse me?'

She turned to find a truly ugly young man staring at her. 'Hello.' Christ, it's Quasimodo without the hump, she thought.

'Dance?'

She couldn't refuse, that wasn't the done thing. Not without a good excuse anyway which she didn't have. She smiled assent and they headed for the floor.

'My name's Richard by the way,' he said as she went into his arms.

'I'm Ellie.'

'Pleased to meet you.'

When he said that she got a whiff of his breath which nearly knocked her sideways. It stank!

'I haven't seen you here before?' he probed.

Ellie answered, keeping her face turned slightly away from him. Then he asked her what she did, which she explained.

'Interesting,' he commented. 'I'm a dock worker myself. Exempt, which is why I'm not in uniform.'

She didn't reply to that, wishing the number would hurry up and be over with. It was manners to accept one dance, but there was no tradition dictated she had to accept two.

Not only did his breath stink, but his personal hygiene wasn't too clever either, she realised. A good bath would have done him the world of good.

When the number finished they politely applauded. 'Will you have another?' he asked eagerly.

'I'm sorry, but I have to get back to my friend,' she lied, at which his face fell.

'Are you sure?'

'Positive,' she stated firmly. 'Thank you.' And with that she walked away leaving him standing there staring after her.

Fortunately she saw a girl she'd been to school with and stopped beside her for a brief chat. When she looked out of the corner of her eye Richard had also left the floor and was talking to some other female which let her off the hook.

What a horrible man, she thought on leaving her school chum who was with a cousin. Josie had remained on the floor making Ellie wonder if she had clicked.

She decided to nip into the ladies for a cigarette and was just about to head in that direction when a couple dancing caught her attention. She couldn't believe it, she simply couldn't, for the couple were none other than George and Connie, Connie with her eyes closed and cheek pressed against George's chest.

'Bitch!' she muttered furiously. 'Bitch!' No wonder Connie had been so strange that morning in Upper Street, making excuses about having to get on so she didn't have to answer her questions about the boyfriend. A boyfriend who now turned out to be bloody George!

Suddenly Ellie felt sick to the very pit of her stomach.

Ellie had waited almost an hour, watching while George and Connie danced together. Her opportunity came when they came off the floor and Connie left George to make for the Ladies'.

Ellie caught up with her halfway down the corridor, coming up behind her and tapping her on the shoulder. 'Hello, Connie.'

Connie blanched. 'Hello, Ellie,' she stuttered.

'Let's go outside. I want a word.'

Connie's eyes flicked first one way, then the other, but she could hardly make a run for it. What would have been the point? 'All right.'

Ellie, still fuming, continued on behind Connie and out of the main door into a balmy July night. 'So tell me about you and George?' she demanded when they'd halted and faced one another.

'What do you want to know?'

Ellie's eyes narrowed. 'You were going out with him when we were still at the office, weren't you? He was the new boyfriend you didn't want to talk about.'

Connie swallowed hard, and nodded.

'What I don't understand is how the pair of you got together when George was supposed to be at sea?'

'Have you got a cigarette?'

'Bugger a cigarette, you've mooched the last one off of me, Connie Fox. Explain,' Ellie hissed.

'George wrote to you from Liverpool, right?'

'Right. He was supposed to sail the next day.'

'Well, he did, only the ship broke down shortly after leaving harbour and had to be towed back in again. It turned out the engines were in need of extensive repair, so the majority of the crew were transferred to other vessels. In George's case it was a small ship doing coastal trips only which meant he could, and still can, get home every week to ten days. We met by chance, here actually, and have been going out together ever since.

'Honestly, Ellie, I didn't pinch him from you, he'd already

broken it off before that night when we both turned up here. As God is my witness, that's the truth.'

Despite what Connie had just said, Ellie still felt betrayed, and somehow humiliated. And still bloody angry.

Connie hung her head. 'I'm sorry, Ellie. I couldn't tell you the truth because I knew it would hurt. We were best mates after all, and you'd been so good to me, going with me to that abortionist woman when I needed a friend by my side.'

'Do you love him?'

When Connie glanced up there were tears in her eyes. 'Yes.'

'And I presume he loves you?'

Connie nodded.

Ellie couldn't resist it. 'Funny how he fell in love with you so quickly after being in love with me, don't you think?'

Connie didn't answer that.

'Are you shagging him?'

'Oh, Ellie,' Connie whispered. 'Don't ask that.'

Ellie's expression became grim. 'Which means you are. There again, you always were a tart. He's hardly the first man you've opened your legs to.'

'I'm not a tart,' Connie sobbed.

'Then what would you call yourself? I say tart, or perhaps you'd prefer slut? Whichever, you're as common as dirt.'

Ellie fought back the urge to slap Connie. It wouldn't have been so bad if Connie had taken up with George some time after she and he had broken up, but to do so almost instantly! That made her blood boil. And to think she'd considered Connie a friend. She should have known better.

'Well, you're welcome to him,' Ellie hissed. 'Good luck to the pair of you.'

And having said that she whirled round and re-entered the Roxy to find Josie and tell her she was going home.

'I see,' Jess mused after Ellie had explained what had happened. 'And I always thought George such a nice lad too.'

'But he didn't double-cross you, Ellie. You've admitted he'd broken it off before taking up with this other girl,' Albert reminded her.

Ellie glared at him. 'That's not the point.'

'Of course it isn't,' Jess chipped in.

Albert was confused. 'Then what is?'

'Connie was my friend, Dad.'

'So?'

'She might have waited a while before taking up with him.'

Albert didn't quite understand the reasoning behind that. 'But she was free and so was he. True, the timing might have been a bit unfortunate but they could hardly help that.'

'Waiting would have been the decent thing to do,' Ellie insisted.

'Quite right,' Jess nodded.

This was beyond him, Albert decided, and went back to reading his paper. He would never comprehend the female mind, not in a million years.

'I'll put the kettle on,' Jess declared brightly, as though that would sort everything.

'She might have waited, the cow,' Ellie repeated.

Albert said nothing.

Ellie had gone to bed early, still upset after the dance, and Albert had gone up a few minutes previously. Now Jess was on her own having promised Albert she'd join him soon.

Trouble was, she wasn't in the least bit tired, her worry and concern for Ellie keeping her wide awake. She hated seeing her daughter so miserable and had said everything she'd thought might help to soothe matters.

Children, she thought. What a worry they were. And it never stopped. From the moment they were born they were just one worry after another, an endless parade of troubles and anxieties.

Jess's eyes strayed to the mantelpiece and the framed picture of Paul standing on it. Well, she didn't have to worry about him any more, she thought bitterly. The poor little sod was dead.

'Dead,' she whispered aloud. Gone. For ever.

311

Rising, she crossed to the photo and picked it up to stare at it. Her Paul. Her darling son. And she'd . . . Jess swallowed. She'd brought him back from Devon for which she would never forgive herself. Not ever.

She carefully replaced the photograph and smiled at it. So many memories, so many good ones.

And at the end, so much heartache.

The following day Jess and Ellie were preparing lunch, a vegetable stew and boiled potatoes, when there was a knock on the outside door. Albert was over in The Florence having his customary Sunday lunchtime drink when not on duty.

'I'll get it,' Jess announced, wiping her hands on her apron, while Ellie continued peeling potatoes.

'It's Julius for you,' Jess declared on returning to the kitchen with him in tow.

'Hi!' he smiled. 'How are you?'

A mess, she thought, for she was still in her nightie and dressing gown having not yet washed or dressed which was unusual for her on a day off.

'Well, as you can see, you've caught me in my glad rags,' she retorted, matching his smile.

Julius laughed. 'Do you want me to come back later?'

She shook her head. 'What can I do for you?'

Ellie left the sink and Jess took over the potato peeling, as curious as Ellie as to why Julius was here.

'We're having a cocktail party at the Embassy next week for some Russians and I wondered if you'd like to come with me?'

'A cocktail party?' Ellie repeated in wonder. She'd never been to one of those, far less one at an Embassy.

'That's right. Friday evening at seven o'clock. There should be about thirty or forty present, including the Ambassador himself. It's a goodwill thing as we're, the White House that is, trying to keep in with the Russkies. Are you free?'

A wide-eyed Jess stared at her daughter, as taken aback as Ellie was.

'I'm free,' Ellie replied.

'Then would you like to go?' He winked. 'There will be some nice food, if that'll tempt you. Nothing serious though, mainly canapés and the like.'

Ellie had no idea what canapés were, never before having heard the word. Tasty bits and pieces, she correctly guessed. 'Sounds wonderful. I'd love to go.'

He nodded. 'That's settled then. I'll pick you up just after six. OK?'

'OK,' she agreed, repeating the Americanism.

'I'll leave you to it then.'

'I'll see you out,' Ellie offered.

'Not in your dressing gown, Ellie. People might get the wrong idea,' he teased.

Ellie blushed bright red as he, laughing, exited the kitchen.

'Well, how about that then?' Jess said after he'd gone. 'Excited?'

'Of course I am. It's something to look forward to.' A look of total panic suddenly came across her face. 'But what am I going to wear?'

After lunch when the dishes had been done and Albert had settled into his chair for a snooze, Jess went up to Ellie's bedroom where she had been busily rummaging through her wardrobe and drawers.

'Find anything?' Jess queried.

Ellie shook her head. 'None of my stuff is right, or classy enough. This will be a posh do remember.'

Jess glanced at the clothes laid out on Ellie's bed, all of them predating the war. 'If we had enough coupons we could try up West,' she said slowly. 'But I'm afraid we don't. Nowhere near enough.'

Ellie looked at the same clothes in despair. 'What am I going to do, Mum? I should have thought of this before accepting.'

'Hmmh,' Jess mused, mentally going through her own wardrobe. But she owned nothing remotely suitable either.

'Damn!' Ellie muttered. She couldn't possibly go in any of these dresses, she'd show herself up, not to mention Julius.

'I have an idea,' Jess said slowly.

'What's that?'

'Put all this away again and don't worry. I think I can sort this out again tomorrow, with a bit of luck that is.'

Despite Ellie pressing her Jess wouldn't say what her idea was, only repeating that Ellie wasn't to worry.

The following evening Ellie arrived home from work to find Albert fretting because Jess wasn't there.

'She was due in half an hour ago and still no sign of her,' a worried Albert declared, glancing yet again at the clock on the mantelpiece. 'I hope nothing's happened.'

'I shouldn't think so, Dad. She's probably had to do a bit of overtime, that's all.'

'Well, it would be a first. She hasn't had to do that up until now,' he frowned.

'There's a war on, Dad, don't forget. Nothing's set in stone.'

Ellie wondered if she should start getting the meal ready, but had no idea what Jess had planned. A look in the cupboard and larder didn't reveal what it might be.

Ellie lit up, and slumped into a chair. Rumour round the station was that the Germans were massing across the Channel for more massive air raids, which might or might not be true. You just never knew where rumours were concerned.

The chap Josie had met at the dance had taken a shine to her and had arranged to meet her to go to the pictures on Wednesday night. His name was Reg and he was a policeman of all things. Josie had pronounced him lovely and was looking forward to seeing him again. Ellie was pleased for her.

'Why don't you make a cup of tea?' Albert suggested. 'That at least would be something.'

'Let me finish my ciggy first, then I'll do it.'

'You're smoking far too many of those things,' Albert admonished. 'You've taken to coughing first thing in the morning.'

'Have I?' Ellie answered innocently, well aware that she had.

Albert glanced again at the clock. Where was Jess? He was starving, his stomach beginning to think his throat had been cut.

It was over an hour later before Jess appeared carrying a cylindrical-shaped object wrapped in brown paper. 'Sorry I'm late,' she apologised. 'But I had a few things to do after work.'

She placed the object on the table. 'That's for you,' she informed Ellie.

'Me?' Ellie couldn't imagine what it was.

'It's part of the idea I told you about yesterday.'

Ellie gasped at what was revealed when she unwrapped the object, a bolt of magnificent black material. 'It's silk,' she croaked, running a hand over it

'Pure silk I'm assured,' Jess qualified. 'Like it?'

'Of course I do. It's beautiful. But what's it for?'

'Your cocktail dress naturally,' Jess replied. 'I nipped round yesterday afternoon and spoke to Mrs Silverman who's agreed to make it for you.' Mrs Silverman was an old Jewish woman Jess had found to alter Ellie's uniform which now fitted perfectly.

'Oh, Mum!' Ellie breathed, eyes shining.

'I can't have a daughter of mine not up to the mark, now can I?' Jess smiled.

Albert was staring in consternation at the material. 'Where did you get it from?' he asked slowly.

'Someone I know,' she replied evasively.

He took a deep breath. 'In other words, the black market. If you don't have enough coupons to buy the dress then you don't have enough for that. True?'

Jess didn't reply.

'You know how much I disapprove of the black market, Jess. And now you've done this behind my back.'

'It's not behind your back,' she prevaricated. 'The material's there for you to see.'

'You *bought* it behind my back, Jess. Don't quibble words with me.'

Jess's expression was one of defiance. 'Rules are made to be broken, Albert, and this is one such time. I have no intention of dealing on the black market ever again, so there!'

Albert, knowing he was beaten, sighed and turned away. 'It is lovely material,' he conceded. 'It should look good on you, Ellie.'

Ellie went to him and pecked his cheek. 'Thanks, Dad.'

'I still don't approve,' he grumbled. 'But the deed's done and that's all there is to it, I suppose. Now what about something to eat around here, I'm starving!'

Jess smiled. 'What would you say if I told you I had three pounds of sausages in my coat pocket?'

'Three pounds, woman, my God, how did you manage that!' His face clouded over. 'Not the black market again I hope?'

'No,' she lied. 'I just got lucky with the butcher.'

The sausages had come from the same source as the silk, but she wasn't admitting that to Albert. She'd snapped them up when offered them.

They were absolutely delicious.

Mrs Silverman was in her early seventies. A tailoress all her working life she was now retired but still did whatever came her way to help make ends meet.

'Very nice,' she nodded approvingly, running a hand over the bolt as Ellie had done. 'You were lucky to get it.'

'It wasn't cheap, I can tell you. But worth every penny I thought,' Jess replied. Neither Ellie nor Albert knew she'd had to pawn a brooch that had belonged to her mother to pay for it, and Mrs Silverman. She hoped one day, if the precious brooch hadn't been sold, to have saved up enough to redeem it. However, that was a chance she'd had to take.

Mrs Silverman didn't inquire into the material's origins, considering it to be none of her business. But she had a shrewd idea.

'Can you do it for this Friday?' Ellie asked anxiously.

'I can do it,' Mrs Silverman smiled. 'Don't you worry your

pretty little head about that. But first, we have to choose a pattern.'

She turned away and crossed over to where her sewing machine stood. 'I've looked out a few that might suit, so shall we see if we can find one you like?'

Mrs Silverman eyed Ellie from top to toe. 'Something fairly simple, I would suggest. That would be best for you in my opinion.'

In the end a pattern was finally decided on, after which Mrs Silverman began measuring Ellie, a procedure, having had years of experience, she did fairly quickly.

'Ellie won't be a moment,' Jess informed Julius who was dressed in a smart charcoal grey suit with pale blue shirt and subdued tie. His topcoat, as he referred to it, was neatly fitting, black and three-quarter length.

'There's no hurry,' Julius replied. 'As long as we're there at a reasonable time.'

Mrs Silverman, good as her word, had finished the dress the previous evening, she and Ellie collecting it and she paying Mrs Silverman. Both she and, more importantly, Ellie were highly delighted with the result. It had been well worth the money.

'Have you heard from your dad?' Albert inquired, Pee Wee still off on tour.

'Yeah, Mom got a call only last night. Dad's fine and enjoyin' himself, havin' a ball as he put it. But missin' Mom.'

'Did he say where he was?'

'A place called Huddersfield, which he's not all that impressed with. But the audiences are good accordin' to him. Real appreciative, and all military. He's lookin' forward to coming back though, he's also missin' Mom's cookin'.'

Jess laughed. 'I can understand that. I only wish I could cook as well as Beulah. She's a whizz in that department.'

Albert frowned at Jess. 'I'd hate it if you went away somewhere. I wouldn't know what to do with myself.'

'You'd be in the pub every night more like,' she teased.

'Not me!' Albert protested. 'Besides, I couldn't afford to be in there every night. That's well beyond my means.'

'Da ra!' Ellie cried, coming into the kitchen.

Julius's large eyes almost popped at the vision before him. He'd never seen Ellie look anything like this, or imagined she could.

'What do you think?' Ellie, suddenly coy, asked him.

He swallowed. 'Holy Toledo. You're an absolute knockout!'

Ellie flushed with pleasure, that being exactly what she'd wanted to hear. 'Like the dress?'

'Sure do. It could have come straight from Paris, France.'

The dress had a softly draped surplice bodice and gently flared skirt with unpressed pleats across the front. There was a self belt and buckle plus a Crown zip placket. The sleeves came to just below the elbow while the skirt ended at the knee.

Ellie had done her hair in a chignon, well pinned into place. She was wearing a pair of nylons from a number Julius had given her, her shoes soft black leather and plain, these brightly polished for the occasion. She wasn't wearing any jewellery as she didn't own any she considered appropriate.

Albert stared in admiration at his daughter. As they'd have said when he was young, she was a dish. He couldn't have been more proud.

Jess picked up the maroon-coloured velvet shoulder cape that Mrs Silverman had insisted Ellie borrow which perfectly complemented the dress. 'Don't forget this.'

Ellie took the cape and put it on. 'Ready when you are, Julius,' she smiled.

Julius shook his head in amazement. 'A knockout,' he repeated. 'When we get there I'm going to have to fight the other guys off.'

Ellie laughed.

'And I mean that. They'll be round you like bears round a honey pot.'

'I'm glad you approve.'

'Hell, yeah.'

'Then shall we?'

'OK, Cinderella, let's go to the ball.'

Cinderella! That was exactly how Ellie felt. Only in her case there were no ugly sisters.

Chapter 24

'They should be there by now,' Albert commented, having noted the time on the mantelpiece clock.

Jess paused in her darning, mending a pair of his socks. 'What's wrong with you tonight? You're ever so restless.'

He shrugged, but didn't reply.

'Why don't you nip over to The Florence and have a couple of pints? That might settle you a bit.'

'Do you want to go?'

Jess shook her head. 'I don't feel like it. But don't let that stop you. Being a Friday night there might be a sing-song later. You always enjoy those.'

True, he thought. He did. 'Nah, I won't bother either. I'll stay home with you.'

Albert fell into a brooding, introspective silence during which he stared at the empty grate. Every so often his eyes flicked back to the clock.

'Albert,' Jess finally said in exasperation. 'I know you. What's wrong? Something obviously is.'

'Nothing's wrong,' he lied.

'Yes there is,' she persisted. 'Now out with it.'

He sighed. 'It's nothing really. At least I don't think it is.'

'What?' she almost screamed.

'Ellie and Julius.'

Jess couldn't see what he was driving at. 'What about them?'

He shifted in embarrassment. 'You don't think tonight is the start of anything do you?'

That had never crossed Jess's mind. Now she considered it. 'To be honest, I've no idea.'

'It just sort of . . . worries me, that's all,' he confessed.

'Why should it do that?' a puzzled Jess queried. 'He's a nice chap, well-mannered with a terrific job. I don't know what he earns but probably a lot more than we realise. American wages, don't forget. So what's to worry about?'

Albert forced himself to say the next bit. 'He's also black, Jess.'

Now she understood, and was appalled. 'Do you hold that against him?'

'Not in the least,' Albert hurriedly replied. 'As you say, he's a nice chap, they don't come nicer. What I don't like is the notion of them getting together. I mean, what if it became serious. What then?'

'Oh, for God's sake, Albert,' Jess snapped in reply. 'He's only taken her to a cocktail party, it's not as if they're about to climb into bed together.'

Albert went puce. 'I should bloody well hope not!'

She couldn't help teasing him. 'Why, because he's black?'

'Ellie wouldn't climb into bed with any man, black, brown, white or tartan. She's been brought up properly, at least I hope she has.'

'I know she has,' Jess stated firmly. 'And you're reading far too much into this. It's only a harmless night out, nothing more. So stop worrying.'

Albert sort of snorted. 'I don't believe in mixed marriages, you see. A recipe for disaster in my book. Each kind should stick to its own. That's the way it should be. How God intended.'

Jess almost burst out laughing. 'You're on intimate terms with the good Lord now, eh? You know his mind on such matters? Honestly, I've never heard anything so ridiculously pompous in my entire life.'

'I am not being pompous,' Albert replied sharply. 'Merely saying what I think and believe. Have you considered children, eh? What about them? What kind of treatment could they expect to get being neither one thing nor the other, neither white or black? The poor little sods would be outcasts, that's what. Probably shunned by both sides. Shunned and mistrusted.'

This was a new side to Albert that Jess had never realised existed. Even after all these years he could still surprise her, and she'd thought she knew him inside out. 'I'm ashamed of you,' she said quietly.

He opened his mouth, then shut it again.

'Thoroughly ashamed,' she qualified.

That shook him. 'I'm only thinking about Ellie, what's best for her. I don't want her to make some terrible mistake.'

'We all have to make our own mistakes, Albert,' Jess stated wisely. 'And whoever listened to advice, especially from their parents? Not many people. And I would remind you Ellie has a mind and will of her own. She'll do what she thinks fit.'

Albert, reluctantly, knew both these points to be so. 'Maybe,' he prevaricated.

'Anyway,' Jess went on, a tone of finality in her voice, 'all this is about absolutely nothing, I'm sure of it. And don't forget, you were the one said Ellie should get out and about more which is precisely what she's doing.' Jess regarded him shrewdly. 'This isn't the jealous father and daughter bit, is it?'

'No it's not,' he replied, thoroughly rattled.

'Are you sure?'

'I wasn't when George was around, was I?'

She had to admit that was true. 'So it's simply about Julius being black?'

Albert nodded.

Jess stood up, she'd had enough of this bigotry. She hadn't forgotten her own wariness and suspicions when the Postons had moved in next door, and that too had been entirely because they were black. But now she'd come to know them she couldn't have asked for nicer or kinder neighbours. As far as she was concerned they were no different to anyone else, apart from the colour of their skins that is.

'I'm going upstairs,' she announced. 'I've listened to enough nonsense for one night.'

'But it's early!' he protested.

'Thoroughly ashamed,' she repeated, and left him to it.

It upset Albert deeply that Jess felt that way about him. He was only looking out for Ellie's best interests after all, that was a caring father's job.

'Damn!' he muttered. He should have kept his big mouth shut, not spoken up. Kept stumm.

He decided he would go to The Florence, he needed a drink after that. For the life of him he couldn't remember the last time he and Jess had argued, it being a rare occasion when it happened.

Without realising what he was doing he slammed the front door shut behind him.

Ellie had never seen such an abundance of rich goodies on one table. Smoked salmon, baked salmon, prime sliced roast beef, other meats – a whole medley of them – exquisitely cut tiny sandwiches, wondrous salads, fruit, cheeses. And all this in wartime when the general populace was on rationing. But then that didn't apply to the American Embassy. It was mind-boggling.

'What are those things?' she whispered to Julius, indicating with a slight jab of a finger.

'Quiches. Egg dishes. They're delicious.'

Quiche was a new one on her. 'And that?'

'Caviar.'

Her eyes widened. She'd heard of caviar but never thought she'd have the opportunity to taste some. She'd read somewhere that it was horrendously expensive.

'And those are spare ribs, a great American favourite – very tasty,' Julius informed her. 'I suggest you try a few.'

'I will, don't worry,' she replied earnestly, which made him laugh.

'Can I make a suggestion?'

'What's that, Julius?'

'I don't wish to sound rude, but we can come back to the table here as often as we like, so don't pile your plate too high to start with, wouldn't look good.'

She nodded that she understood.

'Other than that, the world's your oyster, which are down there by the way.' His little joke amused him.

'What are?'

'Oysters, Ellie.' He pointed, and sure enough there was a huge silver salver covered in opened oysters resting on a bed of chipped ice.

'Ever had any?' he queried, thoroughly enjoying himself.

'No.'

'Well, they're a bit of an acquired taste, rather like caviar. I love both myself.'

'Here goes,' Ellie declared, picking up a plate.

When they'd temporarily finished with the table they moved away, Ellie fascinated as she gazed round the room. The Russians were easily recognisable due to the ill-fitting suits they were wearing and the seriousness of their expressions.

'Which one is the Ambassador?' she asked, before biting into half a stuffed egg, the first egg she'd had in months.

'Second pillar to the left, got it?'

She looked in that direction. 'Got it.'

'He's the guy in the blue suit, the woman standing beside him is his wife.' They were talking to a bald Russian who was gesticulating a great deal.

'That's the head of the Russian delegation he's with,' Julius explained. 'A personal friend of Stalin I believe, and a very important man.'

Ellie was impressed, very much so. There again, the whole

occasion was impressing her enormously. She felt indeed that she was Cinderella at the Ball.

'Hi there, ole buddy, how ya doin'?'

Julius hadn't been aware that he was an ole buddy of Mike Stevenson, they hardly knew one another. 'Hello, Mike.'

Mike beamed at Ellie. 'Well, come on, introduce me to this gorgeous lady,' he requested.

Julius now realised why the 'ole buddy' routine. 'Mike Stevenson, I'd like you to meet Ellie Sykes.'

'Well, hi!' Mike gushed and, taking hold of Ellie's hand, shook it.

'She's English,' Julius said.

'Really?'

'Pleased to meet you, Mr Stevenson,' Ellie nodded in return.

'Mike! Call me Mike. No need to be formal. You know this bozo long?'

She presumed he meant Julius. 'Quite a while now.'

'Uh-huh.'

Julius remained silent, and attentive, while Mike did his best to ingratiate himself with Ellie, who was having none of it.

'I think we'd better circulate,' Julius declared after a few minutes. 'See you around.'

Mike was clearly disappointed as Julius and Ellie moved off. 'You appear to have an admirer there,' Julius commented.

'He seemed pleasant enough. Though somewhat gushy for me.'

Julius laughed. 'A lot of Americans are. They believe that's how to behave.'

'You're not.'

'Thank you. I'll take that as a compliment.'

What a wonderful smile he had, she thought. 'I suppose it was meant as one.'

Julius stopped a passing waiter and helped himself to two glasses of champagne, one of which he handed to Ellie who'd got rid of her now empty plate in the meantime. 'Bottoms up!' he toasted. 'Isn't that what you English say?'

'Some of us.'

The champagne was cold and bursting with bubbles that shot up her nose. Luckily she didn't cough or splutter.

'Like?' Julius queried.

'It's lovely.'

'I can take or leave it. I'd rather have a good shot of bourbon any day.'

Ellie's jaw literally dropped open when she saw who had just entered the room. 'Bloody Nora!' she muttered, for it was no less than the Prime Minister, Winston Churchill himself. He was smaller than she'd imagined.

'What is it?'

She swallowed. 'Over there, heading for your Ambassador.'

Julius followed her gaze. 'I knew he'd been invited, but no one was sure whether or not he could come.' Then, by way of explanation, 'The Russians are even more important to you British than us Yanks at the moment, so it's no wonder he's put himself out.'

Wait till she told Albert, Ellie thought gleefully. He'd have a fit, being an enormous admirer of Churchill's. Come to that, so was she.

'You never said he might be here,' she accused Julius, who shrugged.

'Wasn't certain he would be, so I thought I'd leave it as a surprise if he did show.'

Ellie stared at Churchill now deep in conversation with Ambassador Winant and the bald Russian, unable to believe she was actually in the same room as the great man. This would be a story to tell her children in later years. Providing she had some that was.

'Hi, Julius! Who's your ladyfriend?'

Julius went very still on hearing that. Slowly he turned to face Marybeth who he instantly knew from the glazed look in her eyes was drunk. Or, if not drunk, well on the way to being so. His heart sank, this could be trouble.

He reminded Marybeth that she and Ellie had already met,

Marybeth giving Ellie a long and measured once-over as he did. When Ellie extended a hand she let it hang there.

There was a brief pause, then Marybeth pursed her lips. 'No tits,' she pronounced.

Ellie froze, incredulous that had been said, and at a loss as to what to reply, if indeed she should.

Julius was furious, and about to make a sharp retort when Marybeth burst out laughing and walked, rather unsteadily, away.

'I am sorry,' Julius apologised quietly. 'Goddammit, I am.' The party was spoilt for Ellie, the entire evening ruined by those two words. 'What a cow,' she muttered. 'What an absolute cow.'

Julius could see how deeply upset Ellie was, and rightly so. What Marybeth had done was unforgivable. 'It isn't true,' he assured Ellie.

She stared at him, the beginnings of tears in her eyes, feeling totally humiliated. 'What isn't?'

'What Marybeth said, it isn't true. You've got a lovely figure.'

No tits, she thought in despair, having always considered herself slightly short in that department. That and a bum that was too big.

'I think I'd better go to the ladies if you don't mind.'

'I'll show you the way.'

Taking her by the arm he led her from the room, glimpsing Marybeth enroute with a smirk of satisfaction on her face.

'Do you want to leave?' he asked Ellie when she finally emerged from the restroom.

That was precisely what she did want. 'Would it be all right?'

'Yeah, sure. I've been seen to be here so that's all that matters. We'll blow.'

'I would rather, Julius. I just don't want to go back in there. Sorry.'

'Hey! I'm the one who's sorry, you've no need to apologise. So let's grab our things and be on our way.'

Once outside the Embassy he made a suggestion. 'There's a

little pub nearby that I sometimes use. How about we have a drink?'

'That would be nice.'

'Good,' he approved.

Ellie liked The King's Head, it had a warm and friendly atmosphere. She watched Julius up at the bar ordering, and thought what a pity his evening had also been spoilt. They'd both been enjoying themselves so much too. But at least she'd seen Winston Churchill, had been in the same room as the great man, an unforgettable experience.

'Here we are,' Julius declared on rejoining her. 'No gin I'm afraid but I did manage to get you scotch.'

'Thank you,' she smiled. 'Can I have some water to go with it?'

'Sure thing.'

He hurriedly returned to the bar, coming back again with a small jug. 'Say when?'

'When.'

He put the jug down and sat facing her. 'How do you feel now?'

'Pretty rotten to tell the truth.'

He nodded his sympathy. 'I wish I hadn't taken you now, but how could I have foreseen that?'

She attempted a smile. 'You couldn't possibly, and I wouldn't have missed it for the world. Well, most of the evening anyway.'

He reached across the table and laid a hand over hers. 'I truly am sorry, Ellie. Believe me.'

'Let's forget it, eh?'

'All right. But before we do let me just repeat that what she said was a load of hooey. Bullshit.'

How sweet he was, she thought, as upset about what had happened as she was.

As she'd requested the incident wasn't mentioned again that night.

*　*　*

'You're early!' Albert exclaimed in surprise when Ellie came into the kitchen, waking him up from a doze in his chair.

'It was only a cocktail party, Dad, not a full-blown knees-up.'

He smiled. 'Pardon my ignorance I'm sure. Enjoy yourself?'

'I had a wonderful time.' She certainly wasn't going to tell Albert about Marybeth. And she had had a wonderful time, for the most part. 'And you'll never guess who was there.'

'Who?'

'Someone you admire enormously.'

He was intrigued. 'Well come on, give.'

'Winston Churchill.'

The look of sheer incredulity that came across his face was a delight to see. 'You're taking the micky?'

'No, God's honest truth. He was there.'

'The *Prime Minister*!'

'The very same.'

Albert didn't reply, being lost for words.

'Well?'

'And you actually saw him?'

'Uh-huh.'

'Did you speak?'

Ellie shook her head. 'He was with the American Ambassador and some high-ranking Russian official, all three with their heads together.'

'Wait till I tell my mates at the station about this,' Albert said in awe. 'My daughter at a cocktail party with Winston Churchill!'

'Another thing, Julius got it wrong about the canapés. There was all sorts there to be had. Smoked salmon, turkey, oysters, caviar . . .'

Albert was suddenly ravenously hungry as Ellie reeled off the list of goodies that had been on offer.

Jess glanced across at Albert as the siren sounded for the first time in weeks. Ellie, who was back on nights, was already at work.

Albert's expression became grim. This wasn't unexpected, but a nasty surprise that the Luftwaffe had returned all the same. Jess was thinking she'd have to forego the luxury of her bed yet again for the makeshift, and uncomfortable, one in the shelter.

Albert came to his feet. 'They'll need me at the station,' he declared.

'But you've already done a full shift today,' Jess protested.

'Doesn't matter, you know that. It's all hands to the pumps when those damn things go off.'

Jess also rose. 'I'll get out to the shelter then.'

They both paused to listen when there was the sound of a far-off explosion followed by the unmistakable drone of aircraft overhead. More explosions followed the first.

'Right then,' Albert said abruptly. 'I'm off.' He went to Jess and kissed her on the cheek. 'On you go now, no hanging about.'

'Don't worry, I won't.'

'You'll see me when you see me.'

'Take care, love.'

Albert strode purposefully from the kitchen leaving an anxious Jess staring after him, the lull in the raids having given her, and probably an awful lot of other people, a false sense of security. Now the nightly terror had started all over again.

She quickly gathered a few things together, not forgetting Paul's framed photograph, her most prized possession.

Outside searchlights were criss-crossing a sky also lit up by streams of tracer bullets fired by the many ground batteries. Meanwhile the sirens continued to wail.

Once in the shelter Jess settled down for what she knew from bitter experience would be a long, and harrowing, night. As usual she offered up a silent prayer for Albert and Ellie's safety.

'Hi, hon. I'm home!'

'And ain't you the sight for sore eyes,' Beulah beamed, going to Pee Wee and encompassing him in a meaty embrace.

'Somethin' sure smells good,' he mumbled, face pressed hard against her ample bosom.

'It's tuna casserole. One of your favourites.'

Pee Wee managed to pull himself back a little and gazed into his wife's dark and soulful eyes. 'Miss me?'

'Damn right I did. And you?'

'Every moment.'

'Or was it just ma cookin'?' she teased.

'Well . . .' He played along, teasing also. 'Kinda fifty-fifty, I guess.'

Beulah laughed. She'd been terribly lonely while Pee Wee was away, but that was over now. Her man had returned and God was in His Heaven.

'I could use a cup of coffee,' he smiled.

'Comin' right up.'

While she busied herself with that Pee Wee gazed about him, absolutely delighted to be home again. 'How's things?' he asked.

Beulah shrugged. 'Just like I said when you called. Nothin's changed much. A more or less peaceful day followed by bombin' at night. You get used to it.'

'And Julius?'

'Oh, he's OK. Puttin' in long hours at work, but he says it can't be helped. Says he's gotta do it.'

Pee Wee nodded that he understood. 'I'm tired, hon, we been on the road since early.'

'Then it's straight up to bed for you after you eat.'

He raised an eyebrow. 'Alone?'

'Hell no, I'll be right there alongside.' Another tease. 'Unless you'd prefer otherwise?'

'What do you think?'

Beulah laughed. 'Here's your coffee. The pie's ready whenever you want.'

'I want right now.'

They gazed at one another, she knowing exactly what he meant by that. She felt skittish, almost like a young girl again as she hurried to the cooker.

* * *

Julius had waited to get Marybeth alone, and now his chance had come as she emerged from an office into a corridor empty apart from him.

Marybeth came up short and stared defiantly at him. 'You got something to say, say it,' she challenged.

He had something to say all right. By the time he was finished with her she too was on the verge of tears, just as Ellie had been the night of the cocktail party.

She was shaking all over when he finally walked away. Ellie had been avenged.

Ellie sighed, the paperwork she had to deal with as DSO was seemingly interminable. She no sooner got a load off her desk than it was duly replaced by another stack. Everything had to be accounted for, every call-out reported in detail, requisitions, materials. On and on and on.

And tonight two of the girls hadn't reported in which meant she personally would have to go out if a raid started, which it undoubtedly would.

She bent again to her task, stopping half an hour later when the sirens sounded. At least going out on call was a break from the paperwork, she told herself. A welcome break at that.

Jess grimaced when the same sirens went off, the damn Luftwaffe were late that night, the fourteenth in a row during which they'd pounded London. Another night in the shelter, she thought miserably, wishing there would be a change in the weather which would keep the Luftwaffe away for a couple of peaceful nights at least. Nights she could blissfully sleep all the way through.

She jumped when there was a nearby explosion. Christ, that was close she thought. Better get a move on. And with that she flew to gather up the things she always took with her.

Jess had just got into the shelter when she realised she'd left Paul's photograph behind. 'Stupid bitch,' she muttered. She'd quickly nip back for it.

* * *

High overhead the ack-ack had scored a direct hit on a Junkers bomber, blowing it to bits. The engine detached itself from its housing in what remained of the fuselage and plummeted earthwards.

Jess was just lifting Paul's photo from the mantelpiece when the plane's engine tore through the roof and then the bedroom floor.

She was directly underneath when it landed in the kitchen.

Chapter 25

Julius was lightly dozing having been running through work matters in his mind when the force of the impact threw him out of bed onto the floor where he ended up in a tangle of sheets and blankets.

'Christ!' he swore, as particles of dust and plaster swirled in a maelstrom round his room. The house had been hit.

His next thought was for his mother. Hastily he tossed the bedclothes aside and came groggily to his feet, having banged his head on the floor. Staggering, he left his room and made his way across the corridor to where Beulah slept.

He opened the door to find a thoroughly frightened Beulah sitting up in bed, her bedside light still on and working.

'What happened?' she gasped, her room also filled with swirling dust and plaster. Having asked that she immediately burst into a coughing fit.

'Dunno, Mom. I think we've been bombed.'

He went over to her, grabbed her dressing gown and whirled it round her shoulders. 'We've gotta get out of here. Are you hurt?'

Still coughing, she shook her head.

'Then come on in case this whole place collapses.'

Beulah reached out for the glass of water she habitually kept by her bedside, and gulped down several swallows which successfully cleared her throat. 'You OK?'

'I guess so.' He glanced over his pyjamas – no sign of blood while all his limbs were able to move and were apparently intact.

'Oh Julius,' she sobbed, as the realisation of what had occurred began to sink in.

'Let's go, Mom.'

They stumbled out into the corridor, he leaving her for a few brief seconds while he found his own dressing gown and slippers, then it was down the stairs and out into the street.

Their house was still in one piece, at least as far as he could make out, but next door was a wreck having partially caved in on itself. Several small fires were burning downstairs amidst piles of debris.

'Jess ain't in there,' a wide-eyed Beulah declared. 'She'll be out back in their shelter.'

Neighbours were beginning to foregather, all anxious and horror-struck. 'If it was a bomb it never went off,' someone said. 'I was already out here having just left the drinker.'

'I heard a loud noise, but not an explosion,' someone else, a woman this time, commented. 'Though there was one nearby just before.'

Harry, the pub landlord, appeared. 'I've rung the emergency services,' he informed the still swelling crowd. 'They'll be along when they can.'

Beulah clutched at Julius's arm. 'You can get to Jess through our yard,' she stated. 'Go and see she's OK.'

'Right, I'm on my way.'

Julius dashed back into their own house and moments later was out at the rear where a wooden fence separated the gardens. It wasn't easy, but after a couple of attempts he managed to get over it and drop down the other side.

Trouble was, because of the black-out, he couldn't see all that well. However, he soon found the shelter and stuck his head inside. 'Jess, are you there?'

He frowned when there was no reply. 'Jess?'

When there was still no reply he went into the shelter and flicked on his lighter.

The shelter was empty.

'Albert.'

He glanced round to find it was Danny McGiver who'd spoken. The fire they were desperately trying to bring under control was a large one involving several shops. 'What is it?'

Danny's face might have been carved from stone. 'We've just had word from the station. It's bad news, I'm afraid.'

Fear clutched at Albert's heart. 'Jess, Ellie?'

'Your house has been bombed, though they seem vague about that. Whatever, it's been hit.'

Albert felt as though he'd been punched hard in the stomach. 'Jess?'

'Nothing on her so far. All we know is that your house has been badly damaged. The report says a couple of small fires and the roof in. That's it.'

Jess would be safe, Albert assured himself. She'd have been in the shelter. 'I must get back there right away,' he croaked, his mind both numb and whirling at the same time.

'Of course. On you go, mate.'

Albert handed Danny the hosepipe he was directing and took to his heels. The fire he'd been attending was half a mile away from Florence Street. He ran the whole way without stopping once.

Beulah took it on herself to tell Albert when he arrived at what had been his home. 'Jess ain't in the shelter,' Beulah informed him. 'Had she gone out somewhere?'

Albert shook his head. 'Not that I'm aware. As far as I know she was staying put. At least that's what she said when I left her to go on duty.'

He stared at the remains of his house, he too thinking that if it had been hit by a bomb then the bomb hadn't exploded. 'I'm going in,' he stated.

'I'll come with you,' Julius offered.

'It could be dangerous, son. There might be an UXB in there.' That meant an unexploded bomb.

'Let's go,' Julius replied.

Albert gave him a grateful nod, he might need the help. Harry Clifford and Mike Pratt now stepped forward. 'I'm with you, Albert,' Harry declared.

'Me too,' added Mike Pratt.

A lump rose in Albert's throat. 'Thanks, chaps.'

'You lead the way. You're the expert,' Julius said.

The front door was off its hinges and lying just inside the hall. Albert clambered over it and switched on his torch to light the way.

Julius tried the hall switch, without any result. Odd, he thought, remembering Beulah's bedside lamp had been working.

'Jess!' Albert called out. 'Can you hear me?'

The only sound was that of dripping water as Albert briefly closed his eyes, desperate to go on, and yet reluctant to do so for fear of what he might find. Maybe, just maybe, Jess *had* gone out. He prayed to God that was so.

A little later Beulah clutched herself when a terrible, anguished cry rent the air. The voice was plainly distinguishable as Albert's.

Ellie turned into Florence Street, and immediately halted in her tracks when she saw the cluster of people outside her house, instantly knowing something was terribly wrong. She started to walk again, and then began to run.

The cluster of people, mainly neighbours, parted to let her through, their looks pitying ones.

Workmen were already busy inside shoring up the walls with stout lengths of wood. 'Watch out!' someone in the crowd yelled, and next second a section of slates from what had been the roof clattered onto the pavement and street.

Ellie knew she was in shock having seen the same thing in so many of those she'd been called out to. She could feel hysteria rising up inside her.

Suddenly Julius was by her side. 'Your dad's in our house,' he said quietly.

'And Mum?'

There was no easy way of doing this. He shook his head. 'She was in there when it happened. I'm sorry.'

Tears welled in her eyes. 'Dead?' she asked unnecessarily.

'I'm afraid so, Ellie. If it's any consolation she wouldn't have suffered. It must have been all over in an instant.'

She was dimly aware of Julius taking her arm and guiding her into his house where they found Albert sitting in the Postons' kitchen. The first thing that struck her was how much he'd aged. Within the space of a few short hours he'd become an old man.

'Dad!' she exclaimed, and rushed into his arms where her entire body started violently to shake.

'Sssh, girl, sssh!' Albert crooned. 'There's nothing we can do. Your mum's gone.'

Pee Wee, back hours earlier from The Chicory House, poured a large gin and added a splash of tonic. He waited patiently till he could hand it to Ellie.

Beulah's face had been ravaged by tears, the marks left by them streaked down her cheeks. Her normally huge body appeared somehow deflated, as though air had been let out of it.

'Where's Mum now?' Ellie at last asked.

Albert took a deep breath. Jesus, but this was difficult, the pain inside him excruciating, as if every last nerve in his being had been exposed. 'Still in there. We're waiting for a crane to . . .' He broke off and shook his head, unable to go on.

Julius decided he would have to explain. Going to Ellie he knelt beside her and Albert and did just that, not going into any of the gory details of what he, Albert and the others had discovered. Most of Jess was still underneath the German plane's engine.

Ellie's eyes were bulging as she listened, part of her wanting to open her mouth and scream this wasn't true. And then just scream and scream.

When she looked again at Albert through tear-filled eyes he seemed to have aged even more.

Julius sank onto the barstool and waited for Hazel to come over and serve him. He needed a few drinks before going across the road to see what was what.

'Usual?'

He nodded.

'They took the body away late this afternoon,' Hazel informed him as she poured.

Julius, who'd been at the Embassy all day, digested that.

'On the house,' Hazel said, placing a pint in front of him.

'Thanks.'

'Harry told me you were one of those who went in with Albert.'

'Yeah,' Julius whispered, knowing he'd never forget that sight until his own dying day.

'Harry said it was awful.'

Julius couldn't help but smile. 'That's an English understatement if ever there was.'

'Poor Albert,' Hazel said softly. 'First his son, and now Jess. Poor bloody man.'

'Have you got any spirits, Haze?'

She glanced around. 'Not officially, but hang on.' And with that she disappeared out the back.

When she returned she handed Julius a teacup and saucer. 'So the other customers don't think I'm playing favourites,' she explained.

Julius sipped the scotch the cup contained, shuddering as it hit his empty stomach. He hadn't eaten a thing all day, nor had he wanted to. He still wasn't in the least hungry.

He thought of Ellie and what she must be going through. He'd been thinking about her on and off all day, trying to imagine how he'd have felt if it had been Beulah who'd been killed, particularly in such a gruesome manner. At least, as he'd said to Ellie, it had been instantaneous. That was something to be grateful for.

'What we need are you Yanks in this war,' Hazel declared to Julius while wiping up. 'Just like the last lot. That's what we need all right. Between us we'd soon sort Jerry out.'

Julius glanced at her. 'It's not impossible, Haze.'

She regarded him shrewdly, well aware of where he worked if not exactly what he did there. 'Do you know something?'

'I didn't say that.'

'But your tone implied it.'

He had to be more careful, he told himself. It was unlike him to give anything away. There again, he supposed he could make allowances, excuse himself a little, after the previous night. 'Didn't mean to, Hazel. I simply said it wasn't impossible.'

'Hmmh.' She didn't believe a word of that. 'Well, I only hope you do, and soon.'

Julius hoped so too. In a way this war had now become personal with the death of Jess Sykes.

Julius glanced round the kitchen. 'Where's Ellie?' he queried.

'Upstairs sleepin', the doc gave her a sedative. She's goin' to be stayin' here with us for a while as she can't be next door.'

Julius nodded his understanding and approval. 'What about Albert?'

'He went off some hours ago with a colleague of his called Danny McGiver. He had to fill out some official forms and then he was goin' to McGiver's as we don't have room here for two extra. Anyway, McGiver was insistent Albert beds down at his place.'

Julius ran a hand over his face. He was desperately tired having had virtually no sleep the night before. 'I'm pooped,' he declared wearily.

'Want to eat?'

He shook his head.

'What you had today then?'

'Nothin'. I couldn't face food.'

Beulah wasn't having that. 'Don't matter none, you're gonna have somethin'. I don't want you goin' sick on me, you hear, Julius Poston?'

'I hear, Mom.' He resolved to force himself. 'They got the body out I hear.'

Beulah's face sort of crumpled in on itself. 'Yeah. That was the bit where Ellie kinda went bananas and had to be given a sedative.'

'And Albert?'

'He just cried, son. I hope never to see a grown man cry like that again.'

Julius pulled out a pack of cigarettes and lit up. The smoke he drew deep into his lungs tasted of absolutely nothing at all.

'Can I help you?'

Harry smiled. 'I believe this is where Mr McGiver lives?'

Vera nodded. 'That's so.'

'And Albert Sykes is with you?'

'Are you a friend of his?'

'Landlord of his local.'

'I see,' Vera said, now also smiling. 'Please come in.'

'I won't if you don't mind. How is Albert?'

Vera pulled a face. 'As you'd expect.'

Harry sighed, and took from his overcoat pocket a bottle wrapped in brown paper. 'Give that to him. Say it's from Harry and Hazel at The Florence.'

'Are you sure you won't come in?' Vera queried, accepting the bottle.

'No, I don't want to intrude.'

Vera didn't press further, Harry's mind clearly made up. 'Goodbye then. And thank you on his behalf.'

'Goodbye, Mrs McGiver.'

With that Harry strode off into the night. The bottle he'd given Albert was the last one he currently possessed, and should have been for his own private consumption.

In the circumstances, he hadn't minded parting with it one little bit. It might just bring some comfort to Albert, even if it was of the liquid, and temporary, kind.

As chance would have it, the night following Jess's death was a wild and stormy one which prevented the Luftwaffe from coming. All of London gave a collective sigh of relief at this brief respite.

Julius, who'd gone to bed early, now woke when he heard a floorboard creak out in the corridor. He frowned, wondering who was up and moving about? A glance at the luminous hands on his wristwatch told him it was too early for Pee Wee to have returned, which meant it was either Beulah or Ellie. Now he was awake he decided to find out which.

Ellie was putting the kettle on when he entered the kitchen. She was wearing a shirt of his that Beulah had given her to sleep in, all her own things still being next door.

'Hi!' Julius smiled.

Ellie blushed, realising she was only half dressed, knickers the only other item of clothing she had on. 'I came down for a cup of tea,' she explained, then vaguely gestured to herself. 'Sorry, I don't have a dressing gown here.'

'Don't worry about it. Can I join you in that tea?'

'Of course.'

He sat and studied her. She looked a wreck, not in the least attractive. That was totally understandable considering. He noted she had particularly lovely legs, the first time he'd seen them so exposed.

'Couldn't sleep, uh?'

Ellie glanced over at him. 'I suppose the sedative wore off. Just as well as I was having horrible nightmares.' She shivered.

'Cold?'

'No. Remembering the nightmares.'

Julius pulled out his cigarettes. 'Like one?'

She shook her head. 'Maybe in a minute.'

He lit up. 'Want to talk about them? The nightmares that is.'

She considered that. 'I don't think so.'

'OK. Maybe you'd prefer I leave you alone?'

'No, please don't,' she replied quickly. 'I could use the company.'

He watched her as she laid out cups and saucers, then checked the sugar bowl. 'Milk's in the fridge,' he said. 'If there's any left that is.'

There was. 'Thank goodness for that,' she declared. 'I can't bear tea without.'

She poured water into the pot, swirled it round, then dumped it down the sink. 'I'll never get used to the idea of teabags,' she said, attempting a smile. 'Tea should be loose, not in paper bags.'

'We Americans are weird,' he joked. 'And we usually drink our tea iced.'

'I remember you told me that once. Iced tea, how disgusting.'

He could see she was beginning to relax, which was good. He couldn't imagine what her nightmares had consisted of. She'd called them horrible, probably another example of English understatement. 'As I said, we're weird.'

When the tea was ready she handed him his cup and saucer and holding hers made to sit opposite, stopping abruptly on remembering what she was wearing.

'That's OK,' he smiled, reading her mind. 'I promise not to look.'

Still she hesitated. 'Even so . . .'

He laid his cup and saucer on the floor and then rose, vanishing out of the room. When he returned he was carrying a large towel. 'Drape this over yourself and that'll spare your modesty.'

'Thank you.' How kind and thoughtful he was, she reflected. Always the perfect gentleman.

'Would you like that cigarette now?'

'Please.'

'Is there anythin' you would care to talk about?' he asked when he'd sat again.

'Not really.'

He didn't reply, not pushing it.

'It's Dad I'm really worried about,' she said after a while. 'He and Mum were terribly close.'

'I think you all were.'

'Yes,' she agreed softly. 'As are your family.'

'Very.'

Ellie sighed. 'I still can't believe that Mum's gone. It's as if I'm trapped in one of those nightmares I mentioned, and will soon wake up to find it was exactly that, a nightmare, that Mum's still alive and . . .' She broke off and took a deep breath. 'Only it's no nightmare, is it?'

'I'm afraid not,' he murmured sympathetically.

'It's all too fucking real.'

Her using that word jolted Julius who stared at her in surprise. Judging from her expression Ellie didn't seem to be aware she'd uttered it. Or perhaps she just didn't care.

'Julius . . .' She trailed off.

'What, Ellie?'

She shook her head. 'Nothing. Forget it.'

'What, Ellie?' he persisted.

'Will you do something for me?'

'If I can.'

Her pleading eyes bored into his. 'Will you hold me? Give me a cuddle?'

Again he was surprised. For a second time he laid his cup and saucer aside and stood up, she doing likewise.

She was trembling when he put his arms around her, she nestling a cheek against his chest.

After a few moments he began to gently stroke her hair.

'Ellie! Ellie, wake up, child!'

Ellie blinked open her eyes to see Beulah staring down at her. 'What time is it?' she said huskily.

'Past noon. I brought you a cup of coffee.'

It all came back now. She and Julius downstairs in the kitchen talking for ages. Not speaking about anything in particular, just this and that. At one point he'd even made her laugh. When they'd finally returned to their respective bedrooms he'd kissed her on the forehead before saying goodnight. She'd liked that.

Ellie struggled into a sitting position and gratefully accepted the steaming mug of coffee Beulah gave her.

'What do you plan for today?' Beulah asked.

Ellie thought about that. 'I'll have to go next door and try to salvage some clothes. That's the first thing.'

Beulah frowned. 'Are you sure you want to do that, honey? Why don't I go instead?'

'Because you won't know what's what. Besides . . .' Ellie dropped her gaze. 'I just have to, that's all.'

Beulah understood. Or at least thought she did. 'I got breakfast waiting for you. Would you like a hot tub before or after that?'

Ellie had heard Beulah use the expression before and knew what it meant. 'Afterwards, if breakfast is ready.'

'OK.'

Ellie wondered if she was doing the right thing. But do it she must. For the clothes if nothing else.

Ellie stared in horror at the blood-stained walls and floor of what remained of their kitchen. For a few moments she thought she was going to be sick, but somehow fought it back.

Glancing up she saw the sky through a huge hole where the plane engine had come penetrated the roof, the timbers remaining broken and jagged-edged.

All about her were the contents of her parents' bedroom, the floor of which the engine had also demolished. On her left the smashed chest of drawers and alongside it their wardrobe, its contents spilled out to lie scattered around. Their bed was on its side and jammed against the cooker, the nightie Jess had last worn dangling from exposed springs.

Breath hissed out of Ellie's mouth while her heart was frantically pounding. Why had Jess been in the kitchen instead of the shelter? They'd never know. But if she had gone to the shelter, as she was supposed to have done, then she'd be alive today. So what if the house was in ruins and most of the furniture shattered. Houses, and what went in them, could be replaced. Jess, like Paul before her, couldn't.

Ellie found her eyes drawn back to the floor where the engine had obviously come to rest, and where her mother had died. The large, dark bloodstain bore witness to that.

Ellie sobbed as fresh tears overwhelmed her. Crossing to a chair she sank onto it and bent over to hold her head in her hands.

'Oh, Mum,' she choked. 'Oh, Mum.'

Ellie had never felt so lost or lonely in her entire life.

It was a good turn-out considering so many people had to be at vital war work. Those from Florence Street who could come, had. A tight group of friends and neighbours united in grief with Albert and Ellie.

Julius stared at Ellie who was supporting her father, he clearly on the verge of collapse. A broken man if ever there was. Julius could only guess at the strength of the bond that had been between Albert and Jess. A bond now broken by death.

How strangely radiant Ellie looked, he thought. A light seemed to shine from her as if she'd been touched by the Divine. He found himself wishing he could take her in his arms as he had that night in the kitchen.

With a shock he realised he'd come to care for Ellie. Not just as a friend, but more than that. Much more.

Chapter 26

'I'm putting you on permanent days,' Station Officer Titmuss announced. 'At least for the foreseeable future.'

It was Ellie's first time back at work having been told the moment she arrived to report to the SO.

Ellie frowned. 'Can I ask why?'

SO Titmuss fiddled with a paper clip; should she tell Ellie precisely what was on her mind? She decided not. 'The raids have lessened off again which means you're not needed on the night shift as badly as you were. I think you would accomplish more during days, be more useful.'

'I see,' Ellie murmured, not really seeing at all.

'Besides, we're taking on more personnel, expanding the station, which means I'll now require two DSOs. I was hoping you might recommend someone for promotion?'

Ellie thought about that. 'I would suggest Josie Farnham. Not simply because we're friends, but because, in my opinion, she has all the right qualities for the job. She's a natural.'

The SO nodded her approval. 'Then that's who it'll be. I'll speak to her shortly. Now why don't you go home again and report tomorrow morning sharp at the changeover.'

'Right.'

SO Titmuss cleared her throat. 'I'm sorry I couldn't come to your mother's funeral, it was just impossible for me to get away.'

'I understand.'

'It went well, I believe?'

Ellie shrugged. 'As well as these things can.'

'How's your father?'

Ellie dropped her gaze to stare at the floor. 'Still taking it very badly. They were . . . very much a couple.'

'And yourself, Ellie,' the SO asked softly. 'How are you?'

How the hell do you think! Ellie nearly blurted out. But didn't, that would have been rude. The SO was only showing concern. 'I'm coping. Though it's not easy.'

Titmuss stared at Ellie's tight and drawn face, noting the dark bags under her eyes and the sallowness of her skin. She had a daughter, roughly Ellie's age, who was a nurse at the Charing Cross Hospital. More than once it had crossed her mind how alike, in many ways, Ellie and Charlotte were. Her own husband had died several years previously, after a long drawn-out illness, from cancer of the bowel, so she knew all about loss and grief.

Again the SO nodded her approval. 'Good. Now off you toddle and report back in the morning. The paperwork has got a bit behind while you were off so there's a lot to do.'

'Thank you.'

'And tell someone out there I could use a cup of tea. My throat's as dry as the Sahara.'

Ellie smiled, the SO was a great tea drinker, consuming God knows how many cups a day. It was something of a joke around the station. 'I'll do that.'

SO Titmuss sighed after Ellie had gone. The real reason she wanted Ellie on days was because it was far safer then than working nights when the majority of raids took place. Ellie's father had lost a son and wife within a relatively short space of time, so the best she could do was try to ensure nothing happened to his daughter as well.

Yes, working days was far safer.

* * *

'I've been thinking, wondering,' Danny McGiver said slowly. 'Maybe you should have a sort of holiday.'

Albert stared blankly at his friend. 'What are you talking about?'

'Get away for a while. Have a break. A change of scenery.' Danny guessed he was making a hash of this, but then tact or word usage had never been strong points of his.

'Danny has a point,' Vera chipped in. She and Danny had already discussed this at length.

'But I'll have to return to duty soon,' Albert mildly protested.

Danny took a deep breath. He was going to have to be blunt, no two ways about it. 'Albert, you're not fit enough. It's as simple as that.'

'How do you mean?'

'Jess's death has taken a lot out of you, more than you realise. Mentally as well as physically.'

Albert didn't argue, suspecting that to be true.

'Half the time your hands are shaking,' Danny went on. 'And your concentration's gone to buggery. To be honest, I wouldn't want to be on shift with you. I don't think you're safe for the time being.'

Vera glanced away when she saw the hurt expression on Albert's face.

'You know how much we rely on one another,' Danny continued. 'For our very lives at times.'

Albert swallowed hard. 'Is it that bad?'

Danny nodded.

'I wouldn't want to let anyone down.'

Christ this was painful, Danny thought. But it had to be done, for Albert's good as well as his mates. 'I've had an idea,' he declared.

'What's that?'

'Why don't I have a word with the Union and see if they'll give you some time at Huntington Hall?'

Albert knew all about Huntington Hall which was owned

and run by the Union. It was where firemen went to recuperate after they'd been injured or seriously ill. He couldn't remember exactly where it was but had always heard good things about it.

'So what do you say?' Danny pressed.

'Vera?'

'I think Danny's right. A couple of weeks there, maybe longer, would be just the ticket. Hopefully set you up again.'

Albert ran a hand over his face. 'Are you trying to tell me you've had enough of my being here?'

'Not in the least!' Vera exclaimed. 'You're welcome to stay with us as long as you like. I said that when you arrived, and meant it.'

Albert managed a smile. 'Thanks, Vera. I appreciate that.'

'Of course it's only a suggestion,' Danny declared. 'If the idea doesn't appeal, then fine. But I do mean it when I say I wouldn't be happy working with you at the present. And that's coming from a pal, which you know I am.'

Albert bowed his head, a vision of a laughing, joking Jess in his mind. How he missed her, unbelievably so. It was as if a part of himself had been cut off. 'All right,' he whispered. 'Have a word.'

Danny shot Vera a look of relief, thankful that Albert had listened to sense. 'I'll do that, Albert. First thing.'

'Excuse me,' Albert said and left the room.

'I feel like Judas bloody Iscariot for some reason,' Danny muttered after Albert had gone.

'Judas betrayed his friend,' Vera stated quietly. 'That's not what you're doing at all. Quite the contrary.'

'Well, it feels like it.'

They both looked round when they heard the outside door click shut.

Albert had gone out.

'What!' Beulah exploded, absolutely furious.

'You heard me,' a sheepish Pee Wee replied. 'We's goin' out on tour for another mouth. Maybe six weeks.' He shrugged. 'I can't help it none. The first one was such a huge success Lord Fitzaran has been asked to do it again.'

Beulah swore.

'I'm sorry, hon, but I ain't got no option in the matter. It's already all been agreed.'

'Were you asked?'

Pee Wee knew better than to lie to his wife, she always found out, or just plain knew, if he did. 'Yeah.'

Beulah folded her arms across her massive bosom. 'And what did you say?'

'Hell, Beulah, the other guys wanted to go and I didn't want to let them down. Or Fitzaran, he's been just great since we got here. You know that.'

Beulah had to admit to herself that was true. 'And you'd be playin' for the military?'

'That's it. To help the war effort, as Fitzaran put it.' He reached out and tried to lay a hand on Beulah's crossed arms, she shrugging the hand away.

'Don't be mad, hon,' he pleaded.

'Well, I is.'

'Please?'

Beulah snorted and moved off a few steps, turning her back on him in the process while she thought about this. It had been awful, and desperately lonely, when he'd been away before. And then she'd at least had Jess for occasional company. Now she had to go through it all again, this time without Jess.

'I'll make it up to you, Beulah. I promise.'

'And how will you do that?' she demanded sharply.

'I don't know. But I will. I swears I will.'

She took a deep breath, the beginnings of an idea coming to her. Why not? she thought after a few moments. She'd done it before. Many times. Though, she had to admit, not for a long while now. Nor was she getting any younger, there was that to be taken into account. 'When do you plan leavin'?' she queried, facing him again.

'Week after next.'

'And where you goin'?'

'All over I guess. Includin' Scotland. You know, where the guys wear skirts.'

Despite herself, Beulah almost laughed, finding the idea of men in skirts hilarious. 'No shit?'

'God's honest, Beulah. Skirts made out of plaid I'm told.'

She made a decision. She wasn't going to be left alone a second time. 'Well, OK, but I'm taggin' along this trip. And don't try to argue me out of it none.'

His face broke into a broad smile. 'You mean that, hon?'

'Sure do. It'll be as uncomfortable as hell, always is. But at least we'll be together, and that's what counts.'

'Thanks, hon.'

'Hmmh!'

He went to her and this time she didn't brush his hand away.

Albert sat back in his chair, having just broken the news about Huntington Hall to Ellie. Beulah and Pee Wee were also present.

Ellie wasn't sure what to reply, this being so unexpected. She had to admit her father didn't look at all well, a shadow of his former self. There again, what did she expect? He'd only recently lost his wife.

'I'm looking forward to it,' Albert lied. 'The countryside and all that fresh air. Just what the doctor ordered.'

'And it was Danny McGiver's suggestion?'

Albert nodded. 'To be honest, he doesn't think I'm up to work just yet and that a holiday will do me the world of good.'

'We're takin' a trip as well,' Pee Wee told him. And then explained about the forthcoming tour and that Beulah would be going along with him.

'Sounds smashing!' Albert enthused.

'It certainly won't do you any harm getting out of London for a bit,' Ellie said to Albert, thinking out of London and Islington in particular which held so many memories for him.

'I hope so,' he replied, attempting a smile which was most unconvincing.

Albert stayed another half hour before taking his leave, Ellie accompanying him to the doorway where they had a few private words together. She felt totally wretched as she watched her father disappear off into the black-out, he walking with a stoop that was new since Jess's death.

'Oh Dad,' she whispered.

'Why the long face?' Julius asked when he arrived home. Pee Wee had already left for The Chicory House and Beulah was upstairs. He wasn't eating that night as he'd told Beulah at breakfast he'd be late and therefore would eat at the Embassy.

Ellie explained about her father's visit and Huntington Hall, mentioning how ill her father had looked and the fact his hands had shaken during his entire stay.

Julius listened to this in silence, occasionally nodding his head in sympathy. 'I'd say a drink is what you need, Ellie. How about we go across to The Florence?' he suggested, hoping that might cheer her up.

Ellie couldn't think of anything nicer. 'All right. If you'll just give me a few minutes to get ready.'

He pretended to groan.

'Only a few minutes, honestly.'

'Yeah yeah. OK, on you go.'

A now smiling Ellie hurried from the room.

'Hey, it must be Christmas. They got gin in,' Julius announced, setting a glass in front of Ellie. His was a pint of best.

She tasted the gin and murmured approvingly as it slipped down her throat. 'I needed that,' she declared.

Julius glanced around. The pub was quiet, Hazel behind the bar. 'Your dad was in here either before or after he called on my folks,' he stated.

'Must have been before as I watched him walk up the street when he left.'

'Before then. But he was here according to Hazel.'

Ellie stared into her drink. 'I'm so worried about him, Julius. It's as if . . . as if he's given up the will to live. It frightened me tonight when I saw and spoke to him. It wasn't my dad at all, not really.'

Julius remained silent, desperately sorry for Ellie, wishing he could comfort her in some way other than merely buying her a drink. He had to stop himself from reaching out and taking hold of her hand.

'He'll be OK, you'll see,' Julius replied eventually, thinking how pathetic that sounded. 'Probably love it at this Huntington Hall.'

'God I hope so. I truly do.'

'And he'll be well away from the raids, so there won't be any worry there.'

Ellie smiled at Julius, thinking what a wonderful human being he was. 'I shall see him off at the station. He wasn't keen on that, but I insisted. I can easily arrange an hour or so away from my duties.'

'Even if he isn't keen, as you put it, he'll appreciate that. Especially on the day.' Julius coughed. 'There's something I have to ask. A little delicate perhaps.'

She frowned. 'What?'

'When my folks go that'll leave just the two of us in the house. Does that bother you?'

The same thought had already crossed her mind. 'Not in the least.'

'You sure?'

'Positive. I can't imagine you being anything other than the perfect gentleman. Besides, I trust you.'

That praise pleased him. 'I felt I had to mention it as it obviously never occurred to my folks. There again, they know what I'm like.'

It would be funny, and strange, with only Julius around, Ellie thought, her skin prickling slightly. Not that she'd see much of him as he wasn't home a great deal, often working late. 'As long as you appreciate I can't cook anywhere near as well as your mother,' she warned him. 'I don't exactly shine in that department.'

He laughed. 'Tell you what, we'll cook together. How's that?'

She was amazed. 'You can cook?'

'Yeah, enjoy it too. A lot of it Mom taught me over the years. Easy really, when you know how.'

Ellie simply couldn't imagine Albert cooking. Why, it needed a bomb under his bum for him to even make a cup of tea. Her face immediately dropped realising that had been quite the wrong analogy to make.

'What gives? Did I say somethin'?'

Ellie shook her head, then related what had gone through her mind about a bomb and bum.

'Oh!' he murmured.

Ellie had a long swig of gin, then briefly closed her eyes. 'I often wonder how all this will end. The war I mean. Do you?'

'Yeah.'

'One thing's for certain, nothing will ever be the same again. Can't be.'

'No,' he agreed.

Ellie sniffed. 'Sorry. I'm being foolish now. Letting my emotions get the better of me.'

'Very un-English,' he teased.

'Very.'

'Hey!' he suddenly exclaimed. 'I just remembered. I've brought some cigarettes home. Left them in the car so we'll pick them up when we leave here. OK?'

'OK,' she smiled, thinking how infectious his good humour could be. A right tonic, Jess would have said.

'Another thing, I have a proposition for you.'

She opened her eyes wide, they twinkling. Her turn to tease. 'I thought we agreed you'd be a gentleman, Julius Poston?'

'Oh, nothin' improper,' he grinned. 'Nothin' like that. Are you workin' this weekend?'

She nodded. ''Fraid so.'

'How about the weekend after?'

'I have that off. Or I'm supposed to anyway. It depends on the raids. There's always the possibility I might have to go in after all.'

'Well let's say you don't,' he said. 'How about we go on a picnic? Just the two of us. While the weather's still reasonable and before the Fall sets in.'

'A picnic!'

'You know, where you take food and things, spread a blanket on the grass; eat, drink and generally enjoy yourself?'

Now he was taking the micky. 'Sounds lovely.'

'I'll get all sorts from the Embassy so we can make a proper day of it. Should be fun.'

'Should be,' she agreed. 'But what if it rains?'

'It won't. I give you my word on that. It wouldn't dare.'

Ellie laughed at the absurdity of that. 'Well, if it does we'll simply sit in the car and gorge ourselves there.'

'Hot dog!' he enthused. 'That's exactly what we'll do. But it won't rain. I won't allow it.'

Her mood changed, the laughter going out of her voice to be replaced by sincerity. 'You know something, Julius? You truly are a wonderful person. I mean that.'

He was embarrassed, and delighted at the same time. 'Thank you. You're kinda wonderful yourself.'

Now it was her turn to be embarrassed. Picking up her glass she drained the remainder of her gin. 'The next round's on me,' she declared.

'No it isn't,' he protested.

'Oh yes it is,' she stated firmly, rising to her feet. 'So you just be quiet.'

It took all his self-control not to touch her as she went past. At the funeral he'd realised how much he cared for her. He didn't know how it had happened, certainly not overnight, but somehow he'd fallen in love with Ellie Sykes.

'Platform One is over there,' Ellie declared, pointing. Euston

Station was abustle with people, many of them in uniform. The smell was a combination of smoke and soot.

'I still wish you hadn't come,' Albert complained as they headed in that direction. 'I'm quite capable of putting myself on a train.'

'Oh, stop moaning,' Ellie chided him. 'You sound like an old grouch.'

Albert's suitcase contained clothes that had been donated to him by his mates, he never having gone back to retrieve what he could from the house.

'Do you want to buy a paper?' Ellie asked, glancing at the station clock to check the time.

'I already have one in my inside pocket,' Albert replied.

'Is there anything else you might need?'

'Don't think so.'

Ellie was hating this, even if it was in her father's best interests to go away for a while. With her at the Postons', and him at the McGivers', he'd been close, easily accessible. Now she'd have to keep in touch by writing which wasn't the same thing at all.

They stopped while she bought a platform ticket, and then they were moving along the length of the train looking for a suitable carriage.

'This'll do,' Albert announced on finding an empty one, hoping it would stay empty, apart from himself, as he didn't really want company during his journey.

He opened the door and heaved his case inside, following it to put it on the overhead rack. When he'd done that he rejoined Ellie.

'Now you take care of yourself, you hear?' she declared in a no-nonsense tone of voice.

Albert suddenly smiled. 'You sound just like your mother when you speak like that.'

She smiled also. 'Do I?'

'Oh yes,' he replied quietly. He took a deep breath. 'Don't hang about. I can't bear goodbyes, far less long ones.'

'All right, Dad.'

He took her into his arms and hugged her tight. 'Please don't worry about me. I'll be just fine.'

'Promise?'

'Promise.'

Before releasing her he pecked her on the cheek. 'On you go then.'

'Dad . . .?'

'What, Ellie?'

A choke came into her throat. 'Nothing.'

He knew what she'd been about to say, and it was the same with him about her.

'Don't forget to write,' she said, her voice unsteady.

'I won't. Now be off with you.'

The carriage door slammed shut behind her as she began walking away, feeling as though she'd now lost her entire family. Although, of course, that wasn't true.

Her dad had only gone on holiday, she reminded herself.

'I'm stuffed. Absolutely stuffed!' Ellie declared, flopping back onto the blanket they'd brought. As Julius had predicted it was a beautiful day, the sun shining and the temperature high considering it was the end of September.

Julius laid aside what remained of a chicken leg and wiped his lips with a napkin. 'I reckon I am too. More wine?'

'Not for the moment.'

He pulled out a packet of cigarettes, put two in his mouth, lit them and offered her one. She accepted and took a long, deep drag. She sighed, 'You brought along enough food to feed an army.'

He smiled, but didn't reply.

After a few moments Ellie rolled onto an elbow to stare at him. 'What are you thinking? You're looking very introspective.'

'About you actually,' he replied softly.

She frowned. 'What about me?'

'I was wonderin' what you really thought about black people, and black men in particular?'

'What a strange question,' she mused.

'Is it?' He paused, then said lightly, 'Take me for example. What do you think about me? In the context of being black that is.'

'Well, you certainly are, that can't be denied.' She took another drag on her cigarette and considered what he'd asked. 'I found it disturbing to begin with, not having had any experience of black people before. But now . . . I don't notice it any more I suppose. You're just Julius, the question of colour doesn't enter into it.'

'Are you sure about that?' he further probed.

'Yes I am. I don't think of you as being black at all now, it never crosses my mind. But why do you ask?'

He shrugged.

'Julius?'

Not yet, he thought. The time wasn't ripe. Or was he just being cowardly? He didn't know.

'Curious, that's all,' he replied, and changed the subject.

Albert crossed over to his bedroom window and stared out over the grounds. To his surprise he'd found he liked Huntington Hall, liked it a lot in fact. It was peaceful here, serene almost. And the staff, without exception, couldn't have been nicer. He'd settled in remarkably quickly.

He was also getting on well with the other patients, all firemen like himself. If anything he felt a bit of a fraud being there as some of them were recovering from horrific injuries suffered during the German raids. One poor chap from Coventry had lost both legs and an arm as well as sustaining damage to his sight.

Albert spotted a few of them now, sitting on a bench chatting, having a right old laugh by the looks of things. He decided to go and join them, he too could use a laugh.

He started humming as he left his room, and there was a

spring in his step that hadn't been there when he'd arrived at Huntington Hall.

If Ellie had seen him at that moment she'd have been much relieved.

Chapter 27

Ellie arrived back to find Julius already there pottering round the kitchen. 'You're early!' she exclaimed in surprise.

'Yeah, it was an easy day.' That wasn't true, he'd purposefully hurried through his afternoon's work so he could spend more time with her, but wasn't about to tell Ellie that.

'What was your day like?' he asked.

'So-so. Mounds of paperwork to get through, but thankfully no call-outs.' There hadn't been a raid in over a week, the Germans currently concentrating their bombing further north.

'Coffee?'

'Please.'

Ellie sank onto a chair and lit up. 'I'll be washing my hair tonight, if that's all right with you?'

'Sure.'

'You going out?'

'Hadn't planned to. I might go over the road after a while for a couple. But we'll see.' He had no intentions of doing that unless Ellie came with him.

She watched him as he 'fixed' their coffee, as he called it, admiring the litheness of his movement, and the graceful way he did things. It struck her that he was one of the most handsome men she'd ever known. But more important than that was his

361

attitude to women; he wasn't only unfailingly courteous to them but treated them as equals, a refreshing change to what she'd been used to and brought up with. Not that her father hadn't treated Jess properly, he had. But Albert was a man of his time, and background, where the woman was always second fiddle and whose duty was to be attendant to his needs at all times.

'I thought we'd cook together tonight,' Julius announced.

'Oh?' That pleased her, he'd promised they'd be doing this. 'What do you have in mind?'

'Yankee fried rice.'

Ellie smiled. 'Sounds very exotic.'

'Not really, but it's simple. It'll be another recipe to add to your repertoire.'

'Which, as I warned you, is strictly limited. Cauliflower cheese, stew, bubble and squeak . . .'

'What the hell is that?' he queried with a laugh.

She explained.

'You English sure eat some weird stuff!' he exclaimed, shaking his head in amazement.

'No weirder than some of the things you Americans eat,' she retorted.

'Like what?'

She had frantically to think. 'Meat loaf, your favourite.'

'What's weird about meat loaf? It's mainly minced beef which you English are so fond of.'

He had her there.

'Well? Go on, name somethin'.'

She could hear the triumph in his voice. 'Oh, I don't know offhand,' she said grudgingly, hating to admit defeat.

'Ah ha!' he exclaimed, and beamed at her. 'Gotcha.'

Ellie couldn't have said how it happened, but suddenly they were both roaring with laughter.

He regarded her steadily when he eventually stopped. 'You're fun, Ellie Sykes. Real fun. Great to be with.'

'And so are you,' she replied just as sincerely.

For the space of a few moments they were absolutely still,

staring into one another's eyes. Then Julius broke the spell by turning away. 'If you'll get off your butt I'll start showin' you how to make the rice.'

Ellie took her coffee with her to where he'd begun assembling the ingredients. She was skin-prickly aware when up close of the cologne he was wearing.

Albert entered the day room to find Nurse Cross, a pretty young lady about Ellie's age, busy with a screwdriver. 'What are you doing?' he queried with a frown.

'Trying to fix this shelf before it falls off the wall. It's come loose.'

'Here, let me help you.'

Albert went over and took the screwdriver from her. A quick examination of the offending shelf revealed it was going to need more than a screwdriver to put it right.

'I've no idea how it's happened but the holes the screws go into have widened. To do this properly I'll have to drill new ones. I don't suppose you have a drill handy by any chance?'

Nurse Cross was delighted at Albert's offer of help, not to mention relieved. 'There's bound to be one in the maintenance room. If you'll follow me I'll take you there.'

Albert left the screwdriver on the shelf, as he'd need it later, and followed Nurse Cross out into the corridor. 'I'm a bit puzzled,' he said. 'Why are you doing something like that? Surely there's a man does the odd jobs round here?'

'There was, two of them in fact, but they're both in the Forces now and Matron hasn't been able to replace them. As a result we nurses have to do what we can if anything goes wrong.'

The maintenance room was in the basement, where Albert hadn't been before. Nurse Cross opened the door and flicked on the light. 'Here we are.'

The first thing Albert saw were stacks and stacks of paint cans, a veritable mountain of them. 'Good God,' he murmured. 'Are those empty or full?'

'Full. The whole place was scheduled to be repainted and then the war broke out. They've been lying there ever since.'

'This lot would fetch a pretty penny on the black market,' Albert commented, paint being so difficult to come by since the advent of hostilities.

'I suppose so,' Nurse Cross mused. Then, reprovingly, 'I hope you're not getting any funny ideas, Mr Sykes?'

Albert laughed. 'Not me. I'm dead against the black market, have been all along. No, it was just an observation, that's all.'

Nurse Cross pointed to a couple of old, dilapidated chests of drawers. 'You should find a drill in there somewhere.'

Albert quickly established that the drawers were filled with all manner of tools, and soon found what he was after. 'Just the dab,' he smiled. He then selected a few other items that he'd require and they left the room.

'I'll return this lot when I'm finished,' he assured her.

'Thank you. It'll certainly save me the job, particularly as I'm useless at that sort of thing.'

'My pleasure. I was bored anyway, so this gives me something to do.'

Nurse Cross switched off the light and they made their way back upstairs where she left Albert to get on with it.

Ellie picked up the letter that had just been delivered by the morning post as she was about to set off for work. In the background was the rattle of dishes as Julius washed the breakfast things. She smiled to see the writing was her father's laboured script. Quickly she tore open the envelope and started to read.

Albert, in his own words, was having a whale of a time at Huntington Hall, everyone was friendly, lovely surroundings, etc. etc. He was also feeling a lot better and even putting on a little weight. He finished by hoping she was well and said he was looking forward to hearing from her soon.

'You almost ready?' Julius queried, appearing behind her.

'I just have to put my coat and hat on.' She held up the letter. 'From Dad. Everything's fine and he's enjoying himself.'

'Good,' Julius replied, nodding his approval. It pleased him to see the obvious relief on Ellie's face. 'Now shall we go?'

Ellie tucked the letter into a pocket; she'd re-read it later when she had a free moment.

Julius helped her into her coat, then slipped on his own. After he'd locked the door they made their way to his car and got in.

As had become their custom Julius drove Ellie to the station before going on to the Embassy. 'I was wonderin',' he said as they turned out of Florence Street.

'What?'

'How about we take in a movie tonight?'

She glanced sideways at him. 'There is one on locally I'd like to see. David Copperfield with W.C. Fields. He always makes me laugh.'

'David Copperfield? Well why not! That's settled then, eh?'

'It's a date.'

For the life of her she couldn't think why she'd used that particular word knowing what it meant to Americans. When she glanced again at Julius he was smiling.

'Oh shit!' Julius muttered as the sirens sounded. The movie had only just started.

'I'll have to go home,' Ellie said. 'You know the arrangement.' The arrangement she was referring to was that the station would phone her should she be required. 'You do understand?'

'Of course.'

Quite a few of the audience were now on their feet and moving towards the exits. Some enroute to their shelters, others to the Angel tube, which was close by, to take refuge there.

Once outside they both glanced up to see the usual searchlights criss-crossing the night sky. So far the ack-ack guns hadn't opened up.

They'd almost reached Florence Street when, the sirens having stopped wailing, the All Clear went, bringing both Ellie and Julius up short.

They smiled at one another in the darkness. 'False alarm,' Julius said, thinking of the inconvenience they'd had in leaving the cinema.

'Better that than the real thing,' Ellie replied, turning her collar up against the cold.

'Shall we go back?'

'What do you want to do?'

He hesitated for a few moments. 'Honestly?'

'Honestly.'

'We don't know why the All Clear was sounded, but it is possible the sirens could go again. It's happened in the past.'

Ellie nodded. That was true.

'Let's forget the movie then and go to The Florence instead. That way if they do go again you only have to cross the road.'

Which made sense, Ellie thought. Anyway, the picture was spoilt for her now. If they did return she'd just be sitting there waiting for the bloody sirens to go off a second time. 'All right.'

'Why don't you take my arm? It's treacherous in the black-out and I don't want anythin' happenin' to you.'

She appreciated his concern; twisted ankles and the like had become commonplace since the black-out was imposed. She slipped an arm round his and they proceeded on their way, she wishing he'd made the suggestion earlier. Not for safety's sake, but because she liked the idea of them being arm in arm. It was almost as if they were a couple.

'I'll get tipsy if I have any more,' Ellie declared. They'd been in the pub for nearly an hour and a half during which the sirens had remained silent.

'Oh go on, I'm goin' to have one,' he urged.

Ellie was thoroughly enjoying herself, Julius, as always, great company. They were both drinking shorts, Harry and Hazel, for once, having a seemingly plentiful supply.

'I shouldn't,' she demurred.

'But you will.'

'Oh go on then,' she conceded, and giggled.

Julius went up to the bar and ordered refills, looking back at Ellie whose face was ever so slightly flushed. Adorable, simply adorable, he thought, as she gave him a tiny wave.

'Isn't this far better than the movies?' Julius asked when he rejoined her.

'Much.'

'I think so too.'

'Maybe we can go out again another night?' It was the alcohol making her so forward, she realised. She'd never have asked that when sober.

'Of course. Whenever you wish.'

'OK,' she giggled again, thinking it funny she was using his American expression.

Before they knew it another hour, during which they'd had several more drinks, had flown past and it was approaching closing time.

Ellie finished her G&T and placed the glass firmly on the table. 'That's it. No more otherwise I might fall down.'

'A last cigarette?'

'Is that a ruse to stay on?'

'No.'

'Swear?'

'I swear, Ellie. Only a cigarette, that's all.' The truth was he was loath to break this up, thinking he could have sat there with Ellie all night long.

Cigarettes were duly lit and smoked, after which they both stood, Julius helping Ellie into her coat but deciding to carry his as it was only across the road.

'I'm glad it's you doing that,' Ellie slurred as he put the key in the door.

'Why?'

'Because I don't think I'd manage it.'

'You're not that bad,' he lied as the door swung open and they went inside.

Ellie hung up her coat. 'Well that's me. I'm off to bed where I'll no doubt sleep like the proverbial log.'

'Goodnight, Ellie.'

'Goodnight, Julius. Thanks for a wonderful evening. It was terrific.'

'For me too.'

They were both staring at one another, the mood between them having somehow changed.

'Can I kiss you?'

The breath caught in Ellie's throat to hear that, and her stomach sort of flipped over. She nodded.

It was only a peck, the briefest touching of lips, and then it was all over. Reaching out she laid the tips of her fingers lightly on his cheek, then whirled about and went running up the stairs.

Julius watched her every step of the way, her perfume lingering in his nostrils.

'Come in!' Matron Hapgood, a tallish, angular thin woman, who wore glasses, called out when there was a tap on her office door.

It was Albert. 'Are you free?'

'If you wish to see me.'

'Thank you, Matron.'

She indicated a chair in front of her desk. As he sat she removed her glasses and wiped her eyes. 'Now what can I do for you, Mr Sykes? No complaints I trust?'

He smiled. 'None at all. I've come with a request, that's all.'

The glasses were put back on and she studied him intently. 'Oh?'

'The overflow from the guttering outside my window is very irritating, and I wondered if you'd give me permission to do something about it. I suspect it's only blocked with debris, which happens with gutters, and I'd like to not only clear that but go round the entire guttering and give it a general clean.'

That took Matron by surprise. 'I heard about you fixing the shelf in the day room. Thank you for that.'

Albert nodded. 'My pleasure. Gave me something to do, occupy my mind for a bit.'

'Uh-huh.' Matron was thinking about Albert's proposal. 'Won't it be dangerous up there on a ladder? I mean, I wouldn't want you to hurt yourself.'

Albert laughed. 'I'm a fireman, Matron, I've spent half my life up ladders. I won't fall off, I assure you.'

Matron blushed. 'Yes, of course. How stupid of me.'

'I'm bored you see. Thoroughly enjoying myself here, but bored. I'm a working man, used to doing just that. I'll be far happier being busy.'

Albert wasn't like the rest of her patients, Matron reflected. They were either recovering from injury or illness, whereas in his case he was here to get over the death of his wife. The more she thought about Albert's proposal, the more she approved. It would be good therapy for him. Ideal in fact.

'I've already been in the maintenance room,' Albert went on. 'Everything I might need is there, including overalls which looked more or less my size.'

Matron made a decision. 'All right, Mr Sykes, you carry on.' She wagged a finger at him. 'Just be careful, that's all. I've never lost a patient yet, and don't wish to start now.'

'You won't, Matron, so you can rest easy.' He rubbed his hands together. 'Well, there's no time like the present to get to it. With your permission that is?'

'Granted.'

'Thank you.'

And with that he left Matron Hapgood, heading straight for the maintenance room to sort out what was required.

Ellie arrived in her office to take over from Josie Farnham at the early morning changeover of staff. 'How was last night?' she asked brightly.

'Fine. No raid, no call-outs. I even managed to snatch a few hours sleep.'

'The SO about?'

Josie shook her head. 'But she'll probably be in later knowing her.'

'Anything to report?'

'Not really. With the exception of Annie Croxton who's been taken ill apparently, and admitted to the Royal Free.'

Ellie frowned. 'What's wrong with her?'

'The note her mother sent round didn't say. But, as she's in hospital, I presume it's serious.'

Annie worked on Ellie's day shift and was therefore her responsibility. 'I'll go and see her this evening,' she declared. 'And find out exactly what's what.'

Josie yawned. 'Home to bed for me.'

'I've been meaning to ask,' Ellie went on. 'How are you and Harold getting along? Still going strong?' Harold was the policeman Josie had met at the Poxy Roxy.

'As ever,' Josie smiled. 'He's got himself on nights as well so we see each other during the day. A bit odd perhaps, but you get used to it.'

'Might there be an engagement in the wind?'

Josie winked. 'Possibly. Too soon really to tell, but he seems keen enough. And I certainly am.'

Ellie crossed two fingers and held them up.

'Thanks. Now I'm off. Ta ra!'

'Ta ra!'

Ellie checked her appearance in the mirror, tucking away a few loose hairs, before going out to address the other girls as she did every morning.

Albert came down the ladder to find Matron standing there, where she'd been watching him for the past few minutes. 'That's it done,' he announced. 'All finished.'

'Was it bad?'

He shook his head. 'Not really. But guttering, like lots of other things, does need looking after. What I've done should be done every year. That lot up there hadn't been looked at for quite some time, which was evident. There won't be any overflows now when it rains, I'm delighted to say. And I can stop being irritated.'

Matron smiled. 'If you're willing there are some other jobs that require attending to.'

'Oh?'

'Small ones. General maintenance work, that sort of thing.'

'Well, I'll be happy to see what I can do.'

'This is very kind of you, Mr Sykes. We all appreciate it.'

'Think nothing of it,' Albert acknowledged. 'It's my pleasure.' He hesitated, then said, 'There's something else.'

'What's that?'

'How long am I due to stay here? I got the impression I had another couple of weeks. The Union was rather vague about the actual time allotted.'

'It was left to my discretion,' Matron replied. 'As far as I'm concerned it's up to you.'

Albert nodded that he understood. 'That being the case, why don't I start doing some painting for you? The inside of the building desperately needs it, and there's all that paint just lying there in the maintenance room crying out to be used.'

Matron's face lit up. 'That would be wonderful, Mr Sykes.'

'Then leave it to me. I'll organise everything.'

A treasure, Matron thought gleefully. That's what Albert was. A treasure.

Annie's bed, when Ellie located it, was surrounded by screens. She popped her head round one and smiled.

'Hello, Ellie. Come and sit down.'

Annie looked positively ghastly, Ellie thought as she sat. 'Why the screens?'

'The doctor was doing some more tests. He's finished now, but the screens still haven't been taken away.'

Ellie stared at Annie in concern. 'What's wrong?'

'They don't know yet, I started feeling unwell at home, then began vomiting. Next thing I'd passed out. When our GP was called he insisted I be brought in here.'

'I see.'

'They've already done a number of tests before these latest, but so far they're as baffled as my GP.'

'Well, all I can say is I hope you get better soon.'

Annie gave Ellie a twisted smile. 'I'm glad you've come. Mum was here earlier but had to go home for a while. It's good to have the company.'

Annie was normally a beautiful blonde with gorgeous green eyes and a figure to die for. The hair was now dull and straggly, the eyes as if the light in them had been turned out, and the figure, from what Ellie could see, seemed sort of shrunken. 'I'll stay as long as you like, or they'll let me,' Ellie said.

'Thanks.'

The following afternoon news came to the station that Annie Croxton had passed away the previous night. A post-mortem revealed the cause of death to be a tumour on the brain.

Chapter 28

'Ah, there you are, Mr Sykes,' Matron declared, breezing into the bedroom Albert was painting. 'I was told I'd find you here.'

'Hello, Matron.'

Matron gazed about, nodding her approval. 'You're doing an excellent job.'

Albert continued working. 'Thank you. I enjoy painting. Find it very relaxing. In fact, if I hadn't been a fireman I've sometimes thought I'd have become a painter and decorator.'

Matron shivered. 'It's chilly in here.'

'That's because it's November and the window's wide open. It has to be that otherwise the smell would be unbearable.'

'It's Friday afternoon, Mr Sykes.'

Albert paused to stare at her, wondering why she was stating the obvious. 'I believe it is.'

'Payday in fact.'

What on earth was she talking about?

Matron reached into a side pocket of her uniform to produce two pound notes. 'These are for you.'

Albert was taken aback to say the least. 'I'm not due any wages, Matron. I volunteered, remember?'

'You did indeed, Mr Sykes, for which I'm most appreciative.

373

Nonetheless, I want you to accept this, you've earned every penny of it during the past week.'

Albert laid his brush aside, telling himself not to look a gift horse in the mouth. 'It seems a bit unnecessary to me as there's nowhere to spend money,' he pointed out.

The hint of a smile curled Matron's lips fractionally upwards. 'I presume you came through Loxton on your way here?' That was the name of the nearest village situated about a mile and a half from Huntington Hall.

Albert nodded. 'I did.'

'Well there's a very nice pub there, called The Lamb Inn, which serves excellent ale I understand.'

He could really use a pint, or two, Albert thought. 'Really?'

'And there's a bicycle in the passage leading from the kitchen to the back door, the tradesmen's entrance we refer to it as. Can you ride a bike, Mr Sykes?'

'I can,' Albert mused. 'Though haven't done so in years.'

'I'm sure you'll quickly get the hang of it again. After dinner would be the best time, don't you think?'

'Sounds good to me.'

'Fine then.'

Albert regarded her with amusement. 'You seem to know a lot about men, Matron, no offence meant.' As she didn't wear a wedding ring he presumed she was unmarried.

'I should do, I was brought up with four brothers. Ruffians all. But kindly with it. Not one of them would ever turn down the chance of a pint. Mind you, I haven't seen them in years, but I doubt they've changed their ways.'

Albert accepted the money from her. 'All I can say is thank you.'

'Think nothing of it. And, Mr Sykes, you won't be the first one to use the bicycle for that purpose. It hasn't been unheard of in the past.'

She took a deep breath. 'Now, I'd better get on, lots to do.'

And with that Matron swept from the room leaving a bemused Albert to resume painting.

* * *

Ellie was sitting in front of the fire with her eyes closed, having thought she'd have a doze, but unable to because she was acutely aware of Julius, sitting opposite, staring at her. She didn't have to look to know that was the case, she could feel his gaze. Nor was this the first time she'd been aware of his staring when he thought she wasn't watching.

'Julius?'

'What, Ellie?'

'Why are you staring?'

She opened her eyes just as he was glancing away.

'Was I?' he queried innocently.

'You know you were.'

'Sorry, I didn't mean to.'

Ellie produced her cigarettes. 'Want one?'

'Yeah.'

He came over and helped her to a light before returning to his chair. 'It's cold out there tonight,' he commented.

'Don't change the subject, Julius. Why were you staring at me? You've been doing a lot of that lately, thinking I didn't know, but I did.'

He shifted uncomfortably in his chair, unsure of what to reply.

'Well?' she demanded.

'I'm sorry,' he apologised. 'It won't happen again.' He came suddenly to his feet. 'I'm off over to The Florence for a while. See you later.'

'Julius, don't you dare!' she called out sharply as he made for the door. 'I want an answer.'

He stopped, but kept his back to her. 'Drop it, Ellie. Please.'

'No, I will not.'

'I said please.'

'And I said I want an explanation, Julius Poston. Why do you keep staring at me as if I was some kind of exotic animal or other?'

He was ages in replying. When he did his back remained firmly to her. 'I didn't intend speakin' out, Ellie. Certainly not while you're a guest in our house.'

There was another long pause. 'I'm waiting,' she reminded him, as if she had to.

'It's because I've fallen for you,' he stated quietly.

Ellie went rigid with shock. 'Fallen for me?' she croaked.

'Big-time. No lie.'

Ellie swallowed, then swallowed again. 'Are you saying you love me?'

'I guess.'

'What sort of answer is that. Yes or no?'

'Yes.'

Bloody hell, she thought, still in shock.

'Now can I go?'

Her emotions were in turmoil. This was so unexpected. Or was it? She wasn't sure. 'Turn round,' she further croaked. 'I want to find something out.'

He came about to face her. 'What?'

'Why did I have to force you into telling me that?'

He shrugged. 'All kinds of reasons.'

'Such as?'

'I didn't want to take advantage of us bein' alone in the house while my folks are away.'

'And?' she probed.

'I remember when you said that day when we went on a picnic about not seein' me as a black man any more, but simply as a man. Well that's one thing, us havin' a relationship quite another. Don't you agree? I mean, there are still parts of the States where I'd be lynched for being interested in a white girl far less takin' it further.'

He loved her – those words had burned deeply into her brain and sent her pulse racing. She'd never believed she had a chance with him, not really. Fantasised about it on occasion, but never believed it would come about.

'Ellie?'

He frowned as she got up and came across to him.

'I want you to kiss me, properly this time. As though you meant it.'

'Are you sure?'

She nodded.

He hesitated for a few moments, then took her into his arms.

Ellie felt light-headed when he finally released her, almost staggering on the spot. She'd never known a kiss like it, certainly not with George. His kisses paled by comparison.

'Well?' Julius smiled.

'You can go to the pub now. I want to think about this.'

'OK.'

When he was gone she slumped back into her chair, her mind whirling. What had started as a dull and dreary night had suddenly turned into something very, very different.

While Julius was in The Florence, Albert was standing at the bar of The Lamb Inn. He'd liked the pub the moment he'd walked through the door, its atmosphere cosy, friendly and instantly welcoming. Matron had been right about the beer, a local brew, it was good. Far better than he was used to.

'Passing through?' the barman inquired, polishing a glass.

Albert explained that he'd come from Huntington Hall.

'We occasionally get some of the nurses in here,' the barman said. 'A lively bunch, all out for a laugh.'

Before long Albert found himself chatting to a group of the villagers, feeling completely at ease as if he'd been a regular there for years.

Ellie lay in bed staring at the ceiling, the room in darkness. Julius had returned a short while ago and gone almost immediately to his room.

She couldn't get out of her mind the conversation she'd had with Annie Croxton the night Annie had died. Enjoy your life while you can, Annie had said. For you never knew what tomorrow would bring, especially with a war on.

Well, the latter was certainly true where Annie had been concerned. One moment vibrant and alive, the next ill, the next dead. Albeit in Annie's case it had nothing to do with the war.

Death – she seemed surrounded by it nowadays. Her mother, Paul, old Ma Jenkins from across the road, her two colleagues, Molly Davis and Pat Halfpenny, who'd been burned alive in their vehicle. The countless incidents she'd been called out to where the dead and dying had been all around. The injured who'd died in her vehicle while being taken to hospital, the others – so very many – who'd died after reaching there.

Ellie shivered, which had nothing to do with the temperature. She herself could be next, there was always that possibility. Every time there was a raid, and thank God they'd stopped for a while, her turn could come.

And now Julius said he loved her, which she believed after that kiss downstairs. It was as if her insides had melted, turned to mush, which had never ever happened with George or any other man she'd previously kissed.

It had just seemed so right with Julius. As if, well, as if during the kiss they'd been one person. And if that could happen with a kiss what would it be like should they make love? Her skin prickled all over at the thought.

War changed everything, she told herself. The entire world was turned on its head. She'd been brought up to be a good girl, as Annie had put it. Having sex was something that happened with your husband on your wedding night, and not before. A few liberties perhaps, but not the actual act itself. That was strictly forbidden in the fear of acquiring a reputation, or worse still, being caught out and getting pregnant. The shame of that, for her and her family, would be devastating.

But the world had turned on its head, and who knew what tomorrow would bring? Shouldn't she grab what she could, while she could? Common sense said yes. Screamed it in fact. Loud and clear.

Did she love Julius? She'd never consciously admitted she did, having considered him unobtainable. Only now he wasn't, and he loved her.

That kiss was the key which told her they were right for one another. Indisputably so. Feelings she'd kept locked away had been released, come bubbling to the surface.

She *did* love him, she realised with a jolt. And had never loved George. She'd thought she had at the time, but it hadn't been so, she'd been deluding herself. Julius was the one for her, there was no question about it. None whatsoever. And tomorrow, or the next day, she, or Julius, could be dead, just like all the others.

Her mind made up, Ellie got out of bed and shrugged into her dressing gown. Taking a deep breath she made her way to Julius's door.

Another deep breath and she knocked. 'Julius, are you awake?'

'Yeah,' came the surprised reply.

Ellie opened the door and went inside.

Ellie came awake with a smile on her face, the memories of the previous night instantly flooding back. Beside her Julius was still fast asleep.

She hadn't really known what to expect of lovemaking, but whatever, the reality had far surpassed any preconceptions she might have had.

She felt languid, her body utterly relaxed, a sense of joyous fulfilment encompassing her entire being.

She couldn't have asked for a man to be more tender or gentle with her, he only too well aware it was her first time and wanting her initiation to be a good and rewarding one. And so it had been. It couldn't have been more so.

Reaching out under the covers she ran a hand over his naked buttock, then slid it down between his legs. Hussy, brazen hussy, she thought, her smile widening and becoming knowing.

There had been no embarrassment between them, albeit she'd thought there would be, at least initially. But no. Nothing could have been more natural than their being naked together.

'You know what'll happen if you keep doin' that?' he murmured.

'What?' she replied innocently.

He laughed, a deep rumble that reverberated in the cavern of his chest. 'Well, you'd better stop it, we both have work to go to.'

A glance at the bedside clock told her there was just over half an hour before she normally got up. 'Cuddle me, Julius,' she whispered, releasing him.

He did, savouring the rich scent of her hair. 'Shall I tell you somethin'?'

'What?' she queried dreamily.

'That jibe about your breasts being small. Well they're not, they're absolutely perfect.'

'Oh,' she breathed. 'And what about my bottom?'

'Just the right size, and cute as hell.'

'Thank you.'

'Why? I'm only tellin' the truth.'

The mush was back in her stomach. 'There's still plenty of time, Julius.'

They both made good use of it.

Josie Farnham was sitting perched on the edge of their shared desk when Ellie entered the office. 'You're late,' she frowned. That was most unlike Ellie.

Ellie blushed. 'Sorry. Something came up.' She almost burst out laughing when she realised what she'd said.

'Are you all right?'

'Never more so.'

Josie studied her friend. 'You seem different somehow.'

'Do I?'

'I can't say how, but yes.'

Did it really show? It must for Josie to notice. 'Perhaps it's because I'm happy,' she prevaricated. The truth, if not the whole truth. She wasn't only happy but in love and not a virgin any more.

'Any particular reason?'

Ellie toyed with the idea of telling Josie about her and Julius, then decided not to. It wasn't that she didn't trust Josie, she did, but that was something best kept to herself. 'Just one of those days I suppose,' she replied airily.

Josie didn't believe a word of that, but didn't inquire any further. Ellie's business was her own. Instead she launched into their normal changeover procedure, and was soon on her way home leaving Ellie to it.

Albert took a sip of the tea one of the nurses had just brought him, and wandered over to the open window to stare out.

Being a born and bred townie, and an inner city one at that, his previous experience of the countryside had been extremely limited. But now he was living right in the middle of it he'd come to appreciate the sheer splendour of the land.

How quiet it could be, and peaceful, an ever-changing vista given to many moods. He found it wondrously beautiful.

The animals fascinated him, cows, sheep, and the wild ones he occasionally glimpsed. Why, only the other day he'd actually seen a badger!

And the air, so clean and fresh, often filled with nose-pleasing odours. He smiled – sometimes not so pleasing!

Yes, Albert thought, he could actually live here and not miss London, or Islington, even though the latter had always been his home.

Life moved at a different pace in the country, slower, lacking the hustle and bustle he was used to. Days somehow merged with one another, each seemingly the same, yet at the same time different. And how friendly the people were. He'd thought they might view him, an outsider amongst them, with suspicion, but so far that simply hadn't been the case. They'd accepted him without question.

It would be a sad day when he finally left, he thought ruefully. Back to where he belonged and his job as a fireman. But where to stay? That was the question. He couldn't continue imposing on Danny and Vera, no matter what they said. The alternative was a hostel, many of which had been opened up to accommodate people, like himself, made homeless from the bombing.

Christ, that would be awful. Eating and sleeping with strangers, maybe even having to put up with screaming children night after night. The thought made him shudder.

But he wouldn't be leaving Huntington Hall yet. Matron had said it was up to him when he went, so unless she changed her mind, or circumstances altered, he was staying put for at least a few more weeks. Maybe even longer.

He liked country life. He liked it a lot.

'We can't sleep in your parents' bed!' Ellie protested.

'Whyever not? They aren't usin' it.'

'That's hardly the point. It just wouldn't be right.'

'But it would be more comfortable,' he argued. 'And of course bigger being a double, and a large double at that.'

Ellie had to admit it was difficult the two of them sharing a single bed; this would be far more satisfactory.

'I'll tell you what,' Julius said, a glint in his eye. Going to Ellie he began undoing the buttons of her blouse. 'Why don't we try it out and see?'

'But it isn't even eight o'clock yet.'

'So?'

Her resistance crumbled, she wanted him so badly. In fact she couldn't get enough of him, or he her. She giggled.

'I take it that means yes?'

He removed her blouse and started on her bra. When that too was off he lowered his head and began nuzzling her.

'Oh, Julius,' she whispered. Closing her eyes she gave a soft moan.

Heaven. There was no other word for what followed, sheer heaven.

* * *

Ellie was returning from work when she spotted Connie Fox and George, arm in arm, on the other side of the road. George was speaking and Connie was avidly listening.

Ellie knew if she'd seen them a few weeks back she'd have been jealous. But now? Not one whit of it. On the contrary, she wished them well and every happiness. One thing was certain, they couldn't be any happier than she and Julius. No one could.

She briefly considered going over and saying hello, then decided against it as it would only cause them embarrassment. No, let them be.

Ellie hurried on her way, desperate to be in Julius's arms again. Just to be with him.

'Do you play darts, Albert?'

Albert looked up at the speaker, a chap called Tom whom he'd chatted to on several occasions now. 'As a matter of fact I do.' There was a board at the station which was often used while waiting for a call-out. Tom, like many of the men who came to the pub, worked on a farm which was why he wasn't in the Forces.

'Then can you help us out? One of our regulars can't make it tonight and we have a match against The Bell from Framley. We'd be obliged.' Framley was another village in the area.

'I'd be delighted to play, Tom. Thanks for asking.'

'Good chap. Come on over and have a practice with the rest of us. The Bell team should be arriving shortly.'

'One thing, Tom. I don't have any darts with me.'

'Don't you worry about that. We've got a box of spares. There's bound to be a set that suits.'

Albert was considered the best player at the station, which was something considering the standard of his colleagues. By the end of the evening he'd won his singles game plus his doubles, though they lost the match overall.

He was asked to play again the following week, to which he readily agreed. Before leaving to go back to Huntington Hall he got the distinct impression he was now fully accepted as 'one of the lads'.

That pleased him enormously.

Julius ran a hand over his face, then lit a cigarette. This really wasn't good enough, he chided himself. He had a whole stack of work to get through, but was unable to concentrate on any of it.

The trouble was Ellie, he couldn't get her out of his mind. Whenever he tried to focus on the papers before him his thoughts kept drifting back to her, wondering what she was doing right then, recalling incidents from times they'd been together, she smiling, laughing, clinging to him.

Julius sighed and decided to have a coffee break. 'Ellie.' He said her name aloud, and smiled.

He couldn't wait to see her later.

Matron stood at her window watching Albert cycle off, to The Lamb no doubt which had become a firm favourite of his. Not that that gave her any cause for worry. He never returned drunk, or belligerent in any way. A little merry perhaps, but there was no harm in that. None at all.

He was progressing quickly with the painting, and that morning had started on the day room where he'd made a good beginning.

As she was turning away from the window an idea came to her. One that made her stop and think.

'I've got a couple of complimentary tickets for a show tomorrow night,' Julius announced. 'Want to go?'

'What, do you mean a play?' Ellie queried.

He shook his head. 'A revue. It's called "Sweet and Low" starring Hermione Baddeley and Hermione Gingold. I'm told it's great.'

'Sounds wonderful,' Ellie enthused, already planning what she'd wear. 'Which theatre?'

'The Ambassador's.'

'It'll be fun,' Ellie declared. 'I'm looking forward to it already.'

Julius came over and took her into his arms. 'Me too. But then goin' anywhere with you is fun. As is just bein' with you.'

Her eyes were shining as he bent and kissed her lightly on the lips. 'Love ya, doll.'

'And I love you.'

'For ever and ever.'

'And a day,' she added, thinking with pleasure how romantic Julius could be. There were so many little things he did for her, gestures of appreciation and affection. Why, only the night before she'd gone up to bed to discover a box of chocolates, candy he called it, on her pillow. She hoped he'd never change. Please God.

'Typical woman, always having to have the last word,' he smiled. Then, suddenly all businesslike. 'Right, I'm hungry. Let's eat. I'm goin' to teach you how to cook spaghetti bolognaise.'

'Whatever's that!' she exclaimed.

'Italian. And haven't I had trouble getting the proper ingredients. Luckily one of the chefs at the Embassy owed me a favour and was eventually able to rustle up what I wanted.'

Taking her by the hand he crossed over to the large, brown paper bag he'd brought home. 'OK, let's get started.'

Later Ellie talked him out of putting garlic in it, declaring vehemently that garlic was disgusting and made your breath stink. Only Frenchies and the like used garlic.

Julius thought that was very funny.

Ellie came groggily awake as the bedroom light clicked on. Seconds later she was staring in horror at an open-mouthed Beulah and a clearly amused Pee Wee.

'Holy shit!' Julius exclaimed softly, he too having been woken.

A thoroughly embarrassed Ellie, wishing she could disappear, was only too horribly aware she was stark naked underneath the bedclothes. As was Julius.

'Hi, Mom, hi, Dad!' Julius said, attempting a smile. 'We weren't expectin' you.'

Beulah's glare would have sunk a battleship.

Chapter 29

'What in the name of Sam Hill's goin' on here?' Beulah thundered the moment Julius and Ellie, now both suitably attired, appeared in the kitchen. Pee Wee was standing leaning on the mantelpiece, a glass of scotch in one hand.

'It wasn't what it looked like, Mom,' Julius immediately protested.

Ellie, still acutely embarrassed, face flushed, was staring at the floor. What had happened was a nightmare come true, the only redeeming factor being they hadn't actually been making love when surprised.

Beulah's expression became one of incredulity. 'Well, you sure as hell weren't in bed to discuss the weather, for Christsake!'

'Why don't you sit down, Ellie,' Pee Wee suggested softly.

Ellie did, at the other end of the table to Beulah whose gaze she couldn't meet.

'Anyway, why didn't you call to tell us you were gettin' back?' Julius accused.

'Because the phone's out of order. It's been out all day.'

'Oh!' Julius exclaimed. 'I didn't know that.'

'Well, you do now.' Beulah folded her arms across her massive chest. 'And to think I trusted you, Julius. I should've known, men are all alike.'

387

Julius went over to an opened bottle of scotch, found a glass and poured himself one. 'Ellie?'

She shook her head. If she'd tried to drink scotch in her present state she'd have thrown up.

'As for you, Ellie Sykes,' Beulah bulldozed on, fixing her with a beady stare. 'Your mother would have been downright ashamed of you.'

Ellie's flush deepened to become bright red.

'Hold on, Mom, that isn't fair!' Julius retorted.

'It's fair, OK. Jess was my friend and we talked about all sorts of matters. Now I can't pretend we agreed on everythin', but I sure knew what her views on morality were. What possessed you, girl, eh? Did Julius sweet-talk you into it?'

'No,' Ellie managed to whisper.

'Then what?'

'We're in love, Mom.'

That momentarily deflated Beulah. 'Since when?'

Julius shrugged. 'It just sort of built up I guess. Then it all came out, and that was that.'

'Huh!' Beulah snorted. 'Love, my ass. The pair of you, bein' alone, probably just got the hots for one another.'

'No!' Ellie exclaimed, suddenly finding her voice. 'You're wrong. We do love each other. And it's my fault we started sleeping together. Up until then Julius had been the perfect gentleman.'

Beulah's eyes narrowed. 'Go on?'

Ellie spoke slowly, telling them about Annie Croxton, what Annie had said the night she'd died, and how it had come to her after that she too, because of the war, could die and miss out on so many things she'd always taken for granted would be hers one day.

Beulah's expression softened during this account. 'I see,' she nodded when Ellie was finally finished.

'I believe every word of that,' Pee Wee stated. 'And what's more I agree with it.'

Beulah glanced at him. 'You do?'

'As Ellie put it, war changes everythin'. Hell yeah!'

Julius came across to stand directly behind Ellie, laying his free hand on her shoulder. 'So what happens now?'

'I'll go and live elsewhere,' Ellie offered. 'That's the decent thing to do.'

'No matter what, you two can't go on sharin' a bed here. Irregardless of the rights and wrongs of this, that's final. Jess would turn in her grave if I allowed it.'

'Your father would go apeshit if he found out,' Pee Wee said to Ellie. 'And the poor guy's suffered enough as it is.'

Ellie, recognising the truth of that, nodded her agreement.

'Can she stay and share my bed if we get married?' Julius asked. 'Providin' she'll have me that is.'

Ellie sucked in a breath; this was the first time marriage had been mentioned. She couldn't think of anything she wanted more.

'What do you say to that, Ellie?' Beulah queried.

'I'd like to be asked properly by Julius if you don't mind.'

Pee Wee chuckled. He liked that.

Beulah held up a hand. 'Just one thing before any proposin' goes on. You absolutely certain, Julius? It's a huge step. And I have to say, no mixed marriage I ever heard of has gone easy. You is coloured after all, an' she's a white woman.'

'I'm certain, Mom. As certain as can be.'

'Then you'd better get on with it. Want Pee Wee and I to leave the room?'

Julius shook his head. 'That isn't necessary.'

Ellie closed her eyes for a brief second as Julius placed his glass on the table.

'Ellie?'

She looked up at him, thinking how handsome he was, and how very much she loved him.

'Will you marry me?'

'Yes.'

389

'Amen,' Pee Wee commented.

Julius raised Ellie to her feet and kissed her, not too passion-ately, mindful that his parents were present.

A tear appeared in Beulah's eye which she dashed away. 'Shit, I could sure use a drink,' she declared, and laughed.

'Well, if that don't beat all,' Pee Wee said softly, shaking his head.

When Beulah had been given her drink she and Pee Wee toasted the bride and groom-to-be.

Ellie was positively bursting with happiness. It would be a good marriage, she knew that beyond any shadow of a doubt.

'Engaged!' Josie Farnham squealed. 'You sly old thing!'

It was the following morning and Ellie had just turned up for work to announce her news.

'And who's the lucky man? I didn't even know there was any-one.'

Ellie explained about her and Julius, though she didn't men-tion they'd been sleeping together.

'Well, congratulations,' Josie enthused. 'I'm ever so pleased.'

'Maybe you'll be doing the same yourself before long?'

Josie winked. 'Maybe. It's a distinct possibility I'd say. But come on, tell me what your plans are?'

'We don't have any yet,' Ellie replied. 'He only proposed last night. All I can say is it'll be soon.' She was back in her own bedroom, at Beulah's insistence, Julius in his. Torture for the pair of them now used to the same bed.

'And where, church?'

'I haven't had time to think about that. But probably not.'

'Oh?'

Ellie lit a cigarette, her first of the day, and inhaled deeply. 'This might sound silly, but I don't believe it's right with a war on. I know lots of other women disagree, but a Register Office seems more appropriate in my opinion. Also, don't forget I only recently lost my mum, and brother shortly before that.'

Josie nodded her sympathy. 'I understand.'

Ellie pictured Jess and Paul in her mind's eye, a wave of sadness sweeping over her. Yes, it was far too soon for the fripperies of a white wedding.

At least that's what she thought.

'How much!' Ellie exclaimed, shocked.

The jeweller repeated the price he'd quoted.

'It's far too expensive,' she declared to a smiling Julius.

'But you do like it?'

'Of course. It's gorgeous.'

'And it fits without havin' to be resized.'

True, Ellie reflected, turning her left hand first one way and then the other, the large single diamond shooting off sparks of blue and yellow fire. It was the sort of engagement ring she could only ever have dreamt of.

'Let me worry about the cost,' Julius said. Then, to the jeweller, 'We'll have it.'

The jeweller almost purred with satisfaction. 'A wise choice, sir, if I may say so.'

'Thank you.'

She'd be the envy of every woman she knew, Ellie thought. The girls at the station would be pea green with it. She turned to Julius, her eyes ablaze with excitement. 'You're spoiling me.'

The jeweller discreetly looked away.

'And why not? You deserve to be spoilt.'

Ellie kissed him briefly on the lips, her throat tight with emotion.

'And while we're here we'd better get a couple of gold bands,' Julius said. 'It'll save makin' another trip.'

The jeweller reached into the showcase counter to extract several trays of wedding rings, one gentlemen's, the other ladies'. 'Now is there anything here that's suitable,' he smiled, laying the trays before Julius and a somewhat dazed Ellie. Every few seconds she kept glancing at the ring still on her finger, unable to believe it was actually going to be hers. She was absolutely ecstatic.

When that selection had been made the jeweller put each band into a box. When he asked Ellie about her engagement ring she replied she'd continue wearing it, thank you very much, and take its box with her. After which Julius settled the bill in cash.

'Pleased?' he queried unnecessarily when they were outside again.

'What do you think?'

Julius laughed, Ellie slipping an arm round his as they headed for home.

She hadn't told Julius that was the same shop where George had bought his ring for her. If the jeweller had recognised her he certainly hadn't betrayed the fact by so much as even a flicker.

Ellie glanced yet again at her engagement ring. One thing was certain, this one she wouldn't be throwing away.

Not in a million, trillion years.

'I believe congratulations are in order,' Hazel said to Ellie who'd just come up to the bar. Julius had telephoned to say he was going to be late from work and suggested he meet Ellie in The Florence round about eight o'clock. It was now five to. 'Oh, I say, what a corker of a ring!' Hazel oohed and aahed as she examined it. 'Have you set a date?'

'In three weeks' time at the Caxton Hall in Petty France.'

'Good for you,' Hazel beamed. She took Ellie's order, gin and tonic, and made it a large one.

'That's on the house,' Hazel declared, placing it in front of Ellie. 'All the best.'

Ellie thanked her. 'I'm meeting Julius, he should be in any minute now.'

'Smashing bloke. We all like him. You'll make a lovely couple.' She was still amazed at the news of Ellie marrying a black man, no matter how nice he was. She'd been quite shocked when she'd heard.

Ellie had a sip of her drink.

'So, where are you planning to live?'

'Where we are now, with his mum and dad.'

Hazel pulled a face. 'That'll be a bit cramped, won't it?'

'Yes,' Ellie sighed. 'But we'll just have to manage somehow. We're going to put my bed in Julius's room and place them together. It'll be a bit of a squash, I can tell you.'

It would too, Hazel thought, knowing the houses in the street well. 'Why aren't you trying for a place of your own?'

'We'd love to, but how? Anything that comes available in the area goes straight to those who've been bombed out, and rightly. So there's no hope there.'

'What about other areas?'

'Most of them are as bad, people who've been bombed out are given top priority. Besides, if we moved away it would be difficult for me to get to and from work. I could change stations I suppose, but don't want to do that. The girls I'm with are a terrific lot, and if I did transfer stations I'd probably lose my rank.' She paused, then said, 'Mum was proud I'd been promoted. Very proud.'

'We miss her,' Hazel sympathised softly. 'She was one of the best. Salt of the earth.'

A customer further down the bar gestured to Hazel. 'Excuse me,' she said, and moved away.

At which point Julius arrived and the conversation about where they'd be living was forgotten.

'What am I going to wear?' Ellie said to Beulah in despair, the pair of them of course discussing the forthcoming wedding. 'I've just nothing that's suitable. Nothing at all.'

'Then you're goin' to have to buy new,' Beulah declared.

Ellie laughed. 'How am I to do that? I would need clothes coupons don't forget, damn the rationing, and I've nowhere near enough for a dress.'

Beulah's mind was busily ticking over. 'Shouldn't be too much of a problem, hon.'

'How do you make that out?'

'Julius. Speak to him and he'll get what's necessary. OK, he ain't never got no clothes coupons before, at least not that I know, but he should be able to manage the required number. Uncle Sam, Ellie, don't forget he works for Uncle Sam. There ain't nothin' he can't lay his hands on through that Embassy. At least that's how it seems to me.'

Ellie hadn't thought of that. 'What a wonderful idea. If he can get them, will you come shopping with me?'

Beulah's eyes gleamed. 'You just try and stop me. I'll be there with bells on. Hell yeah!'

Later it dawned on Beulah that she was taking Jess's place in all this, doing things for, and with, Ellie that Jess would have done had she still been alive.

She took it as a compliment. Very much so.

Albert laid the letter from Ellie aside and leant back in his chair to think.

He'd had no idea, not an inkling, that something was going on between Ellie and Julius and now this bombshell. For that's exactly what it was.

And why were they getting married in such a hurry? Could Ellie be pregnant? He'd be furious, not to mention bitterly disappointed, if she was. The main thing of course was that Julius was a black man.

He recalled a conversation he'd once had with Jess when he'd been worried Julius was showing an interest in Ellie, a notion Jess had pooh-poohed. It appeared Jess had been wrong.

He thought about Julius and the Postons. A decent, upright family, that couldn't be denied. And damn fine neighbours, none better. Kindness itself. None of which took away from the fact they were black.

What would Jess have said? he wondered, already knowing the answer. She'd have said that if Ellie and Julius loved one another then that was enough and the colour of his skin didn't matter.

Well, maybe it didn't. Ellie was grown up after all, surely she must know her own mind and what she was doing. Anyway, there was nothing he could do about it except disapprove, which would upset Ellie enormously. And that he didn't want.

Albert sighed. He'd put a brave face on it and go to the wedding, Ellie was his daughter after all. If she was happy then that was all that counted. His own misgivings and prejudices didn't come into it. Or wouldn't, as he wouldn't allow them to. Let them make a go of it with him wishing them well.

A black son-in-law! Who'd have dreamt it.

Julius returned to the kitchen after having gone to answer the phone. 'That was Hazel from across the road,' he said. 'She's asked Ellie and me to go over for a few minutes.'

Ellie frowned. 'What for?'

'She didn't say. Just asked us to go over.'

Ellie looked at Beulah, who shrugged. 'I've no idea, honey.'

'Shall we go then?' Julius said to Ellie.

'Just give me a few minutes to get ready.' She came to her feet. 'I won't be long.'

At least half an hour, Julius reflected wryly, and smiled.

'A flat?' Ellie repeated.

Hazel nodded. 'Upstairs. Small, mind you, a bedroom and sitting room and you'd have to share the bathroom with us. That won't bother Harry and me if it doesn't bother you.'

This had taken both Ellie and Julius completely by surprise, the pair of them bowled over by Hazel's offer.

'We had it done out for our daughter you see,' Hazel went on to explain. 'The idea was she'd still be with us but have a section of the accommodation on her own, more than a mere bedroom. Well, as you know, Ellie, she moved out and so it's free. If you're interested that is?'

'We most certainly are,' Julius replied, thinking this was wonderful and solved all sorts of problems. 'How much are you askin' for rent?'

'You'd better see it first. Wait here a moment.'

Hazel vanished out back to return almost instantly with Harry who declared he'd tend to the bar while Hazel showed them round.

Ellie and Julius followed Hazel up a flight of stairs, along a corridor and then into what Hazel announced was the sitting room.

Ellie glanced around, delighted at what she saw. Comfy chairs, sideboard, standard lamp plus other bits and pieces usually found in a sitting room. 'Very nice,' Ellie commented.

'Now the kitchen,' Hazel said. 'I forgot to mention that. There's not much to it but it's adequate enough.'

That contained a cooker, old but serviceable, sink and a food cupboard. As Hazel had said, it was small, a galley type, but adequate.

'You'll have to eat your meals in the sitting room I'm afraid,' Hazel went on. 'We have a spare drop leaf table and chairs we'll move in if you take it. And by the way, don't worry about linen and the like, there's masses of that.'

The bedroom proved to be almost as big as the sitting room, its main feature being a double bed. 'Well away from our bedroom,' Hazel commented with a twinkle in her eye.

Ellie coloured slightly when she realised what Hazel was getting at. She and Julius could indulge themselves without fear of being overheard.

'The one drawback is you hear the noise from the bar below, but you'd soon get used to that.'

'What about comin' and goin'?' Julius queried.

'There's a back door which can be used at anytime. You'd both have a key for it.'

Julius had a sudden thought. 'One thing is I do require a phone so that I can contact the Embassy, or more importantly, they me.'

'That isn't a problem,' Hazel smiled. 'There's the phone downstairs and an extension in our sitting room. You can use either whenever. And if the Embassy ring and either Harry or I answer then we'll just give you a shout.'

Julius turned to Ellie. 'Well?'

'It's ideal.'

'Then we'll take it, Hazel, and can't thank you enough. Consider the apartment let as from this moment.'

'Right, we'll go back downstairs and hammer out the details.'

Hazel was pleased she'd been able to help. Years before Jess had done her an enormous favour, this was her way of repaying it.

'Sir down, Mr Sykes. What can I do for you?'

Albert explained about Ellie's letter and that he intended returning to London for the wedding.

Matron stared at Albert in concern. 'Does that mean you'll be leaving us then?'

'Oh no,' he hastily replied. 'I'll only be gone a few days. There's still a lot of painting to be done.'

A relieved Matron glanced at her watch. 'I usually have a glass of sherry round about now. Would you care to join me?'

'I don't like sherry I'm afraid,' Albert apologised.

'There's scotch as well?'

'Now that I do like.'

Matron smiled as she came round from behind her desk. 'Neat or with water?'

'Neat please.'

'Do you know the young man in question?' she queried as she did the honours.

'Yes, in fact he and his parents are neighbours. They very kindly took my daughter in after . . .' He trailed off, a stricken look coming across his face, and had a sip of scotch.

'I know what happened. I'm sorry,' Matron said softly.

Albert nodded.

'It must still be very painful for you.'

'Yes,' Albert whispered, and had a larger sip.

'Has being here helped?'

He looked into Matron's warm and sympathetic eyes. 'A lot actually. It's been good to get away from . . . well where it happened. It's so peaceful at Huntington Hall, and quiet. And so very different. To be honest, I'm not sure I'm ready to return to Islington yet, but I'll have to for the wedding. I couldn't miss that.'

'No,' Matron agreed.

'But it's going to be hard. I know that.'

Matron could well imagine. 'I'm glad you've come to see me, Mr Sykes. I wanted a word.'

'Oh?'

'I wonder if you'd consider working here as an employee? Doing more or less what you're doing now, including the usual maintenance jobs that are forever springing up. I'd be willing to pay three pounds a week, plus your board and lodging. You would certainly be doing me, and the nurses, a favour if you accepted.'

This was a surprise, Albert thought. 'Do you mean work here permanently?'

'Long term, short term, that would be entirely up to you. I'd be extremely grateful for either.'

'There is an awful lot of painting still to be done,' Albert mused.

'And the outside after the inside is completed, should that come about.'

Matron was studying Albert intently. 'I've been told that you've made friends in the village. Nurse Isaac mentioned that you've become a member of the pub darts team.'

Albert nodded. 'They're a good bunch in the pub. Enjoyable company. We have great fun on the darts nights.'

'So you wouldn't have to worry about the social side of things if you stayed on, that's already taken care of.'

True enough, Albert thought, severely tempted. 'The only trouble is, Matron, I already have a job. I should really go back to that.'

She'd already foreseen this objection, and expected it to be brought up. 'I can easily arrange the necessary medical papers to relieve you of that duty,' she replied.

'You can?'

'Oh indeed.'

Albert was thinking of his mates at the station, still short-handed with his being away. To duck out entirely wouldn't be fair on them. And what if the heavy bombing started again? Every man jack would be needed.

Albert drained his glass. 'Can I think about it?'

'Of course. Take as long as you wish.'

He placed his now empty glass on her desk. 'I'd better get back to what I was doing.'

'When are you going to London?'

Albert told her.

'I'll arrange transport to take you to the station.'

'Thank you.'

'My pleasure, Mr Sykes. My pleasure.'

Beulah wasn't a fool, they were engaged and had set the date for the wedding after all. Not to mention the fact they'd been sleeping together while she and Pee Wee had been on tour. She'd been young herself once and knew what it was like to be newly in love.

'I'll be goin' to The Chicory House with Pee Wee tonight,' she announced over breakfast. Then, to underline the point, 'So don't expect us back till the wee hours.'

Ellie's heart skipped a beat. She wanted to glance at Julius, but didn't in case Beulah noticed and interpreted it.

'Yeah, OK, Mom,' Julius replied.

Beulah smiled inwardly. 'Now you two better hurry up or you'll be late for work.'

Ellie had been going to have another cup of coffee, but now decided there wasn't time. She couldn't wait for the evening to come round; she and Julius would make good use of it.

Albert had knocked off for a bit to go for a walk, one of his favourite pastimes since coming to Huntington Hall. It still amazed him that he, an out-and-out townie, had come to love, and appreciate, the countryside so much.

He was heading for a nearby river, where he often went, to stroll along its banks. Sometimes, if he was lucky, he'd see fish in the water, trout he'd been told. And only the other week he'd spotted an otter, a rare occurrence in these parts one of the chaps in the darts team had informed him.

It was a cold day so he'd wrapped up warm. Snow had been forecast, but so far none had fallen. Snow in a city was a miserable affair, soon turning to slush. But out here it would just lie, a white blanket stretching for miles in every direction. He knew it would be beautiful when it happened.

He began thinking about his conversation with Matron which he'd been doing on and off since it had taken place. My God, but he was tempted. He'd never felt so physically well in his life since arriving at Huntington Hall, the fresh air like a daily tonic. So different from the fogs and soot-laden atmosphere he was used to at this time of year.

One thing was certain, he didn't have to worry about Ellie any more. She'd be married shortly and starting a new life of her own with Julius, no longer reliant on him, and Jess, as she'd been in the past while growing up. So there was no tie there.

But there was with the station and his mates. He would be letting them down if he was to leave when there was a war on. And what if the raids did resume, as they so easily could? How would he feel, safe and secure in Huntington Hall, while they were out risking their lives? Pretty rotten, that's how.

The main thing he had to do was speak to Danny, find out how things were. He'd already written to Danny and Vera asking to be put up for several nights so they would be expecting him. He'd have the chance to talk then. Find out what was what.

Albert stopped and glanced around. It would be a terrible wrench if he did go back to London to live. He'd miss all this like billy-o.

Ellie lay wrapped in Julius's arms, one hand slowly stroking his flank, the pair of them utterly exhausted after a frantic and frenetic bout of lovemaking.

Julius laughed softly.

'What is it?'

'You.'

Ellie frowned. 'What about me?'

'You've certainly become enthusiastic for someone who was still a virgin only a short while ago.'

That made her smile. 'Are you complaining?'

'Not in the least,' he replied hurriedly. 'If anythin', I approve.'

'Good.'

Ellie snuggled up even closer to him. 'If I'm enthusiastic it's because I love you, and can't get enough of you. You make me so very, very happy.'

'And you me, Ellie.'

She sighed with contentment, thinking how lucky they were to have found one another.

They continued to lie like that, neither wanting to move and break the spell of total completeness that had descended on them.

Albert came out of the Angel tube station and stopped to stare around. Here he was, home.

Familiarity was everywhere, buildings, signs, the faces of passers-by. It was like putting on an old and much cherished suit or set of clothes.

No new damage since he'd left, he noted as he walked along Upper Street. That was good. He stopped briefly at a bombed-out run of shops where he and his mates had worked feverishly to put out a raging fire. Memories from that terrible night, one of the heaviest raids, flickered through his mind. Fortunately, he recalled quite clearly, there hadn't been any casualties.

He halted again outside a baker's that Jess had often used, almost seeing her go inside as she went about her daily shopping.

'Jess,' he muttered softly.

Her ghost was also going to be everywhere.

* * *

As chance would have it Danny was on the night shift and had already been to bed when Albert knocked on their door. Vera answered, giving him a warm welcome, and hug, before ushering him inside.

'My God, but you're looking well!' Danny beamed as he pumped Albert's hand.

'And I feel it. Huntington Hall has done me the world of good.'

'I'll put the kettle on,' Vera declared. 'You must be tired after your journey.'

'It was a long one,' Albert admitted. 'Though what else can you expect in wartime.'

'Take a seat,' Danny said, and did so himself. 'Now I want to hear all about it.'

Albert spoke at length about Huntington Hall and how much he'd come to love the surrounding countryside. He also mentioned the pub and fact he played for the darts team.

'And the Matron has offered you a full-time job there,' Danny repeated when Albert had finally finished.

'Can't take it, of course. Have to get back to the station as you're short-handed.'

'Not any more,' Danny replied. 'A couple of blokes have been drafted in from outlying stations to help plus we've been assigned half a dozen auxiliaries, older retired chaps in the main who've come back into the service. So we've got a full complement again, plus some.'

'I see,' Albert mused.

Danny leant forward in his chair. 'Can I say something?'

'Go ahead.'

'You've paid your price for this war, mate. Jess and Paul, a bloody heavy price too. If you want that job at Huntington Hall I'd grab it with both hands if I was you. You've earned it in my book.'

This revelation about numbers at the station changed matters, Albert thought. If he wished he could go back to Huntington Hall with a clear conscience.

'Well?' Danny prompted.

'I'll have to explain to Jess, talk to her, before I make a final decision.'

Danny wasn't sure what to make of that. He glanced at Vera, busy with cups and saucers, who shrugged.

'Go to the cemetery,' Albert clarified.

Albert waited till Beulah had left the room before asking the question that had been worrying him. 'Are you pregnant, Ellie?'

'No, Dad, I'm not.'

Relief washed through him. 'You're not lying I hope?'

'I'm not pregnant, Dad. I swear.'

He sort of sagged where he sat. It had been important to him that she wasn't. To him, and Jess's memory. 'So why the rush to get married?'

'Because we want to. It's as simple as that. There's a war on after all, why waste time?'

Yes, Albert thought. He could understand that. 'I take it you do love Julius, and he you?'

Ellie smiled. 'As much as any two people can love one another. As much as you loved Mum, and Mum you.'

Albert glanced away so she didn't see the expression on his face. 'That's all right then,' he mumbled.

Ellie crossed over and kissed him on the cheek. 'It's going to be a good marriage, Dad, you'll see.'

He believed her.

'Well that's it, Jess. What I want to do.'

A wind was blowing, stirring the flowers he'd laid on the grave. This was the first time he'd been back since her funeral.

He waited patiently, hoping something would happen, that she'd manage to speak to him in some way.

All of a sudden he knew she understood, and approved. He couldn't have explained how he knew, he just did.

'Thanks, girl,' he whispered. 'I miss you terribly.'

And with that he turned and walked away, never looking back.

The ceremony, by special licence, was short and sweet, the appropriate words said, vows taken, rings exchanged. At the conclusion of which they were pronounced man and wife.

Ellie was dressed in a smart navy blue suit that Beulah had helped her choose, her shoes a matching colour. The blouse she had on was cream-coloured with pretty, rounded, lace-edged cuffs and collar. Everyone agreed she looked absolutely smashing.

A surprise awaited Ellie when they emerged into the street in the shape of Pee Wee's trio, who immediately struck up with 'Moonlit Eyes', Julius having told Pee Wee how fond she was of that particular number and that they'd often played it when Pee Wee and Beulah were on tour.

The trio continued to play, much to the delight of passers-by, while photographs were taken, and then the chauffeur-driven Cadillac, loaned to them for the day by the Embassy, purred into view.

Confetti in abundance was thrown as Ellie and Julius got into the car, she radiant with pleasure and happiness, after which the Caddy moved off, the tin cans that had been tied to its rear clattering noisily.

A watching Albert couldn't have been more proud.

It didn't take long for the reception at The Florence to turn into a knees-up. All the old favourites were being belted out on the piano: 'Roll Out The Barrel', 'Maybe It's Because I'm A Londoner', 'The Lambeth Walk', 'I'm Looking Over A Four-Leaf Clover', 'The White Cliffs Of Dover' . . .

There was no shortage of beer, Harry having managed to lay in a substantial supply, while Julius had arranged for several cases of spirits to be delivered from the Embassy.

Josie Farnham, having re-jigged her duty with the SO, was there, plus other girls from the station. A number of Albert's firemen mates had turned up, though, sadly, not Danny who was on duty. Lots of the neighbours, no invitations required, had come along to join in the fun and wish Ellie and Julius all the very best.

It was in the middle of all this that Hazel appeared at Julius's elbow. 'There's a phone call for you from the Embassy,' she said, having to shout to be heard above the racket.

'Thanks, Haze. I'll be right there.' Julius turned to Ellie. 'It's probably someone calling to congratulate us. I won't be long.'

She kissed him lightly on the lips. 'Don't be.'

'How do you feel?' Albert asked, coming over to stand beside her.

'Terrific. Top of the world.'

He glanced around. 'It reminds me of our reception, your mum's and mine that is. Long time ago now.' For a moment there was a tinge of sadness in his voice when he said that, then it was gone.

When Julius returned to Ellie there was the strangest expression on his face.

'What's wrong?' she instantly demanded.

Instead of replying he held up a hand. 'Ladies and gentlemen, can I have your attention please! I have an important announcement to make.'

Gradually the room fell silent, all eyes on Julius. 'Thank you,' he said at last.

Julius took a deep breath. 'I've just received news that the Japanese have bombed Pearl Harbor, a large American naval base in Hawaii. As from now, the United States is at war on the side of the Allies.'

Eyes popped, mouths dropped open in surprise. This wasn't at all what they'd been expecting to hear. Then, suddenly, pandemonium broke loose as people cheered, clapped and whooped in delight.

'We'll definitely kick Jerry's arse now!' someone shouted.

'God bless the bloody Yanks!' another voice, this one female, cried.

Julius turned to Ellie who was staring at him in astonishment. 'It's true,' he said. 'Thousands have been killed and wounded apparently, many ships sunk. But the important thing is, at long last, we're in the war alongside you British.'

Ellie was sorry for the dead and wounded, but all she could think was that she couldn't have wished for a better wedding present. It was a day to remember. In more ways than one.

Much later, having said his goodbyes, Albert slipped out into Florence Street to stand staring at what remained of the family home. The house where Jess had died, and which held so many memories for him.

Tears were glistening in his eyes when he eventually walked away. He'd be back to visit from time to time, but only to visit. He'd never live in Islington again.

In the morning he'd be catching the train back to Huntington Hall where he'd be telling Matron he was accepting her offer of a job.

He smiled when he remembered there was a darts match on the following night. He was looking forward to that.